A FORTRESS in SHADOW

Other books by Glen Cook

The Heirs of Babylon
The Swordbearer
A Matter of Time
The Dragon Never Sleeps
The Tower of Fear
Sung in Blood

Dread Empire
A Cruel Wind
(Containing *A Shadow of All Night Falling*, *October's Baby* and *All Darkness Met*)
The Wrath of Kings (Containing *Reap the East Wind* and *An Ill Fate Marshalling*, and *Wrath of Kings*)
An Empire Unacquainted with Defeat (Short fiction collection)

Starfishers
Shadowline
Starfishers
Stars' End

Darkwar
Doomstalker
Warlock
Ceremony

The Black Company
The Black Company
Shadows Linger
The White Rose
The Silver Spike
Shadow Games
Dreams of Steel
Bleak Seasons
She Is the Darkness
Water Sleeps
Soldiers Live

The Garrett Files
Sweet Silver Blues
Bitter Gold Hearts
Cold Copper Tears
Old Tin Sorrows
Dread Brass Shadows
Red Iron Nights
Deadly Quicksilver Lies
Petty Pewter Gods
Faded Steel Heat
Angry Lead Skies
Whispering Nickel Idols

Instrumentalities of the Night
The Tyranny of the Night
Lord of the Silent Kingdom

A FORTRESS in SHADOW

A CHRONICLE OF THE DREAD EMPIRE

GLEN COOK

NIGHT SHADE BOOKS
SAN FRANCISCO

Printed in Canada

ISBN: 978-1-59780-100-3

Night Shade Books
Please visit us on the web at
http://www.nightshadebooks.com

Contents

INTRODUCTION

These were the mid-Eighties. Victoria, Vancouver Island, Canada. I was sharing a townhouse flat with Ian C. Esslemont—Cam—down in James Bay. We'd both dropped the academic half of careers in archaeology to pursue the dream of writing and were enrolled in the undergraduate creative writing program at the University of Victoria. Our longstanding friendship was characterized by the convergence of interests, but not always and not in everything, especially what each of us was in the habit of reading.

At the time Cam was immersed in the existentialists of Europe and the magic realist writers of Latin America. I was reading Viet Nam war literature. There were instances of crossover, books and stories we thrust at each other in our enthusiasm. *Going After Cacciato* with its Moebius loop storytelling. Ignácio Brandão's *And Still the Earth,* a magic realist dystopic science fiction novel. We were young, still single, ballsy and ferocious in our literary passions. We were reading stuff that broke the confines of convention and this fuelled our own rather frenzied but probably feeble efforts as young writers.

For all the highfalutin pretensions of that stuff, there was something else going on at the time. We'd both grown up reading fantasy and science fiction. Again, coming at things from two very distinct directions. My earliest serious reading came with the reissue of the novels of Edgar Rice Burroughs (those Frazetta covers...) by Ace and Ballantine; onward to R. E. Howard, Talbot Mundy, H. Rider Haggard, leading finally to what was for me the pinnacle of epic fantasy: Donaldson's *Chronicles of Thomas Covenant*; for science fiction it was Leigh Brackett, Andre Norton, Asimov, Clarke, Zelazny, Harry Harrison, Ursula Le Guin.

Cam's reading list came from another planet.

Back to Victoria. In the midst of all that academic zeal, the late-night writing sessions to meet workshop deadlines, the pissing around at the university pub, the girl-chasing, Cam and I were gaming. From AD&D beginnings on to GURPS, we were busy putting our anthropology backgrounds to an entirely nonsensical use (or so it seemed at the time), fashioning a world that didn't exist but could exist (one of the reasons I have so little hair on my head these days is from tearing most of it out after purchasing the first box-set called Forgotten Realms and unfolding the huge colour map enclosed—only to find it ... well, lacking in certain details relating to principles of geography, cultural anthropology, economics, etc.).

On his move out from Winnipeg, Cam had trucked along a couple boxes—his favourite books, presumably—and so, at last, we come to Glen Cook. There was plenty of beer-drinking in those days so my recollection is hazier than I'd like, but I think the first novel of Glen Cook's that Cam handed to me was *The Black Company*. Might have been *The Starfishers*. What I do recall, however, is what reading *The Black Company* did to me.

I was floored. Recall, we'd been reading literature that broke the rules. And I had been devouring every damned thing ever written by vets of the Viet Nam war, good and bad. Suddenly, here, in my hands, was a work of fantasy that took hold of the genre by its throat and *squeezed*. And even more enticing, it had the voice of the best of the Viet Nam novels I had been reading.

I'd had my fill of evil overlords, princes in shining armour, damsels whose greatest talent was screaming in perfect ascending octaves. If another novel featuring a young farmboy with secret royal bloodlines reached me I was ready to walk into the Pacific and not come back. If I saw one more Dark Lord vowing to lay waste to everything (Now why would any Dark Lord want that?) I was heading for a monastery, tonsure in tow. With but a few exceptions, it seemed that fantasy wanted to stay in the adolescent wish-fulfillment stage, where good was blindingly good and evil absurdly, comically evil. Where everyone spoke in a high diction unintentionally caricaturing something from the Middle Ages.

And then there was Glen Cook. Suddenly, there was ambivalence, there was ambiguity, suspect motivations, heroes with flaws. There were droll, often cynical points of view. There were throwaway lines that could make you howl.

This stuff. It was grown-up. It had wit. It was clever and sly. And it was *dark*.

I do recall descending on the various bookstores in Victoria—and thereafter wherever my archaeology work and other travels took me—hunting down everything Glen Cook had written. And it wasn't easy. There was his science fiction—spectacularly good, hard-bitten and complex. And there were, rare as nuggets of gold, the novels of the Dread Empire. Mystery and wonder began with the damned titles. *A Shadow of All Night Falling*. *Reap the East Wind*. *With Mercy Toward None*. Poetic, arcane phrases. Dark, savage lines. Into these tales I plunged, as avid a fan as any you could imagine. *This* was the fantasy writing I wanted to read. *This* was what I was looking for.

In our gaming sessions, Cam and I played the writing of Glen Cook. Not the specific details of his stories (we were too bound up in creating something unique, even then); but the sensibilities—the characters, their voices—and the pervasive brooding, mysterious atmosphere, the droll commentary, the penchant for outrageous understatement. Fantasy with an older voice, a wiser voice, perhaps. Fantasy with the flaws of the real world coolly, clinically transposed into a place of deadly magic, terrible wars and exhausted refugees.

You could picture some long-lost prince, stepping in from the usual mill of fantasy writing, his plate armour bright and polished, his fair hair luffing in the wind, his teeth bright and his cock boldly bulging his breeches (okay, scratch that last bit), stepping into one of Glen Cook's stories, standing there at the roadside, and some ragtag, exhausted, grim-faced troop of soldiers ride past, every hoof kicking mud and horseshit and worse all over the hapless bystander. Well, I can, anyway. I picture it with a nasty smile.

So, I thank Ian C. Esslemont for pushing on me that first novel by Glen Cook. Thanks, mate, and yeah, you know what's come of all that.

And, with humility and deep respect, I thank Glen Cook for showing what was possible. I've been quoted elsewhere as saying that he had single-handedly changed the field of fantasy—and he has, for me and for many others, writers and readers both. Yet still I wonder, was the genre ready for him back then? Given the struggle I had finding the volumes of the Dread Empire series, I suppose the answer is "no."

Are we ready for him now? I think so. I hope so. Oh, the moribund tropes persist, sagging the bookshelves, groaning with revisitations of that host of clichés so dogging the genre. We're still seeing the life and times of privileged royalty and the evil wizards plotting slaughter (and, presumably, economic suicide). We've still got tens of thousands of ghouls, kobolds or whatnot lurking in subterranean cities desperate for the next foolish adventurer. Dwarves in mountains and elves in forests. Yet, increasingly, we're seeing trope-smashing writers in the genre, the Paul Kearneys, Tim Lebbons, Scott Bakkers, all of whom—consciously or not—are treading in the wake of Glen Cook.

Kudos for Night Shade Books for reviving this extraordinary series, and as for asking me for an introduction to the second volume of the Dread Empire series, well, I never imagined I would ever find myself in such a situation. There is of course no way to know, but I do wonder if I would have found myself on this path, writing the novels I am writing, if not for Glen Cook.

I might have had this idea, about a young farmboy, see? And a lost birthright, and there's this sorcerer named Malefic Malodorous the Mean....

Steven Erikson
Victoria, British Columbia
Canada
April 2007

The Fire in His Hands

Contents

ONE
MAKING OF A MESSIAH

The caravan crept across a stony wadi and meandered upward into the hills. The camels boredly tramped out their graceless steps, defining the milemarks of their lives. Twelve tired beasts and six weary men made up the small, exhausted caravan.

They were nearing the end of their route. After a rest at El Aquila they would recross the Sahel for more salt.

Nine watchers awaited them.

The camels now carried the sweet dates, emeralds of Jebal al Alf Dhulquarneni, and Imperial relics coveted by the traders of Hellin Daimiel. The traders would purchase them with salt recovered from the distant western sea.

An elderly merchant named Sidi al Rhami mastered the caravan. He was captain of a family enterprise. His companions were brothers and cousins and sons. His youngest boy, Micah, just twelve, was making his first transit of the family route.

The watchers didn't care who they were.

Their captain assigned victims. His men stirred uncomfortably in the shimmering heat. The sun's full might blasted down upon them. It was the hottest day in the hottest summer in living memory.

The camels plodded into the deathtrap defile.

The bandits leapt from the rocks. They howled like jackals.

Micah fell instantly, his skull cracked. His ears moaned with the force of the blow. He hardly had time to realize what was happening.

Everywhere the caravan had traveled men had remarked that it was a summer of evil. Never had the sun been so blistering, nor the oases so dry.

It was a summer of evil indeed when men sank to robbing salt merchants. Ancient law and custom decreed them free even of the predations of tax collectors, those bandits legitimized by stealing for the king.

Micah recovered consciousness several hours later. He immediately wished that he had died too. The pain he could endure. He was a child of Hammad al Nakir. The children of the Desert of Death hardened in a fiery furnace.

Plain impotence brought the death wish upon him.

He could not intimidate the vultures. He was too weak. He sat and wept while they and the jackals tore the flesh of his kinsmen and squabbled over delicacies.

Nine men and a camel had perished. The boy was a damned poor bet. His vision doubled and his ears rang whenever he moved. Sometimes he thought he heard voices calling. He ignored everything and stubbornly stumbled toward El Aquila in exhausting little odysseys of a hundred yards.

He kept passing out.

The fifth or sixth time he wakened in a low cave that stank of fox. Pain lanced from temple to temple. He had suffered headaches all his life, but never one as unremitting as this. He moaned. It became a plaintive whine.

"Ah. You're awake. Good. Here. Drink this."

Something that might have been a small, very old man crouched in a deep shadow. A wrinkled hand proffered a tin cup. Its bottom was barely wet with some dark, fragrant liquid.

Micah drained it. Oblivion returned.

Yet he heard a distant voice droning endlessly of faith, God, and the manifest destiny of the children of Hammad al Nakir.

The angel nurtured him for weeks. And droned unceasing litanies of jihad. Sometimes, on moonless nights, he took Micah aboard his winged horse and showed him the wide earth. Argon. Itaskia. Hellin Daimiel. Gog-Ahlan, the fallen. Dunno Scuttari. Necremnos. Throyes. Freyland. Hammad al Nakir itself, the Lesser Kingdoms, and so much more. And the angel repeatedly told him that these lands must again bend the knee to God, as they had done in the day of Empire. God, the eternal, was patient. God was just. God was understanding. And God was distressed by the backsliding of his Chosen. They were no longer bearing the Truth to the nations.

The angel would answer no questions. He merely castigated the children of Hammad al Nakir for having allowed the minions of the Dark One to blunt their will to carry the Truth.

Four centuries before the birth of Micah al Rhami there was a city, Ilkazar, which established dominion over all the west. But its kings were cruel, and too often swayed by the whims of sorcerers interested only in advancing themselves.

An ancient prophecy haunted the wizards of Ilkazar. It declared that the Empire's doom would find it through the agency of a woman. So those grim necromancers persecuted women of Power without mercy.

In the reign of Vilis, the final Emperor, a woman named Smyrena was burned. She left a son. Her persecutors overlooked the child.

That son migrated to Shinsan. He studied with the Tervola and Princes Thaumaturge of the Dread Empire. And then he returned, embittered with the bile of vengeance.

He was a mighty wizard now. He rallied the Empire's foes to his standard. The war was the cruelest that earth remembered. The wizards of Ilkazar were mighty too. The Empire's captains and soldiers were faithful, hardened men. Sorceries stalked the endless nights and devoured nations entire.

The heart of the Empire, then, was rich and fertile. The war left the land a vast, stony plain. The beds of great rivers became channels of lifeless sand. The land earned the name Hammad al Nakir, Desert of Death. The descendants of kings became petty hetmen of tattered bands which perpetrated bloody little butcheries upon one another over mudhole excuses for oases.

One family, the Quesani, established a nominal suzerainty over the desert, bringing an uneasy, oft broken peace. Semi-pacified, the tribes began raising small settlements and refurbishing old shrines.

They were a religious people, the Children of Hammad al Nakir. Only faith that their trials were the will of God gave them the endurance to weather the desert and the savagery of their cousins. Only an unshakable conviction that God would someday relent and restore them to their rightful place among the nations kept them battling.

But the religion of their Imperial forebears was sedentary, a faith for farmers and city dwellers. The theological hierarchies did not fall with the temporal. As generations passed and the Lord did not relent, common folk drifted ever farther from a priesthood unable to shed historical inertia, unable to adapt dogma to the circumstances of a people gone wholly nomadic and grown accustomed to weighing everything in the balance scale of death.

The summer had been the hardest since those immediately following the Fall. Autumn promised no relief. Oases were drying up. Order had begun to evade the grasp of Crown and priesthood. Chaos threatened as desperate men resorted to raid and counterraid and younger priests split with their elders over the meaning of the drought. Undisciplined anger stalked the barren hills and dunes. Dissatisfaction lurked in every shadow.

The land was harkening for the whisper of a new wind. One old man heard a sound. His response would damn and saint him.

Ridyah Imam al Assad's best days were far behind him. He was nearly blind now, after more than fifty years in the priesthood. There was little he could do to serve the Lord any longer. Now the Lord's own must care for him.

Nevertheless, they had given him a sword and set him to guard this slope. He had neither the strength nor the will to employ the weapon. If one of the el Habib came this way, to steal water from the springs and cisterns of Al Ghabha, he would do nothing. He had his weak sight to plead before his superiors.

The old man was true to his faith. He believed that he was but one brother in the Land of Peace and that such good fortune as came his way should be shared with those whom the Lord had called him to guide.

The Al Ghabha Shrine had water. El Aquila had none. He did not understand why his superiors were willing to bare steel to maintain that unnatural balance.

El Aquila lay to his left, a mile away. The squalid village was the headquarters of the el Habib tribe. The Shrine and the monastery where al Assad lived rose two hundred yards behind him. The monastery was the retirement home of the priests of the western desert.

The source of the noise lay somewhere down the rocky slope he was supposed to guard.

Al Assad tottered forward, trusting his ears far more than his cataracted eyes. The sound reached him again. It sounded like the muttering of a man dying on the rack.

He found the boy lying in the shadow of a boulder.

His "Who are you?" and "Do you need help?" elicited no response. He knelt. With his fingers more than his eyes he determined that he had found a victim of the desert.

He shuddered as he felt cracked, scabby, sunburned skin. "A child," he murmured. "And not of El Aquila."

Little remained of the youth. The sun had baked most of the life out of him, desiccating his spirit as well as his body.

"Come, my son. Rise up. You're safe now. You've come to Al Ghabha."

The youth did not respond. Al Assad tried to pull him to his feet. The boy neither helped nor hindered him. The imam could do nothing with him. His will to live had departed. His only response was a muttered incoherency which sounded surprisingly like, "I have walked with the Angel of the Lord. I have seen the ramparts of Paradise." He then lapsed into complete unconsciousness. Al Assad could not rouse him again.

The old man made the long and painful journey back to the monastery, pausing each fifty yards to offer the Lord a prayer that his life be spared till he had carried word of the child's need to his abbot.

His heart had begun skipping beats again. He knew that it would not be long before Death took him into Her arms.

Al Assad no longer feared the Dark Lady. Indeed, his aches and blindness made him look forward to the pain-ease he would find in Her embrace. But he begged an indulgence, that he be allowed to perform this one final righteous deed.

The Lord had laid a charge upon him, and upon the Shrine, by guiding this victim of the desert to him and Shrine land.

Death heard and stayed Her hand. Perhaps She foresaw richer harvests later.

The abbot did not believe him at first, and castigated him for having abandoned his post. "It's an el Habib trick. They're out there stealing water right now." But al Assad convinced the man. And that left the abbot no happier. "The last thing we need is more mouths."

"'Have you bread and your brother naught to eat? Have you water and your brother naught to drink? Then I say this unto you…'"

"Spare me the quotations, Brother Ridyah. He'll be cared for." The abbot shook his head. He got little thrills of anticipation when he thought of the Dark Lady claiming al Assad. The old man was one too-sincere pain in the neck. "See. They're bringing him in now."

The brothers dropped the litter before the abbot, who examined the tormented child. He could not conceal his revulsion. "This is Micah, the son of the salt merchant al Rhami." He was awed.

"But it's been a month since the el Habib found their caravan!" one brother protested. "Nobody could survive the desert that long."

"He spoke of being tended by an angel," al Assad said. "He spoke of seeing the ramparts of Paradise."

The abbot frowned at him.

"The old man is right," one of the brothers said. "He started talking on the way up. About seeing the golden banners on the towers of Paradise. He said that an angel had showed him the wide earth. He says he has been told by the Lord to bring the Chosen back to the Truth."

A shadow crossed the abbot's face. That kind of talk distressed him.

"Maybe he did see an angel," someone suggested.

"Don't be silly," the abbot countered.

"He's alive," al Assad reminded him. "Against all the odds."

"He's been with the bandits."

"The bandits fled across the Sahel. The el Habib tracked them."

"Someone else, then."

"An angel. You don't believe in angels, Brother?"

"Of course I do," the abbot replied hastily. "I just don't think they reveal themselves to salt merchants' sons. It's the desert madness talking through him. He'll forget it when he recovers." The abbot looked around. He was not pleased. The whole Shrine was gathering over the boy, and in too many faces there was a desire to believe. "Achmed. Bring me Mustaf el Habib. No. Wait. Ridyah, you found the boy. You go to the village."

"But why?"

A technicality had occurred to the abbot. It looked like the perfect exit from the difficulties the boy was generating.

"We can't nurse him here. He hasn't been consecrated. And he would have to be well before we could do that."

Al Assad glowered at his superior. Then, with anger to banish his aches and weariness, he set off for the village of El Aquila.

The hetman of the el Habib tribe was no more excited than the abbot. "So you found a kid in the desert? What do you want me to do about it? He's not my problem."

"The unfortunate are all our problems," al Assad replied. "The abbot would speak with you of this one."

The abbot opened with a similar remark in response to a similar statement. He quoted some scripture. Mustaf countered with the quote al Assad had used earlier. The abbot kept his temper with difficulty.

"He's not consecrated."

"Consecrate him. That's your job."

"We can't do that till he recovers his faculties."

"He's nothing to me. And you're even less."

There were hard feelings. It had been but two days since Mustaf had petitioned the abbot for permission to draw water from the Shrine's spring. The abbot had denied him.

Al Assad, cunningly, had brought the chieftain up by way of the Shrine's gardens, where lush flowerbeds in careful arrangements glorified God. Mustaf was in no mood to be charitable.

The abbot was in the jaws of a merciless trap. The laws of good works were the high laws of the Shrine. He dared not abrogate them before his brothers. Not if he wished to retain his post. But neither was he ready to allow this boy to mutter his heretical insanities where they could upset the thinking of his charges.

"My friend, we had hard words over a matter we discussed recently. Perhaps I reached my decision a bit hastily."

Mustaf smiled a predatory smile. "Perhaps."

"Two score barrels of water?" the abbot suggested.

Mustaf started toward the doorway.

Al Assad shook his head sadly. They were going to dicker like merchants while a boy lay dying. He departed in disgust, taking himself to his cell.

Within the hour he surrendered to the embrace of the Dark Lady.

Micah wakened suddenly, rational, intuiting that a long time had passed. His last clear memory was of walking beside his father as their caravan began the last league to El Aquila. Shouts... a blow... pain... reminiscences of madness. There had been an ambush. Where was he now? Why wasn't he dead? An angel... There had been an angel.

Snatches returned. He had been returned to life, to become a missionary to the Chosen. A disciple.

He rose from his pallet. His legs betrayed him immediately. He lay panting for several minutes before finding the strength to crawl to a flapway.

The el Habib had confined him to a tent. They had quarantined him. His words had made Mustaf tremble. The chieftain could sense the blood and pain beyond such mad perspectives.

Micah yanked the flap.

The afternoon sun slapped his face. He threw an arm across his eyes and cried out. That devil orb was trying to murder him again.

"You idiot!" a voice snarled as someone pushed him back inside. "You want to blind yourself?"

The hands that guided him to his pallet became tender. The afterimages faded. He discovered his companion to be a girl.

She was about his own age. She wore no veil.

He shrank away. What was this? Some temptation of the Evil One? Her father would kill him....

"What happened, Meryem? I heard him yell." A youth of about sixteen slipped inside. Micah retreated in earnest.

Then he remembered who and what he was. The hand of the Lord had touched him. He was the Disciple. No one could question his righteousness.

"Our foundling got himself an eyeful of sun." The girl touched Micah's shoulder. He flinched away.

"Back off, Meryem. Save the games for when he can handle them." To Micah he said, "She's father's favorite. The last born. He spoils her. She gets away with murder. Meryem. Please? The veil?"

"Where am I?" Micah asked.

"El Aquila," the youth replied. "In a tent behind the hut of Mustaf abd-Racim ibn Farid el Habib. The Al Ghabha priests found you. You were almost dead. They turned you over to my father. I'm Nassef. The brat is my sister Meryem." He sat down cross-legged facing Micah. "We're supposed to take care of you."

He did not sound enthusiastic.

"You were too much bother for them," the girl said. "That's why they gave you to Father." She sounded bitter.

"What?"

"Our oasis is drying up. The one at the Shrine is still wet, but the abbot won't share his water rights. The holy gardens flourish while the el Habib thirst."

Neither mentioned their sire's pragmatic deal.

"Did you really see an angel?" Meryem asked.

"Yes. I did. He bore me up among the stars and showed me the lands of the earth. He came to me in the hour of my despair and gave me two priceless gifts: my life, and the Truth. And he bade me take the Truth to the Chosen, that they might be freed of the bondage of the past and in turn carry the Word to the infidel."

Nassef flashed a sarcastic look in his sister's direction. Micah saw it plainly.

"You too shall know the Truth, friend Nassef. You shall see the flowering of the Kingdom of Peace. The Lord has returned me to the living with the mission of creating his Kingdom on Earth."

In ages to come there would be countless bitter words spilled over El Murid's returned-to-life remarks. Did he mean a symbolic rebirth, or a literal return from the dead? He would never clarify himself.

Nassef closed his eyes. He was four years older than this naive boy. Those years were an unbridgeable gulf of experience.

He did have the manners to refrain from laughing. "Open the flap a crack, Meryem. Let the sun in little by little, till he can face it."

She did so, and said, "We should bring him something to eat. He hasn't had any solid food yet."

"Nothing heavy. His stomach isn't ready." Nassef had seen victims of the desert before.

"Help me bring it."

"All right. Rest easy, foundling. We'll be right back. Think up an appetite." He followed his sister from the tent.

Meryem paused twenty feet away. Softly, she asked, "He really believes it, doesn't he?"

"About the angel? He's crazy."

"I believe it, too, Nassef. In a way. Because I want to. What he says... I think a lot of people want to hear that kind of thing. I think the abbot sent him down here because he was afraid to listen. And that's why Father won't have him in the house."

"Meryem—"

"What if a lot of people start listening and believing, Nassef?"

Nassef paused thoughtfully. "It's something to think about, isn't it?"

"Yes. Come on. Let's get him something."

El Murid, who was still very much the boy Micah al Rhami, lay staring at the tent above him. He let the leak of sunshine tease his eyes. A compulsion to be on his way, to begin preaching, rose within him. He fought it down. He knew he had to recover completely before he began his ministry.

But he was so impatient!

He knew the wayward habits of the Chosen, now that the angel had opened his eyes. It was imperative that he bring them the Truth as soon as possible. Every life the Dark Lady harvested now meant one more soul lost to the Evil One.

He would begin with El Aquila and Al Ghabha. When these people had been saved he would send them to minister to their neighbors. He himself would travel among the tribes and villages along his father's caravan route. If he could find some way to bring them salt...

"Here we are," Meryem announced. There was a musical note in her voice Micah found strange in one so young.

"Soup again, but this time I brought some bread. You can soak it. Sit up. You'll have to feed yourself this time. Don't eat too fast. You'll make yourself sick. Not too much, either."

"You're kind, Meryem."

"No. Nassef is right. I'm a brat."

"The Lord loves you even so." He began talking softly, persuasively, between bites. Meryem listened in apparent rapture.

He spoke for the first time in the shade of the palms surrounding the el Habib oasis. Little but mud remained of that once reliable waterhole, and that had begun to dry and crack. He made of the oasis a parable paralleling the drying up of the waters of faith in the Lord.

His audience was small. He sat with them as a teacher with students, reasoning with them and instructing them in the faith. Some were men four times his age. They were amazed by his knowledge and clarity of thought.

They threw fine points of dogma into his path like surprise pitfalls, baiting him. He shattered their arguments like a barbarian horde destroying lightly defended cities.

He had been more carefully schooled than he knew.

He made no converts. He had not expected to do so. He wanted to start them gossiping behind his back, unwittingly creating a climate for the sort of speeches that *would* win converts.

The older men went away afraid. They sensed in his words the first spark of a flame that could consume the Children of Hammad al Nakir.

Afterward, El Murid visited Mustaf. "My father's caravan? What became of it?" he asked the chieftain. Mustaf was taken aback, for he did it as an equal, not a child to an elder.

"Ambushed. All wiped out. It was a sad hour in the history of Hammad al Nakir. That I should have lived to see the day wherein men turned upon a salt caravan!"

There was something a little evasive in the way Mustaf had spoken. His eyes had become shifty.

"I have heard that the men of el Habib found the caravan. I have heard that they pursued the bandits."

"This is true. The bandits crossed the Sahel to the country of the western infidel."

Mustaf had become nervous. Micah thought he knew why. The hetman was essentially honorable. He had sent his own people to extract justice for the al Rhami family. But there was a little of the brigand in all the Children of Hammad al Nakir. "Yet there is a camel outside which answers to the name Big Jamal. And another which responds to Cactus. Could it be sheer coincidence that these beasts bear names identical to those of camels which belonged to my father? Is it coincidence that they bear identical markings?"

Mustaf said nothing for nearly a minute. Coals of anger burned briefly in his eyes. No man was pleased to be called to account by a child.

"You are observant, son of al Rhami," he finally replied. "It is true. They were your father's animals. When news came of what had happened, we saddled our best horses and rode swift and hard upon the trail. A crime so hideous could not go unpunished. Though your father's people were not of the el Habib, they were of the Chosen. They were saltmen. The laws shielding them are older than the Empire."

"And there was booty to be had."

"And there was booty, though your father was not a wealthy man. His entire fortune could scarcely repay the cost we paid in horses and lives."

Micah smiled. Mustaf had revealed his bargaining strategy. "You avenged my family?"

"Though our pursuit carried beyond the Sahel. We caught them before the very palisades of the heathen traders. Only two passed the infidels' gates. We were gentlemen. We did not burn their wooden walls. We did not slay the men and enslave the women. We treated with their council of factors, who knew your family of old. We presented our proofs. They took council, then delivered the bandits into our mercy. We were not merciful. They took many days dying, as an example to others who would break laws older than the desert. Perhaps the vultures still pick their bones."

"For that I must thank you, Mustaf. What of my patrimony?"

"We treated with the factors. Perhaps they cheated us. We were but ignorant devils of the sands. Perhaps not. We bore scimitars still stained with the blood of those who had wronged us."

"I doubt that they cheated, Mustaf. It's not their way. And, as you say, they would have been frightened."

"There is a small amount in gold and silver. And the camels did not interest them."

"What were your losses?"

"One man. And my son Nassef was wounded. That boy! You should have seen him! He was a lion! My pride knows no bounds. That such a son should have sprung from my loins! A lion of the desert, my Nassef. He will be a mighty warrior. If he outlives youth's impetuosity. He slew three of them himself." The chieftain glowed in his pride.

"And horses? You mentioned horses."

"Three. Three of our best. We rode hard and swift. And there was a messenger, that we sent to find your father's people, that they might know and make claims. He has not yet returned."

"He has a long journey. It's yours, Mustaf. All yours. I ask but a horse and a small amount of coin with which to begin my ministry."

Mustaf was surprised. "Micah—"

"I am El Murid now. Micah al Rhami is no more. He was a boy who died in the desert. I have returned from the fiery forge as the Disciple."

"You're serious, aren't you?"

El Murid was surprised that there could be any doubt.

"For the sake of the friendship I bore your father, hear me now. Do not pursue this path. It can be naught but a way of tears and sorrow."

"I must, Mustaf. The Lord himself has commanded me."

"I should restrain you. I will not. May the ghost of your father forgive me. I will choose a horse."

"A white horse, if you have one."

"I have one."

Next morning El Murid again taught beneath the palms. He spoke with passion, of the scarcely restrained wrath of God losing all patience with his Chosen's neglect of their duties. The argument of the empty oasis was hard to refute. The fiery summer could not be discounted. Several of his younger listeners remained for a more scholarly question and answer session.

Three days later Nassef whispered from beyond El Murid's tent flap. "Micah? May I come in?"

"Come. Nassef? El Murid?"

"Sorry. Of course." The youth settled himself opposite El Murid. "Father and

I have had an argument. About you."

"I'm sorry to hear that. It isn't a good thing."

"He ordered me to stay away from you. Meryem too. The other parents are going to do the same. They're getting angry. You're calling too many ideas into question. They tolerated you when they thought it was the desert madness talking. But now they're calling you a heretic."

El Murid was stunned. "Me? The Disciple? They accuse me of heresy? How can that be?" Had he not been chosen by the Lord?

"You challenge old ways. Their ways. You accuse them. You accuse the priests of Al Ghabha. They are set in their ways. You can't expect them to say, 'Yes, we are guilty.'"

He had not foreseen that the Evil One would be so cunning as to deflect his own arguments against him. He had underestimated his Enemy. "Thank you, Nassef. You're a true friend to warn me. I will remember. Nassef, I hadn't anticipated this."

"I thought not."

"Go, then. Do not give your father cause for a grievance. I will speak to you later."

Nassef rose and departed, a small, thin smile on his lips.

El Murid prayed for hours. He retreated deep into his young mind. At last the will of the Lord became clear to him.

He looked up the long, stony slope at Al Ghabha. The low hill was barren, as if the darkness up there might creep down to devour any goodness surrounding it.

It was there that his first and most important victory had to be won. What point to winning the el Habib if their traditional spiritual shepherds guided them back to the paths of wrongdoing the moment he traveled on?

"I'm going to the Shrine," he told one of the men of the village, who had come to see what he was doing. "I'm going to preach a sermon there. I shall show them the Truth. Then let them name me heretic to my face, and risk the wrath of the Lord."

"Will that be wise?"

"It must be done. They must declare themselves righteous, or tools of the Evil One."

"I'll tell the others."

El Murid began walking.

The desert religion had contained no real devil figure till El Murid named him. Evil had been the province of a host of demons, ghosts, and fell spirits without leadership. And the paternalistic God of Hammad al Nakir had been but the paterfamilias of a family of gods suspiciously resembling the extended families of the Imperial and desert tribes. The Lord's problems had tended to come from a black-sheep brother who meddled and politicked for the pleasure of causing discord. The religion had retained traces of animism, belief in reincarnation, and ancestor worship.

The scholars at the Rebsamen University in Hellin Daimiel believed the desert gods to be vague echoes of a family that had united the original Seven Tribes and had guided their migration into the land that would one day become the Empire, and later Hammad al Nakir.

El Murid's teachings banished animism, ancestor worship, and reincarnation. They elevated the family chieftain to the position of an omnipotent One True God. His brothers and wives and children became mere angels.

And the meddlesome brother became the Evil One, the master of djinn and ifrits and the patron of all sorcerers. El Murid railed against the practice of witchcraft with a vehemence his listeners found incomprehensible. His principal argument was that it had been sorcery that had brought on the doom of the Empire. The glory of Ilkazar, and a hope for its return, was a theme running through all his teaching.

The primary point of contention at El Aquila was a proscription against praying to the lesser gods. El Murid's listeners were accustomed to petitioning specialists. They were accustomed, especially, to approaching Muhrain, the patron of the region, to whom the Al Ghabha Shrines were dedicated.

The boy's path led him not to Al Ghabha but to the site where the imam, Ridyah, had found him. He did not at first know what drew him thither. Then he thought that he was looking for something.

He had left something there, something that he had forgotten. Something that he had hidden in his last moment of rationality. Something that had been given him by his angel.

Visions of an amulet came in snatches. A potent wrist amulet bearing a living stone. It would be, his angel had told him, the proof he needed to convince unbelievers.

But he could not remember where he had concealed it.

He scrabbled round the sides of the wadi that had prevented him from reaching El Aquila on his own.

"What in the world are you doing?" Nassef asked from above.

"You startled me, Nassef."

"What're you doing?"

"Looking for something. I hid it here. They didn't find it, did they? Did they find anything?"

"Who? The priests? Only a ragged, desert-worn saltman's son. What did you hide?"

"I remember now. A rock that looks like a tortoiseshell. Where is it?"

"There's one over here."

The rock was just a yard from where al Assad had found him. He tried lifting the stone. He did not have the strength.

"Here. Let me help." Nassef nudged him aside. In the process he tore his sleeve on a thorn of a scraggly desert bush. "Oh. Mother's going to brain me."

"Help me."

"Father too, if he finds out I was here."

"Nassef!"

"All right! I'm here." He heaved on the rock. "How did you move it before?"

"I don't know."

Together they heaved the stone onto its back. Nassef asked, "Ah, what is it?"

El Murid gently extracted the amulet from the rocky soil, brushing dirt from its delicate golden wristlet. The stone glowed even in the brilliant morning sun.

"The angel gave it to me. To be my proof to the doubtful."

Nassef was impressed, though he seemed more troubled than elated. In a moment, nervously, he suggested, "You'd better come on. The whole village is going to be at the Shrine."

"They expect to be entertained?"

Noncommittally, Nassef replied, "They think it's going to be interesting."

El Murid had noticed this evasiveness before. Nassef refused to be pinned down. About anything.

They strolled up to Al Ghabha, Nassef gradually lagging. El Murid accepted it. He understood. Nassef had to get along with Mustaf.

Everybody was there, from El Aquila and Al Ghabha alike. The gardens of the Shrines had assumed a carnival air. But he received very few friendly smiles there.

Behind the merriment was a strong current of malice. They had come to see someone hurt.

He had thought that he could teach them, that he could debate the abbot and so expose the folly inherent in the old dogma and old ways. But the mood here was passion. It demanded a passionate response, an emotional demonstration.

He acted without thinking. For the next few minutes he was just another spectator watching El Murid perform.

He threw his arms up and cried, "The Power of the Lord is upon me! The Spirit of God moves me! Witness, you idolaters, you wallowers in sin and weak faith! The hours of the enemies of the Lord are numbered! There is but one God, and I am His Disciple! Follow me or burn in Hell forever!"

He hurled his right fist at the earth. The stone in his amulet blazed furiously.

A lightning bolt flung down from a sky that had not seen a cloud in months. It blasted a ragged scar across the gardens of the Shrine. Singed petals fluttered through the air.

Thunder rolled across the blue. Women screamed. Men clutched their ears. Six more bolts hurtled down like the swift stabbing of a short spear. The lovely flowerbeds were ripped and burned.

In silence El Murid stalked from the grounds, his strides long and purposeful. At that moment he was no child, no man, but a force as terrible as a cyclone.

He descended on El Aquila.

The crowd surged after him, terrified, yet irresistibly drawn. The brothers of the Shrine came too, and they almost never left Al Ghabha.

El Murid marched to the dry oasis. He halted where once sweet waters had lapped at the toes of date palms. "I am the Disciple!" he shrieked. "I am the Instrument of the Lord! I am the Glory, and the Power, incarnate!" He seized up a stone that weighed more than a hundred pounds, hoisted it over his head effortlessly. He heaved it out onto the dried mud.

Thunders tortured the cloudless sky. Lightnings pounded the desert. Women shrieked. Men hid their eyes. And moisture began to darken the hard-baked mud.

El Murid wheeled on Mustaf and the abbot. "Do you label me fool and heretic, then? Speak, Hell serf. Show me the power within you."

The handful of converts he had earlier won gathered to one side. Their faces glowed with awe and something akin to worship.

Nassef hovered in the gap between groups. He had not yet decided which party was truly his.

The abbot refused to be impressed. His defiant stance proclaimed that no demonstration would reach him. He growled, "It's mummery. The power of this Evil One you preach... you've done nothing no skilled sorcerer couldn't have done."

A forbidden word had been hurled into El Murid's face like a gauntlet. A strong, irrational hatred of wizardry had underlain all the youth's teachings so far. It was that part of his doctrine which most confused his audiences, because it seemed to bear little relationship to his other teachings.

El Murid shook with rage. "How dare you?"

"Infidel!" someone shrieked. Others took it up. "Heretic!"

El Murid whirled. Did they mock him?

His converts were shouting at the abbot.

One threw a stone. It opened the priest's forehead, sending him to his knees. A barrage followed. Most of the villagers fled. The abbot's personal attendants, a pair of retarded brothers younger than most of the priests, seized his arms and dragged him away. El Murid's converts went after them, flinging stones.

Mustaf rallied a handful of men and intercepted them. Angry words filled the air. Fists flew. Knives leapt into angry hands.

"Stop it!" El Murid shrieked.

It was the first of the riots which were to follow him like a disease throughout the years. Only his intercession kept lives from being lost.

"Stop!" he thundered, raising his right hand to the sky. His amulet flared, searing faces with its golden glow. "Put up your blades and go home," he told his followers.

The power was still upon him. He was no child. The command in his voice could not be refused. His followers sheathed their blades and backed away. He considered them. They were all young. Some were younger than he. "I did not come among you to have you spill one another's blood." He turned to the chieftain of the el Habib. "Mustaf, I offer my apologies. I did not intend this."

"You preach war. Holy war."

"Against the unbeliever. The heathen nations that rebelled against the Empire. Not brother against brother. Not Chosen against Chosen." He glanced at the young people. He was startled to see several girls among them. "Nor sister against brother, nor son against father. I have come to reunite the Holy Empire in the strength of the Lord, that once again the Chosen might take their rightful place among the nations, secure in the love of the one true God, whom they shall worship as befits the Chosen."

Mustaf shook his head. "I suspect you mean well. But riots and discord will follow wherever you go, Micah al Rhami."

"El Murid. I am the Disciple."

"Contention will be your traveling companion, Micah. And your travels have begun. I will not have this among the el Habib. I take no harsher action than banish you forever from el Habib lands because I consider your family, and your trials in the desert." And—unspoken—because he feared El Murid's amulet.

"I am El Murid!"

"I don't care. Not who you are, or what. I won't have you fomenting violence in my territories. I'll give you the horse and coin you asked, and whatever you need to travel. You'll leave El Aquila this afternoon. I, Mustaf abd-Racim ibn Farid el Habib, have spoken. Do not defy me."

"Father, you can't—"

"Be silent, Meryem. What were you doing with that rabble? Why aren't you with your mother?"

The girl began to argue. Mustaf cut her short. "I've been a fool. You're starting to think you're a man. That is ended, Meryem. From this moment forward you will remain with the women, and do the work of women."

"Father!"

"You heard me. Micah. You heard me too. Start moving."

His converts were ready to resume scuffling. He disappointed them.

"No," he said. "It's not yet time for the Kingdom of Peace to challenge the unrighteous controlling temporal powers, corrupt as they may be. Endure. Our hour will come."

Mustaf reddened. "Boy, don't push me."

El Murid turned. He faced the chieftain of the el Habib. He clasped his hands before him, right over left. The jewel in his amulet blazed at Mustaf. He met the chieftain's gaze without flinching or speaking.

Mustaf yielded first, his eyes going to the amulet. He swallowed and started toward the village.

El Murid followed at a slower pace. His acolytes orbited him, their mouths full of soothing promises. He ignored most of them. His attention was on Nassef, who again was drifting aimlessly between parties, drawn both ways.

Intuition told him that he needed Nassef. The youth could become the cornerstone of his future. He had to win Nassef over before he left.

El Murid was as ambivalent about Nassef as Mustaf's son was about El Murid. Nassef was bright, fearless, hard, and competent. But he had a dark streak in him that frightened the Disciple. Mustaf's son contained as much potential for evil as he did for good.

"No, I won't defy Mustaf," he told his imploring companions. "I've recovered from my debility. It's time I started my travels. I'll return in time. Carry on my work while I'm gone. Show me a model village when I return."

He began one of his gentle teaching sessions, trying to give them the tools they would need to become effective missionaries.

He did not glance back as he rode out of El Aquila. He had only one regret: he had had no opportunity to present Nassef with further arguments. El Aquila had been a beginning.

Not nearly as good a beginning as he had hoped, though. He had not been able to sway anyone important. Priests and temporal leaders simply refused to listen. He would have to find some way to open their ears and minds.

He took the trail that reversed the road his father's caravan had been traveling. He wanted to pause at the place where his family had died.

His angel had told him his work would be hard, that he would be resisted by those who had an investment in the old ways. He had not believed. How could they refuse the Truth? It was so obvious and beautiful that it overwhelmed one.

He was two miles east of El Aquila when he heard hoofbeats. He glanced back. Two riders were overtaking him. He did not immediately recognize them. He had noticed them only momentarily, when they had helped the stoned abbot flee the oasis. What were they doing? He turned his face eastward and tried to ignore them.

His worry would not leave him. It quickly became obvious that they were trailing him. When he looked again he found that they were just a dozen yards behind. Naked steel appeared in their hands.

He kicked his mount's flanks. The white stallion surged forward, almost toppling him. He flung himself forward and clung to the animal's neck with no thought of regaining control.

The riders came after him.

He now knew the fear he had had no time for in the ambush of his father's caravan. He could not believe that the Evil One would have become so desperate so soon.

His flight led him into and through the defile where his family had died. He swept round a mass of bizarrely weathered boulders.

Riders awaited him. His mount sank to its haunches to avoid a collision. El Murid tumbled off. He rolled across the hard earth and scrambled for cover.

He had no weapon. He had trusted in the protection of the Lord.... He began praying.

Hooves thundered down the defile. Men shouted. Steel rang on steel. Someone moaned. Then it ended.

"Come out, Micah," someone shouted into the ensuing silence.

He peeped between boulders. He saw two riderless horses and two bodies lying on the stony earth.

Nassef loomed over them on a big black stallion. His right hand held a bloody blade. Behind him were another three youths from El Aquila, and Meryem and another girl.

El Murid crept out. "Where did you come from?"

"We decided to come with you." Nassef swung down. Contemptuously, he wiped his blade on the chest of one of the dead men. "Priests. They send halfwits to do murder."

The brothers had not been priests themselves, only wards of the Shrine who had been cared for by the abbot in return for doing the donkey work around the monastery.

"But how did you get here?" El Murid demanded.

"Meryem saw them start after you. Some of us were arguing about what to do. That decided us. There's an antelope trail that goes over the hills instead of around. I took that, riding hard. I was sure they would let you get this far, then try to make it look like you'd run foul of bandits again."

El Murid stood over the dead brothers. Tears came to his eyes. They had been but tools of the Evil One, poor things. He knelt and said prayers for their souls, though he had little hope that the Lord would show them any mercy. His was a jealous, vengeful God.

When he had finished, he asked, "What are you going to tell your father?"

"Nothing. We're going with you."

"But…"

"You need somebody, Micah. Hasn't that just been proven?"

El Murid paused thoughtfully, then threw his arms around Nassef. "I'm glad you came, Nassef. I was worried for you."

Nassef reddened. The Children of Hammad al Nakir were often demonstrative, but seldom in the tenderer emotions. "Let's get going," he said. "We've got a long way to travel if we're not going to spend the night in the desert."

El Murid hugged him again. "Thank you, Nassef. I wish you knew how much this means to me." Then he went round clasping the hands of the others, and kissing the hands of the girls.

"I don't rate a hug, eh?" Meryem teased. "Do you love Nassef more?"

Now he was embarrassed. Meryem would not cease playing her games.

He called her bluff. "Come down here."

She did so, so he hugged her. It aggravated Nassef and completely flustered the girl.

El Murid laughed.

One of the youths brought his horse. "Thank you."

So there were seven who began the long trail, the trail of years. El Murid thought it an auspicious number, but the number gave no luck. He would suffer countless nights of frustration and depression before his ministry bore fruit. Too many of the Children of Hammad al Nakir refused him, or were just plain Truth-blind.

But he persisted. And each time he preached he won a heart or two. His following grew, and they too preached.

TWO
SEEDS OF HATRED, ROOTS OF WAR

Haroun was six years old when first he encountered El Murid.

His brother Ali had found himself a perch in a gap in the old garden wall. "God's Whiskers!" Ali squealed. "Khedah. Mustaf. Haroun. Come and look at this."

Their teacher, Megelin Radetic, scowled. "Ali, come down from there."

The boy ignored him.

"How am I supposed to pound anything into the heads of these little savages?" Radetic muttered. "Can't you do anything?" he asked their uncle Fuad.

Fuad's severe lips formed a thin, wicked smile. *Can but won't*, that smile said. He thought his brother Yousif a fool for wasting money on a pansy foreign teacher. "It's Disharhun. What did you expect?"

Radetic shook his head. That was Fuad's latest stock answer.

This barbarous holiday. It meant weeks lost in the already hopeless task of training the Wahlig's brats. They had come damned near three hundred miles, from el Aswad all the way to Al Rhemish, for a festival and prayer. Foolish. True, some important political business would take place behind the scenes.

The scholars of Hellin Daimiel were notorious skeptics. They labeled all faith as farce or fraud.

Megelin Radetic was more skeptical then most. His attitude had generated some bitter arguments with his employer, Yousif, the Wahlig of el Aswad. Fuad had become part of the class scene as a result. Yousif's younger brother and chief bully remained on hand to assure the children's insulation from Hellin Daimiel's stronger heresies.

"Hurry!" Ali insisted. "You'll miss it."

All traffic passing through the Royal Compound, from the pilgrim camps to the Most Holy Mrazkim Shrines, had to follow the one dusty street beyond the wall of Radetic's courtyard-classroom. This was the first time any of his students had joined their fathers during Disharhun. They had never seen Al Rhemish or its holiday displays.

"High Holy Week," Radetic muttered sourly. "Spring Hosting. Who needs it?"

It was his first visit, too. In his quiet way, he was as excited as the children.

He had taken the teaching position in order to study the primitive political processes going on behind the Sahel. The unprecedented challenge of a messianic type like El Murid promised an interesting study of a culture under stress. His field was the study of the evolution of ideals in government, especially the monolithic state trying to survive by adapting to the changing perceptions of subjects believed to be politically disenfranchised. It was a subtle and tricky area of study, and one's conclusions were always subject to attack.

His deal with Yousif had been accounted a great coup at his college, the Rebsamen. The secretive people of Hammad al Nakir were a virgin territory for academic exploitation. Radetic had begun to doubt the opportunity was worth the pain.

Only little Haroun remained attentive. The others jostled Ali for vantage points.

"Oh, go on," Radetic told his one remaining pupil.

Haroun was the sole intellectual candle Radetic had found in this benighted wasteland. Haroun was the only reason Radetic did not tell Yousif to pack up his prejudices and head for Hell. The child had shown tremendous promise.

The rest? Haroun's brothers and cousins, and the children of Yousif's favored followers? Doomed. They would become copies of their fathers. Ignorant, superstitious, bloodthirsty savages. New swordbearers in the endless pavane of raid and skirmish these wild men accounted a worthy life.

Radetic would have confessed it to no man, and least of all himself. He loved the imp called Haroun. He followed the boy and for the thousandth time pondered the mystery of the Wahlig.

Yousif's station roughly equated with that of a duke. He was a cousin of King Aboud. He had every reason to defend the status quo, and much to lose by change. Yet he dreamed of ending the old killing ways, the traditional desert ways, at least in his own demesne. In his quieter, less abrasive way, he was as revolutionary as El Murid.

One of the older boys boosted Haroun to the top of the wall. He stared as if smitten by some great wonder.

Radetic's favorite was slight, dusky, dark-eyed, and hawk-nosed, a child-image of his sire. Even at six he knew his station.

Because he was only a fourth son, Haroun was fated to become his province's chief *shaghûn,* the commander of the handful of sorcerer-soldiers serving with the family cavalry.

Yousif's Wahligate was vast. His forces were numerous, for they nominally included every man able to bear arms. Haroun's responsibilities would be large, his immersion in wizardry deep.

Already Radetic had to share his pupil with witch-teachers from Jebal al Alf Dhulquarneni, the appropriately named Mountains of a Thousand Sorcerers. The great adepts almost always began their studies at the time they were learning to talk, yet seldom came into the fullness of their power till they had passed their prime mating years. The young years were critical to the learning of self-discipline, which had to be attained before the onset of puberty and accompanying distractions.

Radetic wriggled his way into the pack of children. "I'll be damned!"

Fuad pulled him back. "Of that there's no doubt." He assumed Radetic's place. "Holy!... A bare-faced woman! Teacher, you might as well turn them loose. They'll never settle down now. I'd better go tell Yousif that they're here." Fuad's face had taken on the glassy look of a man in rut. Radetic did not doubt that he had an erection.

The ways of the desert were strange, he thought.

Speculation had haunted the Royal Compound for days. Would El Murid really dare come to the Shrines?

Radetic shoved himself into the gap again, staring.

The woman was younger than he had expected. She rode a tall white camel. The fact of her facial nakedness completely eclipsed the presence of the wild-eyed youth on the white mare.

El Murid was, for that matter, overshadowed by the man riding the big black stallion.

That would be Nassef, wouldn't it? Radetic thought. The brawler who led El Murid's dramatically named bodyguard, the Invincibles, and who was the brother of the Disciple's wife.

"El Murid. You're a bold bandit, son," Radetic murmured. He found himself admiring the youth's arrogance. Anyone who thumbed his nose at priesthoods rated with Megelin Radetic.

"Boys. Get down. Go find your fathers. Do you want a whipping?"

Such was the punishment for gazing on a woman's naked face. His pupils fled.

All but Haroun. "Is that really El Murid? The one Father calls Little Devil?"

Radetic nodded. "That's him."

Haroun scampered after his brothers and cousins. "Ali! Wait. Remember when Sabbah came to el Aswad?"

Megelin suspected imminent deviltry. Nothing but bad blood had come of that ill-starred peace conference with Sabbah i Hassan. He stalked his pupils.

He had warned Yousif. He had cast horoscope after horoscope, and each had been blacker than the last. But Yousif had rejected the scientific approach in his own life.

There was a natural yet innocent cruelty in the Children of Hammad al Nakir. Their very language lacked a means of expressing the concept "cruelty to an enemy."

Haroun looked back. He paused when he noticed Radetic watching him. But the urge to impress his brothers overcame good sense. He seized his rudimentary shaghûn's kit and joined their rush into the street.

Radetic followed. He would not be able to prevent their prank, but might finally penetrate the veil of mystery that surrounded the collapse of the negotiations with Sabbah i Hassan.

Its simplicity was frightening.

A shaghûn was as much stage magician as true sorcerer. Haroun spent an hour a day practicing sleight of hand that would awe the credulous one day. Among his simple tools was a peashooter. He could conceal it within a fist and, with a faked cough, blow a pellet into a campfire or a dart at an unsuspecting enemy.

Haroun chose a dart, and put it into the white horse's flank.

She reared and screamed. El Murid fell at Haroun's feet. They locked gazes. El Murid looked puzzled. When he tried to stand, he fell. He had broken an ankle.

Haroun's brothers and cousins began mocking the injured youth.

A quick-witted priest shouted, "An omen! False prophets inevitably fall."

Others took it up. They had been lying in wait, hoping for a chance to embarrass El Murid. Pushing and shoving started between factions.

Haroun and El Murid still stared at one another, as if seeing the future, and seeing it grim.

Nassef spied the peashooter. His sword rang as it cleared his scabbard. Its tip cut a shallow slice an inch above Haroun's right eye. The boy would have died but for Radetic's quick action.

Royalist partisans roared. Weapons materialized. "It's going to get ugly. You little fool. Come up here." Radetic yanked Haroun off the ground and threw him over his shoulder, then hurried toward his employer's tent. During Disharhun everyone, whether making the pilgrimage to Al Rhemish or not, lived the week in tents.

Fuad met them in the street. He had heard a swift-winged rumor of murder. He was angry. A huge man with a savage reputation, Fuad in a rage was a ferocious spectacle. He had his war blade in hand. It looked big enough to behead an ox with a single blow.

"What happened, teacher? Is he all right?"

"Mostly scared. I'd better talk to Yousif." He tried hiding the bleeding. Fuad had less self-control than the usual volatile native.

"He's waiting."

"I should find an injured child every time I want to talk to him."

Fuad gave him a poisonous look.

The shouting and blade waving around El Murid had turned ugly. Fighting was forbidden during Disharhun, but the Children of Hammad al Nakir were not ones to let laws restrict their emotions.

Horsemen bearing round black shields emblazoned with the crude red eagle of the Royal Household descended on the trouble spot.

Radetic hurried on to his employer's quarters.

"What happened?" Yousif demanded as soon as he had determined that

Haroun's wound was minor. He had cleared his tent of the usual hangers-on. "Haroun, you tell it first."

The boy was too frightened to stretch the truth. "I… I used my blow tube. To hit his horse. I didn't know he would get hurt."

"Megelin?"

"That's the gist of it. A practical joke, in poor taste. I'd blame the examples set by his elders. I did, however, hear mention of Sabbah i Hassan beforehand."

"How so?"

"In the context, I believe, of a similar stunt. Your children, you know, are even more primitive and literal-minded than the rest of you."

"Haroun? Is that true?"

"Huh?"

"Did you do the same thing to Sabbah i Hassan?"

Radetic smiled thinly as he watched the boy struggle with the lie trying to break out of the prison of his mouth. "Yes, Father."

Fuad returned to the tent. He seemed to have calmed down.

"Teacher?" Yousif asked.

"Wahlig?"

"What the hell were they doing running the streets? They were supposed to be in class."

"Be serious, Yousif," Fuad interjected. "Don't tell me you're already too old to remember being young." The Wahlig was forty-one. "It's Disharhun. The woman wore no veil. You think the man is a miracle worker?"

Radetic was amazed. Fuad had made it plain that he thought any teacher who did not teach the use of weapons was superfluous. A warrior chieftain needed no other education. Scribes and accountants could be enslaved.

Moreover, he disliked Radetic personally.

What had put him into so good a mood? It worried Radetic.

"Haroun."

The boy approached his father reluctantly, took his spanking without crying. And without contrition.

Yousif was angry. He never punished his children before outsiders. And yet… Radetic suspected that his employer was not entirely displeased.

"Now go find your brothers. Tell them to get back here and stay out of trouble."

The boy ran out. Yousif looked at Fuad. "Bold little brat, isn't he?"

"His father's son, I think. You were the same."

Haroun was Yousif's favorite, though the Wahlig hid it well. Radetic suspected that he had been hired specifically for the benefit of the one boy. The others had been tossed into his classes in a vain hope that a patina of wisdom might stick.

Haroun would have preferred a scholarly life. When away from older brothers he showed the temperament. In fact, he had told Radetic that he wanted to be like him when he grew up. Megelin had been pleased and embarrassed.

For a six-year-old Haroun showed remarkable determination to pursue the mission decreed for him by an accident of birth. He acted twice his age. He was possessed of a stern, stolid fatalism seldom seen in anyone under thirty.

Megelin Radetic hurt a lot for the fated child.

Fuad bubbled over. "Yousif, this is the break we've been waiting for. This time he's given us a good, rock-hard excuse."

Radetic was startled when he suddenly realized that Fuad was talking about El Murid. It was a revelation. He had not suspected that powerful men were actually afraid of the Disciple. Afraid of a fifteen-year-old who, like themselves, had come to Al Rhemish for the rites of Disharhun, and to see his infant daughter christened before the Most Holy Mrazkim Shrines.

They had been lying to him. And to themselves, probably. Just plain old-fashioned whistling in the dark.

All this fuss over religious nonsense.

"Wahlig, this is ridiculous. Barbarous," Radetic grumbled. "Even pathetic. The boy is a madman. He crucifies himself every time he preaches. You don't have to trump up charges. Let him have his High Holy Week. Let him talk. They'll laugh him out of Al Rhemish."

"Let me boot this fish-faced pimp," Fuad growled.

Yousif raised a silencing hand. "Calm down. He has a right to an opinion. Even a wrong one."

Fuad shut up.

Yousif virtually owned his younger brother. Fuad seemed to have no imagination or aspirations of his own. He was a mirror of Yousif, the Wahlig's far-reaching right hand, a sledge used to hammer out another's dreams. Which was not to say that he always agreed. He and Yousif sometimes argued bitterly, especially when the latter was pushing an innovation. Sometimes Fuad won his point. But once a decision had been handed down he would support it to the death.

"Wahlig—"

"Be silent a moment, Megelin. Let me tell you where you're wrong." Yousif rearranged his cushions. "This is going to be long-winded. Get comfortable."

Radetic considered Yousif's tent to be furnished in garish, barbarous taste. The Children of Hammad al Nakir, when they could afford it, surrounded themselves with intense color. The reds, greens, yellows, and blues around Yousif so clashed that Radetic could almost hear their conflict.

"Fuad, see if you can find some refreshments while I start to educate our educator. Megelin, you're wrong because you're too convinced of the correctness of your own viewpoint. When you look around here you don't see a culture. You see barbarians. You hear our religious arguments and can't believe we take them seriously because you can't. I grant you, a lot of my people don't either. But the majority do.

"As for El Murid and his henchman, you see only a deranged boy and a bandit. I see a huge problem. The boy is saying things everyone wants to hear. And believe. And Nassef just might have the genius to carve out El Murid's new Empire. The two together might have an overpowering attraction for our children. Our children, otherwise, have no other hope than to relive our yesterdays.

"You see Nassef as a bandit because he has raided caravans. What makes him remarkable and dangerous isn't the fact of his crimes, but the skill with which he committed them. If he ever rises above theft in God's name to making war in God's name, then God help us. Because he'll probably destroy us.

"Megelin, nobody is going to laugh if El Murid speaks. Nobody. And as a speaker he is as dangerous as Nassef is as a fighter. His speeches are creating the weapons Nassef needs to rise above banditry.

"The boy's movement is at a crossroads. And he knows it. That's why he came to Al Rhemish this year. After Disharhun he'll either be discredited and fade away, or he'll begin sweeping the desert like a sandstorm. If we have to trump up charges to stop that, we will."

Fuad returned with a lemonade-like drink. Megelin and Yousif accepted their portions. Fuad seated himself quietly, out of the way.

Radetic, squatting on a scarlet pillow, took a sip, then said, "And Fuad wonders why I think you a barbarous people."

"My brother has never visited Hellin Daimiel. I have. I can believe that your people would laugh a messiah out of business. You're all cynics. And you don't need that kind of leader.

"We do, Megelin. The heart of me craves an El Murid. He's telling me exactly what my heart wants to hear. I want to believe that we're the Chosen People. I want to believe that it's our destiny to master the world. I want something, anything, to make the centuries since the Fall worthwhile.

"I want to believe that the Fall itself was the work of an Evil One. Fuad wants to believe. My cousin the King would like to believe. Unfortunately, we're old enough to recognize gossamer on the wind. A deadly gossamer.

"Megelin, that boy is a death merchant. He's put it in pretty packages, but he's selling another Fall. If we turn to him, if we break out of Hammad al Nakir in order to convert the pagan and resurrect the Empire, we'll be destroyed. Those of us who have been across the Sahel realize that the world out there isn't the one conquered by Ilkazar.

"We don't have the numbers, the resources, the arms, or the *discipline* of the western kingdoms."

Radetic nodded. These people would be hopelessly overmatched in any war with the west. Warfare, like everything else, evolved. The style of the Children of Hammad al Nakir had evolved in a direction suited only to the desert.

"But his jihad doesn't terrify me yet. That's a long way off," Yousif continued. "The struggle here is what frightens me. He has to win his homeland first. And to do that he will have to tear the belly out of Hammad al Nakir. So. I want to draw his fangs now. By fair means or foul."

"You live by different rules," Radetic observed. It was becoming a favorite saying. "I have to go think about what you've said." He finished his drink, rose, nodded to Fuad, and departed. He seated himself outside the tent flap, in the position for meditation. He listened while Yousif instructed Fuad how to approach King Aboud with news of this opportunity. Embittered by the foolishness of it, the injustice of it, he sealed them out, contemplated his surroundings.

The Royal Compound occupied five acres bordering the southwest flank of the Mrazkim Shrines, which were the religious heart of Hammad al Nakir. Today, because it was Disharhun, the compound was infested with royal relatives, favor seekers, and sycophants. Most of the captains, sheiyeks, and wahligs had brought their entire households. Traders and artisans, hoping to achieve some small advantage over their competitors, virtually besieged the Compound's boundaries. Ambassadors and foreign mercantile factors roamed everywhere. The smells were overwhelming. Men, animals, machines, and insects made noises which melded into an overpowering din.

And beyond the mad anthill of the Compound lay vast encampments of ordinary pilgrims. Their tents swept up the sides of the bowl-shaped valley containing the capital and Shrines. Thousands upon thousands more than customary had made the journey this year—because El Murid's visit had been rumored for months. They had come because they did not want to miss the inevitable collision between dissidence and authority.

Yousif was playing with fire, Radetic reflected as he watched Fuad stride toward Aboud's palatial tent. This monarchy, unlike its predecessor in Ilkazar, did not have the power to rule by decree. Today even the most obnoxious rabble-rouser could not be denied his hour in court, his opportunity to speak in his own defense.

A shy Haroun came to sit with his teacher. He put his hand into Radetic's.

"Sometimes, Haroun, you're too crafty for your own good." There was no rancor in Radetic's voice, though. The gesture touched him, genuine or not.

"I did wrong, Megelin?"

"There's some disagreement." Radetic surveyed the human panorama briefly. "You should think, Haroun. You can't simply act. That is your people's biggest handicap. They yield to impulse without ever considering the consequences."

"I'm sorry, Megelin."

"The hell you are. You're sorry you got caught. You don't care a whit how much you hurt that man."

"He's our enemy."

"How do you know? You never saw him before. You've never talked to him. He's never hurt you."

"Ali said—"

"Ali is like your uncle Fuad. He says a lot. His mouth is always open. And because of that, someday somebody else who doesn't think is going to shove his fist down Ali's throat. How often is he right? How often does pure foolishness come out of that open mouth?"

Radetic was letting his frustrations run wild. He had never encountered a student more unyieldingly unteachable than Ali bin Yousif.

"Then he isn't our enemy?"

"I didn't say that. Of course he is. He's your bitterest enemy. But not because Ali says he is. El Murid is an enemy in his ideals. I don't think he'd harm you physically if he had the chance. He'd just rob you of everything that's important to you. Someday, I hope, you'll understand just how gross a mistake your prank was."

"Fuad's coming."

"So he is. And he looks like an old cat licking cream off her whiskers. It went well, Fuad?"

"Beautifully, teacher. Old Aboud isn't as stupid as I thought. He saw the chance right away." Fuad's grin vanished. "You may be called to testify."

"Then, perhaps, we may be friends no more. I am of the Rebsamen, Fuad. I cannot lie."

"Were we ever friends?" Fuad demanded as he entered the tent.

A chill stalked down Radetic's spine. He was not a brave man.

He was disgusted with himself. He knew that he would lie if Yousif pressed him hard enough.

The court was convened as the traditional Disharhun Court of Nine, the supreme court of Hammad al Nakir. Three jurists were provided by the Royal Household, and another three by the Shrine priests. A final three were common pilgrims selected at random from among the hosts come for the High Holy Days.

It was a stacked court. El Murid was down eight votes before a shred of evidence had been presented.

Someone had bandaged Haroun heavily. He had been coached quickly and well. He lied with a straight face and defiantly traded stares with El Murid and Nassef.

Radetic nearly shrieked in protest when the Court voted to deny a request for permission to cross-examine.

A parade of pilgrims testified after Haroun stepped down. Their testimony bore little relation to the truth of what had happened. It seemed, instead, to follow religious predilection. No one mentioned seeing a peashooter or dart.

Radetic already knew this phase of desert justice well. He had reviewed judicial sessions at el Aswad. The disposition of most cases seemed to depend on which adversary could muster the most relatives to lie for him.

Megelin dreaded having to give his own testimony. His conscience had been ragging him mercilessly. He feared he would not be able to lie.

He was spared the final crisis of conscience. Yousif had passed the word. He was not called. He sat restlessly, and seethed. Such a travesty! The outcome was never in doubt. The decision had been made before the judges heard the charges....

What *were* the charges? Radetic suddenly realized that they had not been formally declared.

They were trying El Murid. Charges did not matter.

El Murid rose. "A petition, my lord judges."

The chief judge, one of Aboud's brothers, looked bored. "What is it this time?"

"Permission to call additional witnesses."

The judge sighed and rubbed his forehead with the heel of his left hand. "This could go on all day." He was speaking to himself, but half the audience heard him plainly. "Who?"

"My wife."

"A woman?"

A murmur of amazement ran through the gallery.

"She is the daughter of a chieftain. She is of the el Habib, who are of the same blood as the Quesan."

"Nevertheless, a woman. And one disowned by her family. Do you mock this Court? Do you compound your crimes by trying to make a farce of the administration of justice? Your request is denied."

Radetic's disgust neared the explosive point. And yet... to his amazement, he saw that even the El Murid factionalists in the audience were appalled by their prophet's suggestion.

Megelin shook his head sadly. There was no hope for these savages.

Fuad pushed a stiffened finger into his ribs. "Keep still, teacher."

The chief judge rose less than two hours after the trial's commencement. Without consulting his fellows privately, he announced, "Micah al Rhami. Nassef, once ibn Mustaf el Habib. It is the judgment of this Court that you are guilty. Therefore, this Court of Nine orders that you be banned forever from all Royal lands and protection, all holy places and protection, and from the Grace of God—unless a future Court of Nine shall find cause for commutation or pardon."

Radetic smiled sardonically. The sentence amounted to political and religious excommunication—with an out. All El Murid had to do was recant.

Had there been any genuine crime the sentence would have been scorned for its mildness. This was a land where they lopped off hands, feet, testicles, ears, and, more often than anything, heads. But the sentence fulfilled the Royal goal. Executed immediately, it would keep El Murid from preaching during Disharhun, to the vast gatherings this year's High Holy Week had drawn.

Radetic chuckled softly. Someone was scared to death of the boy.

Fuad gouged him again.

"My lords! Why hast thou done this to me?" El Murid asked softly, his head bowed.

He does it well, Radetic thought. The pathos in him. He'll win converts with that line.

Suddenly, proudly, El Murid stared the chief magistrate in the eye. "Thy servant hears and obeys, O Law. For does not the Lord say, 'Obey the law, for I am the Law'? At Disharhun's end El Murid shall disappear into the wilderness."

Sighs came from the crowd. It looked like the old order had won its victory.

Nassef shot El Murid a look of pure venom.

And why, Radetic asked himself, hadn't Nassef said a word in their defense? What game was he playing? For that matter, what game was El Murid playing now? He did not seem at all distressed as he laid himself open for further humiliation.

"The Court of Nine orders that the sentence be executed immediately."

That surprised no one. How else to keep El Murid from speaking?

"One hour from now the King's sheriffs will receive orders to seize any of the proscribed, or their families, found within any of the restricted domains."

"That," Megelin murmured, "is too much." Fuad jabbed him again.

Seldom was it that a pivoting point of history could be identified at the precise instant of turning. Radetic recognized one here. A band of frightened men had compounded an action of self-defense with one of spite.

They were trying to rob El Murid of a father's precious opportunity and inalienable right to have his child baptized before the Most Holy Mrazkim Shrines, during Disharhun. El Murid had already announced that he would dedicate his daughter to God on Mashad, the last and most important of the High Holy Days.

Radetic need be no necromancer to predict the long-term results. The meekest of the desert-born would have felt compelled to respond.

In later days El Murid's followers would say that this was the moment when the grim truth of reality finally burst through the curtain of ideals blinding the youth to the hypocrisies of his world.

Radetic suspected that that revelation had come a lot earlier. The youth seemed secretly satisfied with the pronouncement.

Nevertheless, he reddened. The muscles in his neck stood out. "It must be God's will. May the Lord grant his Disciple an opportunity to return to grace."

He spoke softly, but his words were a threat, a promise, and a declaration of schism. Henceforth the Kingdom of Peace would make war on heretics and the enemies of its future.

Radetic could smell the stink of blood and smoke drifting back across the years. He could not understand how El Murid's enemies could fail to see what they had done. Old cynic that he was, he studied El Murid intently. Behind the very real anger there was evidence that the youth had expected this.

He did detect a barely restrained glee in Nassef.

El Murid departed Al Rhemish meekly. But Meryem left word that her daughter would bear no name till she received it before the Mrazkim Shrines themselves. Fuad laughed when he heard. "Women making threats?" he demanded. "Camels will fly before she sees Al Rhemish again."

Yousif was not as sure. Megelin's naggings were forcing him to think. He did not like the thoughts that came to him.

The rioting started before the dust had settled on El Murid's backtrail. More than a hundred pilgrims died. Before the end of Disharhun, El Murid's partisans had defaced the Shrines themselves.

Yousif and Fuad were amazed.

"It's begun," Megelin told his employer. "You should have murdered them. Then it would've been over this week, and in a year he would have been forgotten."

Despite his earlier speech about the emotions involved, Yousif seemed stunned by the reaction of the Disciple's followers. He could not comprehend being so hated by people who did not know him. So the human tragedy goes, men hating without trying to understand, and unable to understand why they are hated.

Later in the week, Radetic cautioned his employer. "There was planning behind this. They anticipated you. Did you happen to notice that neither one of them really tried to defend himself? Especially Nassef? He never said a word through the whole trial. I think you've created a couple of martyrs, and I think you did exactly what they wanted you to do."

"Are you listening, Haroun?" the Wahlig asked. He was keeping the boy close. There were people in the streets who wanted to lay hands on him. "Nassef. He's the dangerous one."

"This rioting will spread," Radetic predicted. "It'll begin to show elements of class struggle, too. Common folk, artisans, and merchants against priests and nobles."

Yousif looked at him oddly.

"I may not understand faith, Yousif. But I understand politics, vested interests and promises for tomorrow."

"What can they do?" Fuad demanded. "A handful of outlaws? The Little Devil's scattered converts? We can hunt them down like wounded jackals."

"I'm afraid Megelin might be right, Fuad. I think Aboud overdid it. He took away their pride. You can't do that to a man. He has to save face somehow. We sent them out like whipped dogs. They *have* to hit back. At least, Nassef does. He's the one with the ego. Think. What would you do if we'd done the same to you?"

Fuad did not think long. He replied, "I see."

Radetic added, "Messiahs tend to take what comes, I think. They see the abuse as part of their witnessing. I've begun to think the jihad El Murid preaches is a metaphoric concept, that he doesn't really see it in terms of blood and death. Not the way Nassef would look at it."

"Still," said Fuad, "all we have to do is go kill them if they try something."

Yousif replied, "I think I can guarantee that Nassef will. We'll just have to judge his strength and try to anticipate him. And, of course, try to kill him. But I have a gut feeling that he won't let us. I have an audience with Aboud tonight. I'd better light a fire under him."

The King, unfortunately, shared Fuad's thinking. For him the El Murid matter was closed.

Yousif and Radetic fussed and worried and, even so, were no less stunned when the blow finally fell.

Even they had grossly underestimated Nassef.

THREE
A Minor Squabble in Another Land and Time

Twenty-three warriors stalked through failing snow, their shoulders downed with white. Ice stiffened the mustaches of those who had them. Towering pines loomed ahead, but here ancient oaks surrounded them like a convocation of gnarled, antlered frost giants squatting, dreaming of blood and fire. Snow masked the altar stone where the priests of the Old Gods had ripped the hearts from screaming virgins. Two boys, Bragi and Haaken, turtled their heads against their shoulders and hurried past.

The trailbreakers fought the deep, soft new snow in iron silence. An arctic wind drove frozen daggers through the heaviest clothing.

Bragi and Haaken had just begun to sport scraggly beards. Some of their companions had winter-white hair. Harald the Half had no shield arm. Yet each man wore the horn helm. Old and young, they were warriors.

They had a cause.

The wind moaned, winging the sad call of a wolf. Bragi shuddered. Some of his companions would be wolf meat soon.

His father Ragnar raised a hand. They stopped. "Smoke," said the man known across Trolledyngja as the Wolf of Draukenbring.

The odor drifted thinly from among the pines. They were near Thane Hjarlma's longhouse. As one, they sat on their hams to rest.

Minutes sped.

"Time," Ragnar said. He was also called Mad Ragnar, a crazy killer known for a thousand miles.

Men checked shields and weapons. Ragnar chose groups to go right and left.

Ragnar's son Bragi, his foster son Haaken, and his friend Bjorn conferred with him briefly. The boys bore clay pots containing carefully nurtured coals. And within them the boys nursed grudges. Their father had ordered them to stay out of the fighting.

Ragnar muttered words of caution and encouragement. "Haaken, you go with Bjorn and Sven. Bragi, stay with me."

The last half mile was the slowest. Bragi kept remembering friendlier visits.

And, last summer, spirited, clandestine tumbles with the Thane's daughter Inger. But now the old King was dead. The succession was in contest.

Hjarlma had declared for the Pretender. His strength had overawed most of his neighbors. Only Ragnar, Mad Ragnar, had remained visibly loyal to the Old House.

The civil war was shredding the tapestry of Trolledyngjan society. Friend slew friend. Ragnar's own father served the Pretender. Families that had been at each other's throats for generations now stood shoulder to shoulder in the battle line.

Every spring in Bragi's memory his father had gone reeving with Hjarlma. Sailing gunwale to gunwale, their dragonships had scourged the southern coasts. They had saved one another's lives. They had celebrated shared wealth. And, in the same chains, they had shared the despair of imprisonment by the Itaskian King.

Now they sought to murder one another, driven by the bitter blood-thirst only politics can generate.

The news had come south on rumor's lightning wings: the Pretender had taken Tonderhofn. The Old House was collapsing.

Hjarlma's men would be celebrating. But the raiders moved carefully. Hjarlma's men had wives, children, and slaves who would be sober.

They penetrated the trenches and stockades. They passed the outbuildings. Fifty feet from the longhouse itself Bragi turned his back into the wind. He dropped dried moss and tree bark into his jar, blew gently. His father and several warriors held out their torches. Others quietly splashed the longhouse with oil.

A man would be stationed at each window. The best fighters would hold the doorway. They would slaughter the drunken rebels as they tried to escape. The Old House's cause, here beneath the brooding, glacier-clawed northern slopes of the Kratchnodian Mountains, would revive at the eleventh hour.

That was Mad Ragnar's plan. It was as bold and ferocious a stroke as ever plotted by the Wolf.

It should have worked.

But Hjarlma was expecting them.

It was a great slaughter anyway. Hjarlma had gotten his warning only seconds before the blow fell. His people were still confused, still trying to shake the mead and find their weapons.

Fire whipped through axed-in windows.

"Stay put!" Ragnar growled at Bragi. "To me!" he thundered at the others.

"Yai! It's Ragnar!" one of Hjarlma's men wailed.

The blond giant attacked with sword in one hand, axe in the other. Not for nothing was he called Mad Ragnar. He went into insane killing rages, became an unstoppable killing machine. It was whispered that his wife, the witch Helga, had spelled him invincible.

Three, four, five of the drunkards fell for each of Ragnar's men. And still he could not win. The odds were too terrible.

The fire had become a liability. Without it driving them to save their families, Hjarlma's men might have surrendered.

Bragi went looking for Haaken.

Haaken's thoughts paralleled his own. He had secured a sword already. They had not been allowed to bring their own. Ragnar had not wanted them getting dangerous ideas.

"What now?" Haaken asked.

"Father won't run. Not yet."

"How did they know?"

"A traitor. Hjarlma must have bought somebody from Draukenbring. Here!"

A rebel, nearly disemboweled, crawled toward them. "Cover me while I get his sword."

They did what had to be done. And felt ghastly afterward.

"Who sold out?"

"I don't know. Or how. But we'll find out."

Then they became too busy to speculate. Several rebels, who had crawled out a window no longer held against them, stumbled their way.

The longhouse burned briskly. Women, children, and slaves screamed inside. Ragnar's men fell back before the weight of their panic.

In a brief exchange, from ambush, Bragi and Haaken slew three men and sent a fourth fleeing into the pines. They received their own first man-wounds.

"Half of us are down," Bragi observed, after studying the main action. "Bors. Rafnir. Tor. Tryggva. Both Haralds. Where's Bjorn?"

Ragnar, roaring and laughing, stood out of the fray like a cave bear beset by hounds. Bodies lay heaped around him.

"We've got to help."

"How?" Haaken was no thinker. He was a follower and doer. A strong-backed, stolid, steadfast lad.

Bragi had all of his mother's intellect and a little of his father's crazy courage. But the situation had rattled him. He did not know what to do. He wanted to run. He did not. With a bellow imitative of Ragnar's, he charged. Fate had made his decision for him.

He had discovered what had become of Bjorn. Ragnar's lieutenant was charging him from behind.

No warning could reach Ragnar's blood-drugged brain. All Bragi could do was race Bjorn to his prey.

He lost the footrace, but prevented the traitor's blow from being fatal. Bjorn's deflected blade entered Ragnar's back kidney high. Ragnar howled and whirled. A wild blow from the haft of his axe bowled Bjorn into a snowdrift.

Then the Wolf's knees buckled.

The rebels whooped, attacking with renewed ferocity. Bragi and Haaken became too busy to avenge their father.

Then twenty rebels wailed.

Ragnar surged to his feet. He roared like one of the great trolls of the high Kratchnodians.

There was a lull as the combatants eyed one another.

The pain had opened the veil across Ragnar's sanity. "A crown has been lost here tonight," he muttered. "Treason always begets more treason. There's nothing more we can do. Gather the wounded."

For a while the rebels licked their wounds and fought the fire. But the raiders, burdened with wounded, gained only a few miles head start.

Nils Stromberg went down and could not get up again. His sons, Thorkel and Olaf, refused to leave him behind. Ragnar bellowed at all three, and lost the argument. They stayed, their faces turned toward the glow of the burning longhouse. No man could deny another his choice of deaths.

Lank Lars Greyhame went next. Then Thake One Hand. Six miles south of Hjarlma's stead, Anders Miklasson slipped down an icy bank into the creek they were following. He went under the ice and drowned before the others could chop through.

He would have frozen anyway. It was that cold, and the others dared not pause to light a fire.

"One by one," Ragnar growled as they piled stones in a crude cairn. "Soon there won't be enough of us left to drive off the wolves."

He did not mean Hjarlma's men. A pack was trailing them. The leader already had made a sally at Jarl Kinson, who kept lagging.

Bragi was exhausted. His wounds, though minor, nagged him like the agonies of a flensing knife in the hand of a master executioner. But he kept silent. He could do no less than his father, whose injury was much greater.

Bragi, Haaken, Ragnar, and five more lived to see the dawn. They evaded Hjarlma and drove the wolves off. Ragnar went to ground in a cave. He sent Bragi and Haaken to scout the nearby forest. The searchers passed near the boys, but without slowing.

Bragi watched them go, Bjorn, the Thane, and fifteen healthy, angry warriors. They were not searching. They were talking about waiting for Ragnar at Draukenbring.

"Hjarlma's not stupid," Ragnar said when he received the news. "Why chase the Wolf all over the woods when you know he has to return to his lair?"

"Mother—"

"She'll be all right. Hjarlma's scared to death of her."

Bragi tried reading behind his father's beard. The man spoke softly, tautly, as if he were in great pain.

"The war is over now," Ragnar told him. "Understand that. The Pretender has won. The Old House is in eclipse. There's no more reason to fight. Only a fool would."

Bragi got the message. He wasn't to waste his life pursuing a lost cause.

He had had fifteen years of practice reading the wisdom behind Ragnar's terse observations.

"They'll abandon him as quickly as they flocked to him. Eventually. They say…" A shudder wracked his massive frame. "They say there's a demand for Trolledyngjans in the south. Over the mountains. Beyond the lands of the bowmen. Past the reeving kingdoms. There's war a-brewing. Bold lads, bright lads, might do well while awaiting a restoration."

Itaskia was the lands of the bowmen. The reeving kingdoms were the necklace of city states hugging the coast down to Simballawein. For half a dozen generations the Trolledyngjan dragonships had gone out when the ice broke at Tonderhofn and Torshofn, to run the gauntlet of the Tongues of Fire and plunder the eastern littoral.

"Under the shingle pine, beside the upper spring. The northwest side. An old, broken hearthstone marks it. You'll find the things you'll need. Take the copper amulet to a man called Yalmar at the Red Hart Inn in Itaskia the City."

"Mother—"

"Can take care of herself, I said. She won't be happy, but she'll manage. I only regret that I won't be able to send her home."

Bragi finally understood. His father was dying. Ragnar had known for a long time.

Tears gathered at the corners of Bragi's eyes. But Haaken and Soren were watching. He had to impress them with his self-control. Especially Haaken, on whose good opinion he depended more than he could admit.

"Prepare well," said Ragnar. "The high passes will be bitter this time of year."

"What about Bjorn?" Haaken demanded. The bastard child that Mad Ragnar had found in the forest, abandoned to the wolves, was not too proud to reveal his feelings.

"Ragnar, you've treated me as your own son. Even in lean years, when there was too little for those of your own blood. I've always honored and obeyed as I would a birth-father. And in this, too, I must obey. But not while Bjorn Backstabber lives. Though my bones be scattered by wolves, though my soul be damned to run with the Wild Hunt, I won't leave while Bjorn's treachery goes unrepaid."

It was a proud oath, a bold oath. Everyone agreed it was worthy of a son of the Wolf. Ragnar and Bragi stared. Soren nodded his admiration. For Haaken, terse to the point of virtual non-communication, a speech of this length amounted to a total baring of the soul. He seldom said as many words in an entire day.

"I haven't forgotten Bjorn. It's his face, smiling, pretending friendship while he took Hjarlma's pay, here in my mind's eye, that keeps me going. He'll die before I do, Haaken. He'll be the torchbearer lighting my path to Hell. Ah. I can see the agony in his eyes. I can smell the fear in him. I can hear him when he urges Hjarlma to hurry and establish the Draukenbring trap. The Wolf lives. He knows the Wolf. And his cubs. He knows that his doom stalks him now.

"We'll leave in the morning, after we've buried old Sven."

Bragi started. He had thought that the old warrior was sleeping.

"A sad end for you, friend of my father," Ragnar muttered to the dead man.

Sven had served the family since the childhood of Bragi's grandfather. He had been friends with the old man for forty years. And then they had parted with blows.

"Maybe they'll be reconciled in the Hall of Heroes," Bragi murmured.

Sven had been a sturdy fighter who had taught Ragnar his weapons and had followed him in his southern ventures. More recently, he had been weapon master to Bragi and Haaken. He would be missed and mourned. Even beyond the enemy banners.

"How did Bjorn warn them?" Haaken asked.

"We'll find out," Ragnar promised. "You boys rest. It'll be hard going. Some of us aren't going to make it."

Six of them reached Draukenbring.

Ragnar gave the steading a wide berth, leading them on into the mountains. Then he brought them home from the south, down a knee of the peak they called Kamer Strotheide. It was a pathway so difficult even Hjarlma and Bjorn would not think to watch it.

Hjarlma was waiting. They could see his sentries from the mountain.

Bragi looked down only long enough to assure himself that Hjarlma had indulged in no destruction.

His mother's witchcraft was held in great dread.

He did not understand why. She was as compassionate, understanding, and loving a woman as any he knew.

Slipping and sliding, they descended to a vale where, in summer, Draukenbring's cattle grazed. They then traveled by wood and ravine toward the longhouse. They halted in the steading's woodlot, a hundred yards from the nearest outbuilding. There they awaited darkness and grew miserably cold.

The inactivity told on Ragnar most. He got stiff.

Bragi worried. His father had grown so pale....

His mind remained a whirl of hope and despair. Ragnar believed he was dying. Yet he went on and on and on, apparently driven by pure will.

It darkened. Ragnar said, "Bragi, the smokehouse. In the middle of the floor, under the sawdust. A metal ring. Pull up on it. The tunnel leads to the house. Don't waste time. I'll send Soren in a minute."

Sword ready, Bragi ran to the smokehouse, stirred through greasy sawdust.

The ring was the handle of a trapdoor. Beneath, a ladder descended into a tunnel. He shook his head. He had known nothing about it. Ragnar had secrets he kept even from his own. He should have been called Fox, not Wolf.

Soren slipped into the smokehouse. Bragi explained. Then Haaken, Sigurd, and Sturla followed. But Ragnar did not come. Sturla brought the Wolf's final instructions.

The tunnel was low and dark. Once Bragi placed a hand onto something furry that squealed and wriggled away. He was to remember that passage as the worst of the homeward journey.

The tunnel ended behind the wall of the ale cellar, its head masked by a huge keg that had to be rolled aside. It was a keg Ragnar had always refused to tap, claiming he was saving it for a special occasion.

The cellar stair led up to a larder where vegetables and meats hung from beams, out of the reach of rodents. Bragi crept up. Someone, cursing, entered the room over his head. He froze.

The abuse was directed at Bragi's mother, Helga. She was not cooperating with Hjarlma's men. They, after the hardships they had faced in the forests, were put out because she refused to do their cooking.

Bragi listened closely. His mother's voice betrayed no fear. But nothing ever disturbed her visibly. She was always the same sedate, gracious, sometimes imperious lady. Before outsiders.

Even with the family she seldom showed anything but tenderness and love.

"Banditry doesn't become you, Snorri. A civilized man, even in the house of his enemy, behaves courteously. Would Ragnar plunder Hjarlma?" She was overhead now.

Bragi could not repress a grin. Damned right Ragnar would plunder Hjarlma. Down to the last cracked iron pot. But Snorri grumbled an apology and stamped away.

The trap rose while the doeskin larder curtain still swayed from Snorri's passage. "You can come up," Helga whispered. "Be quick. You've only got a minute."

"How'd you know?"

"Ssh. Hurry up. Hjarlma, Bjorn, and three others are by the big fireplace. They've been drinking and grumbling because your father has taken so long." Her face darkened when Haaken closed the trap. Bragi had watched her hope die by degrees as each man came up. "Three more are sleeping in the loft. Hjarlma sent the rest out to look for your camp. He expects you to come in just before dawn."

The others prepared to charge. She touched Bragi, then Haaken. "Be careful. Don't lose me everything."

Helga was rare in many ways, not the least of which was that she had borne only one child in a land where women were always pregnant.

She held Bragi a moment. "Did he die well?"

He hated the misdirection. "Stabbed in the back. By Bjorn."

Emotion distorted her features momentarily. And in that instant Bragi glimpsed what others feared. The fires of Hell shown through her eyes.

"Go!" she ordered.

Heart pounding, Bragi led the charge. Fifteen feet separated him from his enemies. Three rebels had no chance to defend themselves. But Hjarlma was as quick as death and Bjorn only a split second slower. The Thane rose like a killer whale from the deeps, dumped a table in Bragi's path, hurled himself to where Ragnar's battle trophies hung. He seized an axe.

Regaining his feet, Bragi realized that the surprise was spent. Hjarlma and Bjorn were ready to fight. Haaken, Sigurd, and Soren were already in the loft. That left only himself and Sturla Ormsson, a man well past his prime, to face two of Trolledyngja's most wicked fighters.

"The cub's as mad as his sire," Hjarlma observed, turning a swordstroke with ease. "Don't get yourself killed, boy. Inger would never forgive me." His remark was a sad commentary on the nature of Man. Had the Old King not died unexpectedly, Hjarlma would have become Bragi's father-in-law. The arrangements had been made last summer.

Don't think, Bragi told himself. Don't listen. Old Sven and his father had beaten those lessons into him with blunted swords. Don't talk back. Either remain absolutely silent or, as Ragnar did, bellow a lot.

Hjarlma knew Ragnar's style well. They had fought side by side too many times. He handled it easily in the Wolf's son.

Bragi entertained no illusions. The Thane was bigger, stronger, craftier, and had far more experience than he. His sole goal became to survive till Haaken had finished in the loft.

Sturla had the same idea, but Bjorn was too quick for him. The traitor's blade broke through his guard. He staggered back.

Two pairs of ice-blue eyes stared into Bragi's own.

"Kill the pup," Bjorn growled. His fear was plain to hear.

As stately as one of the caravels the longships pursued down the southern coasts, Helga glided between them.

"Stand aside, witch woman."

Helga locked gazes with the Thane. Her lips moved without speaking. Hjarlma did not back down, but neither did he press. She turned to Bjorn. The traitor went pale, could not meet her terrible eyes.

Haaken jumped from the loft, snatched a spear from a far wall. Soren and Sigurd came down by the ladder, but nearly as fast.

"Time has run out," Hjarlma observed laconically. "We have to go." He directed Bjorn to the door. "Should've expected them to slip the picket." He whipped his axe past Helga, struck the sword from Bragi's hand, creased the youth's cheek on the backstroke. "Be more civil when I return, boy. Or be gone."

Bragi sighed as the wings of death withdrew. Hjarlma had done all he dared because of old friendship.

The fear of Ragnar haunted Bjorn's eyes throughout the encounter. He kept looking round as if expecting the Wolf to materialize out of fireplace smoke. He was eager to flee. He and Hjarlma plunged into the night, where the snow had begun to fall again.

Helga started tending Bragi's cheek and berating him for not having killed Bjorn.

"Bjorn hasn't escaped the storm yet," Bragi told her.

Haaken, Soren, and Sigurd lingered near the doorway. They kept it open a crack. The women, children, and old folks of the stead, who had done their best to remain invisible during the skirmish, tended Sturla or wept softly for those who had not returned.

There was no joy in Ragnar's longhouse, only the numbness that follows disaster.

Draukenbring had come to the end of its years, but the realization of that fact had not yet struck home. The survivors faced uprooting, diaspora, and persecution by the Pretender's adherents.

The falling snow muted the cries and clanging of weapons, but not completely. "There," Bragi told his mother. One of his father's howling war cries had torn the belly out of the night.

Ragnar soon staggered through the doorway, bloody from chin to knee. Much was his own. He had his stomach opened by an axe stroke.

With a peal of mad laughter he held Bjorn's head high, like a lantern in the night. Bjorn's horror remained fixed on his features.

Ragnar mouthed one of his battle cries, then collapsed.

Bragi, Haaken, and Helga were beside him instantly. But it was too late. His will had, finally, broken.

Helga plucked at the ice in his hair and beard, ran fingers lightly over his face. A tear dribbled down her cheek. Bragi and Haaken withdrew. Even in her loss the plunder-bride from the south could not shed her pride, could not reveal the real depth of her feelings.

Bragi and Haaken crowded the main fire, and shared their misery.

The funeral was managed in haste. It was an expediency, unworthy of the dead man, rushed because Hjarlma would return. It should have been a warrior's funeral with pyres and ricks, following a week of mourning and ritual.

Instead, Bragi, Haaken, Sigurd, and Soren carried Ragnar up Kamer Strotheide, above the tree- and summer snowlines, and placed him, seated upright, in a stone cairn facing both Draukenbring and the more distant Tonderhofn.

"Someday," Bragi promised as he and Haaken placed the last stone. "Someday we'll come back and do it right."

"Someday," Haaken agreed.

It would be a long tomorrow, they knew.

They shed their tears, alone together there, then went down the mountain to begin the new life.

"This is how he managed it," said Helga, while watching her sons chop at the frozen earth by the broken hearthstone. She held a golden bracelet, slim but ornately wrought. "It's half of a pair. Hjarlma wore the other. Each reacted to the other's approach. When Bjorn drew close, Hjarlma realized that Ragnar was coming."

Bragi grunted. He did not care now.

"I think I hit it," Haaken said.

Bragi started digging with his hands. He soon exposed a small chest.

Sigurd and Soren arrived with the packs. The four surviving warriors would go south from the shingle pine.

The chest proved to be shallow and light. It was not locked. Little lay within. A small bag of southern coins, another of gemstones, an ornate dagger, a small parchment scroll on which a crude map had been inscribed hastily. And a copper amulet.

"You keep the valuables," Bragi told his mother.

"No. Ragnar had his reasons for keeping these things together. And of treasure he left me plenty elsewhere."

Bragi considered. His father had been secretive. The forest round Draukenbring might be filled with pots of gold. "All right." He pushed the things into his pack.

Then came the moment he had dreaded, the time to take the first southward step. He stared at his mother. She stared at him. Haaken stared at the ground.

The cord was hard to cut.

For the first time in memory Helga revealed her feelings in public—though she did not exactly go to pieces.

She pulled Haaken to her, held him for nearly two minutes, whispering. Bragi caught the sparkling of a tear. She brushed it away irritably as she released her foster son. Embarrassed, Bragi looked away. But there was no evading emotion. Sigurd and Soren were, once again, parting with their own families.

His mother's embrace engulfed him. She held him tighter than he had thought possible. She had always seemed so small and frail.

"Be careful," she said. And what less banal was there to say? At such a parting, probably forever, there were no words to convey true feelings. Language was the tool of commerce, not love.

"And take care of Haaken. Bring him home." No doubt she had told Haaken the same thing. She pulled away, unclasped a locket she had worn for as long as Bragi could remember. She fastened it round his neck. "If you have no other hope, take this to the House of Bastanos in the Street of the Dolls in Hellin Daimiel. Give it to the concierge, as an introduction to the lord of that house. He'll send it inside. One of the partners will come to question you. Tell him:

'Elhabe an dantice, elhabe an cawine.*
Ci hibde clarice, elhabe an savan.
Ci magden trebil, elhabe din bachel.'

He'll understand."

She made him repeat the verse till she was sure he had memorized it.

"Good. No more can be done. Just don't trust anyone you don't have to. And come home as soon as you can. I'll be here waiting."

She kissed him. In public. She had not done that since he had been a toddler. Then she kissed Haaken. She had never done that at all. Before either could react, she ordered, "Now go. While you can. Before we look more foolish than we already do."

Bragi shouldered his pack and started toward Kamer Strotheide. Their way led round its knee. Sometimes he looked up toward Ragnar's cairn. Only once did he look back.

The women and children and old people were abandoning the steading that had been home to generations. Most would flee to relatives elsewhere. A lot of people were on the move during these times of trouble. They should be able to disappear and elude the spite of the Pretender's men.

He wondered where his mother would go....

Forever afterward he wished that, like Haaken, he had refused to look. He could, then, have remembered Draukenbring as a place alive, as a last hope and refuge quietly awaiting him in the northland.

FOUR

A CLASH OF SABERS

Nassef looked back once. Heat waves made the bowl of Al Rhemish a tent city writhing beneath dancing ghosts. A muted roar echoed from the valley. He smiled. "Karim," he called gently.

A hard-looking man whose face had been scarred by the pox joined him. "Sir?"

"Go back down there. Visit our people. The ones who met us when we came in. Tell them to keep the riots going. Tell them I need an extended distraction. And tell them to pick five hundred willing warriors and send them after us. In small groups, so they're not noticed leaving. Understand?"

"Yes." Karim smiled. He was missing two front teeth. Another was broken at an angle. He was an old rogue. He had seen his battles. Even his gray-speckled beard seemed war lorn.

Nassef watched Karim descend the stony slope. The former bandit was one of their more valuable converts. Nassef was sure Karim's value would increase as the struggle widened and became more bitter.

He swung his mount and trotted after his sister and brother-in-law.

El Murid's party consisted of almost fifty people. Most were bodyguards, his white-robed Invincibles, who had been guaranteed a place in Paradise if they died in El Murid's behalf.

They made Nassef uneasy. They had eyes madder than those of their prophet.

They were fanatically devoted. El Murid had had to bend the full might of his will to keep them from storming the Royal Compound after the trial.

Nassef assumed his post at El Murid's right hand. "It went better than we hoped," he said. "The boy's attack was a godsend."

"Indeed it was. To tell the truth, Nassef, I was reluctant to do it your way. But only the intercession of the Lord Himself could have made it so easy. Only He could have brought about an attack so timely."

"I'm sorry about the ankle. Does it bother you much?"

"It pains me terribly. But I can endure it. Yassir gave me an herbal for the pain, and bound it. If I stay off it, I'll be good as new before long."

"During that farce of a trial… For a minute I thought you were going to give in."

"For a minute I did. I'm as subject as anyone else to the wiles of the Evil One. But I found my strength, and the lapse made the outcome sweeter. You see how the Lord moves us to His will? We do His work even when we think we're turning our backs on Him."

Nassef stared across the barren hills. Finally, he replied, "It's hard to accept a defeat hoping it will yield a greater victory someday. My friend, my prophet, they signed their death warrants today."

"I'm no prophet, Nassef. Just a disciple of the Lord's way. And I want no deaths that can be avoided. Even King Aboud and the High Priests may someday seek the path of righteousness."

"Of course. I was speaking figuratively. Saying that by their actions they have doomed their cause."

"It is often thus with the minions of the Evil One. The more they struggle, the more they contribute to the Lord's work. What about the raid? Are you *sure* we can pull it off?"

"I sent Karim back to Al Rhemish. If our people do what we ask, if they keep the riots going and send us five hundred warriors, we can. There'll be no one to stop us. All the lords came to Al Rhemish to see our humiliation. The riots will occupy them through Mashad. We'll have a week's lead."

"I just wish we could have christened the baby."

"That was a pity. We'll return, Lord. We'll see it done, some Mashad. I promise it."

For once Nassef's words burned with total sincerity, with absolute conviction.

The by-ways of the desert were long, lonely, and slow, especially for a man apart from other men. There was no one for El Murid to confide in, to dream with, except Meryem. The Invincibles were too much in awe of him, too worshipful. Nassef and his handful of followers remained engrossed in their scheming against tomorrow. The riders who overtook them, coming from Al Rhemish by tens and twenties, were all strangers. The fast friends who had been his first converts, the others who had come with him out of El Aquila, were all dead, sainted.

Nassef's struggles on his behalf took their toll.

The Disciple rode beside the white camel, his child in his lap. "She's such a peaceful, tiny thing," he marveled. "A miracle. The Lord has been good to us, Meryem." He winced.

"Your ankle?"

"Yes."

"You'd better let me take her back, then."

"No. These moments are too rare already. And they're going to become rarer still." After a minute alone with his thoughts, "How long will it be before I can set aside my staff?"

"What do you mean?"

"How long before our success is achieved? How long till I can settle down and lead a normal life with you and her? We've been riding these hidden trails for three years. It seems like thirty."

"Never, my love. Never. And as a wife I loathe to admit it. But when the angel spoke to you, you became El Murid for all time. So long as the Lord sees fit to leave you among the living, that long must you remain the Disciple."

"I know. I know. It's just the mortal within me wishing for something it can't have."

They rode without speaking for a while. Then El Murid said, "Meryem, I'm lonely. I don't have anyone but you."

"You have half the desert. Who brings us food and water from the settlements? Who carries the Truth into provinces we've never seen?"

"I mean a friend. A simple, ordinary, personal friend. Somebody I can just play with, as I did when I was a child. Somebody I can talk to. Somebody who can share the fears and hopes of a man, not somebody smitten by the dreams of El Murid. Surely you've felt the same things since Fata died."

"Yes. Being the woman of El Murid is lonely, too." After a time, "But you have Nassef."

"Nassef is your brother. I won't speak ill of him to you. I do love him as if he were my own brother. I forgive him like a brother. But we'll never be real friends, Meryem. We'll just be allies."

Meryem did not argue. She knew it was true. Nassef, too, had no one else in whom to confide. No friendship would blossom between her husband and brother while they remained unsure of each other.

It had been a long, hard ride. In the end, Nassef had pushed hard. Everyone was tired except Nassef himself, who seemed immune to fatigue.

"There it is," El Murid whispered in wonder. He forgot the pain in his ankle. "Sebil el Selib."

The light of a three-quarters moon illuminated the mountain-flanked meadow which was second only to Al Rhemish in the hearts of the Children of Hammad al Nakir. Long ago, it had been second only to Ilkazar in the hearts of their Imperial ancestors.

A very old fortress overlooked the meadow, and the shrine and cloisters it contained. There were no lights to be seen anywhere.

The name Sebil el Selib meant Path of the Cross. It had come into being because of the event memorialized by the shrine.

It was in that meadow that, on the first day of the Year 1 in the common dating, the Empire had been born. The first emperor had made himself secure in his power by crucifying a thousand opponents there. The path of the name was the trail winding through the pass, along which the doomed nobles had had to bear the instruments of their destruction. From the meadow that trail wound on, connecting the old Inner Provinces with the cities along the coast of the Sea of Kotsüm.

The weathered fortress, dating from the early Imperial era, guarded the pass, not the shrine and cloisters over which it brooded.

"Here the father of our dream found life," El Murid told Nassef. "Here the First Empire was born. Let our own gasp its first breath on the same bedclothing."

Nassef said nothing. He was looking with awe on a place drenched with history. It seemed too plain, too simple, to be so important.

Al Rhemish had given him the same feeling.

It amazed him that ordinary places could, in time, attain such a hold on men's imaginations.

"Nassef."

"Yes?"

"Are we ready?"

"Yes. Karim will take the Invincibles down first. They'll scale the walls and open the gate to the rest. I'll send smaller forces to seize the shrine and cloisters."

"Nassef?"

"I hear you."

"I'm no warrior. No general. I am but the instrument of the Lord. But I'd like to make a small adjustment to your plan. I'd like you to close the road to the coast. And to leave a detachment with me. I don't want anyone to escape."

Nassef thought that he had misunderstood. El Murid was always after him to spare and forgive their enemies.

"I thought about it all the way here. The Lord has no friends in this place. They're soldiers of the King and acolytes of the false path. Moreover, a clear, unequivocal message has to be sent to those who yield to the seductions of the Evil One. Last night I prayed for guidance, and it came to me that our Second Empire must also have its birth in the blood of its enemies, on the site where the First Empire was born."

Nassef was surprised, but not dismayed. "As you say, so shall it be."

"Slay them all, Nassef. Even to the babes in arms. Let no man, from this day forth, think that he can evade the wrath of the Lord."

"As you say."

"You may begin." But before Nassef had taken a dozen steps, El Murid called, "Nassef."

"Yes?"

"In this moment, before the armed struggle begins, I name you my war captain. I entitle you Scourge of God. Wear the title well."

"I will. Have no fear."

The attack went forth with the speed and precision that had become hallmarks of Nassef's caravan raids. Many of the fortress's garrison died in their bedrolls.

El Murid sat his horse on the elevation and awaited fugitives or news. In his heart he nursed a black seed of fear. If he failed here, if the defenders of the fortress drove him away, then his mission might never recover. Nothing impressed the men of the desert so much as boldness and success. Nothing daunted them so much as failure.

No fugitives came. Neither did any news till, as dawn began coloring the sky over the mountains before him, Nassef's man Karim rode up.

"My Lord Disciple," said Karim, "your war captain sends me to report that the fortress, shrine, and all cloisters are in our hands. Our enemies have been gathered in the meadow. He begs you to come accept them as a gift of his love."

"Thank you, Karim. Tell him I'm on my way."

Nassef awaited him on a knoll overlooking the captives. There were at least two thousand of them. Many were from the fortress, but most were from the cloisters, innocent pilgrims who had come here to celebrate Disharhun and who had not yet departed for their homes.

The garrison had been a large one. The only other useful pass through Jebal al Alf Dhulquarneni lay hundreds of miles to the north. The Hidden Ones permitted passage at no other points. The defense was big because the passage taxes were important to the Crown.

The stronghold's defenders lived their entire lives there. Some of the garrison families went back to Imperial times. Women and children lived in the castle with the men.

El Murid looked down on the captives. They looked up at him. Few recognized him till Meryem, veilless, on her white camel, came up beside him. They began to buzz in excitement. An officer of the garrison shouted something placatory, offering his men's parole. El Murid peered at him. He searched his heart for mercy. He could find none. He gave Nassef the signal to begin.

The horsemen rode round the prisoners, chopping with their sabers. The prisoners screamed. They tried to run. There was nowhere to go except to climb atop one another. Some dashed through the circle of death, only to be ridden down by pickets awaiting them outside. A few warriors hurled themselves at the horsemen, trying to make a brave end.

Thus it was that a man named Beloul escaped the massacre.

He was one of the under officers of the garrison, a man about Nassef's age. He came of a family which traced its roots well back into the Imperial era. Fighting like a demon, Beloul seized both horse and sword, then cut his way through the pickets. He bluffed a charge toward El Murid. While the Invincibles rushed to protect their prophet, he galloped through the pass into the desert.

Nassef sent four men after him. None ever returned.

Beloul carried the news to el Aswad. Messengers immediately streaked from the Wahlig's castle.

"Is this really necessary?" Meryem asked when the slaughter was halfway done.

"I think so. I think my enemies… the enemies of the Lord will find it in-structive."

It took longer than he expected, and eventually proved more than he could stomach. He turned away when the Invincibles dismounted to drag the corpses of mothers aside to get at the children they had shielded with their bodies. "Let's look at the shrine," he said. "I want to see my throne."

Nassef came to report while he knelt, praying, before the Malachite Throne.

Ancient artisans had sculpted that seat from the boulder on which the first emperor had sat while watching the crucifixions of his enemies. It was the second most potent power symbol in Hammad al Nakir. Only the Peacock Throne, salvaged from the ruins of Ilkazar and transported to Al Rhemish, had a greater hold on men's minds.

Nassef waited patiently. When El Murid completed his prayers, his war cap-tain told him, "It's done. I've ordered the men to rest. In a few hours I'll begin the burying. Tonight I'll send scouts back into the desert."

El Murid frowned. "Why?"

"We're within the domains of the Wahlig of el Aswad. They say he's decisive and smart. He'll attack us as soon as he hears what's happened."

"You know him?"

"By sight. So do you. That was his son who attacked you in Al Rhemish. Yousif was the one who arranged our trial."

"I remember him. A thin, cruel-faced man. Eyes of jet, and hard as diamonds. A true champion of the Evil One."

"My Lord Disciple, do you realize what we've accomplished today?" A sud-den awe filled Nassef's voice.

"We captured the Malachite Throne."

"And more. Much, much more. Today we became a major power in Ham-mad al Nakir. Because of the Throne, and its location. So long as we hold Sebil el Selib, we're a factor they have to reckon in every decision they make at Al Rhemish. So long as we hold this pass we virtually isolate the desert provinces from the coast of the Sea of Kotsüm. We deny Aboud all the strength and wealth of the coast in his struggle to defy the will of the Lord."

Nassef was right. The seacoast was the one area of the core Empire that had not suffered heavily during the Fall. It had not become a wasteland. In modern times its cities were virtually autonomous, though they shared the language and cultural roots of Hammad al Nakir. They paid lip service and tributary fealty to King Aboud and the Quesani, mainly so their wild cousins of the desert would leave them alone. Politically, they had little to gain by opposing El Murid, and would come up losers if they supported him.

If they did and he failed, they would have won the hatred of the ruling Quesani family. If they supported him and he succeeded, they would be expected to squander their wealth and manpower in his holy war against the infidel states surrounding Hammad al Nakir.

They could be counted on, for a while, to remain outside the power equation. Nassef's selection of Sebil el Selib as his first target had been the best possible.

Geopolitics and economics aside, the seizure should have a strong psychological effect. Thousands should turn to El Murid. Other thousands should cool toward the Royal cause.

"I have one question, Nassef. Can we keep what we've won?"

"These men will die for you."

"I know that. It doesn't answer my question. There's a field full of men who died for Aboud outside. They didn't hold the pass."

"We won't be taken by surprise."

Nassef was only half right. The Wahlig of el Aswad responded quicker than he expected.

The pickets had scarcely gone out when one on a lathered horse returned to say that several hundred horsemen were right behind him.

They swooped down from the northwest. Nassef had expected to be attacked from el Aswad, so had distributed his pickets and skirmishers to the southwest. But Yousif had heard about Sebil el Selib while coming home from Al Rhemish. He had decided to strike back immediately, using his escort.

The swift strike, the sneak attack, the hit and run, were traditional desert warfare, founded on centuries of tribal feuding.

Yousif arrived long before the pickets could be recalled, thereby denying Nassef a quarter of his strength.

Fighting raged through the pass and down into the meadow. Yousif's warriors were skilled and disciplined household troops who spent their lives in training and maneuver. The Wahlig was a master of light cavalry technique. He pushed Nassef's larger force into the fortress and cloisters.

El Murid and his Invincibles became isolated in the shrine, defending the Malachite Throne. As soon as he learned the Disciple's whereabouts, Yousif concentrated on the shrine. He wanted the serpent's head.

Facing the Wahlig across twenty feet of bloody floor, El Murid shouted, "We will die before we yield one inch, Hell serf. Though your master send up all the devils of his fiery abode... Yea, though he hurl against us all the legions of the damned, we will not be dismayed. The Lord is with us. Ours is the confidence of the righteous, the assurance of the saved."

A big, muscular man said to the Wahlig, "I'll be damned. Yousif, he really believes that drivel."

"Of course he does, Fuad. Belief in himself is what makes a maniac dangerous."

El Murid was puzzled. Could they doubt his sincerity? The Truth was the Truth. They could accept or refuse it, but never brand it a lie.

"Slay them," he told the Invincibles, though they were grossly outnumbered. The Lord would deliver them.

His fanatics attacked like hunger-maddened wolves. Yousif's warriors went down like wheat before the scythe. The Wahlig himself went to his knees with a grievous wound. His troops wavered.

Fuad rallied them with his war cries. His scimitar flickered like a mirage, so swiftly did it cut and stab.

The Invincibles did as El Murid said. They held each inch they had taken. They did not yield, but they died.

Gingerly, still believing that the Lord would deliver him, El Murid descended from the Malachite Throne. He collected a fallen blade.

Now the Invincibles were falling like scythed wheat. El Murid began to doubt.... He would not! Were he to be martyred here, it would be the will of the Lord.

His sole regret was that he might leave this pale without seeing Meryem and his daughter again. They were trapped in the fortress with Nassef....

But Nassef was trapped no longer. Yousif's assault on the shrine had given him time to organize. He went over to the attack. His sally scattered Yousif's forces on the meadow.

He, Karim, and a score of their best burst into the shrine. The tide of fighting shifted.

"God is merciful!" El Murid thundered, daring to cross blades with a warrior. The man struck the weapon from his hand.

Nassef was there in an instant, turning the warrior's attack.

Fuad hurled that warrior aside and faced Nassef. "Let's see the color of your guts, bandit."

Nassef attacked. He wore a thin, cruel, confident smile.

Their blades danced a deadly morisco. Neither could penetrate the other's guard. Each seemed astonished by the other's skill.

"Fuad. Fuad," Yousif gasped from between supporting warriors. "Break off."

Fuad stepped back, wiped sweat from his face. "Let me finish him."

"We have to go. While we still have the strength to rescue our wounded."

"Yousif—"

"Now, Fuad. They've beaten us. All we can do here is die. And there'd be no point to that. Come on."

"Next time, bandit," Fuad growled. "I've seen the weakness in your style." He spit in Nassef's face.

The desert people could be demonstrative. Especially in matters of hatred and war.

"You won't live long enough to take advantage, son of a jackal." When Nassef reached a certain level of anger he achieved an icy self-control. He had done so now. Clearly, for the benefit of everyone present, he said, "Karim. Put an assassin into el Aswad. Let this heap of camel dung be the target. You. Hell serf Fuad. You think about that. Wonder when he—or she—will strike." He smiled his thin, cruel smile. "Karim. They wish to depart. Let them run like the whipped dogs they are. Let us amuse ourselves with the sight of them running with their tails between their legs."

Once the enemy had departed, El Murid sighed, limped back up, and collapsed into the Malachite Throne. "That was close, Nassef."

"Too close. Why didn't you use the amulet? You could have destroyed one of our worst enemies."

El Murid raised his arm. He stared at the glowing jewel. He had not called on its power since his demonstration at El Aquila. The people of the el Habib were still talking about the day that he had restored their dry oasis.

"It didn't occur to me. It truly didn't. I suppose the Lord touched me, telling me that you were coming. I never doubted our victory."

"As you say, it worked out. And as long as you don't use it, they won't be reminded. They won't be trying to find ways to counter it."

"Why did you tell Karim to let them go?"

"We've lost too many men. There's no sense spending more lives after we've won. They'll be back, stronger than this time. We'll need every man then."

"What was that about an assassin?"

"A ploy. Let them become afraid to turn their backs on each other. Let them become frightened of shadows. Let fear sap their strength and will."

"How clever you are. Nassef, my brother, don't you ever speak without first calculating some long-term effect for your words?"

"With my friends. Isn't it one of your teachings that words are the mightiest weapons of the Kingdom of Peace?"

"That's true. Words of Truth. But, Nassef, sometimes I think you're mocking me. Even when you save my life…"

Nassef stared at the floor. "Forgive me, my Lord Disciple. It's my manner, my way of speaking. It's a curse. When I was little I couldn't tease the other children. I couldn't tell jokes. They always took me seriously. And when I was serious, they thought I was sneering."

"What are we to do now, Nassef? We have the Malachite Throne. We have Sebil el Selib. And that will bring all the enemies of the Lord upon us."

"We can defend ourselves and trust in the Lord. I'll send messengers to our supporters asking for warriors and arms. I'll strengthen our defenses. We'll erect another fortress here. The Throne has to be protected too."

"You're right. Nassef, I'm afraid we'll be here a long time. Sebil el Selib is a trap in a way. It's given us two astonishing victories, but to survive we'll have to hang on to what we've taken. I'm afraid they'll simply bottle us up here."

"They'll try. But they'll never manage it completely. Their own system will work against them. As long as they can summon the tribal levies for only forty-five days a year, we'll pretty much be free to come and go the rest of the time. Assuming I receive your blessing, I plan to have partisan bands hitting and running wherever we have willing converts. That'll keep the full-time warriors busy elsewhere. It'll give us a chance to build our foundation here."

El Murid peered at him thoughtfully. After a time he observed, "You seem to have your plans thoroughly worked out."

"I've lain awake during a lot of lonely nights these three years, Lord."

"I suppose you have. When are you going to take a wife, Nassef?"

Nassef was taken aback. "I haven't considered it. After we've established the Kingdom of Peace, maybe."

El Murid peered at him again. "Nassef, I'm tired. Tonight and tomorrow we rest. The next day we resume our work. You, your wars. Me, my preparations for the Kingdom they will establish. I'll want you to find me scribes and architects. I want to set down a code of laws, and I want a special palace built to house the Malachite Throne. Also, I want to erect a stele in the meadow. On it I'll inscribe the names of the faithful who fall in the Lord's cause, that their names be immortal both here and in Paradise."

"As you say. I like the stele. Perhaps if you set aside the top for the Invincibles?"

"Yes. Have somebody remember the names of everyone who died here. They'll be the first inscribed."

Later, before he retired, El Murid led Meryem, and carried his daughter, to the highest rampart of the old fortress. "My loves," he said, "one tiny splinter of the dream has come to life. The Kingdom of Peace exists, although its bounds lie no farther than I can see. Someday all the earth will acknowledge the Lord."

Cradling the baby in his left arm, he slipped his right around Meryem's waist. She leaned against him, shivering in the cool mountain breeze.

"Come," she said after a time. "Let me remind you that you're also a man." She smiled up at him. The spoiled brat of the el Habib had grown into a woman who loved him as a man.

That night they conceived a boy-child.

FIVE

A FORTRESS IN SHADOW

Megelin Radetic walked the stony slopes below the tired walls of el Aswad, the Eastern Fortress. Haroun tagged along, scattering his attention as small boys will, yet clinging to the one adult who had time for him. A scarred old veteran dogged them both, his sword always in hand.

Haroun had not spoken for days. He had become lost inside his own young mind. Now, at least, he chose to speak, as Radetic paused to stare out across the sere, inhospitable land. "Megelin, is Father going to die?"

"I don't think so. The physicians are hopeful."

"Megelin?"

"What?" It was time to be gentle. He knelt.

"Why did he kill them? The pilgrims at the shrine."

Radetic resumed walking. "I don't know. If anyone but El Murid had given the order, I'd guess for spite."

They moved round the flank of the mountain. On its eastern face they encountered Haroun's brother Ali. Ali was seated on a boulder. He stared at Jebal al Alf Dhulquarneni, as if his thoughts might conjure the Hidden Ones from their secret strongholds.

Radetic stared too. He wondered what the wizards of the mountains thought of recent events. Presumably they would pursue tradition and ignore their neighbors. They had been up there since time immemorial. They bothered no one who did not bring them trouble. Even the mighty Empire had let them be, and they had remained aloof from its death throes.

Haroun murmured, "Megelin, I'm afraid."

Ali started to make a cutting remark.

"He's right, Ali. It's a time for fear. We have to fear Nassef for his sword, and El Murid for his Word. They make a deadly combination. And we must fear this, too: that the Sword might become master of the Word, rather than the reverse. Go, then, and try to capture the whirlwind."

Ali frowned. Old Radetic was in one of his ambiguous moods.

Ali was cast more in the mold of his uncle than of his brother or father. He was no thinker. Haroun understood Radetic plainly.

Yousif had reached el Aswad only hours behind the returning family caravan. His force had been savaged, and he had come within a mouse's whisker of death.

The caravan had not come through unscathed. Yousif had left no guards. Disorganized bands of Nassef's pickets had tried their luck plundering.

Even Megelin Radetic had taken up arms in the running fight.

He gripped his left bicep. He had taken a light saber slash. The wound still ached.

He smiled. How he had amazed his assailant with his counterattack!

Fuad still could not assimilate the fact that his brother's tame intellectual knew which end of a sword to grab. Nor did he know what to make of the fact that the teacher had taken charge of old men, boys, women, and camel drovers and had whipped hell out of tough young warriors.

Radetic found his incredulity amusing. He had told Fuad, "We study more than flowers at the Rebsamen." The remark referred to Fuad's bewilderment the time when he had discovered that Megelin was cataloging and making color drawings of desert wildflowers.

Ali descended from his perch. "Megelin?"

"Yes?"

"I'm scared too."

"We all are, Ali."

Ali glared at Haroun. "If you tell, I'll pound you."

Haroun snatched up a jagged rock. "Come on, Ali."

"Boys. Save it for El Murid."

"He's asking for it," Haroun replied.

"You little snot—"

"I said knock it off. Haroun, come on. Ali was here first."

Ali stuck out his tongue.

Radetic strolled away wondering what Haroun did fear. People did not intimidate him. "Let's go back to the castle, Haroun. It's time we did a little studying."

El Aswad was a regional name which popular usage also applied to its capital fortress. The Imperial builders of the original featureless square stronghold had called it the "Eastern Fortress." Under the Empire it had been the headquarters of a major military command.

The castle was bigger now, though less important. Every generation did a little something to make it more impregnable. Rounded towers had been added to the original walls. Curtain walls and supporting towers had been appended to its north side, enclosing the whole of the mountaintop. Still farther north, connected to the main castle by the curtains, commanding the mountain's most gentle slope, stood a massive square sub-fortress.

The other three faces of the mountain were barren, rocky, and often precipitous. The surface rock was soft and loose. Weather had been gnawing away for ages. Tortuously curved layers of sedimentary rock showed the progress of ancient ages. The children of Yousif's courtiers and soldiers loved scrounging the slopes for fossils, for which Radetic paid a candy bounty.

Radetic found the castle a miserable place to live. It was either too cold and drafty, or too hot and stuffy. The roofs and walls leaked during the rare rains. The sanitary facilities were primitive, and furniture virtually nonexistent. There was not one bath in the entire place. Hellin Daimiel was known for its communal baths. The only closable door he had ever seen was the one barring entry into the women's quarters.

He often longed for the comfort and privacy of his tiny apartment at the university.

Despite its drawbacks as a home, the castle served its intended function. Its granaries, cisterns, and arsenals could support its garrison almost indefinitely. It commanded a view of vast territories. It had never been conquered by siege or storm.

Radetic paused at the gate and surveyed the miles of stony land surrounding the fortress. "Haroun, you know what I'd like to look out there and see? Just once? A tree."

Weeks passed. Fuad sent out a summons to the tribal levies. On the morning they were to muster, Haroun wakened his teacher. "What do you want?" Radetic growled, squinting one-eyed at the dawn light crawling through his apartment window. "Better be good. No normal human being ought to be up at this hour."

"Uncle Fuad is going to meet the levies. I thought you'd want to be there."

Radetic groaned, swung his legs out of bed. "Want to? No. You've seen one mob of fellahin, you've seen them all. But I suppose I'd better go, if only to keep your uncle from doing anything he'll regret. How many showed up?" He had had doubts that a call from Fuad would elicit the same response as a call from the Wahlig.

Haroun looked disappointed. "Not good. But they're still coming in. Maybe some were delayed."

"Uh? Pretty bad, eh? Here. Hand me those sandals."

The levies were assembling on the slope leading to el Aswad's main gate. Not all had arrived, as Haroun had said, but the few dust clouds approaching indicated that Fuad would be disappointed by the response to his call. "Not a third of what he has a right to expect," Megelin observed.

"Some of those eaters of camel droppings have gone over to the bandits." Fuad had come out. He scowled at the assembling host. "Cowardice is spreading like the pox."

Radetic replied, "I wouldn't think them that fickle."

"They are, fishwife. And those that haven't deserted are hiding in their tents like old women, afraid to take a stand. Their excuse to my brother will be that he didn't issue the call himself. I ought to ride out and punish them. Bloody crones."

"Maybe you ought to wait a few days," Radetic suggested. "Send another round of messengers and have them talk tough."

"What good will that do? They want to hide behind their women's skirts, let them. I'll mock them when I return with El Murid's head on my lance. Beloul! Assemble the sheiyeks."

The captain Beloul inclined his head and descended the slope. He passed among the contingents. Chieftains started uphill by twos and threes. Fuad did not greet any of them warmly, though he knew them all and had been riding with them for years. His black scowl compelled them to hold their tongues and keep their distance.

When the last arrived, joining the circle surrounding Fuad, Radetic, Haroun, and Fuad's officers, Fuad turned slowly. "So this is it. Only you have the guts to face these boy bandits. Taha. Rifaa. Qaboos. All of you. I promise you my brother will remember this. And he'll not forget the faces we don't see here today."

Someone suggested, "Maybe we ought to give the others more time."

"More time, Feras? Will the Disciple give *us* more time? No! We strike. No game. No subtleties. We hit them like a hammer. And we bring their heads back to decorate the walls. Every motherlorn one."

Radetic muttered, "Fierce this morning, aren't we?"

Fuad rewarded him with an ugly look. "You'll find out fierce, teacher. Keep nagging. Beloul. Order the column according to plan. Just drop the places of the cowards who didn't show."

"Fuad," Radetic whispered, "I really think you ought to reconsider this."

"We ride when the column is in order," Fuad countered. "There will be no more discussion. We will be victorious or we will fail. I wouldn't want to be in the sandals of those cowards if we fail and I survive. Get away from me, teacher. You don't have anything to tell me."

Hours later Megelin watched the column pass out of sight. "I did what I could, Haroun. But he's too damned stubborn to hear reason."

"You don't think he'll win?"

Radetic shrugged. "Anything is possible. Maybe he'll get lucky."

A messenger located Megelin in his classroom two days after Fuad's departure. "The Lord Yousif has awakened. He asks your attendance."

Radetic was irritated by the interruption, but could not ignore the summons. "Ali. I'm leaving you in charge while I see your father. Keep on with the lesson."

Outside, the messenger chuckled. "You set them a grim taskmaster."

"I know. It's the only way I can get him to learn anything. He doesn't want his students thinking they're smarter than he is."

"Would that I had had such an opportunity when I was young."

"Ah." Radetic smiled gently. Yousif's subterfuge was working. Before children could be educated their elders had to be convinced that there was some point to education. "How is he?"

"Quite well, considering. But he's tough. This is a tough family. The desert has never been kind here."

"I can see that." Megelin had heard the same remark so often, even where the desert had been kind, that he suspected it was a homily.

Yousif was sitting up, arguing with a physician who wanted him to lie down. "Ah. Megelin. Here at last. Save me from the mercies of this old woman."

"The old woman probably knows more about what your body needs than you do, Wahlig."

"You all stick together, don't you? Well, no matter. Come here. Take one of these cushions. I can't use them all."

Radetic sat. He could not conceal his discomfort. He was too old to adapt to the desert custom of sitting cross-legged on cushions.

Yousif ignored his discomfort. "I've been away from this world a long time. It makes a man take stock. You know what I mean?"

"I think so, Wahlig."

"My first job in this second life is to get you to stop acting like a servant. We have things to talk about, Megelin. I think the first should be friendship."

"Wahlig?"

"You brought my caravan through."

"Nonsense."

"I've spoken with Muamar. We won't argue it. I'm grateful. It hadn't occurred to me that I might be leaving enemies behind me."

"My life was in danger, too."

"That's one way of looking at it. Whichever view you choose, my wives and children came through safely. I consider your effort an act of friendship. I do as I'm done by, Megelin."

Radetic could not stifle a wry smile. "Thank you." The gratitude of princes was notoriously short-lived.

"Megelin, you show expertise in surprising directions. I value a man who has skills beyond those demanded by his profession."

"Score a point for education."

"Indeed. Tell me. What do you think of Fuad's expedition?"

"I haven't been over the ground, except on the chicken tracks you call maps. He had a thousand men. Maybe he'll get lucky."

"He outnumbers them three or four to one."

"The numbers might be enough to make his hammer blows more convincing than Nassef's finesse. Your brother isn't a thinker."

"How well I know. Tell me, why are you so impressed with Nassef?"

"He has the subtle touch of genius. In a western context his threat to send an assassin to el Aswad would have been brilliant. Here it's a waste of inspiration."

"I don't see it. That was just talk by somebody who got spit on."

"That's the flaw in his subtlety."

"What?"

"There's no one here subtle enough to see the implications of the threat. Is the assassin here already? If not, how will he get in? And so on."

"You westerners are a devious race. We're more direct."

"I've noticed. But Nassef and El Murid are working on a different level. Their behavior betrays careful calculation. They occupied Sebil el Selib knowing your strength and probable response."

"Meaning?"

"Meaning they're confident they can hold it. There's no point in their taking something they can't keep. Not at this point in their growth."

"You give them too much credit."

"You don't give them enough. Despite everything you told me at Al Rhemish, you haven't really convinced yourself that these people are anything more than bandits led by a madman. Do you recall what you said? About El Murid selling the snake oil everyone wants to buy? I've reflected on that, and I think it's even truer than you know."

"What would you have me do?"

"There are a lot of possibilities." Radetic suggested several, all of which Yousif rejected as impractical or politically unfeasible. "Then be direct. Murder El Murid. People will scream, but they will forget quickly enough. And Nassef won't be able to survive without him. Not at this point."

"I plan to try. Assuming Fuad fails. You haven't given me a thing."

"I know I'm overlooking the financial and political difficulties. You asked for options. I laid out what I see. Hell, it's even remotely possible we could ignore them till they all die of indifference."

"Megelin, my recovery wasn't spontaneous. I've been lying here, for two days, aching more in mind than in body. I've thought of it all. And the only workable option is to fight and hope we get lucky. If we can't get lucky, then we'll try to keep them contained."

"This is depressing. We're talking ourselves into accepting a defeat before the event."

"Drop it, then. Megelin?"

"Yes?"

"You can do one thing to brighten my life."

"Wahlig?"

"Stay here when your contract is up. I may need the outsider's viewpoint desperately before this is over."

Radetic was surprised. This was the first time ever that Yousif had treated him with more than minimal respect. "I'll consider it, Wahlig. I'd better go. I left Ali in charge of my class."

Yousif chuckled. "Yes, you'd better."

"I'm a political historian, Haroun," Megelin explained. "That's why I'm going to stay. Why I have to stay. I can't leave during the political storm of the century, can I?"

The boy seemed slightly disappointed. Radetic understood, but did not have it in him to lay out the true, emotional bases for lengthening his stay. He did not understand all his motives himself.

"You see, I'm the only one here at the heart of it. History is written by prejudiced parties, Haroun. By winners, usually. This is a unique opportunity to capture the truth."

Haroun looked at him sideways, wearing an amused little smile. After a moment, Megelin chuckled. "You devil. You see right through me, don't you?"

He had his excuse, though. It would be good enough to prolong his stay as grim weeks piled into months and years.

Haroun whipped into Megelin's room, almost falling as he swung through the door, almost overturning the little table where the scholar was poring over his notes, inscribing one of his regular missives to a friend in Hellin Daimiel. "What is it, child?"

"Uncle Fuad is coming."

Radetic asked his next question by raising an eyebrow. Haroun understood. "No."

Radetic sighed, pushed his papers back. "I didn't think so. There would have been messengers carrying his brags. Let's go down to the gate."

The troops were dragging in when Radetic arrived. Megelin located Fuad. The Wahlig's brother was tired, deflated, and had exhausted his stock of contrariness. He answered questions dully, frankly, apparently not caring how bad the answers might make him look. "Just get it down the way it happened, teacher," he muttered at one point. "Just write it up the way it happened. We came up one company short. One stinking company. One fresh company, in reserve, and we would have had them." Stalking toward his brother's quarters, he added, "One company from any one of those whoreson sheiyeks who didn't show at muster. There's going to be some new chieftains in el Aswad."

Three months later Yousif issued his own call to arms. It took Megelin by surprise. "Why?" he demanded. "And why didn't you tell me?" He was severely piqued because the Wahlig had not consulted him.

"Because," Yousif replied, donning a teasing grin. "Because I wanted to deal with your protests at one sitting, instead of endlessly."

Hardly mollified, Radetic demanded, "Why this hosting? That's the important question."

"Because I need to assert my primacy over the tribes. They need to be shown that I'm still strong, that I remain in command. We children of the desert are a lot like your forest wolves, Megelin. I'm the leader of the pack. If I stumble, if I reveal any weakness, if I hesitate, I'm lost. I have no desire to attack El Murid. The time isn't right, as you no doubt would have told me endlessly had you been informed earlier. But the eyes of a hundred chieftains are on el Aswad, waiting to see my response to my wounding and Fuad's defeat. Not to mention the turnout for Fuad's hosting."

Megelin now recalled the busy comings and goings of recent weeks, movements he hadn't thought significant at the time. Messengers, of course. But, too, he had seen several of Yousif's most devoted captains leading sizable patrols into the waste. Not one of those had as yet returned. "I presume your representatives will be in place when the call reaches certain sheiyeks of questionable devotion."

Yousif chuckled. "Gently put, teacher. And true."

"I suppose my wisest course is to keep my mouth shut, then. It's an ancient truism: what is logical and practical isn't always politic. And vice versa."

"Truer in this land than anywhere else, Megelin. Truer here than anywhere. How have my son's lessons been progressing?" He did not clarify which son. They understood one another plainly on that score.

Radetic searched for the right words. He decided he could do no better nor worse than to be straightforward. There were no witnesses. The Wahlig was tolerant in private. "I say it's a pity he wasn't born in a civilized land. He's brilliant, Wahlig. Positively brilliant. The sorrow is, he has been shaped by this savage kingdom. Already. He could become a great man. Or a great villain. He has it in him. Let us direct that thrust to greatness."

Yousif harumphed, stared into the distance, finally remarked, "Were it not for the situation, I would consider sending him to your Rebsamen. Perhaps that can be accomplished later. After this wicked little devil is put down."

Radetic studied Yousif from the corner of his eye. There was a halo of destiny about the Wahlig at the moment, an aura, a smell, and Yousif sensed it himself. His stance said he knew the future he faced was not the one he had described.

Yousif's expedition against the usurpers of Sebil el Selib, though stronger than Fuad's, suffered the fate of his brother's. Once again the loyalists came up that one fresh company short of strength enough to recover the Malachite Throne. In his determination to retain an image as strong and hard, Yousif pressed his attack far longer than was reasonable, well beyond the point when it became obvious that he would fail.

The bitter fighting brutalized both loyalist and rebel. Its outcome generated repercussions which only injured the loyalist stance. As the news swept the desert ever more opportunists gravitated to El Murid's standard. Nassef sent out a call. Recruits drifted to him. He began teaching them his own devilish style of warfare.

Yousif adopted more reactionary tactics, screening the trails from Sebil el Selib, using his household warriors to pursue enemy bands moving in and out.

Spies sent disturbing reports about new fortifications.

"We can abandon any hope of ever rooting them out," Radetic prophesied one day three years after the loss of the pass. Intelligence had just been received concerning the rapid growth of the fortress-palace guarding the Malachite Throne. The report also claimed that El Murid now had a full-time following of a thousand warriors, half of whom belonged to the fanatic Invincibles.

Nassef and his henchman Karim had begun slipping in and out to advise and occasionally direct the marauders plundering the desert in El Murid's name.

"They're like ghosts," Fuad murmured one day. "Yousif, you should have let me kill Nassef when I had the chance. He's everywhere and nowhere, and I can't get him to fight."

"Do I detect a case of the guerrilla warfare blues?" Radetic asked. "Of course Nassef won't stand still. He'd get whipped if he did. Give him a target he can't resist. Have a surprise waiting."

"His spies would warn him two days before we decided to do it," Yousif replied.

"I know. The real hope is that you can get him or El Murid with a knife in the kidneys."

"We've tried," Fuad growled.

"Keep trying. We're losing a little ground every day. They're wearing us down. As long as Aboud looks at it as a scuffle between Yousif and El Murid, and won't see how it spills over into the rest of the kingdom, our best bet is to hang on and pray that they do something fatally stupid before we do."

"How's your monograph coming, Megelin?" Yousif asked.

The monograph's incompleteness was Radetic's stated excuse for staying on. He reddened. Gripping Haroun's shoulder, he replied, "Damned slow. The war keeps getting in the way. I hardly have time to teach, let alone get any writing done."

Time had made of Radetic much more than a tutor. In some ways he had become the power behind the Wahlig. Yousif sought his advice ever more often, and followed it with increasing frequency.

El Murid had recognized Radetic's new importance in a recent sermon, naming him as one of the thirteen Barons of Hell on earth, minions the Evil One had sent up to abuse the faithful. Megelin had been surprised to discover his noble standing. He thought Yousif more deserving.

Radetic was guiding Yousif's policy into a Fabian mode, getting the Wahlig to husband his strength and buy time. He hoped the Crown would recover its senses, or that Nassef would do something to defeat himself.

He composed countless admonitory letters, over Yousif's seal, to virtually everyone close to Aboud. He found a few sympathizers, but Crown Prince Farid was the only one in any position to influence Royal policy.

Young Haroun was growing, though more in mind than in stature. His father had begun to fear that he would become the family runt. Megelin soothed him with remarks about late bloomers. He had abandoned any pretense of educating anyone else. He no longer had time to coax and coddle Yousif's stubborner sons and nephews.

His concentration on the one child won him no friends. Not when he took the boy away from his regular shaghûnry studies and chores to accompany him on botanical and geological field trips. Not when he answered questions about the other children's talents honestly.

Other than Yousif and Haroun, Megelin had just one real friend in el Aswad, his bodyguard, Muamar.

Muamar enjoyed the field trips and studies more than did Haroun. For him they were play. The old warrior had reached that stage in life where mental challenges were more easily negotiated than physical. He responded to them with a heart never seen in the young.

In the fourth year the rebels made a small mistake. Fuad emerged triumphant, having trapped and slain nearly three hundred marauders. The victory guaranteed a respite from guerrilla activity. Yousif declared a holiday in his brother's honor.

Women were summoned from their quarters to dance. Yousif, Fuad, and most of the captains brought out their favorite wives. The voices of kanoons, ouds, derbeckis, and zils filled the hall with music. Radetic found it strident, harsh, and discordant.

Laughter abounded. Even Radetic hazarded a few jokes, but his efforts were too esoteric for his audience. They preferred long-winded, intimately detailed tales about rogues who cuckolded pompous husbands and about nitwits who believed anything their wives and daughters told them.

There was no wine to modulate the merriment, but the air was sour with a mildly narcotic smoke produced in special braziers.

Haroun sat beside Radetic, taking it all in with wide, neutral eyes. Radetic wondered if the boy was becoming one of life's perpetual observers.

"Ho! Megelin! You old woman," Fuad called. "Get up and show us one of your infidel jigs."

Radetic was in a daring mood. He liberated a flute from a musician and danced a clumsy flamenco to his own abominable accompaniment. He laughed with the rest when he finished.

"Now you, Fuad. Put on the zils and show the ladies how it's done."

Fuad took the dare, without zils. He performed a wild sword dance which won a roar of applause.

The hall was packed with victorious warriors. With the women dancing, then the teacher and the Wahlig's brother doing their stunts, no one had any attention left over. Nobody noticed the slow drift of three men toward the leaders....

Till they sprang, one each at Yousif, Fuad, and Radetic.

Each lifted a silver dagger overhead. Fuad stopped his with his dancing sword. Yousif evaded his by throwing himself into the screaming mob.

Muamar flung himself into the path of the third assassin. The silver dagger slashed his cheek as the killer desperately tried to reach Radetic.

Muamar's wound was bloody, but should have done no more than leave a thin scar. But the old warrior froze. His eyes grew huge. A gurgling whine crossed his lips. Then he fell, stone-dead.

The assassin drove toward Radetic again, struggling past grasping hands and flashing weapons. His dagger burned with a weird blue light.

"Sorcery!" a woman screamed.

The uproar redoubled.

Haroun kicked the assassin in the groin. It was as savage a blow as a ten-year-old could deliver. The knife wielder ignored him.

Neither he nor his companions seemed to notice the blows raining upon them. Six of Yousif's men perished before the assassins could be stopped.

Shaking, Radetic gasped, "I've never seen anything like it! What kind of men are they?"

"Back! Damn it, clear away!" Yousif bellowed. "Gamel! Mustaf! Beloul!" he roared at three of his captains. "Clear the hall. Get the women to their quarters.

Don't touch them!" he snarled at a man who had rolled one of the assassins onto his back.

The three silver daggers lay on the dark stone floor, glowing blue.

Fuad crouched over the man who had come after him. He was pale. His hands shook. "Nassef said he would send an assassin."

"He waited long enough," Yousif growled.

"This isn't El Murid's style," Radetic murmured. "There's sorcery in this. It hasn't been six months since he preached that sermon against wizardry."

"Nassef. It has to be Nassef's doing," Fuad insisted.

Something about one assassin caught Radetic's eye. He dropped to one knee, lengthened a tear in the man's clothing, gazed at his chest. "Come here. Look at this."

A tiny tattoo lay over the man's heart. It was not clear, but seemed to be two letters of the desert alphabet intertwined.

The tattoo faded away as they studied it.

"What the hell?" Fuad growled. He jumped to another assassin, hacked his clothing. "Nothing on this one." He went to the third. "Hey. This one's still alive." Again he cut cloth. "And he's got the same mark."

"Gamel. Send for the physician," Yousif ordered. "Maybe we can keep him alive long enough to get some answers."

While they were looking at the tattoo, Haroun collected one of the daggers. A blue nimbus formed round his hand. He held the flat of the blade to the light of a lamp.

"What are you doing?" Yousif demanded. "Put that down."

"It's harmless, Father. The light is just a spell unraveling."

"What?"

"There was a spell on the blade. This one includes Uncle Fuad's name. I'm trying to read the rest, if you'll let me. It's hard. It's fading away, and it's in the language of Ilkazar."

"If there's sorcery…"

"The blue is the sorcery giving up energy as it decays, Father. Because the knives cut the wrong men. They're just daggers now."

Haroun's assertions did not reassure Yousif. "Put the damned thing down."

"He just died," Fuad said of the third assassin. "Oh. There it goes."

The man's tattoo faded in thirty seconds.

"What are we into here?" Yousif asked the air. The air did not reply.

Haroun's shaghûnry instructors confirmed the boy's comments about the daggers. Spells had been placed on the blades to make even a slight cut fatal. But they could make nothing of the vanishing tattoos. Nor could they, with their most potent conjuring, determine whence the assassins had come.

The physician determined that the men had taken drugs. And everyone could see that they had bound their limbs and genitals tightly, severely restricting circulation. They had been both fearless and immune to pain when they had attacked.

"Whoever sent them has himself a potent weapon," Radetic observed. "Yousif, you'd better tell the gate watch to stay alert."

Once the excitement died and there was no other concern to stay him, Megelin knelt over Muamar and wept. "You were a true friend, old warrior," he murmured. "Thank you."

Fuad, of all people, placed a comforting hand on his shoulder. "He was a good man, Megelin. We'll all miss him."

The teacher glanced up. He was surprised to see a tear on Fuad's cheek. "He was my weapons master when I was Haroun's age. As he was Haroun's." For Fuad that seemed to be ample explanation.

The man called Beloul, who, subjective centuries ago, had escaped the disaster at Sebil el Selib, examined the dead men. He was now one of Yousif's most savage captains. In his time, too, he had gone back into Sebil el Selib as one of the Wahlig's spies.

"These are El Murid's men," he said. "This one is Shehab el-Medi, a captain of the Invincibles. He was almost as crazy as the Disciple."

"So," said Yousif. "The mystery deepens. They're El Murid's special bullies. Nobody gives them orders but the man himself. And yet it's only been six months since he outlawed any kind of sorcery. Curious."

The Disciple had, in fact, declared a death sentence upon all witches, warlocks, shamans, shaghûns, diviners, and anyone who practiced any kind of occultism. He had charged Nassef with the eradication of sorcery wherever his troops found it.

"He's insane," Beloul observed. "He doesn't have to be logically consistent."

Radetic had thought at the time that the Disciple's declaration made a grim kind of sense. The Kingdom of Peace had won no converts among the wise. Men with the Power were almost universally his enemies. They aided the Royal cause where they could. That they were generally ineffectual reflected the level of competence of the sorcerers of Hammad al Nakir. The talent had been very nearly eradicated during the fury of the Fall.

Radetic again thought of the Hidden Ones. Would El Murid be fool enough to try expelling them from Jebal al Alf Dhulquarneni?

That was too much to hope. Like most of the Children of Hammad al Nakir, he probably did not think of them at all.

El Aswad buried its dead and went on, as it had done for years. A month later a spy brought news which illuminated the assassination attempt.

El Murid had instructed his Invincibles to found a secret order within the bodyguard. The available details convinced Radetic that it was a mystery cult. It called itself the Harish, and was extreme in its secrecy. Members were organized in pyramided "brotherhoods" of three men, only one of whom knew any cultist above the three in the hierarchy. The tattoo was El Murid's personal seal. It was formed from the initial letters of "Beloved of God," and meant that the bearer was guaranteed a place in Paradise. It supposedly faded when the cultist's soul ascended.

"That's spooky," Fuad observed, and seemed perfectly willing to write the idea off as another example of El Murid's insanity.

"It is," Yousif agreed. "It's also damned dangerous if they're all as willing to die as our three were."

They were. Dredging the dark corners of his mind, El Murid had created a dread new instrument for the furthering of his mission.

Nine weeks later Radetic received a long letter from an old schoolmate, Tortin Perntigan, who had become a professor of mercantile theory. Meaning he was a glorified accounting instructor.

He mulled it for days before taking it to Yousif.

"You look strange," the Wahlig told him. "Like a man who's just seen his best friend and worst enemy murder each other."

"Maybe I have. I've received a letter from home."

"An emergency? You don't have to leave?" Yousif seemed alarmed by the prospect. Megelin's pride responded warmly.

"No. I'm not going anywhere. The letter… It'll take some explanation." Quickly, Megelin explained that Perntigan was a long-time friend, that they had been close since entering the Rebsamen together nearly three decades ago. "He's the one costing you so much when I send my fat packets of mail." Yousif was a tight man with a copper, like all his desert brethren, and repeatedly protested the expense of Megelin's communications with his distant colleagues. "I've been sending him fragments of my monograph as I write it, along with my natural observations, notes, thoughts, speculations, and what have you. To ensure that not everything will be lost if tragedy strikes. Knowledge is too precious."

"I seem to recall having heard that argument."

"Yes. Well. Perntigan, old gossip that he is, responds by keeping me informed of the latest from Hellin Daimiel."

Sourly, Yousif observed, "It gratifies me no end that you're able to stay in touch. Though it beggars me. Now, what piece of foul gossip has this expensive excuse for scholarly chitchat brought me?"

"As you are aware, Hellin Daimiel is the financial axis of the west—though the standing is being challenged by Itaskian consortiums—"

"Get on with it, Megelin. Bad news is like a dead camel. It gets no pleasanter for being let lie."

"Yes, Wahlig. Perntigan is obsessed with a phenomenon the bankers have begun calling 'the Kasr Helal Gold Seam.' Kasr Helal is a fortified Daimiellian trading village on the edge of the Sahel. The same one where, I believe, the Disciple's father traded for salt—"

"Megelin! You're still dancing around it."

"Very well. Of late large amounts of new specie have been reaching Hellin Daimiel, channeled through Kasr Helal. Thus the name Kasr Helal Gold Seam.

According to Perntigan, the House of Bastanos—the largest of the Daimiellian international banks—has accepted deposits equaling a million Daimiellian ducats. And that's just one bank. He sent a long list of queries about what is happening inside Hammad al Nakir. His excuse is that he is a student of finance. His motive, of course, is that he hopes somehow to profit."

"Can't we somehow get to the point of all this? What're you getting at? The fact that this money is coming out of the desert?"

"Exactly. Which is the root of the mystery. There is a trader's axiom that says specie is as scarce as frog fur in the desert. In this land debts are almost always paid in service or kind. Are they not? What silver and gold there is has a tendency to remain motionless." Radetic indicated the rings and bracelets Yousif wore. They formed a considerable portion of the Wahlig's personal fortune. The men of Hammad al Nakir customarily wore or hid whatever valuable metals they possessed. They yielded them up only in the direst extremity. "The movement out of the desert of fortunes of the scale Perntigan describes represents a huge financial anomaly. There is a great deal of trepidation among the bankers, though they profit. They foresee some titanic economic disaster."

Yousif simply looked puzzled. Half of what Radetic was saying had to be couched in the tongue of Hellin Daimiel. The desert language hadn't much of a financial vocabulary. And, though Yousif spoke some Daimiellian, he did not comprehend merchants' cant.

"Perntigan questioned his contacts in the banking establishment. He assembled a list of names associated with the suspect deposits. Along with another list of questions. You put everything he wrote together and it implies a rather disturbing process."

"I see that somebody is sending a hell of a lot of wealth out of the kingdom."

Radetic nodded. Finally. About five minutes behind, but finally. "Exactly. The whos and whys are what make the news interesting."

Yousif puzzled for a few seconds, then started to speak. Haroun tugged at his clothing. "Father? May I?"

The Wahlig grinned. "Of course. Let's see if this old fussbudget is worth his keep. Show us what he's taught you."

Radetic smiled too. The boy was showing signs of overcoming his innate reserve.

Haroun proclaimed, "There are only two people who could have that much money. The King and El Murid."

"Your reasoning?" Radetic demanded.

"The King because he accepts money instead of service. Also, he collects some rents and trade taxes. And El Murid because he has been looting people for years."

Yousif peered at Radetic. "Well? I take it from your look that he's wrong. Explain."

"Not really. He just hasn't reasoned closely enough. Tortin indicates that the Quesani family did make a big deposit. It was used to purchase properties on the Auszura Littoral. That's a stretch of seacoast north of Dunno Scuttari. It's a sort of elephant's graveyard of deposed princes. The purchase makes it look like somebody at Al Rhemish is covering the Quesani bets."

"Not Aboud. He doesn't have the foresight."

"Farid, perhaps? No matter. That was only a small part of the flow, and not what was bothering Tortin. What did bother him came from two other sources. The loot Haroun mentioned without carrying his reasoning to the point where he mentioned that it hasn't been El Murid doing the pillaging. The depositors have been Karim, el-Kader, el Nadim, and that bunch."

"Nassef's bandits-turned-generals. That's good news, Megelin. We could make the Scourge of God damned uncomfortable by spreading that around. In fact, the Invincibles might end his tale if he's been slipping something over on El Murid."

Radetic was not cheered by the opportunity. "Our side is vulnerable too."

"Aboud's money? It's his. He can do what he wants with it. Besides, he isn't looting the realm."

"Not Aboud. The priesthood. They've been sending out as much bullion as Nassef's gang. Which means they're stripping the holy places and melting the gold and silver down. What would the faithful do if they found out that they're being robbed by their own priests? El Murid can explain Nassef, more or less. Soldiers pillage their enemies. We can't shed ourselves of the priesthood.

"A lot of people already damn Nassef without damning El Murid. They consider him the Disciple's compromise with fate. They figure he'll disappear if El Murid's Kingdom of Peace becomes a reality."

"Looks like Nassef is worried about it too. He and his boys are putting a little away for their old age."

"Don't you think the priesthood's behavior will win El Murid a lot of converts?"

"Absolutely. I'll write Aboud."

"Who is under the thumbs of the priests. Who will give you the same answer he's been giving you since this mess started. If he bothers to answer at all."

"You're right. Of course. We'll just have to intimidate a few priests. Cover it up." Yousif closed his eyes wearily. "Megelin, what do you do when your allies are more trouble than your enemies?"

"I don't know, Wahlig. I really don't. Stupidity and incompetence create their own special rewards. All I foresee is deterioration and more deterioration, and most of it moral. Maybe Hammad al Nakir *needs* the purifying flame of an El Murid."

Haroun gripped Radetic's elbow. "Don't give up yet, Megelin."

The boy's face had assumed an expression of stubborn determination. It made him seem far older than his years.

Radetic thought it a pity that a child had to grow up in the fires of this particularly chaotic furnace.

SIX
INTO STRANGE KINGDOMS

Gaunt, shivering, Bragi and Haaken paused at the crest of the last high pass.

"Already spring down there," Bragi observed. He extended an arm to support his brother. "That green must be a hardwood forest."

"How long?" Haaken croaked.

"Three days? Five? Not long."

"Hah!"

There had been days when they had not made a mile. Like yesterday. After burying Soren in the hard earth, they had fought the snowy mountain till exhaustion had forced a halt.

Sigurd had passed almost a month ago. The crossing had taken two months.

"Can't make it," Haaken gasped. "Go on without me."

He had suggested it before. "We've got it whipped now, Haaken. All downhill from here."

"Tired, Bragi. Got to rest. Make it while you can. I'll catch up."

"Come on. Step. Step. Step."

The foothills were hot compared to the high range. The boys camped there a week, regaining their strength. Game was scarce.

They had begun to encounter signs of the foothill tribes. Once they passed the ruin of a small log fortress. It had been burned within the month.

"We should be near Itaskia's Duchy Greyfells," Bragi said around a rabbit's leg. "This trail should run into the highway Father called the North Road. That's a straight run to Itaskia the City."

Itaskia the kingdom and its capital bore the same name. This was the case with several states. Each had grown round a strong city-survivor of the Fall.

"Wish you'd stop being so damned optimistic," Haaken grumbled. He attacked the rabbit like a starved bear. "We can't even speak the language. And we're Trolledyngjans. If bandits don't get us, the Itaskians will."

"You should ease up on the pessimism. Damned if I don't think all you'd see is a hernia if we found a pot of gold."

"Can't go through life expecting everything to work out. You expect the worst, you're ready for anything."

"What do *you* want to do?"

"I stopped making plans when Father died."

Bragi had no plan either beyond following his father's sketchy suggestions. What happened after they found this Yalmar?

"Haaken, all I know is what Father said."

"Then we just have to keep on till something happens."

It happened next morning.

Haaken paused to urinate. Bragi ambled on ahead and was alone when the hillmen leapt out of the brush.

Their stone-tipped spears turned on his mail shirt, which his father had told him to wear whenever he traveled. They pulled him down and drew knives.

Haaken arrived, axe whining. He slew two before the others realized he was there.

Bragi scrambled away, regained his feet, finally used his sword.

A survivor tried to flee. Sword and axe stopped him.

"What the hell?" Haaken gasped.

"Meant to rob me, I guess," Bragi wheezed, shaking. "That was too close."

"I warned you."

"Let's ditch them and get out of here."

"Listen!"

Hoofbeats. Approaching.

"Into the brush," Bragi said.

"Up a tree," Haaken countered. "Ragnar said people never look up."

Within a minute they were high in an old oak. Their packs seemed weightless during the climb.

The dead still lay scattered on the trail.

Six horsemen appeared. An officer, four soldiers, and one civilian.

"Itaskians," Bragi whispered.

"What the hell?" the officer demanded, reining in. The youths did not understand Itaskian, but guessed his meaning.

The soldiers drew swords. The civilian dismounted, examining the battleground.

"Majneric's men. They ambushed two travelers. Within the past few minutes. The travelers are in a black oak about thirty feet to your left."

"Who'd be out here when Majneric's loose?"

"You'll have to ask. Use bows. They shouldn't resist the invitation."

"Just so. Sergeant."

The soldiers sheathed their blades, readied bows. Bragi and Haaken exchanged looks.

"Nobody ever looks up, eh?" Bragi growled, looking down four shafts. The scout beckoned.

When Bragi reached the ground he found his foster brother with axe in hand, defiant.

"They're just pups," the sergeant observed.

"These were the two?" the officer asked.

"The same," said the civilian. "Look like Trolledyngjans. They teach them young up there." The woodsman held out his palms. "Let's talk in peace," he said in accented Trolledyngjan.

"What's going to happen?" Bragi asked. Shakes threatened to shame him.

"Depends on you. What happened here? What brings you south?"

Bragi told it all. The scout translated.

The Itaskians chattered briefly, then the interpreter said, "Sir Cleve is inclined to generosity. Because of those." He indicated the dead. "We've been after their band for weeks. We deliver their heads to the Duke, we'll get off patrol for a while. But he doesn't know about this Pretender. He wants to look in your packs."

Haaken growled softly.

"Easy, son. We won't rob you."

"Do what he says, Haaken."

A minute later, "Good. Now move back five paces."

The leader examined their things. Bragi's heirlooms generated questions.

"Our father gave them to us before he died. He told us to take them to a man in the City."

"What man?"

"Someone named Yalmar."

The officer asked, "You think they're telling the truth?"

"Too scared not to. This Yalmar probably fences for the coast raiders. Their father probably saw this succession crisis coming and made arrangements."

"What should we do with them?"

"We have no quarrel with them, sir. And they've done us a favor."

"They're Trolledyngjans," the sergeant observed. "Ought to hang them as a warning to the next bunch."

"A point," the officer agreed. "But I've no stomach for it. Not children."

"These children killed four men, sir."

"Majneric's men."

"What's going on?" Bragi asked nervously.

The scout chuckled. "Sergeant Weatherkind wants to hang you. Sir Cleve, on the other hand, is willing to let you go. Provided you let him have these bodies."

"That's fine by us."

"Watch that sergeant," said Haaken. "He'll get us killed yet." The soldier was arguing something with his commander.

"He wants Sir Cleve to confiscate your packs."

"Friendly sort."

"He's from West Wapentake, where the raiders strike first every spring."

"Look out!" Haaken dove into Bragi's legs.

But the sergeant's arrow was not meant for his brother. It brought a howl from down the trail.

Twenty hillmen charged from the forest.

The youths and scout braced for the charge. And Bragi marveled at the way it melted before the Itaskians' arrows.

It was a lesson he would not forget.

A few of those hillmen bore stolen weapons, mail, and shields. The first to reach Bragi was one such, and skilled with his blade. Haaken's axe, screaming across after slashing a spearman, saved Bragi.

While Sir Cleve and his soldiers sorted themselves out, the youths and woods-man dropped three more hillmen.

The remainder scattered before the horsemen, who harried them into the forest. "Finish the wounded before they escape," Sir Cleve called back.

"This is some day's work," the scout observed once the grisly business ended. "A quarter of Majneric's men dead within an hour. Makes a week spent chasing them worthwhile."

"Why?" Bragi asked.

"What? Ah. Hard times in the hills. Majneric brought his bucks down to raid. Can't really hate them for it. They're trying to take care of their families. At the expense of ours. We caught them near Mendalayas, killed a dozen. They scattered. We started hunting them down. Have to make this raiding too expensive for them."

The soldiers returned. They had corpses across their saddles and prisoners on tethers. Sir Cleve spoke.

"He says thanks for the help. Some of us would've been killed if you hadn't been in their way."

Even the sergeant seemed well disposed.

"Now's the time to make any requests. He's happy. He'll be in good odor when the Duke hears about this."

"Could he give us some kind of traveling pass? To get us to the City?"

"Good thinking, lad. I'll see."

They were ready to travel when the knight finished writing.

Later, after his lips stopped quivering, Bragi started whistling. But his brother never stopped looking back.

Haaken was still watching for a change of heart when they reached the capital.

The Red Hart Inn was a slum tavern. It was large, rambling, boisterous, and appeared on the verge of collapse. Evening shadows masked its more disreputable features.

The clientele fell silent at their advent. Fifty pairs of eyes stared. Some were curious, some wary, some challenging, none friendly.

"I don't think we belong here," Haaken whispered.

"Easy," Bragi cautioned, concealing his own nervousness. "Yalmar?"

No response.

He tried again. "Is there a man named Yalmar here? I come from Ragnar of Draukenbring."

The Itaskians muttered amongst themselves.

"Come here." A man beckoned from shadows at the rear.

The murmur picked up. Bragi avoided hard eyes. These were men Haaken and he had best not offend.

"In here."

The speaker was lean, stooped, ginger-haired, about thirty-five. He limped, but looked as tough as the others.

"I'm Yalmar. You named Ragnar of Draukenbring. Would that be the Wolf?"

"Yes."

"So?"

"He sent us."

"Why?"

"How do we know you're Yalmar?"

"How do I know you're from Ragnar?"

"He sent proof."

"A map? A dagger, and an amulet of Ilkazar?"

"Yes."

Yalmar's grin revealed surprisingly perfect teeth. "So. How is the crazy bastard? We swung some profitable deals, us two. I picked the ships. He took them. I fenced the goods."

Haaken grunted sullenly.

"What's with him?"

"Ragnar's dead. He was our father."

"The infamous Bragi and Haaken. You've got no idea how he bored me silly bragging you up. Passed over, eh? I'm sorry. And not just for the loss of a profitable partnership. He was my friend."

Neither youth responded. Bragi studied the man. This was an honest inn-keeper? How far could he be trusted?

Their silence unsettled Yalmar. "So. What do you want? Or are you just going to sit there like a couple of clams?"

"I don't know," Bragi said. "Father was dying. He said to go to you, you owed him. We're here."

"I noticed. Better begin at the beginning, then. Maybe give me an idea what he was thinking."

Bragi told the story. It did not hurt as much now.

"I see," Yalmar said when he finished. He pinched his nose, tugged his golden chin whiskers, frowned. "You got any skills? Carpentry? Masonry? Smithery?"

Bragi shook his head.

"Thought not. All you people do is fight. Not your safest way to make a living. And it don't leave you many openings here. Been at peace for fifteen years. And nobody in my business would use you. Too visible. And bodyguarding is out. Not enough experience. Tell you what. Give me a couple days. I'll put you up meantime. Upstairs. Try to stay out of sight. I'll put the word out that you're protected, but that won't keep the drunks from cutting you up. Or the police from breaking in to find out why I'm keeping Trolledyngjans."

With no better option available, Bragi and Haaken agreed.

They spent a week at the Red Hart. Yalmar told them things about Ragnar they had never heard at home. The Itaskian proved likable, despite an over-powering tyranny when he made them study his language.

Strange, hard men visited Yalmar late at night, though he steadfastly denied their existence. It finally dawned on Bragi that Yalmar did not trust them completely either.

One night he asked, "About the amulet, map, and dagger…"

Yalmar laid a finger across his lips. He checked the windows and doors. "They're why I owe your father. If I have to run, I can go knowing he provided means elsewhere. Now forget about it. The Brothers would be displeased. There's honor on the Inside. There's fear or friendship. Your father and I were friends."

Later, he told them, "I'm sorry. There's nothing for you here. I'd say go south. Try to catch on with the Mercenary's Guild. High Crag is taking on recruits."

Next afternoon, Haaken grumped, "This loafing is getting old, Bragi. What're we going to do?"

Bragi touched his mother's locket. "There's Hellin Daimiel. I'll talk to Yalmar."

The day following, Yalmar announced, "I've gotten you guard jobs with a caravan leaving tomorrow. There's a job you can do for me while you're at it. A man named Magnolo will be traveling with the caravan. He'll be carrying something for me. I don't trust him. Watch him." He added some details. "If he takes the package to anyone but Stavros, kill him."

Grimly, Bragi nodded.

"Bragi?" Haaken asked.

"Yeah?" Bragi poked the coals of their campfire, watched them glow briefly brighter.

"I kind of wish we didn't kill that guy Magnolo."

The man Yalmar had set them to watch had delivered the Itaskian's package to a house in the fanciest quarter in Hellin Daimiel. In their enthusiasm to fulfill their charge the youths had not only killed Magnolo, they had injured the gentleman he had visited and had killed one of the bodyguards. Aghast, panicky, they had fled the city.

"I'm hungry," Haaken complained.

"Don't seem to be much game in these parts, does there?"

They had made camp on a rocky hill eight miles northeast of Hellin Daimiel, in the only uncultivated area they could find. Hellin Daimiel was an old city. Its environs had been tamed for ages. Small game, especially agricultural pests, had been eradicated. The youths had eaten nothing but fish for three days, and those were treasures hard-won from irrigation canals.

"What're we going to do?"

Haaken sounded a little frightened.

Bragi did not mention it. He was scared too. They were on their own in a foreign, indifferent land.

"I don't know. I really don't."

"We don't have too many choices."

"I know."

"We can't just stay here. Not only will we starve, we're Trolledyngjan. Some-body's going to jump us for that."

"Yeah. I know." They had had their run-ins already. Trolledyngjans were not popular anywhere near the sea.

"We could go ahead and try the Mercenary's Guild."

"I just don't like the sound of that. All that marching around and saying 'Yes sir, no sir, by your leave, sir.' I don't think I could take it. I'd pop somebody in the snot box and get myself hung."

"It doesn't sound so bad to me. We could try it. They say you don't have to stay if you don't like it. It isn't like joining a regular army."

"Maybe. Okay? I've been thinking about something else." Bragi rose and moved to a large boulder. He leaned against it and peered out across the plain surrounding Hellin Daimiel.

Even by night the view reflected the studious planning characteristic of these peculiar people. The lights of the planned villages where the farm laborers lived made points on the interstices of a grid. The grid was more clearly discernible by day, in the form of carefully maintained roads and irrigation canals. The city itself was a galaxy in the background.

A whippoorwill struck up its repetitive commentary somewhere downslope. Another vocalized agreement from a distance. A gentle breeze climbed the slope, bringing with it scents of crops still a few weeks short of being stealably ripe.

The lights died away till Bragi was alone with the darkness and stars. They formed an immense silver girdle overhead. He stared at them till one broke free and streaked down the sky. It raced toward Hellin Daimiel.

He shrugged. An omen was an omen. He went and sat across the coals from his brother, who seemed to be asleep sitting up. Softly, he said, "I wonder where Mother is now."

Haaken shook all over, and for a moment Bragi was scared something had happened. Haaken was the sort who could become deathly ill without saying a word.

His concern was short-lived. There was enough light in the fire to betray the tears on Haaken's cheeks.

Bragi said nothing. He was homesick too.

After a time, he remarked, "She gave me this locket." He waited till he had Haaken's attention. "She told me we should take it to some people in Hellin Daimiel. To the House of Bastanos."

"That's not people. That's what they call a bank. Where rich men go to bor-row money."

"Oh?" He had to think about that. After a few seconds, "People run it, don't they? Maybe that's what she meant. Anyway, we could find out about it before we tried the Guild."

"No. It's too hot down there. They'll hang us. Besides, I don't think Mother wanted us to go there. Not really. Not unless there was nowhere else we could go."

"The excitement should have died down."

"You're fooling yourself, Bragi. I say try the Guild."

"You scared of Hellin Daimiel?" Bragi was. The city was too huge, too foreign, too dangerous.

"Yes. I don't mind admitting it. It's too different to just jump into. Too easy for us to get into something we can't handle because we don't know better. That's why I say go with the Guild."

Bragi saw Haaken's reasoning. The Guild would provide a base of safety while they learned southern ways.

He fingered his mother's gift, battled homesickness and temporized. "In the morning. We'll decide after we've slept on it."

He did not sleep well.

SEVEN
WADI EL KUF

El Murid stalked around Sebil el Selib like a tiger caged. Would this imprisonment never end? Would that villain Yousif never crack? The desert was on his side, if his advisers were to be believed. Nassef claimed he could stamp his foot and twenty thousand warriors would respond.

Why, then, did the Kingdom of Peace still extend no farther than he could see? Like the Lord Himself, he was running short on patience.

The pressure had been building for months. He was growing increasingly frustrated, increasingly suspicious of Nassef and his gang of self-made generals. He had told no one, not even Meryem, but he had begun to believe that Nassef was keeping him here intentionally, isolating him from his people. He was not sure why Nassef should want it that way.

Sometimes he took his son or daughter along on his walks, explaining the wonders of God's handiwork to them. Over Nassef's objections he had had several scholars brought in to explain some of the less obvious miracles of nature. And he had begun learning to read and write so that he could promulgate his laws in his own hand.

But usually he roamed alone, accompanied only by the Invincibles. The Invincibles were necessary. The minions of the Evil One had tried to murder him a dozen times. Sometimes it seemed his enemies had more men in his camp than he did.

He would greet soldiers by name, study the ever growing barracks-city, or inspect the new truck gardens being terraced into the hillsides. The army was devouring the available flatland. The gardens did not provide enough, but they helped. Every vegetable raised here meant one fewer that had to be bought on the coast and transported through the pass. And the fieldwork kept idle hands from turning to the Evil One.

It rained the day El Murid decided to end his confinement. It was not a pleasant rain, but one of those driving, bitter storms that beat down the spirit as easily as they beat down grass and leaves. The rains passed, but left the sky and his mood low, gray, and oppressive, with the potential of turning foul.

He summoned the captains of the Invincibles.

His bodyguard now consisted of three thousand men. It formed a personal army independent of that which Nassef commanded. The quiet, mostly name-less men who formed its brotherhood were absolutely faithful and completely incorruptible.

They had, for the past year, been undertaking operations of their own out in the desert. Unlike Nassef's men, they did not concentrate on attacking and looting loyalists. They moved into preponderantly friendly areas and stayed, assuming both administrative and defense functions. They spoke for the Lord, but contained their enthusiasm, proselytizing by example. They did not bother local loyalists as long as the loyalists observed a strict pacifism and tended their own business. The areas they occupied were largely free of strife. They had skirmished with Nassef's men on several occasions because they refused to allow anyone to disturb the peace of their lands.

Once the commanders assembled, El Murid said, "My brother, the Scourge of God, has returned. Has he not?"

"Last night, Disciple," someone volunteered.

"He hasn't come to see me. Someone go get him."

A half-minute after an emissary departed, the Disciple added archly, "I'd be indebted if someone could manage to borrow a Harish kill dagger." Though he knew who the senior members of the cult were, and had several in his pres-ence, he wanted to allow them their secrecy. They were useful. "We'll leave it lying around as a reminder of where the final authority lies."

El Murid's formal audience chamber, before the Malachite Throne, was large and formularized. He had a bent toward show and structure. Petition-ers had to come before him and stand at one of several podium-like pieces of furniture, wait their turn to be recognized, then present their plea and any important evidence.

At twenty-two El Murid was a hard, strong-willed, dictatorial leader—once he had suffered through his private hells of indecision. He no longer brooked defiance. The men and women of Sebil el Selib lived to the letter of his laws.

Less than two minutes passed before an Invincible placed a kill dagger on an evidence stand near the chief petitioner's podium. El Murid smiled his approval and suggested that the man move the blade slightly, so that it could not be seen from the Malachite Throne.

They waited.

Nassef stalked in sullenly. His lips were tight and pale. The Invincible accompanying him wore a smug look. El Murid guessed that there had been an argument, and Nassef had been compelled to concede.

Nassef strode to the central petitioner's podium. He was too angry to examine his surroundings immediately. El Murid could almost read the complaints marshaling behind his brow.

Then Nassef noticed the Invincibles standing stiffly in the shadows. Some of his anger and arrogance deserted him.

"Your war-general at your command, my Lord Disciple."

Nassef went through a further subtle deflation when he spied the kill dagger. Its placement made it appear to be a personal message from the cult, unknown to El Murid himself.

There was a quiet power struggle developing between Nassef and the Invincibles. El Murid, scarcely as ignorant as some of his followers thought, was aware of it, and hoped to use it to dampen Nassef's tendency toward independence.

Sometimes he thought that his brother-in-law was trying to carve out his own private empire.

What El Murid really wanted was a lever on Nassef that he could use to pry himself free of Sebil el Selib.

He could not stand to remain tied down much longer.

He mentioned none of the real grievances he had with his war-general. "Scourge of God, you've boasted that you could muster twenty thousand warriors with a word."

"That's true, Enlightened One."

El Murid controlled an impulse to grin. Nassef was going to lay it on heavy. "War general, speak that word. Gather your warriors. I've decided to move on Al Rhemish."

Nassef did not reply immediately. He surveyed the Invincibles. He found no sympathy in their eyes. They were El Murid's hounds. They would respond to his will no matter what he commanded. He looked at the dagger. He looked at El Murid. "It shall be as you command, my Lord Disciple. I'll send the summons as soon as I leave." He chewed his lower lip.

El Murid was mildly surprised. He had not expected Nassef to yield this easily. "Go, then. I'm sure you have a lot to do. I want to start as soon as possible."

"Indeed, Enlightened One. Moving an army to Al Rhemish will take a great deal of preparation. The desert is no friend to the soldier."

"It's a work of the Evil One. Naturally, it serves him. But it can be conquered, even as he can."

Nassef did not respond. He bowed and departed.

El Murid kept tabs. Not all the Invincibles wore white robes and mustered with their companies. A few remained secret members of the fraternity, providing intelligence for their commanders.

Nassef kept his word. He sent his messengers. He gathered his captains.

They plunged into the problems inherent in marching a large army across a wasteland.

Satisfied, El Murid almost forgot him.

Then he stole one of his rare evenings with his family.

The Disciple's private life would have scandalized the conservative Invincibles. But he had learned from his attempt to have Meryem testify at his trial. He and she kept their abnormal equality concealed behind closed doors.

His New Castle apartments were sumptuous. Though it would serve as a cistern in time of siege, he even had a large pool in which to relax and bathe.

Meryem met him with the excited smile that had come to mean so much to him. "I was afraid something would keep you."

"Not tonight. Tonight I need you more than they need me." He closed the door and kissed her. "You're a patient woman. A miracle. You've changed so much since El Aquila."

She smiled up at him. "Men change us. Come on. There's no one but family tonight. I'm even doing the cooking myself so the outside can't get in."

He followed her into the next room—and stiffened.

Nassef sat with their son Sidi and the still-unnamed girl, telling them some outrageous tale of the desert. El Murid pursed his lips unhappily, but settled to his cushion without a word. Nassef was Meryem's brother, and the children loved him. Especially the girl. Sometimes she would sneak out and follow her uncle all over the valley. She could not believe that her father's enemies were capable of attacking him through her.

"It'll be a while," Meryem told him. "Why don't you relax in the pool? You haven't had a chance all week."

"Me too!" Sidi yelped.

El Murid laughed. "You're going to grow scales like a fish if you spend any more time in the water. All right. Come on. Nassef, when we reach the sea we'll make Sidi our admiral. I can't keep him away from the water."

Nassef rose. "I'll join you. This old skin hasn't been clean for two months. Sidi, I've got a job for you. Show me how to swim. I might need to know if your father is going to take us to the sea."

"What about me?" the girl demanded. She hated the water, but did not want to let her uncle out of her sight. She was beginning to remind her father of her mother at an earlier age.

"You're a girl," Sidi told her. His tone suggested that that was cause enough for her to be thrown into stocks, let alone banned from the bath.

"You might melt, sugar," her father told her. "Let's go, men."

Lying in the cool water, letting it buoy him up, allowed him a relaxation that was missing even in Meryem's arms.

He relaxed for half an hour. Sidi and Nassef squealed and splashed and laughed and dunked one another. Then he said, "All right, Nassef. Now."

His brother-in-law did not pretend to misunderstand. He hoisted Sidi to the edge of the pool. "Time to get out. Dry yourself off, get dressed and go help your mother."

"How come I have to leave whenever anybody wants to talk?"

"Do as he says, son," El Murid told him. "And make sure you're good and dry before you get dressed."

Sidi was gone in a minute. Nassef said, "I'm beginning to be sorry that I never married. I miss having children."

"You're not too old."

"No. But I'm in the wrong business. Taking a wife would be tempting fate too much, wouldn't it? Fuad would catch me the first time I took the field."

"Maybe you're right. Maybe a soldier shouldn't marry. Too much strain on the family."

Nassef said nothing for several seconds. Then, "We're alone. No ears to hear. No hearts to offend. Can we speak as brothers? As the two who rode out of El Aquila together, and who fought the desert side by side? Simply as Nassef and Micah, men who have too much in common to be at odds?"

"It's a family occasion. Try to keep it at a family level."

"I will. You married my sister, who is my only true friend in this world. I am your brother.

"I'm deeply troubled. We're embarking on a doomed enterprise. My brother, I tell you this out of my love for you, and for no other reason. We can't take Al Rhemish. Not yet."

El Murid conquered his anger. Nassef was following the rules. He could do no less. "I don't understand why not. I look and I listen. I see hosts pass through Sebil el Selib. I hear that we can summon a horde to our banner. I'm told that much of the desert is with us."

"Perfectly true. Though I can't say how much of the desert is on our side. More with us than with our enemies, I think. But it's a big desert. Most people don't care one way or the other. What they really want is for us and the Royalists both to leave them alone."

"Why, then, do you urge me to delay? That's the argument you want to present, isn't it? And I remind you of your own observation that we're alone. You can be as frank as you like."

"All right. Stated simply, twenty thousand warriors don't make an army just by gathering in the same place. My forces are only now beginning to coalesce. My men aren't used to operating in large groups. Neither are the Invincibles. And the men from areas that we've controlled a long time have lost their battle edge. Moreover, there isn't a man among us, myself included, who has the experience to manage a large force."

"Are you claiming we'll be defeated?"

"No. I'm telling you that we'd be risking it, and that the risk will go down every day that we put off fighting them on their own terms. Which we would be. They would know we were coming. They have their spies. And they have men who *do* know how armies work."

El Murid said nothing for a minute. First he tried to assess Nassef's sincerity. He could not fault it. Nor could he challenge his brother-in-law's arguments. His frustration at being trapped in Sebil el Selib returned.

He could stand his containment no more. He would tolerate it not one minute longer than it would take to assemble the host.

"My heart tells me to go ahead."

"That's your decision? It's final?"

"It is."

Nassef sighed. "Then I'll do everything I can. Maybe we'll be lucky. I do have one suggestion. When the time comes, take command yourself."

El Murid scrutinized his brother-in-law narrowly.

"Not because I want to shirk responsibility for any defeat. Because the warriors will fight harder for the Disciple than they will for the Scourge of God. That might be the margin between victory and defeat."

Again El Murid had the feeling that Nassef was being sincere. "So be it. Let's go see if Meryem is ready for dinner."

It was a quiet family meal, with few words spoken. El Murid spent much of it examining his ambivalent feelings toward Nassef. As always, Nassef was hard to pin down.

Nassef had argued no harder than a man of conscience should have. Had El Murid misjudged his brother-in-law? Was the news reaching him becoming distorted by the Invincible minds through which it passed?

His frustration mounted as the days turned into weeks. The army grew, but the process was so damnably slow! His advisers frequently reminded him that his followers had to come long distances, often pursued by Royalists, and as they approached Sebil el Selib they had to contend with Yousif s patrols.

But the time came at last. The morning when he could kiss Meryem good-bye and tell her that when next they met it would be within the Most Holy Mrazkim Shrines themselves.

More than twenty thousand men responded to Nassef's call. Their tents were everywhere. Sebil el Selib reminded El Murid of Al Rhemish during Disharhun.

Yousif's people had been quiet for nine days. They had ceased contesting the passage of the warrior bands. Nassef had been telling anyone who would listen that he did not like it, that it was a sign that the Wahlig had something up his sleeve.

Then the news came. Yousif had mustered every man he could, some five thousand, and had installed himself at the oasis near Wadi el Kuf. His neighbors had loaned him another two thousand men.

"We'll have to fight him there," Nassef told El Murid. "There's no choice. We can't get to Al Rhemish without watering there. This is what he's been waiting for all these years. The chance to get us into a conventional battle. It looks like he wants that chance so badly that he doesn't care about the numbers."

"Give him what he wants. Let's rid ourselves of him once and for all."

Nassef guessed right most of the time. But he had erred in calling in all of El Murid's supporters. By so doing he stripped the desert of his sources of intelligence. He and El Murid would not learn the truth about Yousif's stand till it was too late.

Nassef selected twenty thousand men. El Murid took twenty-five hundred Invincibles. They left a substantial force to defend the pass in their absence.

It was a morning many days after departure. The sun hung low in the east. They moved up on the waterhole by Wadi el Kuf.

The wadi was a shallow, broad valley a mile and a half east of the waterhole. It was filled with bizarre natural formations. It was the wildest badland in all Hammad al Nakir.

Nassef and El Murid raised the Lord's standard atop a low hill a mile south of the oasis, and an equal distance from the wadi. They studied the enemy, who was waiting on horseback.

"They don't seem impressed by our numbers," Nassef observed.

"What do you suggest?"

"It seems straightforward. Hold the Invincibles here, in reserve. Send the rest in one wave and overwhelm them."

"This is a strange land, Nassef. It's so silent."

The stillness did seem supernatural. Thirty thousand men and nearly as many animals faced one another, and even the flies were quiet.

El Murid glanced at the wadi. It was a shadowy forest of grotesque sandstone formations: steeples, pylons, giant dumbbells standing on end. He shuddered as he considered that devil's playground.

"We're ready," Nassef said.

"Go ahead."

Nassef turned to Karim, el-Kader, and the others. "On my signal."

His captains trotted their horses down to the divisions they commanded.

Nassef gave his signal.

The horde surged forward.

Yousif's men waited without moving. They had arrows ready on the strings of their saddle bows.

"Something's wrong," the Scourge of God muttered. "I can feel it."

"Nassef?" El Murid queried in a voice gone small and tentative. "Do you hear drums?"

"It's the hoofbeats...."

El Murid did hear drums. "Nassef!" His right arm stabbed out like a javelin thrust.

The devil's garden of Wadi el Kuf had begun to disgorge a demon horde.

"Oh, my God!" Nassef moaned. "My God, no."

King Aboud had harkened to Yousif's importunities at last. He had sent Prince

Farid to Wadi el Kuf with five thousand of the desert's finest soldiers, many of them equipped after the fashion of western knights. With Farid, in tactical command, was Sir Tury Hawkwind of the Mercenary's Guild. Hawkwind had brought a thousand of his brethren. They were arrayed in western-style lances of a heavy cavalryman, his esquire, two light and one heavy infantrymen.

Nassef had time to think, to react. Heavy cavalry could not charge at breakneck speed across a mile of desert and up a slight hill. And Hawkwind obviously meant to bring his shock power to bear.

"What do we do?" El Murid asked.

"I think it's time for the amulet," Nassef replied. "That's the only weapon that will help now."

El Murid raised his arm. Without a word he showed Nassef his naked wrist.

"Where the hell is it?" Nassef demanded.

Softly, "At Sebil el Selib. I left it. I was so excited about coming, I forgot it." He had not worn the amulet for years, preferring to keep it safe within the shrines.

Nassef sighed, shook his head wearily. "Lord, choose a company of Invincibles and flee. I'll buy you all the time I can."

"Flee? Are you mad?"

"This battle is lost, Lord. All that remains is to salvage as much as we can. Don't stay, and deprive the movement of its reason for existing."

El Murid shook his head stubbornly. "I see no defeat. Only more trouble than we anticipated originally. We still outnumber them, Nassef. And no matter what, I won't leave the field while men are dying for me. Not when they have it in their hearts that I am commanding them. What would they think of my courage?"

Nassef shrugged. "We can but die with honor, then. I suggest you form the Invincibles to meet the coming charge." A moment later, after studying the enemy banners, he murmured thoughtfully, "I wonder what Hawkwind is doing here."

"Trust in the Lord, Nassef. He will deliver them unto us. We have the numbers, and Him on our side. What more could we ask?"

Nassef stifled an angry response. He helped guide the Invincibles into a new disposition.

At the oasis, at least, it seemed that El Murid's confidence was justified. Yousif's force was surrounded.

"Who's this Hawkwind?"

"A Guildsman. Perhaps their best general."

"Guildsman?" El Murid's ignorance of the world outside Hammad al Nakir was immense.

"A brotherhood of warriors. Not unlike the Invincibles. Called the Mercenary's Guild. They're also a little like the Harish, and yet like nothing we know.

They own no allegiance except to one another. After Itaskia, they're probably the greatest military power in the west, yet they have no homeland but a castle called High Crag. When their generals frown, princes cringe. Just their decision to fight for someone sometimes stops a war before it starts."

"How do you know? When have you ever had time to learn?"

"I pay people to learn things for me. I've got spies all over the west."

"Why?"

"Because you want to go there someday. I'm preparing the way. But it's all irrelevant if we don't get out of this alive."

Hawkwind's force was close enough to start increasing its pace.

None of the Invincibles had seen knights before. They neither understood nor sufficiently feared what they faced. When their master gave the signal, they charged. They trusted in the Lord and their name.

Hawkwind increased his pace again.

The long lances and heavy horses hit the Invincibles like a stone wall. The Royalists passed through and over them, and crushed them, and in ten minutes were turning and forming for a charge into the rear of the horde beleaguering Yousif.

Neither Nassef nor El Murid said a word. It was even worse than Nassef had expected. The Wahlig of el Aswad was in a bad way. But once help arrived the battle became a rebel slaughter.

Hawkwind placed a screen of infantry between himself and the remnants of the Invincibles. He placed another of light horse between himself and the oasis, with extended and slightly C-shaped wings. Then he started hammering with his armored horsemen. Charge. Melee. Withdraw. Reform. Charge.

El Murid was too stubborn to accept reality. Nassef's troops, down in the witch's cauldron, were too confused to realize what was happening.

Hawkwind set about systematically exterminating them.

At one point Nassef wept. "My Lord," he pleaded, "let me go down there. Let me try to break them out."

"We can't lose," El Murid murmured in reply, more to himself than to his war-general. "We have the numbers. The Lord is with us."

Nassef cursed softly.

The sun moved to the west. Hawkwind extended his wings, completing a thin encirclement against which Nassef's warriors collided randomly, like flies against the walls of a bottle. He put more and more strength into the circle, daring El Murid to try something with his battered Invincibles. The Wahlig's men filtered out of the cauldron and became part of the circle.

Some of Nassef's men tried to surrender, but Prince Farid had ordered his to take no prisoners.

"They have taken away our last ounce of choice," Nassef moaned. "We have to throw these pitiful few hundreds in to give those men down there a chance to escape."

"Nassef?"

"What?" The voice of the Scourge of God was both sorrowful and angry.

"I'm sorry. I was wrong. The time wasn't right. I listened to myself instead of to the Voice of God. Take command. Do what you can to save what you can. O Lord Almighty, forgive me for my arrogance. Pardon me for my vanity."

"No."

"What? Why?"

"I'll tell you what to do, but you do the leading. This is no time to show weakness. Salvage some respect from the disaster. Do that and we can always say that they tricked us, that the Evil One blinded our eyes."

"Nassef! You're right, of course. What should we do?"

Fifteen minutes later the survivors of the Invincibles hurled themselves against Hawkwind's circle. They did not strike toward the center, but cut a shallow chord meant to break the widest possible gap.

Nassef's warriors began flooding through while the gap was still opening. El Murid and his brother-in-law rode at the head of the charge.

El Murid flailed about him with his sword. The clash of weapons, the screams of horses and men, were overwhelming, maddening. The dust choked him. It stung his eyes. A horse plunged against his, nearly unseating him. A wild swordstroke, partially turned by Nassef, cut his left arm, leaving a shallow, bloody wound. For an instant he was amazed at the lack of immediate pain.

Nassef struck about himself like some war djinn just released from Hell. The Invincibles did their desperate best to keep their prophet from coming to harm, but...

"Now!" Nassef shrieked at him. "Give the order to fly. To the wadi. We can lose them in the rocks." Most of Nassef's men were away. The circle was collapsing toward El Murid and the Scourge of God.

El Murid vacillated.

A random swarm of arrows rained from the cloudless sky. One buried itself in his mount's eye.

The beast screamed and reared. El Murid flew through the air. The earth came up and hit him like a flying boulder. A horse trampled his right arm.

He heard the snapping of bone over his own shriek. He tried to rise. His gaze met that of a Guild infantryman who was calmly working his way through the chaos, braining wounded Invincibles with a massive war hammer.

"Micah!" Nassef screamed at him. "Get up! Grab hold of my leg!"

He found the will and strength. Nassef started away.

"Hang on tight. Bounce high."

He did.

Behind him, another hundred Invincibles gave their lives to make sure he got away.

Once into the wadi, Nassef flung himself from his mount, seized El Murid's left hand. "Come on! We've got to disappear before they get organized."

The sounds of battle died swiftly as they fled deeper into the grotesque wilderness. El Murid did not know if distance or final defeat were responsible, but he feared the worst.

They kept to terrain no horse could penetrate. Their enemies would have to come for them on foot if they insisted on pressing the pursuit.

It was almost dark when Nassef found the fox den. Two badly wounded warriors crowded it already, but they made room. Nassef did his best to eliminate traces outside.

The first hunters came only a short time later. They were in a hurry, chasing game still on the wing. Other parties passed during the next few hours. Occasional shouts and metallic clashings echoed through the wadi.

During each stillness Nassef did what he could for the two warriors. He did not expect either to live. When it seemed that the pursuit had ended, he worked on El Murid's arm.

The fracture was not as bad as it had seemed. The bone had broken cleanly, without being crushed.

It was midnight when the pain subsided enough for El Murid to ask, "What do we do now, Nassef?" His voice was vague, his mind airy. Nassef had given him an opiate.

"We start over. We build it again, from the ground. We don't hurry it. At least we won't have to capture Sebil el Selib again."

"Can we do it?"

"Of course. We've lost a battle, that's all. We're young. Time and the Lord are on our side. Be quiet!"

He was at the mouth of the den, masking the others with his body and dark clothing. He could see the flickering light of torches playing among the rocks.

Men followed the light.

One complained, "I'm tired. How long do we have to keep this up?"

Another replied, "Until we get them. They're in here and I don't intend to let them out."

Nassef knew that second voice. It belonged to that stubborn brother of the Wahlig, Fuad. Hatred welled within him.

One of the wounded warriors chose that moment to die. His comrade thought quickly enough to smother his death rattle with a corner of his robe.

"Why didn't you bring the damned amulet?" Nassef demanded testily, after the danger had passed. "It would have made the difference."

The Disciple barely heard through his pain. He gritted the truth between clenched teeth. "I was a fool, wasn't I? The angel gave it to me for moments like those. Why didn't you say something before we left? You knew I was keeping it safe in the shrine."

"I didn't think of it. Why should I? It's not mine. We've been a pair of prize idiots, brother. And it looks like we're going to pay the ancient price of idiocy."

The devil Fuad did not give up for four days. Hardly a minute passed when there was not some Royalist hunter within hearing of the den. Before their trial ended, Nassef and El Murid were drinking their own urine in a grave they shared with two decaying corpses. The body poisons filling the urine made them so sick it seemed certain they were but trading a quick death for a slow one.

EIGHT
THE CASTLE TENACIOUS AND RESOLUTE

There is great rejoicing in Sebil el Selib," Fuad snarled as he stalked toward Yousif, Radetic, and the Wahlig's captains. A heavy layer of trail dust covered him. "Nassef and the Disciple have returned. They survived."

The cords in Yousif's neck stood out. His face darkened. He rose slowly, then suddenly hurled his platter across the room. "Damn it!" he roared. "And damn that fool Aboud! When they finally take Al Rhemish and strangle him, I hope I'm there to laugh in his halfwit's face."

Wadi el Kuf had been the limit of Royal aid. Nothing Yousif had done or said had been sufficient to excite Prince Farid into exceeding his orders and following through. The opportunity had been there, to pursue and slay, to re-cover Sebil el Selib. But Farid had had his instructions, and had been satisfied himself that El Murid and Nassef were dead.

Farid's father was old and fat and none too bright. He loved his comforts and could see nothing beyond tomorrow. He did not want his son wasting money or lives.

There had been a time when Aboud had been a renowned warrior and captain. He had driven the Throyens from the disputed territories along the northern end of the eastern shore. But that had been long ago. Time, that old traitor, slows and weakens all men, and makes them less inclined to seek hazard.

"Thank God for Farid," Yousif sighed, his rage spent. "No one else could have gotten us the help we needed at Wadi el Kuf. Megelin? What now?"

"We step back a few years and go on."

"The same thing?"

"The same. And don't count on them making any more mistakes. They've had their one and gotten away with it. El Murid will take the lesson to heart. He'll listen to Nassef now."

Nearly eight thousand of Nassef's men had escaped Wadi el Kuf. They were back in the desert now, stunned, but a foundation for a new guerrilla infra-structure.

"We should have attacked Sebil el Selib while they were still demoralized," Yousif growled. "We should've hit them and kept on hitting till they gave up. None of the leaders were there."

"Hit them with what?" Fuad asked caustically. "We were lucky they didn't come after us."

Yousif's forces had been battered and exhausted after the battle. Getting themselves home had been the most difficult task they could handle.

Fuad added, "They would have if anybody had been there to tell them what to do."

Yousif's anger evaporated. He could not sustain it in the face of the truth.

The years had taken their toll. El Aswad was approaching its limit. Yousif had done all he could, but his best had not been enough. From Wadi el Kuf onward he foresaw nothing but a downhill slide. His last hope had been that El Murid and his generals had perished. But Fuad's news accounted for the last of the missing leaders. They were all alive. The fury of Wadi el Kuf had consumed none but the expendable.

"Megelin," Yousif said, "think for the enemy. What will he do now?"

"I don't know, Wahlig. They say Nassef is vindictive. We'll probably get a lot of attention. Beyond that guess, you might as well read sheep's entrails."

Yousif said nothing for several minutes. Then, "I'm going to concede the initiative again. We'll keep up the patrols and ambushes, but avoid contact most of the time. We'll stall. Concentrate on surviving. Try to lure them into a debilitating siege of the Eastern Fortress. Aboud is old. He's got the gout. He can't live forever. I talked to Farid. He's on our side. He'll be less sedentary. He can see the shape of things. He'd give us what we need if he wore the Crown."

But neither fate nor Nassef would play the game according to Yousif's wishes. In the year after Wadi el Kuf Yousif's men seldom saw their enemies. They could not be found even when hunted. Nassef seemed to have forgotten that el Aswad existed. With the exception of the patrolled zone immediately before the mouth of Sebil el Selib, security and peace reigned in the Wahligate.

The quiet drove Yousif and Fuad to distraction. They worried constantly. What did the silence mean?

Haroun and Radetic went on their first fieldtrip in almost two years. Megelin wanted to look for rare wildflowers. His search took them into a canyon which meandered deep into Jebal al Alf Dhulquarneni.

Haroun worried about offending the Hidden Ones. He tried to mask his nervousness behind uncharacteristic chatter. That generally took the form of trying to get Radetic to illuminate the enemy's behavior.

Exasperated, Radetic finally growled, "I don't know, Haroun. The Sword rules the Word these days. And Nassef is a big unknown. I can't begin to guess his motives, let alone predict his moves. One minute he looks like El Murid's most devoted follower, the next like a bandit looting the desert, and a second after that he seems to be a man quietly finagling himself an empire. All I can say is wait. He'll make everything painfully clear someday."

One painful piece of news had sullied a restful winter. El Murid had appointed Nassef commander of the Invincibles for a period of five years. Spies said that the Scourge of God had launched an immediate purge, that Nassef was redesigning the bodyguard to his own specifications.

The Sword apparently mastered the Word completely now.

Nassef's campaign plans became less murky once Haroun and Radetic returned to el Aswad. They were given no chance to recuperate from the hardships of the trail. Guards hustled them directly to the Wahlig.

"Well, he's finally made a move, Megelin," Yousif declared as they approached. "He's shown his hand. And it was the last thing anybody expected."

Radetic dropped gingerly to a cushion. "What did he do?"

"All that strength he's been gathering? That's been piling up so fast our spies figured he was going to take a stab at us this summer? He used it to attack to the east."

"The east? But—"

"Souk el Arba has fallen already. He's besieging Es Souanna. His riders have reached Ras al Jan. Souk el Arba didn't resist. They sent a committee to welcome him. Our agents say our cousins on the coast are tripping over each other they're so eager to join him. He's promising everybody the loot of Al Rhemish and the Inner Provinces."

"In other words, the east has decided its future lies with El Murid."

"They've had a lot of time to preach there. And to make deals. Aboud hasn't done much to hold their loyalties. In fact, I expect Throyes to cut us off completely now."

The only way Al Rhemish could reach its eastern supporters was by using the same narrow, northern pass which gave desert merchants access to Throyes. The Throyens were racially and linguistically akin to the Children of Hammad al Nakir, but had not recognized an external suzerainty since the Fall. The city had been founded as a naval and mercantile port by Ilkazar.

There had been no fighting for years, but the city still claimed territories on the northern shores of the east coast. Since Sebil el Selib Throyes had been nibbling away at the lands Aboud had reconquered in his youth. The Royal lines of communication now had to pass through areas patrolled by unfriendly troops.

"I imagine they'll occupy in earnest as soon as they hear what's happened," Radetic agreed. "How strong a garrison did Nassef leave? Did El Murid go with him?"

"Fuad's checking it now."

Fuad was doing more than checking. He was conducting el Aswad's first assault on the pass in years. His initial progress report arrived early next day.

Haroun came to drag Radetic out of his quarters. "Come on, Megelin! Uncle Fuad took them by surprise. Get up! Father needs you."

Radetic rubbed sleep from his eyes. "Fuad did what?" He began to dress, donning desert-style clothing. The last of his own western garb had gone to rags years earlier. "Never going to get used to this women's wear," he muttered. "Maybe I should have something sent out. Bah. That would make it too easy for assassins to find their target."

"Come on!" Haroun bubbled. "He surprised them. He got through their picket lines and cut them off so nobody knew he was coming. He caught them working in their fields and killed a whole lot. Come on. Father needs to know what you think we should do."

Haroun could not stop jabbering. He revealed most of Yousif's surprise before he and Radetic located the Wahlig in the parapet of the tower on the north wall. Yousif was staring northward, toward Sebil el Selib.

With a mixture of luck, planning, and cunning, Fuad had outmaneuvered El Murid's patrols and had broken into Sebil el Selib. He had killed or captured hundreds before the survivors could seal up the two fortresses, and had killed and captured hundreds more afterward, because in their panic the gatekeepers had locked them out. Fuad and the survivors were trading stares over the walls of the castles. Fuad did not have the strength to storm either. While he awaited advice from home he was destroying everything he could. He expected Nassef to send help soon. He wanted to leave the enemy nothing when he withdrew.

"What do you think we should do, Megelin?" Yousif asked.

"Send for help. Especially to Prince Farid. Explain the situation. Tell him that if he hurries we have a chance to cut them off on the coast. That might be as good as killing them."

"I've done that. I was thinking in more direct terms. What can we do up there? While we're waiting for Farid and Nassef?"

Radetic considered. "I'd have to see the fortresses myself. I might notice a weakness you've overlooked."

The western style of warfare was more given to castles and siegework than that of Hammad al Nakir. The men of the desert were inclined to run away when outnumbered rather than to retreat into a fortress. Most of the extant fortifications were Imperial hand-me-downs weak from long neglect.

"You can join me, then. I'm leaving in an hour. Taking every man who can hoist himself onto a horse."

"Father?"

Yousif eyed his son. He knew what the boy wanted, but made him ask anyway. "What, Haroun?"

"Can I go? If Megelin does?"

The Wahlig glanced at Radetic, who said, "It's all right with me if it's all right with you."

"Go get your things, son."

Haroun left with the excitement of a small whirlwind. Radetic observed, "It's time he got a glimpse of the realities."

"That's why I told him he could go. He accused me of letting Ali have all the fun this morning. I want him to see that Ali isn't enjoying himself."

"How much more muscle can you give Fuad?"

"Not much. Maybe three hundred men."

"Hardly enough."

"Then hope that my messengers get lucky."

Two days later Megelin saw Sebil el Selib for the first time. He was surprised.

He had been hearing about it for eight years. He had built a mental picture that only vaguely resembled reality.

"How easy it is to destroy," he told Haroun. "You see what your uncle has done? In a few days he's undone the labor of years."

Fields had been ruined. Hillside terraces had been undermined and allowed to collapse. Fuad's men were still forcing their prisoners to destroy, daring the inmates of the two fortresses to try stopping them. Fuad was saving the vast barracks-city east of the new fortress to become a burning greeting for Nassef's return.

Radetic studied the situation for several hours. Then he located Fuad and asked, "Is El Murid here?"

"Went with Nassef. To preach to new converts. He left his family, though. They're in the New Castle."

Radetic glanced at the huge fortress. "We couldn't take that. The old stronghold we might. We can pound it a little, anyway. If we can come up with the lumber to build siege engines."

Fuad found the lumber in the barracks.

Radetic gathered the Wahlig's officers. "We probably won't have time for much before Nassef returns," he told them. "But we won't get anywhere if we don't try." Those men had been involved in the war so long that other ways of life now seemed alien. "What the Wahlig wants is a low-risk assault on these fortifications. We're likely to have little luck with the New Castle. It's up to modern standards and it's in good repair. The old castle isn't. It'll be our primary target.

"We'll build a variety of siege engines, beginning with trebuchets and mangonels. We'll start gathering suitable stones, lumber and so forth, right away.

"We'll work on the old castle wall a few yards to the left of the barbican. That's a recent addition, and they weakened the wall during construction.

"I'll want to keep several things going at once. Especially some obvious practice with scaling ladders, turtles, rams, and siege towers. We'll build the turtles right away and bunch them in the meadow as close to the old castle as we can. We'll use them to conceal the head of a mine we'll run under the weak section of wall. We'll dispose of the earth at night."

Radetic's siege strategy was extensive. It would require every available body, including Fuad's prisoners. But as he revealed it, the faces of Yousif's officers darkened. He was asking warriors to do the work of slaves. It was beneath their dignity. He considered their hostile faces. "Haroun," he whispered, "fetch your father."

The Wahlig did his convincing for him.

Yousif came to Megelin three days later, while Radetic was inspecting his projects. "How long till you drop that wall, Megelin? We're running out of time. Nassef should be on his way by now." There was little force in the Wahlig's voice. He seemed dazed.

"I'm having trouble. The soft earth doesn't run all the way to the foundations. I'm running a mine to the New Castle, too, but I don't have much hope for it. Those walls were engineered by westerners. You can tell that from the camber of the base."

"What?"

"The way it slopes out at the bottom. Instead of coming straight down. It increases the thickness and coherence of the wall, making mining difficult."

"Nevertheless, Megelin."

"Yes, Wahlig. We'll persist. Any news from Al Rhemish?"

Yousif became more sour. His lined, rugged, aquiline face darkened. "The messenger returned an hour ago."

Radetic watched as his hastily constructed trebuchets hurled a barrage against the old castle. One of the engines groaned and fell apart. The rocks rumbled against the castle. The wall shuddered. A merlon stone slid off the battlements and plunged downward. Cracks had begun to show in the wall. "The engines might be enough. If I can keep them working. What's the bad news?"

"Aboud says we have to chase Nassef off the coast. He was pretty definite about it."

"Did he have any suggestions? How much help is he going to send?"

"None. And no ideas either. Just a flat-out order to do the job."

Radetic peered at Yousif. The Wahlig's face had gone gray with despair.

"This is the beginning of the end, Megelin. Unless you can produce a miracle here. They've abandoned us."

Radetic thought he understood. "You could pretend the letter never arrived. You can't commit suicide."

"Megelin, I can't. I'm a man of honor. I don't think I could explain that to a westerner. Even a westerner who has been around as long as you. You see my men there? They know I'm fighting a losing battle. But they stick with me year after year. They don't see that they have any choice. Neither have I. Pledges of honor have been made. Aboud's orders leave me no room for maneuver. I have to try to beat Nassef even when I know that I can't."

"Haroun? Are you listening?"

"Yes, Megelin." The youth was as close as Radetic's shadow. As always. He followed his teacher everywhere, watching with those wide, curious eyes, logging every detail of the siegework in an infallible memory.

"Pay attention to this. Listen to your father. He's talking about paying the price of an absolute and inflexible concept of duty. Don't ever push a man into the corner he's in. And don't ever let yourself get shoved into one like it. Yousif, there has to be a way around destroying yourself because of Aboud's stupidity."

"It's our way, Megelin. It's mine. I have to do *something*."

"Isn't this something?" Radetic swept an arm round to include everything happening in Sebil el Selib. "Isn't this enough? We've been bled white. We just don't have our strength anymore. Yousif!"

The Wahlig stepped back from his sudden intensity. "What?"

"I get the feeling you're thinking about going on through the pass. To meet Nassef and martyr yourself in some big last battle. Don't do it. Don't waste yourself."

"Megelin—"

"At least set your schedule so you can do it after you've finished here. Would that violate the spirit of Aboud's orders? Only a fool leaves behind an enemy who can close a trap on him later."

Yousif mused. "You're right, of course. You always are. I'm not thinking this morning. I'm so tired of fighting and Aboud's indifference that part of me just wants to hurry the end."

"Have you explored the pass? Is there a narrow passage where you could ambush Nassef? Where you could roll boulders down on him? This is our last great cry of defiance, Yousif. Why don't we make it memorable *without* getting ourselves martyred?"

"All right."

The Wahlig departed. He seemed less depressed.

Radetic watched as the trebuchet crews cranked the arms of the engines back to throwing position. They were clumsy and slow. "Damn!" he muttered. "What I wouldn't give for a company of Guildsmen."

Fuad materialized. "I don't know what you said to Yousif, but thanks. He was ready to throw himself on his sword."

"Not much, really."

"He told you the news?"

"That Aboud isn't going to help? Yes. Damn the fool anyway. I thought sure Farid would talk him into sending us something."

"The Crown Prince won't be talking anybody into anything anymore. Didn't he tell you? Farid is dead."

Very carefully, like an old cat searching for just the right place to curl up, Radetic looked round and chose himself a stone on which to sit. "He's dead? Farid?"

Fuad nodded.

"He had help making his exit? The Harish finally got him?"

The cult was trying to exterminate the Quesani family. They failed more often than they succeeded, but scared hell out of the family by trying. Farid had become a favorite target. He had escaped their attentions three times.

"Not this time. This time Nassef sent his own expert. He slipped Karim and a couple of hundred Invincibles into the wastes north of Al Rhemish. Last week they ambushed Farid while he was lion hunting. It was a big hunt."

"That's sad. It really is. Sometimes I think there really is a God who's on El Murid's side."

"You don't know how sad it is. They didn't just kill Farid. I said it was a big hunt. They got most of his brothers, his retainers, a bunch of Aboud's officers and ministers, and the Wahlig of Es Sofala and a lot of his people."

"Good heavens. A disaster."

"A hell of a coup if you're Nassef. He's carved the heart out of the Quesani. You know who's left? Who our beloved Crown Prince is now? Ahmed."

"Ahmed? I don't know the name."

"With reason. He's a nothing. I wish I didn't know him. He's a damned woman, if you ask me. I wouldn't be surprised if he prefers boys."

"No wonder Yousif was so grim."

"Megelin?" Haroun piped. "Does that mean it's over? Uncle Fuad? Did we lose the war when we weren't looking?"

Fuad laughed sourly. "A good turn of phrase, Haroun. A fine way to say it. Yes."

"No," Radetic countered. "It's never over till you surrender. In your own heart."

Fuad laughed again. "Bravely spoken, teacher. Fine talk. But it doesn't change the facts."

Radetic shrugged. "Haroun, let's see if they're ready with that spoon trebuchet."

The crew was cranking the machine for a test shot when they arrived. Radetic watched while they ignited a bundle of brush, tipped it into the spoon, then flipped the blazing missile over the New Castle wall.

"Will it start a fire, Megelin?"

"Probably not. But it'll keep them nervous."

"Why do it, then?"

"Battles can be won in men's minds, Haroun. That's what I meant when I told your uncle it's not over till you surrender in your heart. The sword isn't the only weapon that will wear an enemy down."

"Oh." Haroun's face took on that look he got when he wanted to remember something forever.

Two days passed. And still Nassef did not come. Megelin could feel the contempt radiating from the coast. Nassef did not consider them dangerous.

He would learn.

Megelin sent for Yousif, who wore a bright expression when he appeared. The Wahlig seemed to have made peace with himself.

"I'm going to bring her down now," Radetic told him. He gave a signal. "Fuad, get the men ready. The way we rehearsed it."

Fuad muttered something uncomplimentary and stalked off. A gust of activity swept the valley. It became a gale. Yousif's warriors gathered for the assault.

The trebuchets ceased pounding the old castle. The wall had held, but barely.

The engine crews dragged their machines around to face the New Castle.

An hour passed. Yousif became impatient. "When's something going to happen?" he demanded.

Radetic indicated smoke trailing out of cracks at the base of the wall. "When you mine a wall you have to shore it up with timbers. When you're ready to bring it down you fill the chamber underneath with brush and set it afire. It takes time for the timbers to burn through. Ah. Here we go."

A deep-throated grinding assailed the air. The cracks grew. Pieces of masonry popped out of the wall. Then, with a startling suddenness, a twenty-foot-wide section dropped straight down, virtually disappearing into the earth.

"Perfect!" Radetic enthused. "Absolutely perfect. Fuad!" he shouted. "Go ahead! Attack now!" He turned to Yousif. "Don't forget to watch the New Castle for a sally."

The gutting of the old fortress took under four hours. It was almost a disappointment. There weren't enough defenders to slow the assault.

Radetic turned his attention to El Murid's New Castle immediately. The capture of the old was barely complete when word came that an enemy column was in the pass. Yousif roared off to spring the ambush Radetic had suggested.

The tardiness and weakness of the relief column underscored Nassef's contempt for el Aswad. He did not come himself. He sent el Nadim and two thousand green recruits from the coast. Yousif carved them up.

Nassef himself came four days later. He brought twenty thousand men and did not spare their lives. It took him just eight days to reverse roles and surround el Aswad.

The siege of the Eastern Fortress persisted for thirty months and four days. It was as cruel to the enemy as Yousif had hoped. El-Kader, in command of the besiegers, though nearly as competent as Nassef himself, simply could not overcome Yousif, his environment, and the sickness that ravaged his camp.

El-Kader's own most potent weapon, starvation, remained untested because Nassef was unable to spare the besieging army sufficiently long.

Nassef himself remained on the coast. After the successes at Es Souanna and Souk el Arba he found the going more difficult. The narrow, rich, densely populated littoral was nearly four hundred miles long. Those miles revealed a lot of towns and cities with no sympathy for El Murid's cause.

And there was Throyes.

El Murid was compelled to fight a foreign war before he had won over his own people.

When it came, the Throyen land grab was so brazen and extensive that El Murid found it politically unendurable. The nationalist sentiment it generated forced him to react.

Nassef's need for warriors on that front drew the besiegers away from el Aswad. He left just a thousand men in the province, commanded by Karim. They were to distract Yousif from Sebil el Selib.

Once his environs were open Yousif began corresponding with neighbors and Royalists whose thinking paralleled his own. The Kasr Helal Gold Seam was reborn. Trustworthy friends and acquaintances of Megelin Radetic made quiet arrangements in the west.

To an extent, the defenders of the Eastern Fortress had surrendered in their hearts.

Yousif stood in a windswept parapet watching the smoke of a brush fire burning twenty miles south of el Aswad. It was a huge blaze. Fuad was using it to herd one of Karim's battalions into a deathtrap. Haroun, practicing his shaghûnry at last, was with his uncle.

The boy had been a tremendous asset since the end of the siege. He always accompanied his uncle now. His shaghûnry instructors said he had enormous potential. They had taken him to their limits without pushing him to his own.

The Wahlig spied a rider coming from the northwest. Another whining message from Aboud? He did not bother going down to find out.

His Royal cousin was becoming a royal aggravation. His bluster, wishful thinking, and vain edicts would not alter the situation one iota.

Radetic joined him a few minutes later. He looked grim. He was becoming ever more dour and remote as el Aswad's position became ever less tenable.

"Another command to victory?" Yousif asked.

"More like a petition this time. But he has started to realize what's happening. After all this time. I mean, Nassef has got to be more than a bandit if he can fight a war with Throyes. Doesn't he?"

"Eh?" Yousif turned. "You mean he said something positive? That he's going to take us seriously? Now that it's too late?"

"A little. A little too little too late. He's hired Hawkwind again. He's sending him out here."

"Hawkwind? Why a mercenary?"

"He didn't explain. Maybe because no one else would come. The messenger says the negotiations have been on since Prince Farid's death. For three years! Hawkwind was reluctant. But Aboud finally made a sufficiently convincing presentation to the Guild generals, and paid over a handsome retainer. And he put huge bounties on El Murid, Nassef, Karim, and that lot. Hawkwind is on his way already."

Yousif paced. "How many men?"

"I don't know. I was told a substantial force."

"Enough to change anything?"

"I doubt it. We both know there will be no more victories like Wadi el Kuf."

"But why won't he send Royal troops?"

"I think all is not well in the Royal camp. Some wahligs apparently refuse to send men into the witch's cauldron. They want to sit tight and let El Murid come to them. It seems if he wanted to send anyone, it had to be mercenaries. He did the best he could in the circumstances he faces."

"But not enough." Yousif smote the weathered, lichened stone of the parapet.

"No. Not enough." Radetic studied the smoke from the brush fire. "Is

Haroun out there?"

"Yes. Fuad says he's doing well. Is there more news? You looked grim when you arrived."

Radetic kept his own counsel for a few minutes. Then, "Prince Hefni was killed."

"A pity. The Harish again?"

"Yes."

Hefni had been the last of Aboud's sons, excepting Crown Prince Ahmed. He had been much like his brother Farid. There were rumors that Aboud wished Hefni were Crown Prince instead of Ahmed, and that Ahmed was being pressured to abdicate in his favor.

"The Quesani are going to become extinct."

"Wahlig…"

Yousif turned slowly. "Don't tell me any more bad news, Megelin. I don't think I could stand what I think you're going to say."

"I don't want to. But I have to. Now or later."

Yousif peered at the fire. In time, he murmured, "Out with it, then. I don't want to break down in front of everybody."

"Your sons, Rafih and Yousif. They were killed in the attack on Hefni. They acquitted themselves well."

The two had been in Al Rhemish for several years, serving in the Royal Court. It was a common practice for nobles to send junior sons to court.

"So. Now I have only Ali and Haroun." He stared. For a moment it seemed the cloud of smoke was a response to his baleful glare. "Look away from me, teacher."

Radetic turned his back. The man had a right to solitude while he shed his tears.

After a time, Yousif remarked, "Aboud won't be able to handle this. He'll do something stupid." He sounded like a man begging for help. He was not talking about Aboud.

Radetic shrugged. "The behavior of others has always been beyond my control. Unfortunately."

"I'd better go tell their mother. It's not a task I savor."

Megelin moved nervously, came to a decision. "Would you look at this first?" He offered Yousif a chart on which he had penned names, titles, and connecting lines in a tiny, tight hand. It constituted a who's who of Hammad al Nakir.

"A chart of succession?" Over a period of ten years Yousif had sneakily picked up enough reading ability to puzzle his way through simple texts. He was good at names.

"Yes."

"So?" Every nobleman kept one. The chart was critical in determining precedence and protocol.

"Permit me." Radetic laid the chart out on a merlon. He produced a stick of drawing charcoal. "Let's scratch out the names of people who aren't with us anymore."

His hand moved like the swift-stabbing hand of Death.

Dolefully, Yousif remarked, "That many? I hadn't realized. It's bad, isn't it?"

"Anything apparent?"

"The better classes are being slaughtered."

"Yes. But that's not what I wanted you to see."

Yousif leaned closer to the chart, then backed away. His eyes were weakening.

"I see," he said. His voice was sadder than ever. "All of a sudden I'm third in the succession. If anything happens to Ahmed…"

"Some of our most devoted allies might expedite his meeting with the angels."

The Crown Prince had all of his father's faults, and none of the virtues that had made Aboud a respected king earlier in his reign. He was thoroughly disliked. Some of his enemies even accused him of being a secret adherent of El Murid.

His life would become worthless the moment Aboud's health started to fail. The behind-the-scenes manipulators at Al Rhemish would hold an "abdication by dagger."

"And," Radetic added, "going by the way you people figure these things, Ali is fourth in line, Haroun fifth, Fuad sixth, and his sons in line after him."

"Megelin, I know how you think. You've got a double-level puzzle here. You're getting at something more. Out with it. I'm not in the mood for intellectual gymnastics."

"All right. If by some ill fortune your family is destroyed—say during a successful siege—the succession would shift to the western cousins of the Quesani. Specifically, to a certain Mustaf el Habib, who must be pretty old by now."

"So?"

"This particular gentleman is the father of a rebel named Nassef."

Yousif seized the chart. He stared and stared. "By damn! You're right. How come nobody ever saw it before?"

"Because it's not exactly obvious. Mustaf el Habib is a damned obscure royal relative. And Nassef is as cunning as El Murid's Evil One. His moves remain strictly explicable within the context of his service to the Disciple. Why should anyone expect a threat from this direction? Would you like to bet that El Murid hasn't the vaguest notion that the Scourge of God could become King?"

"No. Hell no. Megelin, somebody has got to kill that man. He's more dangerous than El Murid."

"Possibly. He does think on his feet. El Murid was ready to set the Harish on him before Wadi el Kuf. Six months later he took over the Invincibles."

"Well, I've got a surprise for both of them. It'll so amaze them that they'll waste six months trying to figure it out. It might even panic Nassef into abandoning his eastern wars." Yousif laughed a little madly. "How soon will Hawkwind arrive?"

"I couldn't guess. They should be coming by now, but it's a long haul from High Crag."

"I hope it's soon. I do hope it's soon."

NINE
RIPENING SOLDIERS

High Crag was an ancient, draughty stone pile surmounting a wind- and sea-battered headland.

"The Gates of Hell," Bragi gasped as his training company double-timed uphill, toward the fortress. For three months he and his brother had been in the hands of merciless veterans. Seldom had they had a moment to call their own.

They had found themselves a new friend. He was the only other Trolledyngjan in their Itaskian-speaking company. He called himself Reskird Kildragon. "It was just a small dragon," he was wont to say. "And thereby hangs a tale." But, though Reskird almost never shut up, he never told that tale. He hailed from Jandrfyre, a town on the Trolledyngjan coast opposite the Tongues of Fire. He was as loquacious as Haaken was reticent.

"No," Kildragon replied to Bragi's remark. "Hell would look good from here."

"Knock off the chatter up there," Sergeant Sanguinet thundered. "You barbarians got breath to waste, I'll send you round the course again."

Kildragon had come south with a raiding fleet the previous summer. It had been one of the few to sail during the succession troubles. An Itaskian warship had rammed it off Libiannin. He had managed to swim to shore, the only survivor. Of necessity, he had learned southern ways fast.

"Still a scroungy-looking lot you've got there, Torc," the gatekeeper called as they double-timed into the Guild stronghold.

"I'll get them weeded out yet, Andy."

The three months had been a pitiless weeding through exhaustion of body and will.

"Wichard's about had it," Reskird murmured as the Itaskian ahead of him stumbled.

Bragi grunted. He and Haaken had weathered the grind well. Trolledyngja had schooled them for it. Haaken seemed right at home. The structured military life suited him perfectly. Bragi was less comfortable. He just did not like a Yes sir, No sir, Do it by the numbers approach to life.

"We'll get him through. He's got guts," Bragi whispered. Despite his reservations, Ragnarson had been designated recruit corporal in charge of his squad. He had a sneaking suspicion that the assignment was more of Sanguinet's torment, though the sergeant claimed he had been given the position because he could yell louder than anyone else.

After bathing and shaving they mustered for Recruits' Mess. Their mealtimes were one of the few occasions when they could relax and talk.

Haaken was in a mood. "You want to leave, Bragi?"

"Leave? What?"

"The Guild."

A recruit could do so whenever he decided the life was not for him. Any Guildsman could leave. But few who survived the training and shielding abandoned the brotherhood. The preliminary weeding was thorough.

The Citadel wanted no physical or moral weaklings in its command.

"Hell no. With six days to go? I'll finish if I have to do it walking on my hands."

The name Guild was a popular misnomer. The organization was not a Guild at all. It was a brotherhood of warriors bound together by honor, discipline, and an exaggerated set of military codes. It showed elements of monasticism, though it bowed to neither god nor prince. It was a kingdom spanning scores of kingdoms, consisting of men from countless lands who had renounced every allegiance save that to their brothers in arms.

The ruling council of nine generals, all of whom had once entered the Guild as the recruits were now, had reached their stations on merit. A complete contempt for quality of birth was one of the cultural chasms separating the Guild from the rest of the world. There were princes in the ranks and farmers' sons in the Citadel.

The Guild had phenomenal political leverage. The fates of principalities turned on High Crag's decision to accept or reject a commission offering. The order was wealthy. Its services were not cheap. It often accepted payment in lands and livings. It held income properties everywhere. If the nine old men in the Citadel became unhappy, princes hastened to learn how they had offended. Elite, powerful, the Guild was like nothing else in existence. It held a strong attraction for youths seeking a mission, a place in something bigger than themselves. Just belonging set a man a notch above his contemporaries. It marked him as the best.

The brotherhood was also a mystery cult. It had seven circles of initiation. Certain promotional levels demanded a prior passage to a circle closer to enlightenment. The nine generals were the truly illuminated.

An organization so powerful and secretive naturally accumulated detractors. Those claimed that the true nature and goals of the brotherhood were known only to the old generals in the Citadel.

There was truth in the allegation, but not enough to make the order an object of terror or reprisal.

Bragi, Haaken, and Reskird did not care how others saw the Guild. They had bought the message of pride sold them from the moment they had entered High Crag's gate.

In six days they would belong.

"Where do you think we'll be posted?" Reskird asked.

They had been sent to barracks immediately following supper. Their companions were abuzz, speculating about the unprecedented event. They used the time to catch up on their brass and boot polishing. Sergeant Sanguinet was obsessed with shininess.

"All I want is out of this dump," Haaken grumbled. "Penny to a pound, this is what Hell is like."

"Think we'll get lucky?" Reskird persisted. He smoothed straight, fine ginger hair that refused to stay in place. "One of the famous outfits? We're doing good."

Kildragon did not look Trolledyngjan. He was tall but on the lean side, with delicate features and feminine hands. He seemed more typically Itaskian.

"Hawkwind? Lauder? The White Company?" he babbled.

Bragi shrugged. "Wichard's got a chance at the White. If we can get him through. It's spooky, the way he can use a bow."

"It's the regiments for us," Haaken grumbled. "Lauder and Hawkwind don't take Greens."

"I'd guess the regiment in Simballawein," Bragi said. "That's where the war scare is."

"Farther south," Haaken complained. "And it's still summer."

"Me," said Reskird, "I think we ought to kiss Sanguinet's ass so he'll recommend us for Octylya." Sardygo, the Prince of Octylya, maintained a Guild bodyguard consisting entirely of Trolledyngjans.

A demonic creature looking nine feet tall and seven wide lumbered into the barracks room. "Kiss it all you want, boy. I'm still getting rid of you before you get your shield."

Ragnarson squawked a startled, "'Ten-shut!"

"Failing that, Kildragon, I'll get you the honeybucket concession for the whole damned castle."

Reskird did not cringe. This was what passed for light banter with the sergeant.

Sanguinet stalked round the cramped little room occupied by Bragi's squad. He poked fingers into cracks. He thumped hammocks. He hunted mercilessly, and could find nothing to bitch about.

"Ragnarson!"

"Sir?"

"You making fun of me, boy?"

"Sir? I don't understand, sir."

"You're playing some kind of game. It's too perfect. Your squad is always too perfect." He grinned wickedly. "So maybe I'll change the rules."

Corporal Trubacik stuck his head in the doorway. "Sarge? The Old Man wants you. Said make it yesterday."

"What is it now?"

"Another messenger came in. Looks set. He's expecting word from the Citadel."

"Damn it all to Hell! The rumor was right. And us stuck with Greens." The demon stalked out in the wake of his apprentice.

"What was that all about?" Bragi wondered. Haaken and Reskird shrugged.

Kildragon said, "We've got to give him something to gnash his teeth on, Bragi. He's foaming at the mouth because you won't give him anything."

"Not going to, either. I don't like his game. As long as I'm stuck with it, I'm going to play it better than he does. All that growl is just for show, anyway. My father did the same thing. Bet you he isn't half a hardass once we've won our shields."

"Harumph!" Haaken opined.

Rumors flew like panicky pigeons at breakfast. The old men in the Citadel had accepted a big commission. The drill instructors did not deny that. The recruit company would be included. The noncoms would not confirm or deny that. Going on from that point, virtually every imaginable possibility was aired. Sanguinet and Trubacik apparently knew the truth, but they weren't talking. The sergeant was pale, and he roared more than normal. He altered the training routine to include more weapons practice and drill to battlefield signals.

"We're going," Bragi guessed, stomach heavy. "And he expects action. The enemy won't be anybody who'll fold when he hears we're in the field."

Haaken grunted affirmatively. Reskird observed, "He's scared."

Bragi grumbled, "Hell, you can't blame him. His life will depend on us. And we've never been in combat."

"He should have more faith in his ability as an instructor."

"Would you, in his boots?"

Reskird shrugged. "No. You never know what a man will do till he's stuck in a situation. We're the only ones in the outfit who've ever been in a real fight."

There was no official comment till evening parade. Then a colonel from the Citadel addressed the assembled troops, veterans and recruits alike. He said, yes, a commission had been accepted. A thousand men would be involved. General Hawkwind would command. Details he kept to himself, perhaps for security reasons. He urged all brothers not actively participating to remember Hawkwind's force in their prayers.

"Hawkwind!" Reskird enthused. "What a break. First time out and we get the grand master. You hear what he did at Balewyne last year? Beat the whole Kisten army with five hundred men."

Bragi grunted. "With five hundred veterans from his own and the White Company."

"You're as bad as Haaken. Know that? What about Wadi el Kuf? Fifteen thousand enemy dead on the field. He's never lost a battle."

"Always a first time," Haaken grumbled.

"I don't believe you. How soon you think we'll head out?"

The word passed through the barracks that night: the recruit company would complete its training. Five days of Hell remained.

"So much for marching off to war, Reskird." Bragi whispered after lights out. "You're full of it, you know that? Enjoy the obstacle course."

One regular company departed two days later, bound for a rendezvous with Hawkwind somewhere to the south. Word spread quickly: the recruit company would have to catch up on the road. Grim faces appeared. The pace would be hard. Graduation would provide no respite.

Corporal Trubacik was amused. "You're all young men. In prime shape, I hear. You should be able to do it walking backward."

Bragi said little the next few days. He went through the exercises and drills numbly. Haaken finally asked, "You all right? Sure you don't want to bow out?"

"I started it. I'll finish it. I just have trouble when I think about dying out there. Wherever." They had not been told where they were going.

Bragi could not buy all the brotherhood of the Guild. He felt solidarity with his squad and company, of course. That was one function of the training program. A group went through Hell together and learned to depend upon one another. But the larger belonging that made the Guild had not infected him. The honor and nobility had not become tangible to him. And that worried him. Those things were important to both his superiors and to his comrades. They made the Guild what it was.

He tried hard to sell himself. It was like trying to force sleep. Self-defeating.

It seemed to take forever arriving, but Shielding Day did come. All the grand old men, the great and famous generals, came down from the Citadel to review the recruits and make speeches. They kept their remarks refreshingly brief. The Castellan, the senior member of the order present, apologized because the recruits would have no opportunity to enjoy the leave traditional after completing training.

Then came the final ceremony, when each new Guildsman was awarded the shield of a Guild footsoldier. Each had to go before the assembly to accept. Trainees who had excelled received honor ribbons with their shields. Bragi was awarded one for having had the best squad during inspections.

The award embarrassed him terribly. He hustled back into line. His comrades grinned wolfishly. He knew he would not hear the end of it soon. He examined shield and ribbons, found a lump rising in his throat, felt his pride swelling. "Damn," he murmured. "They got to me after all."

Corporal Trubacik bellowed, "Up and at them, lads. Up and at them. It's another glorious day in the outfit." He whipped blankets off the new young soldiers. "Let's go. Let's go. You know the drill. Company formation in half an hour." Out the door he went, leaving the lamp turned a little higher.

"Damn," Reskird said. "Ain't nothing changed. I hoped we'd at least get to sleep in."

Bragi did not say anything. He got his soap and razor and stumbled to the lavatory. His head was stuffed up and his temper was foul. He washed and shaved in silence, refusing to respond to jibes about his ribbon.

"Fall in!" Trubacik bellowed across the parade yard. "Platoon leaders, report!" The platoon sergeants turned and bellowed for reports from the squads. Bragi reported all present and accounted for without checking. Nobody had missed muster yet.

He was more interested in a number of men lounging behind Sanguinet. Why were they here? What were they up to?

Minutes later his heart sank. The hangers-around proved to be veterans assigned as squad leaders. Though he had known it vain, he had hoped to retain that status himself.

Each squad departed as it received its new corporal. Bragi's went to a wiry little Itaskian named Birdsong, who led them to the quartermasters. He did not have much to say at first, just watched while the quartermasters replaced gear worn or damaged during training. Each recruit received an extra pair of boots.

"I don't like this," Reskird grumbled. "Extra boots means somebody figures us to wear out a lot of shoe leather."

Bragi glanced at Birdsong. The little corporal smiled. Smiling made his mustache wiggle like a brown caterpillar.

The armorers came after the quartermasters. They exchanged training weapons for battle weapons. Breastplates were issued. Bragi and Haaken went two rounds with an armorer who wanted to relieve them of the swords they had brought down from Trolledyngja. Birdsong interceded. He understood the importance of heirloom blades.

"But they're not standard!" the armorer protested.

And Birdsong, "But your budget will come up on the long side."

End of dispute.

There were two more stops. The kitchens, for field rations, where Reskird moaned at the size of the issue, and the paymaster, where Reskird's protests were noteworthy by their absence.

Individual Guildsmen did not receive a large stipend. Not compared to other troops. Belonging was their great reward. But on this occasion the old men in the Citadel had awarded a substantial bounty because the trainees had been deprived of graduation leave. Each man also received a month's advance, which was customary on taking the field.

Then it was time to gather in the courtyard again. There were other squads passing through the system. Birdsong took the opportunity to acquaint himself with his men. He proved to be a tad pompous, a lot self-conscious, a little unsure of himself. In short, he suffered the usual insecurities of anyone new to a supervisory role.

Bragi told Haaken, "I think I'm going to like him."

Haaken shrugged, indifferent. But Reskird threatened to drag his feet because he thought Bragi should have retained the squad leader's post.

Bragi told him, "You do and I'll crack your back."

Sanguinet returned to the drill yard on horseback, accompanied by Trubacik and the other noncoms who had guided the company through training. They wore new belts and badges proclaiming their elevated status. Sanguinet had been promoted to lieutenant.

"Fall in!" Sergeant Trubacik roared. "We're moving out." And in five minutes, with the sun still barely above the horizon, the march began.

It was rougher than any training hike. Dawn to dusk, forty and fifty miles every day, eating pemmican, dried fruit, and toasted grain, drinking only water, and occasionally nibbling such fruits as could be purchased from wayside farmers. Living off the land was prohibited, except catch-as-catch-can in the forests. Guildsmen did not plunder, even to support themselves. They were schooled to consider themselves gentlemen, above the savageries of national soldiers.

Kildragon complained. The northern custom was totally opposite.

Day followed day. Mile followed mile. They headed south, ever south, into ever warmer lands. They gained on the veteran company, but couldn't seem to catch it.

A horse troop joined them south and east of Hellin Daimiel. Their dust filled the lungs, parched the throat, and caked upon dried, cracking lips.

"I don't like this," Haaken grumbled as they reached a crossroads and turned eastward. "There ain't nothing out this way."

Kildragon grumped back. "What I don't like is getting screwed out of my shielding liberty. I had plans."

"You've said that a hundred times. If you can't sing a new song, don't sing at all."

"We'll make up for it," Bragi promised. "After the victory, when we're heroes." He laughed a laugh he did not feel. That morning Sanguinet had assigned the Birdsong squad to the primus, or front battle line.

Sanguinet had grinned over the announcement, explaining, "You do good, gentlemen, you work hard, and you reap your reward."

Thus Bragi learned a basic fact: the more a man does, and the better he does it, the more is expected of him. The rewards and gratifications come either as afterthoughts or as carrots meant to get the old mule moving after it realizes that it has been taken.

Bragi was no coward. There was little that he feared. But he had not inherited his father's battle lust. He was not eager to remain in the primus, which bore the brunt of combat.

"Look on the bright side," Reskird said. "We get to loaf around on guard duty when the other guys have to dig the trenches and pitch camp."

"Bah! Some silver lining." Bragi had a broad lazy streak, but in this case did not feel that escape from the drudge work was sufficient compensation.

Birdsong watched over his shoulder, mustache wriggling. Bragi bared his teeth and growled. Birdsong laughed. "You know what they say. A bitching soldier is a happy soldier."

"Then Reskird is the happiest fool on earth," Haaken grumbled. "A hog up to his collar in slops."

Birdsong chuckled. "Every rule has its exceptions."

"Where are we going, Corporal?" Bragi asked.

"They haven't told me yet. But we're headed east. There isn't anything east of here but the border forts facing the Sahel."

"The Sahel? What's that?"

"The outer edge of Hammad al Nakir. That means the Desert of Death."

"Oh, that sounds great."

"You'll love it. Most godforsaken land you'll ever see." His eyes went vague.

"You been there?"

"I was at Wadi el Kuf with the general. We took this route then."

Bragi exchanged glances with his brother.

"Ha!" Reskird cried, suddenly enthusiastic. He started babbling cheerfully about Hawkwind's victory.

Bragi and Haaken had listened to other veterans of the battle. It hadn't been the picnic Reskird thought. Haaken suggested Kildragon attempt a difficult autoerotic feat.

They finally overhauled the other infantry company a day from the assembly point, a fortified town called Kasr el Helal. The veterans grinned a lot during night camp. They had made the overtaking intentionally difficult.

Hawkwind and the remainder of the regiment were waiting at Kasr el Helal. Also on hand were several caravans hoping to slip into Hammad al Nakir in the regiment's safety shadow, and two hundred Royalist warriors sent to guide the Guildsmen. Bragi and Haaken found the desert men incredibly odd.

Hawkwind allowed a day's rest at Kasr el Helal. Then the savage march resumed. Bragi soon understood why extra boots had been issued. Rumor said they had eight hundred miles to march, to some place called the Eastern Fortress. The actual distance was closer to five hundred miles, but it was long enough.

The pace started slowly enough, passing through the wild, barren hills of the Sahel. The desert riders ranged far afield. The column traveled ready for combat. The primitive locals were fanatic adherents of the enemy, somebody called El Murid.

The natives never offered battle. The Guildsmen never saw them. They saw almost no natives anywhere during the first twenty-seven days of the desert crossing.

Hawkwind conducted repeated exercises during the march. The heavy support train acquired at Kasr el Helal was a severe drag on speed. Yet its professional camp followers, cooks, and workers made military life easier to bear. Hawkwind, though, kept those people as segregated as he dared, fearing an infection of indiscipline. Their discipline was pure chaos compared to that of the Guildsmen.

The youths from the north examined the barrens day after day. "I'll never get used to this," Bragi said.

Haaken admitted, "It scares me. Makes me feel like I'm going to fall off the world, or something."

Bragi tried to see a bright side. "Somebody wants to attack us, we'll see them coming."

He was only partly right. Twenty-seven days out of Kasr el Helal, Reskird suddenly yelled, "Pay up, Haaken."

"What?"

"The van riders are coming in." Kildragon pointed. The native outriders were rushing toward the column like leaves aflutter on a brisk March wind. "That means a fight."

Bragi looked at Haaken meaningfully. "You suckered him out of a month's pay, eh?" An hour earlier word had come back that they could expect to be within sight of their destination before nightfall. Haaken had begun crowing about how he had hornswoggled Reskird into betting they would see action before they arrived.

Haaken suggested they both attempt the sexually impossible. He grumbled, "Those Invincibles wouldn't be this close to the castle anyway."

"They're between us and the Fortress," Reskird said. "We have to break through. Pay me now, Haaken. Be hard to collect if you get taken dead."

"Don't you ever shut up? You got a mouth like a crow."

"You do have a way with words, Reskird," Bragi agreed.

Horsemen indistinguishable from the outriders crested a ridgeline ahead. They studied the column, then flew back the way they had come.

Hawkwind halted. The officers conferred, dispersed. Soon Bragi and his companions were double-timing into the selected formation, which was a broad, shallow line of heavy infantry with the native horsemen on the flanks. Bowmen scattered behind the infantry. The heavy horse, still donning armor and preparing mounts, massed behind the center. The camp followers circled wagons behind them to provide a fortress into which to retreat.

Birdsong dressed the squad. "Looking good, lads," he said. "First action. Show the lieutenant we can handle it." Sanguinet insisted they couldn't whip their weight in old women.

"Set your shields. Stand ready with spears. Third rank. Stand by with your javelins."

Bragi watched the ridgeline and worried about his courage. This was no proper way for a man to fight....

Riders crested the hill. They swept toward the Guildsmen, hoofbeats rising into a continuous thunder. Bragi crouched behind his shield and awaited the order to set his spear. Some of his squadmates seemed to be wavering, certain they did not dare hold against the rush.

The riders sheered off toward the flanks. Arrows from short saddle bows pattered against shields, crossing paths with a flight from longer Guild bows. Horses screamed. Men cursed and wailed. Bragi could see no casualties on his side.

An arrow chunked into his shield. A quarter inch of sharp steel peeped through. A second shaft caromed off the peak of his helmet, elicited a startled curse behind him. He scrunched down another inch.

The earth shuddered continuously. Dust poured over him. The taunting riders were racing past just thirty yards away.

He could not restrain his curiosity. He popped up for a peek over the rim of his shield.

An arrow plunked him squarely, smashing the iron of his helmet against his forehead. He tumbled onto his butt, losing his shield. Another arrow streaked through the gap in the shield wall, creased the inside of his right thigh. "Damn," he muttered, before it started hurting. "An inch higher and..."

Reskird and Haaken shifted their shields, narrowing the gap till a man from the second rank could assume Bragi's place. Hands grabbed Ragnarson, dragged him backward. In a moment he was cursing at the feet of the bowmen. One shouted, "Get back to the wagons, lad."

He didn't make it halfway before the encounter ended. The enemy tried to turn the flanks. The friendly natives pushed them back. Trumpets sounded. Hawkwind led the heavy horse through aisles in the infantry, formed for a charge. The enemy flew away, vanishing over the hill as swiftly as he had come. He remembered Wadi el Kuf, and had no taste for another bout with the men in iron.

Though Bragi had perceived their undisciplined rush as an endless tide, there had been no more than five hundred of the riders. Outnumbered by a disciplined foe, they had done nothing but probe. Even so, several dozen fallen comrades were left scattered across the regiment's front. Bragi was one of only four casualties on the Guild side.

The camp followers rushed out to cut throats and loot. The Guildsmen remained standing at arms while their native auxiliaries went scouting again.

Bragi settled down with his back against a wagon wheel, cursing himself for the stupidity that had gotten him hurt. All he had had to do was keep his head down, just as he had been taught.

"Some people will do anything to get out of walking."

He looked up, lips taut. His wound hurt bad now.

Sanguinet dropped to one knee. "Might have known you'd be the first one hurt. Let me look at it." He grinned. "Close, eh? Don't look that bad, though." He squeezed Bragi's shoulder. "There's a reason behind every lesson we try to teach. Hope you learned something today. You paid a cheap enough price." He smiled. "I'll send the surgeon around. You'll need stitches. Ride the chow dray the rest of the way in."

"Do I have to do KP? Sir?"

"Got to pull your weight somewhere."

"I'll walk, then. Just stay with my squad."

"You'll do what you're told, son. Laziness isn't a good enough excuse for losing a leg."

"Sir—"

"You have your orders, Ragnarson. Don't compound foolishness with more foolishness." Today Sanguinet spoke as a Guildsman to a brother, not as a drillmaster belittling a recruit.

Birdsong let Haaken and Reskird drop back to visit, the afternoon the regiment started the long climb up the slope leading to the Eastern Fortress. They lifted him down off the chow wagon so he could look at the castle.

"Gods. It's big," he said.

"They call it the Eastern Fortress," Reskird told him. "Been here for like eight hundred years, or something, and them all the time adding on."

Bragi looked around. How did the people of Hammad al Nakir survive in such desolation?

The castle turned out its garrison in welcome. Ranks of silent men, dark of eye and skin, often beakish of nose, observed them without expression. Bragi sensed their disdain. They were all old, weathered veterans. He tried hard not to limp.

If he could impress them no other way, his size ought to stir some awe. He was six inches taller and fifty pounds heavier than the biggest.

Nowhere did he see a woman, and children were scarce. "This is the reception the old-timers talk about when Guildsmen come to the rescue?" he muttered. "Where are the flowers? Where are the cheers? Where are the eager damsels? Haaken, I'm not going to like it here. I've seen brighter people at funerals."

Haaken had his shoulders hunched defensively. He grunted his agreement.

The column passed through the castle gate, into a stronghold as spartan as its defenders. Everything inside looked dry and dusty, and was colored shades of brown. Dull shades of brown. The companies fell in one behind another in a large drill yard, under the hard eyes of a group watching from an inner rampart. "Those guys must be the ones who hired us," Bragi guessed. He studied them. They did not look any different from their followers. To him, very strange.

Reskird murmured, "Two things I'd give up what Haaken owes me to see. A tree. And a smile on just one of their ugly faces."

The group on the wall came down and joined Hawkwind. Time passed. Bragi wished they would get on with it. After all that desert all he wanted was a gallon of beer and a soft place to lie down.

Things started moving. Men led the horses away. The front company filed through an inner gate. Bragi surveyed the fortress again, scowled. Not damned likely to be any comfortable barracks here.

One by one, the companies ahead marched away. Then it was the recruits' turn. A lean native youth approached Sanguinet and spoke briefly. The lieutenant turned and started bellowing. The company filed out.

The quarters were worse than Bragi had imagined. Two hundred men had to crowd into space meant for maybe seventy. Only a serpent would be able to slide in or out after taps. He tried not to think of the horror consequent to an alarm sounding after dark.

Even officers and noncoms got shoved into that overcrowded cage. There was no room at all for gear. That they left outside.

The growling and cursing died a little. Reskird muttered that he didn't have room enough to get breath to bitch. Their youthful guide said, "I offer my father's apologies for these quarters. You came earlier than expected, and at a time when many of our warriors are away, fighting the Disciple. You will be moving to better quarters as soon as they can be furnished. Some may move tomorrow. Your commander is already meeting with my father concerning duty rosters. Men who are assigned stations far from here will be moved nearer immediately." He spoke Itaskian with a nasal accent, but much more purely than Bragi or his brother.

His gaze crossed Bragi's. Both youths stared for a moment, startled, as if seeing something unexpected. Once their eyes moved on, Bragi shook his head as though trying to clear it.

"What's the matter?" Haaken demanded.

"I don't know. It's like I saw… I don't know." And he didn't. And yet, the impact had been such that he was now sure this slim, dark, strange young man would play an important part in his life.

Haaken was intrigued. There was more life in his eyes than there had been for months. "You've got that look, Bragi. What is it?"

"What look?"

"The same look Mother got when she was Seeing."

Bragi snorted, making light of their mother's alleged ability to see the future. "If she'd been able to See, Haaken, we wouldn't be here."

"Why not? She could've known. She wouldn't have said anything if there wasn't anything she could do. Would she?"

"That was all bullshit. She just put on an act to scare people into doing things her way. She faked it, Haaken."

"Who's bullshitting who? You know better than that."

"Want to hold it down back there, you Ragnarsons?" Sanguinet bellowed. "Or at least speak Itaskian so the rest of us can get in on it?"

Bragi reddened. He glanced at the lieutenant, averted his gaze from the man's taut face. His eye fell on the young guide again. Again he had that *frisson*, and the youth seemed to have suffered a similar response. He was just regaining his equilibrium. Curious. Maybe his mother was in his blood after all.

The youth said, "I am Haroun bin Yousif. My father is Wahlig of el Aswad. What you would call a duke. During your stay here, unless I am needed elsewhere, I will remain attached to your company as interpreter and go-between. Is there a word for that in Itaskian?" he said in an aside to Sanguinet.

The lieutenant shrugged. Itaskian was not his native tongue either.

"Liaison," Sergeant Trubacik volunteered.

"Yes. I recall now. Liaison. If you have problems requiring communication with my people, see me. Especially in matters of dispute. We are of contrasting cultures. Probably my people seem as strange to you as you do to them. But we must stand side by side against the Disciple...."

"Rah rah rah," Reskird muttered, a little too loudly. "Three cheers for our side. Why doesn't he tell us what's so special about this El Murid character?"

In a voice dripping with honey, easygoing Corporal Birdsong said, "That will be four hours of extra duty, Kildragon. Want to try for more?"

Reskird gulped, sealed his lips.

Haroun continued, "I, and my tutor, Megelin Radetic, whom I shall introduce later, are the only men here who speak Itaskian. If you find yourself desperate to communicate, and you can speak Daimiellian, try that. Many of our men have worked the caravans and speak a little Daimiellian. But talk slowly, and be patient."

Haaken lifted a hand. "Back here. Where can we get something to drink?"

"There is a cistern." Haroun turned to Sanguinet, who expanded upon the critical question in a soft voice. He looked puzzled. Then he said, "The drinking of spirited beverages is forbidden. Our religion does not allow it."

Grumble mumble growl. "Holy shit," somebody shouted. "What the hell kind of hole is this? No women. No booze. Hot and dirty... Hell. For this we should risk our lives?"

The youth looked baffled. He turned to Sanguinet for help. Bragi prodded Haaken, who was within reach of the loudest complainer. Haaken took hold of the man's shoulder muscle and squeezed. His protests died.

Sergeant Trubacik called out, "Any problems, you see me or Haroun here. At ease. Settle in. Lieutenant suggests you roam around and get to know the place. Duty assignments will come out tomorrow. That's it."

"You'd better believe I'm going to roam around," Reskird muttered. "This is so tight it would give me the shakes, only there isn't room to shiver."

"Yeah. Me too," Bragi said. "Come on, Haaken. Let's catch that Haroun. I want to talk to him." But it took them ten minutes to get out of the barracks room. By then the youth had disappeared. So the brothers went up on the wall and looked out on the barren land and wondered why anyone would fight to defend it.

Haaken, unwittingly prophetic, observed, "What I'd fight for is to get out."

"There he is, down there," Bragi said, spotting Haroun "Let's go."

But they missed him again. And thus they began their first commission as soldiers of the Guild.

Ten

Salt Lake Encounter

El Murid had been up late discussing the coastal war. His aching limbs left him in no mood to be wakened prematurely. "What is it?" he snapped at the insistent slave. "It had better be important, or... Well, out with it!"

The man gulped. The Disciple's temper had grown ever fiercer since Wadi el Kuf. "Lord..." He burst right into it, talking almost too fast to follow. "Lord, Mowaffak Hali insists on seeing you. He's just returned from patrol. He won't be put off."

El Murid grumbled and scowled. "Hali? Hali?" He could not associate a face with the name.

"Mowaffak Hali, Lord. The elder Hali. The Invincible." The slave eyed him oddly, as if bemused because he could not recall a man as important as this visitor.

"All right. Show him in. And if it's another petty squabble over precedence between the regulars and the Invincibles, I'll crucify you both." He beckoned a second slave. "Clothing."

He was dressing when the Invincible strode in, advancing like a trail-dirty thunderhead, brow furrowed. El Murid remembered him now. One of his favorites among the Invincibles. One of his best men. One of the most determinedly faithful. And, in all likelihood, one of the high brethren of the Harish, too.

"Mowaffak, my brother. A pleasure to see you again."

Hali halted a few paces away. "My apologies, Lord. I wouldn't disturb you for anything less than a disaster."

El Murid's lips stretched in a rictus of a smile, cracking because they were dry. "Disaster? What now?"

"The rumors are true. Aboud has engaged Hawkwind again."

El Murid's stomach knotted. He fought to keep his fear off his face. They had whipped him like a cur at Wadi el Kuf. They had branded terror upon his soul. He could not be reminded without cringing. "Hawkwind?" he croaked.

"I saw them with my own eyes, Lord. I was leading the Fourth through the gap between el Aswad and the Great Erg. My scouts reported the presence of a large body of foreigners. I took the battalion forward, and engaged briefly. They drove us off like swatting away flies."

El Murid swallowed. Memories of Wadi el Kuf swarmed, helter-skelter, chaotic. He simply could not think straight.

Hali interpreted his silence as a patient wait for continued illumination. "There were a thousand of them, Lord, including many lances of heavy cavalry, and a large baggage train. They have come to fight a long campaign. I kept patrols close till they entered el Aswad, but could gather little more information. Their column was screened by Aboud's best light cavalry. I trust our agents in the Eastern Fortress will provide better reports."

El Murid just could not grasp the news. Finally, he croaked, "It *was* Hawkwind? You're sure?"

"I was at Wadi el Kuf, Lord. I haven't forgotten his banners."

"Nor I, Mowaffak. Nor I." The shock began to recede. "So. Aboud is frightened enough to hire foreigners. Why, Mowaffak? Because the Scourge of God has the temerity to defend Hammad al Nakir against Throyen predations?"

"I think not, Lord. I think the King wants revenge." Hali's tone was strained. He was hinting round the edge of something.

"Aboud has a special reason for wishing us ill? Beyond a desire to perpetuate his dynasty of darkness?"

"That's the point, Lord. There can be no dynasty. With Prince Farid dead he is left no successor but Ahmed. Our friends and the Royalists alike consider Ahmed a bad joke."

"Farid is dead? When did that happen?"

"Long ago, Lord. Karim himself undertook the mission."

"Our people did it? Karim? Meaning the Scourge of God sent him?" He hadn't heard a word about this. Why did they keep the unpleasant news secret? "What else is Nassef doing? What else don't I know?"

"He is destroying the Quesani, Lord. Using the Invincibles, mainly. But perhaps he felt Farid was too important a task to entrust to anyone but his personal assassin."

El Murid turned away, both to conceal his anger at Nassef and his disgust with Hali's obvious politicking. The Invincibles loathed Nassef. They were convinced he was the bandit the Royalists claimed.

"The Scourge of God is somewhere near Throyes. Too busy to bother with this."

"This is a task for the Invincibles, Lord."

"Have we so many otherwise unemployed, Mowaffak? Much as I loathe the Wahlig, his destruction isn't first on the list of works that need accomplishing."

"Lord—"

"Your brotherhood will participate, Mowaffak. El Nadim is in the valley. Send him to me."

"As you command, Lord." Hali's tone was sour. He started to protest entrusting Nassef's henchman with so critical a task, thought better of it, bowed himself out.

Wearily, El Murid rose. A servant scooted his way, one hand extended in an unspoken offer of help. The Disciple waved the man off. He now knew he would never recover completely. Wadi el Kuf had made of him an old man before his time.

Hot anger hit him. Yousif! Hawkwind! They had stolen his youth. The years could not soften his rage. He would destroy them. The two were in one place now, eggs in one nest. He had been patient, and the Lord had given him his reward. The eagle would descend, and rend its prey.

One smashing blow. One bold stroke, and the desert would be free. This time there would be no doubt about el Aswad. War with Throyes notwithstanding.

Pain stabbed through his leg. The ankle never had healed right. He flung his arms out for balance, and that stimulated the pain in the arm that had been broken. He groaned. Why wouldn't the bones heal? Why wouldn't they stop hurting?

The servant caught him before he fell, tried to guide him to his throne. "No," he said. "Take me to my wife. Have el Nadim meet me there."

Meryem took him from his helper, led him to a large cushion and helped him lie down. "Your injuries again?"

He drew her to him, held her for a long minute. "Yes."

"You were angry again, weren't you? It only gets bad when you get angry."

"You know me too well, woman."

"What was it this time?"

"Nothing. Everything. Too much. Bickering between the Invincibles and regular soldiers. Nassef's going off on his own again. Aboud sending mercenaries to reinforce el Aswad."

"No."

"Yes. A thousand of them. Under Hawkwind."

"He's the one?"

"From Wadi el Kuf. Yes. The most brilliant tactician of our age, some say."

"Are we in danger, then?"

"Of course!" he snapped. "Can you picture Yousif having a weapon like that and not using it?" He was shaking, frightened. The root of his anger was his fear. He needed reassurance, needed help to banish the doubts. "Where are the children? I need to see the children."

He felt settled before el Nadim arrived.

The general was as nondescript a man as the desert produced. Like all Nassef's henchmen, his background was suspect. The Invincibles said he had begun as a cutpurse, and had descended into darker ways from that. He was a puzzle to the Disciple. He was not known for his genius in the field, unlike others of Nassef's intimates, and, if the grudging reports were to be believed, he was a true believer. Yet he remained a favorite of Nassef, entrusted with commands where imagination was less needed than a legate dedicated to executing his orders.

"You summoned me, Lord?"

"Sit." The Disciple contemplated his visitor. "I have a task for you."

"Lord?"

"You've heard the news? That the King has sent mercenaries to el Aswad?"

"There are rumors, Lord. They say Hawkwind is the commander."

"That's true." El Murid grimaced, stricken by sudden pain. "A thousand mercenaries, and Hawkwind. I'm sure you appreciate the threat."

El Nadim nodded. "It's an opportune moment for the Wahlig, Lord, what with the Scourge of God away battling the accursed Throyen."

"I want to beat Yousif at his own game. To go out and meet him."

"Lord? I'm afraid—"

"I know the arguments. I've been meditating on them since the news arrived. Tell me this. How large a force could we raise if we called in our patrols, stripped Sebil el Selib of its garrison, drafted untrained recruits, armed slaves willing to fight in exchange for their freedom, and what have you?"

"Three thousand. Maybe four. Mostly unmounted. On foot they'd have little chance against Guild infantry."

"Perhaps. How many mounted veterans?"

"No more than a third, Lord. And the garrisons here are made up of old men."

"Yes. The Scourge of God persists in taking Sebil el Selib's best defenders. Go. Call in the scouts and raiders. See how many men you can arm."

"You insist on doing this, Lord?"

"Not at all. I insist on examining the possibility. We need make no decision till we see what strength we can muster. Go now."

"As you command, Lord."

Meryem joined him as el Nadim departed. "Is this wise?" she asked. "The last time you overruled your commanders—"

"I don't intend to overrule anyone. Prick them into action, perhaps. Lay suggestions before them, yes. But, if, in their wisdom, they foresee disaster, I'll yield."

"You want to embarrass Yousif and Hawkwind the way they embarrassed you, don't you?"

He was startled. The woman was psychic. She had reached down inside him and touched a secret truth he had not wholly recognized himself. "You know me too well."

Meryem smiled, enfolded him in her arms, rested her cheek against his chest. "How could it be otherwise? We grew up together."

El Murid smiled. "I wish there were some rest from my labors."

"So long as the wicked do not rest, neither may we. Spoken by the Disciple on the occasion of his return from the movement's greatest disaster. Don't yield now."

El Nadim approached the Malachite Throne. He bowed, glanced at the Invincibles attending the Disciple. His face remained blank. "I have assembled every possible man, Lord."

"How many?"

"Thirty-eight hundred. We could raise another two thousand if we waited for the arrival of the garrisons of the nearest coastal towns, which I have ordered here. But by the time they joined us it would be too late. The Wahlig won't await the completion of our preparations. He will use his new strength soon."

El Murid glanced at Mowaffak Hali. Hali nodded. He could find no fault with el Nadim's preparations. Mowaffak was a master at finding fault.

El Nadim endured the moment without wincing, without acknowledging his awareness that his every move was closely scrutinized.

"What of my suggestions?" El Murid asked.

"Entirely workable, Lord." El Nadim could not conceal a certain surprise at his master's having seen a military potential missed by his captains.

Hali said, "The question becomes how quickly the Wahlig will move, Lord."

"What about the men? We've dug deep and taken the dregs. Will they stand up to a fight?"

El Nadim shrugged. "That can be answered only in battle. I fear the answer, though."

"Mowaffak?"

"You're demanding a lot. They have faith but no confidence. Only a quick, clear success at the outset will hold them together."

El Murid left the throne, limped to the shrine where his angel's amulet lay. He grasped it in both hands, raised it above his head. The jewel's flare filled the hall. "This time, gentlemen, the fist of heaven will strike with us. There will be no Wadi el Kuf."

He saw doubt. He saw unhappiness. Neither el Nadim nor Hali wanted him along. They feared he would become more burden than help. Nor had they witnessed the drama at the el Habib oasis. For them the amulet was more symbol than reality, without proven efficacy.

"There will be no Wadi el Kuf," he declared. "And I won't be a burden. I'll neither overrule your commands nor interfere with your operations. I'll be just another soldier. Just a weapon."

"As you will, Lord," el Nadim replied, without enthusiasm.

"Shall we attempt it?" El Murid asked.

El Nadim responded, "It's face them here or face them there, Lord. There we'll have the advantage of having done the unexpected."

"Then let's stop talking and start doing."

The country was wild. Chaos had frolicked there, leaving the hills strewn with perilous tumbles of boulders. El Nadim halted at the eastern end of a white plain which was the only memory of an ancient salt lake. The road to Sebil el Selib crawled along its southern flank. The general ordered camp made.

He rode onward with the Disciple, Hali, and the Disciple's bodyguards to examine the salt pan. After a time he remarked, "You were right, Lord. It's a good place to meet them."

El Murid dismounted. He squatted, wet a finger, touched it to the salt, then tasted.

"As I thought. Not mined because it's bad salt. Poisons in it." Childhood memories came, haunted him momentarily. He shook them off. The salt merchant's son was another being, simply someone with whom he shared memories.

He surveyed his surroundings. The hills were not as tall as he had imagined them, and less rich with cover. And the pan looked all too favorable for western cavalry. He offered his doubts.

"Let's hope they see only what's visible, Lord," el Nadim replied. "They'll beat themselves." Hali, puzzled, refused to ask the questions puzzling him. El Nadim did not enlighten him. El Murid suspected he was being deliberately vague. When the dust settled the Invincible would be able to stake no claim on having engineered any victory.

The party continued westward. At the far end of the lakebed el Nadim told Hali, "Choose five hundred Invincibles and hide in those rocks. After dark. Travel the reverse slope so you leave no traces. Take water rations for five days. Don't break cover till the Guild infantry closes with my line."

"And if they don't?" Hali demanded.

"Then we'll have won anyway. They have to retreat or break through. They won't have the water to wait us out. Either way we embarrass them."

El Murid fretted. He would bear the odium if this failed. If it succeeded, el Nadim would harvest the credit. That didn't seem fair. He smiled wearily. He was getting as bad as his followers.

Hali remarked, "Our scouts say they're on the march, Lord. We won't wait long."

"Very well." He checked the altitude of the sun. "Time for prayers, gentlemen."

Hawkwind and the Wahlig reached the western end of the salt pan the following afternoon. Invincible horsemen blocked the road and skirmished with Yousif's riders till the Royalists elected to make camp.

Confidence filled that camp. The Wahlig had more and better men. He exercised only the caution necessary to abort a night assault.

El Murid missed the skirmishing. El Nadim had assigned him a small force placed well west of Hali's, where the road to the lakebed wound between steep hills. The Disciple suspected the general simply wanted him out of the way, though his companions were the cream of the Invincibles.

He did not sleep that night. He could not shake the specter of Wadi el Kuf—and this, though a smaller action, could generate even more devastating repercussions. Sebil el Selib would be vulnerable till the troops arrived from the coast. It would fall to a featherweight attack. He was terrified. He had bet too much on one pass of the dice. But it was too late to stand down.

He prayed often and hard, beseeching the Lord's aid in his most desperate hour.

El Nadim roused his men before dawn. He addressed them passionately while they ate a cold breakfast, claiming the whole future of the movement hinged on their courage. He then arrayed his infantry across the end of the pan, with horsemen stationed on the wings. The slave volunteers he posted in front of his primary line, carrying shovels as well as weapons. His army was in place when dawn broke. A morning breeze rose from behind him.

He assembled his officers. "Keep the men to the standards," he told them. "Set an example. If the Lord won't yield us the day, let's die facing our enemies."

He had expressed the same sentiments to the troops, only now he indicated a willingness to cut down any officer who forgot his courage. He told his cavalry commanders, "The breeze is rising. Begin."

Moments later horsemen began riding back and forth ahead of the infantry. The westbound wind filled with alkaline dust. Horns and drums sounded in the distance. The enemy formed ranks. El Nadim smiled. The Wahlig would challenge him. He moistened a finger, felt the breeze. Not as strong as he had hoped. The dust was not carrying as well as he desired. "Trumpets," he snapped. "Speed them up."

Bugles called. The cavalrymen urged their mounts to a trot, kicking up more salty dust. El Nadim turned. The sun was about to break over a low, distant mountain, into enemy eyes.

He examined what he could see of the Wahlig's dispositions. Guild infantry in the center. Light horse on the wings and behind. And the heavy cavalry forming for the first charge, that should be enough to shatter his line. Good again. They were doing the obvious. Exactly what he wanted.

The breeze was not rising. "Trumpets. Speed them up again. Messenger. I want the slave volunteers to start digging."

The volunteers used their shovels to hurl the fine, salty earth skyward, putting more dust into the air.

Let them breathe that, el Nadim thought. Let them become parched of throat and sore of eye. Let them want nothing so badly as they want to break away for a drink. He glanced back. The sun was up. Let them advance into the face of that, glaring off the white lakebed.

Let the men in iron come, he thought, half-blinded as they charge....

"They're coming, General," an aide announced.

Distant trumpets called. Dust boiled up as the chargers started forward. "Recall," el Nadim ordered. "Let them bury their infantry themselves."

His trumpets sounded. The cavalry fled to the wings. The slave volunteers retreated through the front to form a reserve.

The enemy advanced, armor gleaming through the dust, pennons fluttering boldly. "You're great, Hawkwind," el Nadim murmured. "But even you can become overconfident."

His heart hammered. It was going exactly as he wanted. But would that be enough?

The Wahlig's light horse followed the heavy cavalry, eager to fall on the scattered, terror-stricken infantry Hawkwind's charge would leave in its wake.

Both waves went to the gallop.

And when they were two thirds of the way across the lakebed they fell into el Nadim's trap, the trap suggested by a saltman's son.

It was no man-made trap. Nature herself had placed it there. Out where the old lake had been deepest a bit of water remained trapped beneath a concealing crust of salt and debris. It was seldom more than two feet deep, but that was enough.

The charging horses, already running shakily on the powdery lakebed, reached the water, broke through the crust. Their impetus was broken. Many of the warhorses fell or dumped their riders. Yousif's light horse hit from behind, worsening the confusion.

El Nadim signaled the advance. His men poured missile fire into the uproar. Selected veterans ran ahead to hamstring horses and finish dismounted riders.

El Nadim's horsemen circled the confusion and assaulted Yousif's men from their flanks.

The enemy broke. El Nadim's horsemen harried them back to their lines, killing scores, then flew back to their stations on their infantry's flanks, howling victoriously.

"Don't sing yet," the general muttered. "The worst is to come."

The historians would declare the honors even. Casualties were about equal. But Guildsmen had been hurled back, and rendered incapable of delivering another massed charge.

El Nadim backed away from the brine. "Water for everyone," he ordered. "Horses too. Officers, get those standards aligned. I want every man in his proper position. See to the javelins. Slave volunteers out front with the shovels." The breeze was stronger. The sun had turned the lakebed into a gleaming mirror over which heat waves shimmered. He doubted the enemy could see him.

"Come on, Yousif," el Nadim muttered. "Don't stall."

The Wahlig decided to attack before the dust and heat completely debilitated his men. The Guild infantry began its advance.

"Now we find out." El Nadim moved up to the edge of the brine. When the enemy came in range, he ordered javelins thrown. The Guildsmen took the missiles on their shields, suffering little harm. But the javelins dropped into the water, where they floated haft up and tangled feet. The Guild line grew increasingly ragged.

The slave volunteers used slings to hurl stones over their comrades' heads, further sapping enemy morale.

"Now, Hali," el Nadim murmured. "Now is your time."

And in the distance white boiled out of the rocks and swept down on the enemy's camp and mounts and reserves. The Invincibles were outnumbered, but surprise was with them. They drove off most of the horses and slaughtered hundreds of unprepared warriors before Yousif forced them back into the shelter of the rocks.

El Nadim was pleased. Execution had been perfect, and the rear attack threat remained.

But now the Guildsmen were slogging up out of the brine. His own men were half-ready to flee. He galloped across the rear of the line, shouting, "Hold them! Thirst is our ally."

The lines met. His men reeled back a step, then steadied up. Only a handful lost their courage. He chevied most back into the line with strokes from the flat of his blade.

The Guildsmen were as tough as ever. Without the heat, the sun in their eyes, the bitter dust, without their thirst, it would have been no contest.

The Guildsmen who had waded the deepest water appeared less than perfectly efficient. They had lost the cohesion of their shield wall, could not get it together again. El Nadim galloped back to his slave volunteers, ordered half to add their weight to that part of the line.

Javelins and stones rained on that sector. El Nadim's troops pushed forward by sheer body weight. The Guild line bowed. El Nadim signaled his cavalry.

The majority went to challenge the Wahlig's men, still busy skirmishing with Hali's Invincibles. A handful crossed behind the Guild line to harass Hawkwind's reserves and his least steady company.

Slowly, slowly, a fracture developed in the mercenary line. El Nadim bellowed with joy, gathered the rest of his reserves and plunged into the fray.

El Murid tried to follow the battle from a remote perch. He could tell little through the dust and heat shimmer. Nevertheless, it felt right. He gathered his officers and told them. They began placing their men.

The Guildsmen fought as well as ever they had, as magnificently in defeat as in victory. El Nadim could not rout them. But he drove them into their camp, then broke off to rest his men and water his mounts.

The victors laughed and congratulated one another, battered though they were. They had beaten Hawkwind! El Nadim withdrew them to their original stations and dared the enemy to try again.

Hawkwind and the Wahlig chose to withdraw. One Guild company contained Hali while the main force moved out, headed west.

In the gloaming a man approached El Murid. "They come, Lord. El Nadim did turn them back."

"The Lord is great." The Disciple could not stifle a grin. "Good. Spread the word."

The clatter of hooves and tramp of boots swelled in the darkness. A sour aura of disappointment reached the Disciple where he crouched, praying. A small unit passed below. The vanguard, he thought. He had to await the main force....

The time came. For a long minute terror paralyzed him. He could not shake his recollections of that fox den…. Not again. Never again. Not even for the Lord…

He leapt up and screamed, "There is but one God, and he is our Lord!" And, "Attend me now, O Angel of the Lord!"

His amulet blazed, illuminating the slope. He flung his arm down. Lightning hammered the canyon walls. Boulders flew around like toys at the hand of a petulant child. The earth quivered, shivered, shook. The far slope groaned in protest, then collapsed.

The roar of falling rock obliterated the cries from below.

When the rumbling stopped El Murid ordered the Invincibles down to finish the survivors.

He settled on a stone and wept, releasing all the fear that had plagued him for days.

ELEVEN
LIGHTNING STRIKES

"Come on, Reskird. You're dogging it."

Haroun cocked his head. That was the one called Bragi. The northern youths argued all the time. The more so since their company had cracked on the battle line. The one called Reskird was wounded. His friends ragged him mercilessly while they helped him walk.

The clang of weapons round the rearguard redoubled. The Disciple's men were keyed to a fever pitch by their success. He wished he could drop back and use his shaghûn's skills, but his father insisted he remain with his Guild charges.

This feuding between northmen was irritating. He dismounted. "Put him on my horse. Then you won't have to carry him."

The one called Haaken grumbled, "Fool probably never learned to ride. You ever been on a horse, Reskird?"

Kildragon's response was as testy. "I know one's arse when I…"

A brilliant light flared on the slope to the south. A man screamed words Haroun did not catch. Then the lightning came.

Boulders thundered into the column. Horses reared, screamed, bolted. Men cried out. Confusion quickly became panic.

Haroun retained his self-control. He faced the light, began mumbling a spell.…

A fist-sized stone struck his chest. The wind fled him. He felt bones crack. Red pain flooded him. Hands grabbed him, kept him from falling, hoisted him. He groaned once, then darkness descended.

A sliver of moon hung low in the east. Haroun saw nothing else, and that only as through a glass of murky water.…

"He's coming around." That was one of the northerners. He forced his vision to focus, rolled his head. The brothers squatted beside him. Haaken had his arm in a light sling. He appeared to be covered with dried blood.

Around them, now, Haroun discerned other shapes, men sitting quietly, waiting. "What happened?"

Bragi said, "Some sorcerer dumped a mountain on us."

"I know that. After that."

"We threw you on the horse and headed for the wizard just as his men charged us. We cut our way through and wound up here with the general. More men keep turning up. Your father is out looking for strays."

"How bad was it?"

The mercenary shrugged. He was floating on the edge of shock. For that matter, everyone around them seemed dulled, turned inward. It had been bad, then. A major defeat, consuming all the hopes raised by the advent of the Guildsmen.

Haroun tried to rise. Haaken made him lie still. "Broken ribs," he growled. "You'll poke a hole in your lung."

"But my father—"

"Sit on him," Bragi suggested.

Haaken said, "Your old man's gotten along without you so far."

Still Haroun tried to rise. Pain bolted across his chest. Lying still was the only way to beat it.

"That's better," Bragi said.

"You cut your way out? Through the Invincibles?" He vaguely recalled a clash of arms and flashes of men in white.

"They're not so hot when they're not on their horses," Haaken said. "Go to sleep. Getting excited won't do you no good."

Despite himself, Haroun followed that advice. His body insisted.

Yousif was standing over him when next he wakened. His father's left arm was heavily bandaged. His clothing was tattered and bloody. Fuad was there too, apparently unharmed, but Haroun had no eyes for his uncle. Wearily, his father was interrogating the Guildsmen through Megelin Radetic.

His father looked so old! So tired. So filled with despair.

Haroun croaked, "Megelin," overjoyed that fate had not seen fit to slay the old man. His death would have made the disaster complete.

His father knelt and gripped his shoulder, as demonstrative a gesture as the man could manage. Then duty called him elsewhere. Megelin stayed, seated cross-legged, talking softly. Haroun understood only a third of what he heard. The old scholar seemed to be talking about economic forces in one of the western kingdoms and deliberately ignoring present straits. Sleep closed in again.

When next he wakened the sun had risen. He was lying on a rolling litter. He could see no one who was not injured. His mercenary saviors had vanished.

Megelin appeared, drawn by some signal from the bearers. "Where is everybody, Megelin?"

Radetic replied, "Those who are able are trying to stall the pursuit."

"They're close?"

"Very. They smell blood. They want to finish it."

But Sir Tury Hawkwind in defeat proved more magnificent than Sir Tury Hawkwind achieving victory. The defeated column reached el Aswad safely.

Physicians set and bound Haroun's ribs. He was up and around almost immediately, against medical advice, blindly trying to encompass the enormity of the disaster.

Two thirds of the force had been lost. Most had been slain in the landslide and following attack. "But that's history," his father told him. "Now the enemy is at the gate and we don't have enough soldiers to man the walls."

It was true. El Nadim had pressed the chase right to the gate and though he did not have the manpower to undertake a proper siege, he had begun siegework. He had erected a fortified camp and begun constructing engines. His men were digging a ditch and erecting a barricade across the road. That looked like the first step toward circumvallation.

"What are they up to?" Haroun asked Megelin. "Three thousand men can't take el Aswad."

Radetic was glum. "You forget. Nothing is impossible to the True Believer."

"But how?"

"Recall the night attack."

"The lightning. A sorcerer that knocked a mountain down. But El Murid hates sorcery."

"True. Yet one sorcery is entwined in his legend. It hasn't been seen since shortly after he stumbled out of the desert."

"The amulet that he claims his angel gave him? I thought that was all made up."

"It happened. Apparently he's decided to use it again. I'd guess our walls will be his next target."

"El Murid is out there?"

"He is."

"Then Father ought to sortie. If we killed him..."

"Nothing would please them more than to have him try."

"But—"

"I discussed this with your father and General Hawkwind. They've decided to let el Aswad take its punishment. Let them break the wall. The amulet will be useless in close fighting."

Haroun did not like the strategy. It depended too much on the enemy doing the expected, too much on his not receiving reinforcements. But he protested no more. He had a glimmering of a scheme, and did not want to make Megelin suspicious.

"Did you ask Father about those Guildsmen?"

"I mentioned it. He'll do something when he gets time."

Haroun was pleased. Bragi and Haaken had saved his life. They deserved a reward. "Thank you."

"Have you completed those geometry exercises?" Radetic had no mercy. There was no break in the studies, even for convalescence.

"I've been busy...."

"Busy malingering. Go to your quarters. Don't come out till you have solutions you're prepared to defend."

"There's the old guy," Haaken said.

Bragi turned, watched Megelin Radetic make his way along the battlements. Radetic paused to talk to each soldier. "He remind you a little of Grandfather?"

"Keep an eye on those fools out there," Haaken said. "Or Sanguinet will eat you alive."

Little had been said about the recruit company's failure in battle. No fatigues or punishments had been enforced. Rumor said Hawkwind believed the recruits had done well, considering the terrain and concentrated resistance they had faced.

The veterans were less understanding. Their general's record had been sullied. Hundreds of comrades were dead. They didn't care that the briny water had been thigh deep, nor that the recruits had borne the brunt of the fury of El Murid's army. They saw more recruits surviving than members of any other company, and they were not pleased.

Radetic reached the youths. He paused between them, leaned on a merlon. Below, el Nadim's men were hard at work. "Confident as ants, aren't they?"

"Maybe they got reasons," Haaken grumbled.

Bragi did not respond. He did not know how to take the older man. Radetic was important here, yet seldom acted it. He did ask, "How's Haroun?"

"Mending. The Wahlig sends his regards. He'll thank you personally when he has a free moment."

"Okay."

"So enthusiastic! He's a generous man. Haroun is his favorite son."

"The only thing I could get enthusiastic about is getting out of here."

Radetic made a thoughtful "Hmm?" sound.

"It's hot and dry and there's nothing out there but miles and miles of nothing."

"My patrimony for a decent tree. I feel the same sometimes." Radetic patted Bragi's shoulder. "Homesick, lad?"

Bragi blustered—then poured out his story. Radetic looked interested, and encouraged him whenever he faltered.

He *was* homesick. Much as he pretended otherwise, he was just a boy forced into a man's role. He missed his people.

Bragi related his feelings about the defeat. Radetic patted his shoulder again. "No need to feel shame there. The general was surprised you held up so well. If there's any blame due, it belongs to him and the Wahlig. They got cocky.

And you soldiers paid the price. I'd better move along."

Bragi did not understand what the old scholar had done, but he did feel better. And Haaken didn't look half as glum.

Sergeant Trubacik arrived moments later. "The lieutenant wants you, Ragnarson. Get your butt down there."

"But—"

"Go."

Bragi went. He shivered all the way, though the day was a scorcher. Now it begins, he thought. Now the repercussions set in.

Sanguinet was set up in a storeroom off the stables. It was a dark, musty room, badly lighted by a single lantern. Bragi knocked on the doorframe. "Ragnarson, sir."

"Come in. Close the door."

Bragi did as he was told, wishing he were elsewhere. He could tell himself it didn't matter what these people thought, that *he* knew he had done his best, but it did matter. It mattered very much.

Sanguinet stared for fifteen seconds. Then, "Birdsong died this morning."

"I'm sorry, sir."

"So am I. He was a good man. Not much imagination, but he could hold a squad together."

"Yes sir."

"I'm preparing the report. You were there. Tell me how it happened."

"We was slogging through that salt water. A stone nicked his elbow. He dropped his shield. Before he got it up again a javelin hit right at the edge of his breastplate. Went in under his arm and got his lung, I guess."

"You took over?"

"Yes sir. The guys were kind of used to me telling them what to do. From training."

"You had only one other casualty?"

"Kildragon, sir." Reskird had gotten excited, broken formation to get at a particular enemy, and had paid the price of indiscipline.

"Corporal Stone commanded the squad on your left. He says you held your ground."

"I tried.... We tried, sir. But we couldn't stand fast when everybody else was pulling back."

"No. You couldn't. All right, Ragnarson. You may have the makings. I'm entering the promotion in the record. Pay and a half from the day Birdsong was wounded."

"Sir?" He thought he had missed something.

"You're taking over. Permanent promotion. Subject to the general's approval. Go back to your men, Corporal."

For half a minute Bragi stood there, dazed, wanting to argue, to protest, or something. This was not what he had expected.

"I said you're dismissed, Ragnarson."

"Yes sir." He bumbled out, returned to his post.

"Congratulations," Trubacik said, and hobbled off.

"What was that?" Haaken asked.

Bragi tried to explain, but did not understand. He just could not see himself as deserving.

Each afternoon el Nadim drew his men up in formation, offering battle. Each afternoon the defenders of el Aswad refused his challenge. This afternoon started no differently. El Nadim advanced to within extreme bowshot. He sent a herald to demand the surrender of el Aswad. The Wahlig sent him back empty-handed.

The besiegers then customarily withdrew a few hundred yards. Once a lack of response was assured they resumed their labors.

Not this time. El Nadim did not back down. He and the Disciple came to the van. The Disciple raised a fist to the sky. His amulet waxed brighter, till he seemed only a shadow of a man caught in the heart of eye-searing fire.

The lightning struck. Ten thousand boulders from the barren countryside leapt into the air and poured down on the Eastern Fortress. The lightning struck again, lashing the satellite guarding the approach and the curtain walls connecting it with the main fortress. The defenders launched flights of arrows, none of which reached their marks. The pillar of light remained rooted. The doors of heaven remained open, pouring out the fury of a dozen storms.

A section of wall collapsed, some stones bounding away down the slope, plowing furrows through the enemy ranks.

The Invincibles sent up a mighty war cry and surged forward. They scrambled up the mounds of rubble, pelted by missiles from the battlements. The going was slow. The rubble was piled high and was treacherous underfoot.

The Wahlig formed a force inside the break, and called for Hawkwind, who was more familiar with this sort of fighting.

The Disciple and most of el Nadim's army began moving across the slope, toward the fortress's western face.

The Invincibles attained the summit of the rubble and rushed down into a storm of arrows and javelins. They crashed into the Wahlig's men. Yousif's sketchy line dissolved. A melee ensued. The Disciple's troops continued to pour in, regular soldiers following the more dedicated Invincibles. One band turned to assault the gate.

The Disciple summoned the fury of heaven again. Lightning hammered the taller, stubborner western wall of el Aswad.

The northmen were stationed on the main fortress's north wall, near its juncture with the west wall, away from the fighting. Haroun joined them. "Damn them," he said. "They were smart. They made it impossible for Father to sortie."

Neither Bragi nor Haaken responded. They were completely involved in themselves, expecting Sanguinet's order to fall in and move into the fighting. They jumped each time lightning struck, though the Disciple's point of attack was well away.

No order came.

A wide section of western rampart gave way.

In the outlying sub-fortress Hawkwind launched a counterattack. He overwhelmed the enemy there, rushed into the main fortress, attacked the enemy entering through the west wall. The fighting there was among buildings and sheds, with little room for maneuver. It was confused and savage.

Hawkwind cordoned the breeched area, then pushed forward, slowly compressing the invaders. The last were evicted before sunset. The day's combat produced roughly equal losses for each side.

The defenders began clearing rubble and erecting a secondary barrier behind the gap in the west wall. The sub-fortress they decided to abandon.

The hour was late but Bragi was still at his post. There were no reliefs. Haaken was napping. So it went all around the wall. Every other man sleeping. The night was still but for the sounds of construction work.

Haroun strolled out of the night. He said, "Tomorrow they'll be rested and we'll be exhausted. My father thinks tomorrow may be the end."

Bragi grunted. El Nadim was thinking. Just wear the defense down. Morale was at a low ebb anyway, with the Wahlig's men convinced that the struggle was hopeless.

"We need help," Haroun said. "But help isn't going to come. The tribal leaders are deserting us."

Again Bragi grunted.

"They will join el Nadim. The desert will fill with men eager for the plunder of el Aswad. Something has to be done."

"Your father is doing what he can."

"Not everything. I have talents he won't use. He's afraid I'd get hurt. I could turn it around if he'd let me."

"How?"

"I came to thank you. For what you did out there."

"No thanks needed. Anyway, you already did."

"There's a debt now. My family always pays its debts."

Bragi didn't argue. He had a low opinion of human gratitude, though. Look at his father and the Thane. No two men ever owed one another more.

Haroun ambled off, seemingly distracted. The whole encounter was puzzling. Bragi decided Haroun needed a keeper.

Haroun was back within the hour. He carried a rope and small black bag. "What are you up to?" Bragi demanded when Haroun tied the rope to a merlon.

"Going to give the Disciple some of his own back."

"Who told you to? I didn't get any orders about you going out."

"I told me." Haroun pitched the rope into the darkness. "I'll be back before anybody misses me."

"The hell. I can't let you..."

Haroun was gone.

Bragi leaned forward. "You don't know what you're doing. Look at you. You don't even know how to rappel."

Haaken woke up. "What're you making all that racket for?" he grumbled. "They coming?"

"No. It's that Haroun. He just went over the wall."

"Call the sergeant of the guard. Don't stand there squawking like an old hen."

"Then he'd get in trouble."

"So? What's it to you?"

"I like him."

"He's deserting, ain't he?"

"No. He's going after El Murid."

Haaken levered himself upright, stared down into the darkness. Haroun had disappeared. "Damned fool if you ask me."

"I'm going after him."

"What? You're crazy. They could hang you for leaving your post. He's dumb enough to go down there, leave him go. No skin off our noses."

Bragi debated. He liked what he had seen of Haroun. But the youth had a romantic streak that would get him killed. "He's alone out there, Haaken. I'm going." He arranged his weapons so he could descend without them getting in his way.

Haaken sighed, began arranging his own weapons.

"What're you doing?"

"I'm going to let you go by yourself? My own brother?"

Bragi argued. Haaken snarled back. The debate became so heated their squadmates came to investigate. And in moments the whole squad was talking about accompanying Bragi.

That gave him pause. It was one thing to risk his own neck, quite another to lead the squad into an action his superiors would not approve.

What motivated the men, anyway? He wasn't sure. But, then, he didn't know why he was going himself. "It's your necks if we get found out," he said. "Stay or go. It's up to you." He grabbed Haroun's rope, swung over the edge, began descending. Halfway down the rope jerked. He spied a manshape against the stars. "Damned Haaken," he muttered. And smiled, feeling warm within.

He crouched among the boulders at the foot of the wall, trying to recall an easy approach to the Disciple's encampment, wondering if anyone up top would spot him and think he was the enemy. Haaken joined him. A third man dropped to one knee on his right. Then a fourth and fifth arrived, and more, till the whole squad gathered. "You idiots," he whispered. "All right. Keep it quiet, unless you want somebody up there to plink you." He stole forward, trying to approximate the route he suspected Haroun had taken.

The fates were kind. The watch on the wall did not spot them. That no longer a worry, Bragi became concerned about enemy pickets.

He stole within bowshot of the enemy encampment without finding Haroun. "He hornswoggled you," Haaken said. "He cut and ran."

"Not him. He's around somewhere, going to pull some stunt." He looked back, eyeing the fortress from the foe's perspective. It was a huge, forbidding outline, looming against the stars like the edge of a giant's ragged saw. Not a light shown anywhere. The construction crews had finished their work. "Spread out. We'll wait here till something happens."

The enemy camp was quiet, though fires glowed behind the stockade. An occasional sentry appeared, silhouetted by the glow.

"Bragi!" somebody hissed. "Over there."

"I see it."

Just a whisper of pale lilac light limned a boulder momentarily. A lilac bead dribbled toward the camp stockade. Defying gravity, it floated upward.

A sentry tilted forward, dropped off the wall. He struck earth with a soft crump.

"What're we into here?" Haaken demanded. "That's sorcery, Bragi. Killing sorcery. Maybe we ought to go back."

Bragi rested a steadying hand on Haaken's forearm. Another lilac glimmer appeared. Another bead danced toward the camp. Another sentry fell from the stockade, dying in utter silence.

Something scraped on stone. Staring intently slightly to one side of the sound, Bragi discerned a shadow sliding toward the wall. "That's him. He's going in." He rose.

"You're not going too?" Haaken whispered.

"No." That would be certain suicide, wouldn't it? "I was going to catch him. But it's too late, isn't it?"

TWELVE

NIGHTWORKS

Haroun crouched at the foot of the stockade, uncoiled with all the spring he could exact from young muscles. His fingers found purchase on top. He hung for a moment, listening. No alarm. No footsteps hastening his way. He hoisted himself till his eyes were an inch above the edge.

There were still a few fires burning, and a few men around them. Most were preparing wholesale breakfasts. Evidently El Murid meant to start early. No sentry was nearby.

He heaved upward. Part of the wall gave way, dribbling down with what seemed to him an incredible racket. The stockade was constructed of materials no better than sticks and stones mortared together with moistened clay. The clay was now dry, becoming powdery. He scrabbled for another handhold, rolled across the top, and dropped onto a rickety catwalk, slithered into a shadow. He remained as still as stone then, awaiting an alarm and forming a mental map he would not forget in the heat of action.

No one noticed the noise he'd made.

How soon would the sentries be missed? Surely not long. Ten minutes? That might be too tight. He had to locate the Disciple before he could strike.

Before he moved on he assumed the camouflage of a minor spell that would avert the unsuspecting eye, making him effectively invisible till he did something blatant.

He dropped to the ground, stole along the wall till he could move into the camp in the shelter of tent shadows. He harkened to his weakling shaghûn's senses, trying to locate the Disciple through the aura of his amulet. Only a vague sense of direction came, centerward. He needed no sorcery to guess that. He wished he'd had more time with his instructors, had been able to study with the masters, and had attained a higher level of proficiency. But there had been so many things to learn, and so little time for study....

There! That way. The throb of the amulet was strongest thither.

He moved like a panther, shadow in shadow. That romantic undercurrent welled up. He imagined himself more than what he was, nominated himself a mighty avenger. Dangerous as his undertaking was, he was not afraid. Fright did not occur to him. His fearlessness was the fearlessness of folly.

The camp center was set off from the remainder by a twenty-yard width of barren earth. Beyond stood a half-dozen tents guarded by twenty Invincibles. These sentries were posted too close to slip past.

He could not pick out the tent occupied by the Disciple. Time fled. Any minute the absent sentries would be missed. He had to *do* something.

He made the lilac magic, sent several of the tiny, deadly balls hunting. And kept sending them as fast as he could create them.

There was no other way. There would be an alarm, and an alert, and mad confusion. In it he might get close enough to do the deed.

An Invincible shouted. Not one of those touched by a violet pellet, of course. Those would make no sound again, ever.

Still creating and releasing the killing pellets, Haroun crept forward... and found himself face to face with a giant in white. A giant not misled by his feeble spell of concealment. A scimitar howled down. Haroun hurled himself aside, stumbled into a low tent, tripped, scrambled into a shadow, crouched, stared back at the Invincible. The man lost him, but only for an instant. Scimitar raised, he charged.

Haroun drew his blade.

The camp was coming to life. Men shouted questions. In the circle guarded by Invincibles—a dozen of whom lay dead—tent flaps whipped open. Officers demanded reports. Haroun spotted a man who had to be el Nadim. He tried to unleash another lilac bead. But the giant was upon him again.

He blocked a stroke so strong his whole arm went numb. The Invincible left himself open to a counterstroke, but Haroun hadn't the strength to deliver it.

Another blow fell. Haroun rolled with it. Again he could not take advantage of an opportunity. His weapon had been forced too far out of position.

Men shouted at his opponent, who shouted back.

The third stroke was as overwhelming as its predecessors. This time Haroun kicked as his blade was driven down and away. His toe connected with the giant's knee. The man staggered. He was slow getting his guard up. Haroun struck before he did so.

Haroun whirled and ran a short way, banging bewildered warriors out of his way. He dived into a shadow behind a tent. The tent was unoccupied. He slithered under the fabric's edge.

The uproar grew. There were cries that the Wahlig was attacking. Men rushed to the stockade. As many ran hither and thither in panic. A very few sought the interloper who had slain the Disciple's guards.

The halloo moved away. Haroun peeped outside, saw no one. He crept out and slid from shadow to shadow, toward the Disciple's tent. He knew which it was now.

Behind him flames rose. In their panic some of the enemy had scattered a fire. Some tents had caught. The blaze was spreading.

The fallen Invincibles had been replaced. Haroun cursed. There was no way, now, that he could deliver the stroke he had been anticipating all day.

He would have to use the Power. He hadn't wanted to do that. He wanted the Disciple to see death coming, wanted the man to look into his eyes and recognize the boy from Al Rhemish. Wanted him to know who as well as why.

The lilac killer would not do. It would take the nearest Invincible, not a man cowering inside a tent. It had to be something else. His arsenal of petty magicks contained little that was apt. Again he cursed the chain of circumstance that had prevented his achieving his full potential as a shaghûn.

He selected a spell that would induce the symptoms of typhoid, ran through the chants softly, visualized the El Murid he recalled from Al Rhemish. He loosed the spell.

A cry of agony answered it.

Some Invincibles rushed to their master. And some rushed toward Haroun.

"What the hell is going on?" Haaken asked.

"I don't know," Bragi replied. "But he's sure got them stirred up."

"Maybe we ought to help. Maybe if they think they're under attack he can get out in the confusion."

Bragi doubted that. He had written Haroun off. The decision he faced was whether or not to rush back to el Aswad in hopes he hadn't been missed. It had to be too late. Might as well do some good here.

Some of the enemy were fleeing the camp. Within, the fires were spreading. Horses were making panic noises.

"All right. Let's go. Harass the ones running away. You guys with the bows. Shoot a few over the wall."

Alarms awakened Megelin Radetic. Groggy, he staggered from his cubicle, his seldom used sword dragging. A night attack? He hadn't anticipated that. It wasn't to the Disciple's advantage. The man merely needed to wear the defense down with hammerings like yesterday's.

He paused, listened. Plenty of people running around yelling, but no thunder. No crash of lightning striking the fortress. Maybe it wasn't an attack.

What, then?

He reached the north court to find it aboil with men rushing out the gate. He grabbed a soldier. "What's happening?" The man pulled away. So did the next he caught. Nobody wanted to spare a moment. Radetic dragged his weary bones to the ramparts.

The Disciple's camp was ablaze. Men were scurrying everywhere. Animals were stampeding with the men. There was fighting. The defenders of el Aswad were falling on their foes in a great disorderly rush. The anthill simile occurred to him. "Trite," he murmured.

It took Megelin just seconds to guess how it had started. "Haroun! You fool!" He panicked. His own Haroun.... He practically threw himself off the wall in his haste to get down there.

The observer within was amused. *The boy isn't your child,* it said. *He's only on loan to you.*

Even so, his heart was ripped by fear that the boy had destroyed himself in some romantic scheme for rescuing his father's fortunes.

Bragi kept his men close together, unbroken by the human stampede. Two score bodies lay around them. The enemy was easy in this state.

A rabble from the fortress arrived, as disorganized as the foe, but with blood in their eyes. The area became a slaughter yard. Bragi urged his men toward the gateway.

Entering was easy. The enemy simply ran away or piled over the stockade. Guildsmen and the Wahlig's warriors followed Bragi's squad.

What now? Where to look? Haroun wanted the Disciple. El Murid's quarters should be near the center of camp. "This way. On the double." Haaken kept the men together while Bragi ran off to the right, skirting the fires. His squad left a trail of enemy injured. Wild-eyed horses proved a greater danger than enemy weapons.

Bragi found an aisle of encampment unthreatened by flames. He turned toward the camp's heart.

Haroun stifled a cry when the Invincibles slammed him to the earth at El Murid's feet. He spat at their chieftain. The man cuffed him.

"The Wahlig's brat, Lord."

"You're sure, Mowaffak?"

"The very one who attacked you in Al Rhemish."

"He was just a boy."

"That was a long time ago, Lord. He's learned more shaghûn tricks, it seems."

Haroun watched the Disciple's face darken. He compared it with the face he recalled. The man had aged beyond his years. He looked *old*. "You'd damn me when you use a fouler sorcery yourself?"

The Invincible hit him again. Blood filled his mouth. He bit down on the pain, spat scarlet on the man's robe. "Pig eater."

"You delude yourself. I use no sorcery." El Murid puffed up with offended dignity. "I call upon the might of the Lord, as vested in me by his angel."

"Somebody is deluding himself."

El Nadim arrived. "Lord, the camp is total chaos. The fires can't be contained. Guild soldiers are inside the stockade. We'd best get out."

The Disciple's face darkened further. "No."

"Lord!" Mowaffak snapped. "Be reasonable. This scum panicked the men. The enemy are upon us. We can't make a fight of it. It's get out or be destroyed. Now, before the panic infects the Invincibles."

El Nadim agreed. "We can rally the survivors on the road, then return." He exchanged a look with the Invincible.

Haroun caught it. Both knew there would be no second attempt on the fortress. This night would see their strength leeched. "None of you will escape," he gurgled. "You're dead men." Big talk. But maybe they *would* be destroyed. He heard the fighting now.

Agony lanced across the Disciple's features. Bodyguards rushed to support him. The Invincible captain snarled, "Get him onto a horse. Get everybody you can mounted. Riding double if you have to." He faced Haroun. "What did you do to him?"

Haroun said nothing.

The Invincible hit him. "What did you do?"

Haroun gritted his teeth and willed the pain away.

The blows fell steadily. The Invincible became workmanlike, telling him the pain would stop only when he undid whatever he had done.

The minutes felt like hours. The pain got worse and worse. Only stubbornness kept Haroun from yielding.

An Invincible rushed up. "They're headed this way."

"How close?"

"Right behind me."

The captain dragged Haroun to his feet. "We'll take him along. Is the Lord safe?"

"They're leaving through the back way now, sir. The general and some of his men are with them."

"Help me carry him." Haroun hadn't the strength to support himself. He sagged between the men, his feet trailing in the dirt. He could not see well, now. Everything was out of focus, distorted and fire-tinted.

He was going to die. They would make him break the spell, then they would kill him....

He was not afraid. Despite the pain, he felt only triumph.

"There he is!" Bragi yelled. "The white robes have him. Let's go." He charged, bloody sword overhead.

One of the Invincibles looked back. His eyes widened. He ran. The other turned, assessed the situation, released Haroun and drew a dagger. He grabbed the youth's hair, pulled his head back for a throat slash.

Bragi threw his sword. It smacked the white robe's shoulder, doing no harm, but did foil the murder attempt.

Bragi went for the Invincible's legs. Haaken roared and wound up for a two-handed swordstroke. The white robe flung Haroun into their path. Bragi smashed into the youth. Haaken leapt over. The Invincible tripped him, flung the next Guildsman down atop him, sprinted into the night. Bragi's squadmates charged after him.

Bragi untangled himself. "What a mess. Haaken?"

"Right here."

"Look at this. They really worked him over."

"He asked for it. Better see if I can make a litter."

"Asked for it? You don't have a sympathetic bone in your body."

"Not for fools."

"Not that big a fool. He broke the siege." The fighting in the camp was slackening. The Disciple's men were fleeing. Had the Wahlig been able to mount a controlled pursuit none would have escaped. In the chaos, Hali and el Nadim rallied enough men to shield El Murid's withdrawal.

"That's two I owe you," Haroun croaked. Bragi and Haaken stood over him, flexing muscles tightened from carrying the litter.

"Yeah," Bragi grumbled. "Getting to be a habit."

"Here comes the old guy," Haaken whispered.

Radetic came puffing up, features oddly adance in the firelight. He dropped to his knees beside Haroun.

"Don't let the blood worry you," Bragi said. "They just slapped him around."

Haroun tried to grin. "I almost got him, Megelin. Stuck him with a spell, anyway. He's going to hurt a lot."

Radetic shook his head. Bragi said, "Let's get rolling. Hoist him up, Haaken."

Two riders came up, stared down. "Father," Haroun croaked.

"Haroun." The Wahlig eyed Radetic. "He start this, Megelin?"

"He did."

The Wahlig sucked spittle between his teeth. "I see." He considered Bragi and Haaken. "Aren't these the lads who brought him out of the pass?"

"The same. Making a career, aren't they?"

"So it would seem. See to Haroun's injuries, then get their stories. And I'll want to talk to you once we're finished down here."

"As you will."

"Fuad. Let's go." The Wahlig and his brother rode on into the confusion.

"Can we go now?" Bragi asked.

"By all means." Megelin eyed Haroun, who could not conceal his trepidation. "It'll be all right, lad. But you did get out of hand. Just as you did at Al Rhemish."

Haroun forced a laugh. "Didn't have a choice."

"That's debatable. Nevertheless, it turned out well. Assuming we save your teeth. I hope you have it out of your system now."

"What?"

"The rebellion. The foolishness. You're young. You have a lot of years left, if you don't squander them. These lads won't always be around."

Haroun closed his eyes, shivered. He *had* been a fool, throwing himself in like he was one of El Murid's Invincibles, with never a thought to how he would get away. There were a lot of tomorrows, and through thoughtlessness he'd nearly squandered his share. He owed the northerners more than he had realized.

Megelin scowled.

"Well?" the Wahlig demanded.

Radetic looked at Hawkwind. The general's leathery countenance remained blank. His vote was "present," nothing more. Megelin considered Fuad. The Wahlig's brother was abubble with rage. He had an ally there, but he and Fuad made a pathetic marriage of purpose.

Megelin recalled an instructor who had intimidated him terribly in his youth. It had taken him a decade to conquer his unreasoning fright. And only then had he been able to analyze what the man had done. He adopted the fellow's method now.

"For more years than I care to recall I have slaved thanklessly in this armpit of the world." Excessive ferocity and bombast were the keys, accompanied by exaggerated gestures and body movement. These wakened the father-fear in one's listeners. "Time and again have you asked my advice. Time and again have you ignored it. Time and again have I prepared to return home, only to have my will thwarted. I have fought for you. I have suffered for you. I have wasted a career for you. I have endured ceaseless, senseless humiliation at the hands of your family and men. All for the sake of salvaging a rockpile in the middle of nowhere, a rockpile that protects a godforsaken wasteland, inhabited only by barbarians, from the predations of bandits whose mercies the land most assuredly deserves."

His blood was rising, responding to years of frustration. "How many hundreds, nay, how many thousands of men have lost their lives over this abomination upon a hill? I have grown old here. Old before my time. Your sons have grown up here, made ancient by endless hatred and treachery and war. And now you want to abandon the place to the Disciple. For shame!"

Radetic planted himself in front of the Wahlig, fists on hips. He almost grinned. Even Fuad was shaken by his fury. "What have we lived for? What have we died for? If we go now, have we not wasted all those years and sacrifices?"

"We fought for an ideal, Megelin." Yousif's voice was soft and tired. "And we lost. The Disciple did not overthrow us physically. We ran him off again. But the ideal lies dead beneath his heel. The tribes are deserting us. They know where the strength lies, where the future lies. With the man we couldn't kill. With the man who, in a few weeks, will command hordes eager to swarm over our broken walls to plunder our homes, defile our women, and murder our children. There is nothing we can do here—unless we want to die valiantly in a lost cause, like the knights in your western romances."

Megelin could not sustain his anger in the face of the truth. He and Fuad were being stubborn out of sentiment and pride. Death could be the lone reward for harkening to either. The Wahligate was lost in all but name.

Yousif continued, "Things aren't yet hopeless up north. Aboud opened his eyes enough to see the need for the general. Maybe reports from his own men, who have *seen* the enemy, will widen the crack in the wall around his reason. He still commands the strength and faith of the kingdom—if he'd just use them."

Torment and despair muddied the Wahlig's words, pain he would never confess. The decision to flee had cost him. It may have broken him as a man.

"You'll have your will, Lord. I haven't the strength to deny it. But I fear you'll find more heartbreak in Al Rhemish. There's nothing else to say. I must pack. It would be a sin if my labors of years were destroyed by ignorant fools in white."

For an instant torment controlled the Wahlig. His face reflected the horrors of Hell. But he steadied himself, like the great lord he was. "Go, then, teacher. I'm sorry I've been a disappointment."

"Not that, Wahlig. Not ever." Radetic surveyed the others. Hawkwind remained inscrutable. Fuad was a study in inner conflict, an almost trite portrait of a man compelling himself to remain silent.

"Megelin," Yousif called as Radetic neared the door. "Travel with Haroun. I have very little else left."

Radetic nodded, stamped out.

"There you go," Kildragon said. "March all the way from High Crag, forced march, killing ourselves, so we can save this dump, and what do we do? Walk away. Why do they always let the morons do the military planning?"

"Listen to the old strategist," Haaken mocked. "He don't have sense enough to hold his spot in the line, but he knows better than the general and Haroun's old man, who've only been leading armies since before he was a twinkle in his father's eye."

"Keep it down," Bragi said. "We're supposed to be sneaking out of here."

"With all this racket? You could probably hear these wagons four miles away, they're making so much noise."

The Wahlig's horsemen had ridden out at nightfall, several hours earlier, in hopes of scouring the area of enemy spies. Now the main column was under way. The Guildsmen would guard its rear. The Wahlig hoped his getaway would not be noticed till he could not be overhauled.

"Ragnarson."

Bragi faced Lieutenant Sanguinet. "Sir?"

"Too much noise from your crowd. Tell Kildragon to keep it down or I'll leave him for the jackals."

"Yes sir. I'll gag him if I have to, sir."

That should have been it. But Sanguinet remained rooted, staring. Bragi began to wilt. Once the man finally did leave, Bragi told Haaken, "He knows. He has to pretend he don't on account of if he doesn't he'll have to do something about it. Even if we did save the Wahlig's kid. We're going to be walking on eggs. He'll be looking to get us on something else. Reskird, you better pretend you never learned to run your mouth."

"What did I do? I just said what everybody is thinking."

"Everybody else has sense enough to keep it to themselves. Let's move out." Bragi left el Aswad and never looked back. A glance over his shoulder would have been a glance into his past, and he did not want to rue his decision to enlist. A fool's decision, that, but he was here now, and he was of that stubborn sort which insists on enduring the consequences of its acts.

Looking ahead, he saw nothing promising. He expected to shed his life's blood somewhere on the sand of this savage, alien, incomprehensible land.

Haroun did look back. He had no choice. The litter he rode, despite insisting he could ride a horse, faced the castle.

He wept. He had known no other home, and was certain he'd never see it again. He wept for his father and Fuad, for whom el Aswad meant even more. He wept for all the valiant ancestors who had held the Eastern Fortress, never yielding in their trust. And he wept for the future, intimations of which had begun to reach him already.

Megelin joined him, and walked beside him, sharing a silence no words could give more meaning.

Before dawn arrived the column vanished into the Great Erg, unmarked by a single unfriendly eye.

THIRTEEN
ANGEL

Stunned by unexpected shifts of fortune, El Murid retreated into his fastness in Sebil el Selib. He did but one thing before further retreating into the fastnesses of his mind: he summoned Nassef from the Throyen front. He did so in a message sufficiently strong that it would be subject to no misinterpretation. Nassef must appear or face the wrath of the Harish.

Nassef made record time, urged on more by the Disciple's tone than by what he actually said. He feared El Murid might fall apart. He was not reassured when he arrived. His brother-in-law acted as if he did not exist.

For six days the Disciple sat on the Malachite Throne and ignored everyone. He drank little and ate less while venturing deep into labyrinths of self. Both Nassef and Meryem became deeply disturbed.

Nassef. Cynical Nassef. Unbelieving Nassef. He was half the problem. He was an infidel in the service of the Lord. El Murid prayed that his God forgive him for compromising. He should have shed the man a decade ago. But there was Meryem to reckon with, and there was Nassef's unmatched skills as a general. And, finally, there was the grim chance that some of the Invincibles now felt more loyal to their commander than to their prophet. It had been a mistake to hand them over to Nassef.

But the heretics within would have to wait till he had cast down the foes of the Lord without.

But Nassef… He took bribes from Royalists willing to buy their lives. He sold pardons. He appropriated properties for himself and his henchmen. He was building a personal following. If only indirectly, he was suborning the movement. Someday he might try to grab it all. Nassef was the Evil One's Disciple within the Lord's camp.

But no spiritual malaise had driven El Murid into the wasteland of his soul. No. Nor was it so much the debacle before the Eastern Fortress. That hadn't proven as bad a defeat as it had seemed at the time. The enemy had loafed at the pursuit, fearing another ambush. The cause of his inturning was the decampment of the Wahlig of el Aswad.

It had come too suddenly, and was too out of character. The man was a sticker, a fighter, not a runner. Flight made no sense after his having resisted so bitterly for so long.

Yousif's withdrawal left the Disciple without focus. His plans, for so long, had been thwarted by one man's stubbornness, that he had given up looking beyond Yousif's defeat. He did not know what to do.

Yousif was gone, but he remained foremost in El Murid's mind. Why had he gone? What did he know? Finally, the Disciple summoned Nassef and put the question.

"I don't know," Nassef replied. "I've interviewed el Nadim and Hali repeatedly. I've talked to most of the men. I've lost a week's sleep over it. And I can't tell you a thing. Aboud certainly didn't summon him. Nothing is happening at Al Rhemish." Nothing that transpired in the capital escaped Nassef. He had an agent in the Royal Tent itself.

"Then he knows only what we do," El Murid mused. "What fact is he interpreting differently?"

"That foreign devil Radetic is behind it."

"Perhaps. The outland idolaters must hate me. They must sense the hand of God upon me. They must feel, in His wrath, the knowledge that I shall be the instrument of their chastisement. They are the slaves of the Evil One, struggling to prolong his sway over their wicked kingdoms."

Was that a suppressed smirk on Nassef's lips?

"Papa?"

The girl was skipping. His first impulse was to swat her for insolemnity before the fanes. But it had been an age since he had given her any attention.

Nassef remarked, "The child is a savage sometimes."

"And when was laughter an abomination unto the Lord? Leave us." He let her slide into his lap. "What is it, darling?" She was nearly twelve now.

Had it been that long? Life was whistling by, and he seemed little nearer fulfilling his destiny. That unholy Yousif. Nassef had had so many successes, but they had meant nothing as long as the Wahlig had kept the movement bottled up in Sebil el Selib.

"Oh, nothing. I just wanted to see if you were done thinking yet." She snuggled, moving in his lap.

He was shamed by the impulse the Evil One sent fluttering across his mind. Dark-winged vampire. Not with his own daughter.

She was on the precipice: womanhood was but a moment away. Soon her breasts would begin to swell, her hips to broaden. She would be marriageable. Already his followers were scandalized because he allowed her the run of Sebil el Selib, unveiled, and often permitted her to accompany Nassef on his safer journeys.

He suspected Nassef wanted her himself.

And still she had no name.

"You know I don't believe that, sweetheart. Something besides your grouchy old papa brought you here." He was acutely aware of the disapproval of the priests tending the shrines.

"Well…"

"I can't say yes or no till you tell me."

In a staccato burst, "Fatima promised me she'd teach me to dance if you said it was okay. Please? Oh, please, Papa, can I? Please?"

"Slow down. Slow down."

Fatima was Meryem's body servant, and a successful piece of propaganda. A reformed prostitute, she was living proof that all who came seeking were found worthy in the eyes of El Murid's Lord. Even women.

It was El Murid's most radical departure from orthodox dogma, and he was having trouble selling it still.

Women had been doubly disadvantaged since the Fall. A woman had brought the nation to its present desperate plight. Now the most rigidly fundamentalist of men allowed their wives in their presence only for purposes of procreation. Even relative liberals like Yousif of el Aswad kept their women cloistered and on the extreme fringes of their lives. The daughters of the poor were sometimes strangled at birth, or sold to slavers who trained them for resale as prostitutes.

A prostitute, socially, was as far beneath a wife as a wife was beneath a husband.

Yet even in Hammad al Nakir Nature had her way with the young. "This is serious." Little girls seldom became interested in dances unless also interested in interesting boys in girls. Then they were little girls no more. And the boys were no longer boys.

It was time to speak to Meryem about veils.

"Time, he rides a swift steed, little one." He sighed. "So soon come and gone. Everything past in the wink of an eye."

She began twisting her face into a pout, sure she was about to be refused.

"Let me think. Give me a few days, will you?"

"All right," she said brightly. His asking for a delay was, inevitably, the prelude to his giving in. She kissed him, scooted off his lap, became all skinny, windmilling arms and legs as she ran away.

Disapproving priestly stares followed her passage.

"Hadj!" El Murid called to his chief bodyguard. "We're going to make a journey. Prepare."

Far south of Sebil el Selib, south of el Aswad, stood a mountain rising slightly separate from the mother range called Jebal al Alf Dhulquarneni. It was called Jebal al Djinn, Mountain of Demons, or, sometimes, the Horned Mountain. When seen from the southwest it resembled a great horned head rising from the desert. It was there El Murid met his angel when he felt lost enough to require face to face advice. He'd never wondered why the Lord's messenger had chosen a meeting place so remote and of such evil repute.

The Disciple's faith in his angel was tried severely during a long, solitary ascent which left his body feeling tortured. Would the messenger even respond after all this time? El Murid had not come seeking him since before his ill-starred visit to Al Rhemish. But the angel had promised. On Jebal al Djinn, though, even the promises of angels seemed suspect.

The mountain was not a good place. It was cursed. No one knew why any longer, but the evil inhabiting the stones and trees remained, palpably beating upon any intruder. Each visit more than the last, El Murid wished his mentor had chosen somewhere more benevolent.

He hardened his resolve. Evil had to be defied in its very fastnesses. How else could the righteous gain the strength to resist the Darkness when it came against their own strongholds?

His doubts grew as a night and most of a day creaked past and there was no response from his heavenly interlocutor. Another evening was gathering. His campfire was sending shadows playing tag over barren rock.

The emissary arrived in a display of thunder and lightning that could be seen for leagues around. He raced his winged steed three times around the horned peaks before alighting fifty yards from the Disciple's fire. El Murid rose. He gazed at his own feet respectfully.

The angel, who persisted in assuming the shape of a small old man, limped toward him over the shattered basalt. Slung across his back was a cornucopia-shaped instrument which looked far too massive for his strength.

He swung his burden down, sat upon it. "I thought I would hear from you sooner."

El Murid's heart fluttered. The angel intimidated him as much now as when he had been a boy in the desert so long ago. "There was no need. Everything was going the way it should."

"If a little slowly, eh?"

El Murid glanced up shyly. A shrewd look had narrowed the angel's eyes. "Slowly, yes. I got in a hurry. Wadi el Kuf taught me the folly of trying to force something before its time."

"What's happened now?"

El Murid was puzzled because the angel had to ask. He told of Yousif's strange flight after the recent siege, and of an impending crisis in his own household. He begged for guidance.

"Your next move is obvious. I'm surprised you summoned me. Nassef could have told you. Gather your might and strike. Take Al Rhemish. Who will stop you if the Wahlig is gone? Seize the Shrines and your family problem will resolve itself."

"But—"

"I see. Once burned, twice cautious. Twice burned, petrified. There will be no Wadi el Kuf. No surprises from children deft with the Power. Tell Nassef that I will be watching personally. Then unleash him. He has the genius to pull it off." He sketched a plan, displaying a knowledge of desert affairs and personalities which quieted the Disciple's doubts. "Before we part, I'll give you another token."

The old man slipped off his seat and knelt. He whispered to the horn, then hoisted it and shook it. Something tumbled from its bell. "Have Nassef transmit this to his agent in the Royal Tent. The rest will follow if he strikes a week later."

El Murid accepted a small teakwood box. He stared at it, baffled.

The old man dashed to his mount and took wing. El Murid shouted after him. He had only begun to discuss his problems.

The winged horse swooped round the horned peaks. Thunder rolled. Lightning clawed the sky. Gouts of fire hurtled back and forth between the horns. Two blasts smashed together and erupted upward, forming some giant sign El Murid could not make out because it was directly overhead.

The blinding light faded slowly. And when El Murid could see once more, no sign of the angel could be found. He returned to his fire and sat muttering to himself, staring at the teakwood box.

After debating several seconds, he opened it. "Finger cymbals?" he asked the night.

The box contained an exquisite set of zils, worthy of a woman who danced before kings.

"Zils?" he muttered. What on earth? But a messenger of the Lord could not be wrong. Could he?

He searched the sky again, but the angel was gone.

Decades would pass before he encountered the emissary again.

"Zils," he muttered, and stared down the mountain at the campfires where Nassef and the Invincibles waited. His brother-in-law's face filled his mind. Something would have to be done. After Al Rhemish had been taken?

"Nassef, attend me," he called weakly when he finally stumbled into camp. It was late, but Nassef was awake, studying crude maps by fire and moonlight.

El Murid's brother-in-law joined him. With the exception of the Disciple's chief bodyguard, everyone else withdrew. "You look terrible," Nassef said.

"It's the curse. I hurt all over. The ankle. The arm. Every joint."

"Better get something to eat." Nassef glanced up the mountain, frowned. "And some sleep probably wouldn't hurt."

"Not now. I have things to tell you. I spoke with the angel."

"And?" Nassef's eyes were narrow.

"He told me what I wanted to hear. That the Al Rhemish apricot is ripe for the plucking."

"Lord—"

"More listening and less interrupting, please, Nassef. There'll be no Wadi el Kuf this time. I don't mean to try sweeping them away with sheer numbers. We'll use the tactics you developed. We'll move by night, along the trails Karim followed when you sent him to slay Farid."

If he expected a reaction from Nassef he was disappointed. Nassef merely nodded thoughtfully.

He still wondered about that incident. Aboud's hysteria had been predictable, though his turning to mercenaries had come as a surprise. Hali had provided a detailed report on the attack. Karim's force had sustained startlingly heavy casualties. The man should have brought more of his soldiers home. But, then, Karim was Nassef's creature, and the Invincibles who had accompanied him were not.

"But first, these have to be delivered to your agent in the Royal Tent."

Nassef opened the box, then peered up at the horned mountain. Just three people knew who that agent was. He and the agent were two of those. The third was not El Murid. The Disciple, he was sure, had been unaware that such an agent existed. "Zils?" he asked.

"The angel gave them to me. They must be special. Carry out his instructions. Nassef?"

"Uhm?"

"What's the situation on the coast?"

"Under control."

"Do we really dare try Al Rhemish with just the Invincibles?"

"We can *try* anything. It would be a bold stroke. Unexpected. I don't think a move that way will complicate the eastern situation. It's winding down there. I had Karim take over. He'll subdue the Throyens. They were ready to talk when I left. A few weeks of Karim's attentions and they'll accept any terms. And el-Kader has shattered the last resistance at the south end of the littoral. El Nadim will hold Sebil el Selib. With Yousif gone there will be no trouble out of el Aswad."

The Disciple sighed. "Finally. After all those years. Why did Yousif run, Nassef?"

That was the critical question. "I wish I knew. It keeps me wondering what he has up his sleeve. Yes. We'll try for Al Rhemish. It's worth a try even if it doesn't work. It'll be a spoiling raid if nothing else. Yousif will be more dangerous there than he was at el Aswad, where his resources were limited."

El Murid still carried Yousif's taunting note. He studied it for the hundredth time, fixed though every word was in his memory.

"My dear Micah," he read aloud. "Circumstances compel me to be away from my home temporarily. I beg to leave it in your curatorship, knowing you will attend it carefully in my absence. Do feel free to enjoy its luxuries during your stay. May you anticipate all your tomorrows with as much eagerness as I anticipate mine.

"Your Obedient Servant, Yousif Allaf Sayed, Wahlig of el Aswad."

"Still a mystery to me," Nassef said.

"He's mocking us, Nassef. He's telling us he knows a secret."

"Or Radetic wants us to think he does."

"Radetic?"

"The foreigner must have composed that. Yousif isn't that subtle. It smells like a sneaky bluff."

"Maybe."

"Let's not play his game. Forget the message. In Al Rhemish he can whisper the words of the Evil One directly into the King's ear. He can gather the Royalist strength against us."

"Yes. Of course. We must do as the angel says, and strike hard, now, at the very nest of the vipers."

"Whatever his reasons, Lord, I think Yousif made a mistake. Without him to block the road I don't think the Royalists can stop us. As long as we don't meet them head-on, in a test of strength. They retain the advantages they had at Wadi el Kuf."

"Gather the rest of the Invincibles. This year in Al Rhemish for Disharhun."

"It will be a delight, Lord. I'll begin now. Give my love to Meryem and the children."

El Murid sat silently and alone till long after Nassef's departure. The critical hour was at hand. He had to wrest the most from it. His angel had suggested that the resolution of many troubles lay in the taking of Al Rhemish. And he had begun to get a glimmering of what could be done.

"Hadj."

"My Lord?"

"Find Mowaffak Hali. Bring him to me."

"Yes, my Lord."

"My Lord Disciple?" Hali asked as he approached. "You wanted me?"

"I have news for you, Mowaffak. And a task."

"At your command, Lord."

"I know. Thank you. Especially for your patience while it was necessary that the Scourge of God direct the blades of the Invincibles."

"We tried to understand the need, Lord."

"You saw the light on the mountain?"

"I did, Lord. You spoke with the angel?"

"Yes. He told me it's time the Invincibles liberated the Most Holy Mrazkim Shrines."

"Ah. Then the Kingdom of Peace is at hand."

"Almost. Mowaffak, it seems to me that worldly elements crept into the Invincibles during my brother's tenure. Perhaps this is our opportunity to expunge those. The fighting at Al Rhemish will be bitter. Many Invincibles will perish. If those who are the most trustworthy are elsewhere, on a secret mission…"

He said no more. Mowaffak understood. He wore one of the crudest smiles the Disciple had ever seen.

"I see. What would that mission be, Lord?"

"Use your imagination. Choose your men and inform me of the nature of the task I've assigned you. And we'll celebrate Disharhun in Al Rhemish."

Hali kept smiling. "It shall be as you command, Lord."

"Peace be with you, Mowaffak."

"And with you, Lord." Hali departed. He walked taller than El Murid had seen in some time.

After a time, the Disciple called softly, "Hadj."

"Lord?"

"Find the physician. I need him."

"Lord?"

"The mountain was too much for me. The pain... I need him."

The physician appeared almost immediately. He had been sleeping, and had clothed himself hastily and sloppily. "My Lord?" He did not look happy.

"Esmat, I'm in pain. Terrible pain. My ankle. My arm. My joints. Give me something."

"My Lord, it's that curse. You need to have the curse removed. A philter wouldn't be wise. I've given you too many opiates lately. You're running a risk of addiction."

"Don't argue with me, Esmat. I can't cope with my responsibilities if I'm continuously preoccupied with pain."

Esmat relented. He was not a strong man.

El Murid leaned back and let himself drift in the warm, womblike security of the narcotic.

Someday he would have to find a physician who could outwit his injuries and the curse of the Wahlig's brat. The pain bouts came every day now, and Esmat's dosages had more and more difficulty banishing them.

The desert was vast and lonely, just as it had been during the advance on Sebil el Selib so long ago, and as it had been during the desperate flight from Wadi el Kuf. It seemed to have lost its usual natural indifference, to have become actively hostile. But El Murid refused to be daunted. He enjoyed the passage, seeing whole new vistas, wild new beauties.

It was a matter of years no more. Just days remained. Hours and days, and the Kingdom of Peace would become a reality. In hours and days he could turn his mind to his true mission, the resurrection of the Empire, the reunification of the lands of yore in the Faith.

The days and hours of the infidel were numbered. Those sons of the Evil One were doomed. The Dark One's long ascendancy was about to end.

Rising excitement made a new man of him. He became more outgoing. He bustled here and there, chattering, fussing, joking with the Invincibles. Meryem complained that he was destroying his sublime image.

He began to recognize landmarks seen years ago.

The bowl-shaped valley was nearby. And not a soul had challenged them. The angel had been right. And Nassef had been as competent as ever, slipping them past Royalist pickets as if they were an army of ghosts.

He laughed delightedly when he glimpsed the spires of the Shrines from the lip of the valley, standing like towers of silver in the moonlight.

The hour had come. The Kingdom was at hand. "Thank you, Yousif," he whispered. "You outfoxed yourself this time."

FOURTEEN
STOLEN DREAMS

To Haroun it seemed Al Rhemish hadn't changed at all. The dust, the filth, the vermin, the noise were all exactly as he recalled them. The heat was as savage as ever, reflecting in off the walls of the valley. Hawkers cried their wares through the press of tents. Women screeched at children and other women. Men made sullen by oppressive temperatures exploded violently when tempers collided. If there was any change at all, it was that there were fewer people than during his previous visit. That would change as Disharhun approached, he knew. And the tension would heighten as the capital became more crowded.

There was a malaise in the air now, a continuous low-grade aggravation which went beyond what one would expect. No one put it into words, but the appearance of the Wahlig of el Aswad, with his household and troops, had initiated a process yet to run its course: stirring guilt and shame amongst those who had done nothing to aid or support Yousif's long fight in the south. His presence reminded them, and they resented it. A pale shadow of fear, too, haunted the capital. The reality of the threat posed by El Murid could no longer be denied except by a willful closing of the eyes.

"And that's what they're doing," Radetic told Haroun. "Blinding themselves. It's the nature of Man to hope something will go away if it's ignored."

"Some of them act like it's our fault. We did everything we could. What more do they want?"

"That, too, is human nature. Man is a born villain, narrow, shortsighted, and ungrateful."

Haroun cocked an eye at his teacher, smiled sarcastically. "I've never heard you so sour, Megelin."

"I've learned some bitter lessons out here. And I fear they'll apply equally to the so-called civilized people back home."

"What's going on over there?" There was a stir around his father's tent. He spied men bearing the shields of the Royal Household.

"Let's find out."

They encountered Fuad near the tent. He looked puzzled.

"What is it?" Haroun asked.

"Ahmed. He's asked your father and Ali to be his guests tonight. With the King."

Radetic chuckled. "Surprised?"

"After the way they've ignored us since the first few nights, yes."

A chill trickled down Haroun's spine. His gaze swept the surrounding hills. Nightfall was not far off. Shadows were gathering. He had a sense of foreboding.

"Tell Yousif to keep his views to himself," Radetic suggested. "They're not socially acceptable right now. Aboud is old and slow and needs time to adjust to the loss of the southern desert."

"He'd get used to it faster if that idiot Ahmed would get out of the way."

"Maybe. Haroun, what's the matter?"

"I don't know. Something strange. Like this isn't any ordinary night coming on."

"Allegorical thought, no doubt. Beware your dreams tonight. Fuad, do tell the Wahlig not to get exercised. If he wants to make headway with Aboud he has to become acceptable company first."

"I'll tell him." Fuad departed wearing one of his most fearsome scowls.

"Come, Haroun. You can help with the papers."

Haroun's shoulders tightened. Radetic had no end of papers and notes, all totally disorganized. He could spend years getting them sorted—by which time another mountain would have collected.

He glanced at the hills again. They seemed unfriendly, almost cold.

Lalla was the pearl of Aboud's harem. Though she was a scant eighteen, and without benefit of marriage, she was the most powerful woman in Al Rhemish. The capital was drenched in a flood of songs praising her grace and beauty. Aboud was mad for her, a slave to her whim. There were rumors that he would make her a wife.

She had been a gift, years ago, from a minor Wahlig on the lost coast of the Sea of Kotsüm. She had not caught Aboud's attention till recently.

Aboud was an infatuated, silly, and proud child. He wasted few opportunities to flaunt delights only he should have known in their entirety, taunting his court with his favorite toy. Night after night he summoned her from his seraglio and had her dance before the assembled nobles.

Yousif gazed on her lithe form. He appreciated Lalla as much as did any man, but at that moment his thoughts were far away and fraught with guilt. His heart would not accept the conclusion of his reason. He could not shake despair over having abandoned his trust and ancestral home.

He and his son Ali were guests of Crown Prince Ahmed. Ahmed was the only member of the court not yet disgusted with his attempts to initiate a major campaign against the Disciple.

Yousif was restless. There was a wrongness afoot in Al Rhemish, though it was nothing he found concrete. The feeling had been growing all week, and tonight it was strong enough to make his skin crawl.

There was a wrongness, too, about Ahmed. Especially when he looked at Lalla. His lust lay naked in his eyes, but there was more. He seemed agitated, and could not restrain a wicked, greedy smile. Yousif feared that smile foreshadowed grief.

Lalla spun close, shaking her lithe, smooth young hips inches from his eyes.

His malaise lessened. When Lalla danced, even his cares soon faded. Her beauty had a narcotic quality.

How Ahmed stared! As though he had sampled those delights and become so addicted that he would kill to make them his own. Madness backlighted his gaze.

Nervousness had given Yousif a strange sensitivity to the undercurrents flowing around him. A paranoid sensitivity, he chided himself. Ahmed was not alone in staring. The faces of a dozen wild sons of the waste told him they would kill to possess the dancer.

He began to grow uneasy again. Even Lalla's melodious zils could not still his troubled heart completely. It had been a bad day. News had come from the south, at last, and it was not good.

El Murid had climbed the Horned Mountain. Something ominous had occurred there. A fire in the sky had been seen for a hundred miles. El Murid had come down decisive and determined. He had summoned the tribes to his banner, to help extirpate the Royalists' evil. And rumor said thousands were responding, inspired by the awesome display over the evil mountain.

There was also word that the Scourge of God had left his forces in the littoral. He had gathered the Invincibles and was on the move. The fox was loose in the henyard, and no one in Al Rhemish apparently cared.

A magical wall erected on foundations of willful blindness isolated the bowl valley containing Al Rhemish. Reality could not penetrate that rampart of wishful thinking. The Royalist overlords had retreated from the world and immersed themselves in their pleasures. Even the hardest, the most practical, the most pragmatic among them were becoming as dissolute as the Crown Prince.

Yousif was bewildered. He had known most of these men for decades. There were dark forces at work here—how else to explain what was happening? They seemed to have resigned themselves, were seizing what pleasure they could before the end.

But all was not lost. Any fool could see that. Here in the north there were enough loyal warriors to crush El Murid twice over.

Yousif cast a covert glance at his host. The Crown Prince was a sour note, a distinct off-pitch element in the festivities. Why had Ahmed insisted his remote southern cousins be his guests tonight? Why was he so nakedly excited and lustful?

Aboud could be pardoned his dissipations. He hadn't many years left, and was terrified of the Dark Lady. He was trying to recapture the ghost of his youth. But Ahmed, Ahmed had no excuse.

Yousif had polled the more hardheaded Royalist nobility. His brother wahligs agreed that Ahmed was a disaster in the making. He had assumed a dangerous influence over his father since Farid's death. His suggestions had resulted in several minor defeats by guerrillas operating near Al Rhemish. But those same hardheads would do nothing when Yousif suggested they take the initiative....

Kingdom and Crown were decomposing while yet alive. The stench of corruption filled the land. And no one would lift a hand to halt the process. The pity of it all was that Aboud was so much stronger than El Murid. A determined, decisive leader could destroy the Disciple easily.

His anger stirred his adrenaline. He swore. "He can be put down!"

His neighbors looked at him askance. They did that a lot. He'd earned a reputation as a single-minded boor of a country cousin already.

"Really, Yousif," Aboud admonished softly. "Not while Lalla is dancing."

Yousif's glance flicked from the King to his heir. Ahmed wore a wicked smile. A moment later he slipped quietly away.

Yousif wondered no more than a moment. Ringing zils and shimmering veils and flashes of satiny skin at last captured his undivided attention. Lalla was dancing just for him.

"Would you quit that?" Reskird snapped. "You're driving me crazy."

"Quit what?" Bragi asked, halting.

"Pacing. Back and forth, back and forth. Think you were ready to have a kid."

Haaken grunted agreement. "What's the matter?"

Bragi hadn't been conscious of his pacing. "I don't know. Nervous energy. This place gives me the creeps."

The mercenaries had pitched camp on the western wall of the bowl, separate from the rest of Al Rhemish, but not separate enough to suit the men. There were strong tensions between native and outsider. The Guildsmen mainly stayed to themselves and radiated contempt for the barbarism of Al Rhemish and its people.

Reskird said, "I heard we won't be here much longer. That they're going to pay us off and let us go."

"Can't be too soon for me," Haaken said.

Bragi sat down, but didn't stay seated long. In moments he was circling the fire again.

"There you go again," Reskird snarled.

"You're making *me* nervous," Haaken said. "Go for a walk or something."

Bragi paused. "Yeah. Maybe I will. Maybe I can find Haroun, see how he's doing. Haven't seen him since we got here."

"Good idea. Look out you don't have to save his ass again." Reskird and Haaken laughed.

Bragi scanned the star-limned hills, uncertain what he was seeking. The air had an odd feel, as though a storm were in the offing. "Yeah. That's what I'll do."

"Don't take too long," Haaken admonished. "We've got midnight guard."

Bragi hitched his pants and walked away, his pace brisk. He was out of camp in minutes, passing among the tents of pilgrims here for Disharhun. By the time he reached the permanent part of town his nervousness had dwindled. He became preoccupied with the problem of locating Haroun among people whose language he did not speak. He had no idea where the Wahlig had pitched camp.

His wanderings took him to the wall enclosing the Most Holy Mrazkim Shrines. He forgot his quest and became a simple sightseer. He hadn't been into town before. Even by night the alien architecture was bemusing.

Haroun could not sleep. Nor was he alone. All Al Rhemish was restless. Fuad had been sharpening his sword since sundown. Megelin paced constantly. Haroun was tired of the old man's nattering. Radetic's customary verbal precision was absent. He rambled through vast, unrelated territories. Nervous energy was building up, and could not discharge itself in any special direction.

The first startled cries gave purpose, provided relief at last. They burst from their tents into the moonlight. The compound was a-crawl with white-robed Invincibles.

"Where the hell did they come from?" Fuad demanded. "Altaf! Beloul! To me!"

"Megelin, what's happening?"

"El Murid is here, Haroun. Back for Disharhun, it would seem."

In minutes the fighting was general, and chaotic. Royalists and Invincibles fought where they found one another, the majority on both sides acting with no goal greater than surviving the attack of the foe.

"The King is dead!"

Ten thousand throats took up that demoralizing cry. Some Royalist partisans shed their arms and fled. The rot Yousif had sensed now betrayed how deeply it had gnawed the fiber of Royalist courage.

"Ahmed betrayed his father!"

That declaration of filial treachery was more demoralizing than news of the King's demise. How could a man fight when the heir of his sovereign was one of the enemy?

"Father is it, then," Haroun told Radetic.

"Absolutely." Megelin seemed bemused. "But he's…"

"I'll find him," Fuad growled. "He'll need me. He's got nobody but Ali to guard his back." He hit the nearest Invincibles like a windmill of razor steel.

"Fuad!" Radetic shouted. "Come back here! You can't do anything."

Fuad could hear nothing.

Haroun started after him. Radetic seized his arm. "Don't you be a fool too."

"Megelin—"

"No. That's stupid. Think. You're just heartbeats from the throne. After your father and Ali, who else? Nobody. Not Ahmed. Never Ahmed. Ahmed is a dead man no matter who wins. Nassef will want him living less than we do."

Haroun tried to break away. Radetic's grip held. "Guards," he called. "Stay with us." Several of the Wahlig's men obeyed. They had overheard Radetic. "There has to be a pretender, Haroun. Otherwise the Royalist cause is dead.

After you, Nassef has next claim."

White robes kept pouring into Al Rhemish. Confusion and panic ran before them. Twice Megelin and the guards beat off attacks. Radetic kept gathering Royalists.

A company of Invincibles appeared, hunting Yousif's family. They were determined. Radetic fought like a demon, revealing tricks of the sword seldom seen outside Rebsamen practice halls. His stubbornness inspired the men he had assembled. Haroun fought beside him, trying to win a minute's respite so he could employ his shaghûn's skills. The Invincibles gave him no chance. His companions began to falter.

Haroun tried to dig into his kit anyway. A swordtip buzzed past his ear. He fumbled the kit, lost it.

The Invincibles couldn't be stopped. He was going to die....

An unholy bellow slammed the belly of the night. Swinging his sword with both hands, Bragi Ragnarson hit the Invincibles from behind. In seconds half a dozen went down. Some scrambled away from his insanity. The northerner attacked those who remained, pounding through their sabers with his heavy sword.

They broke too. Haroun laughed hysterically. "Three times," he gasped to Megelin. "Three times!" He staggered toward Bragi. The northerner waved his sword and called the Invincibles cowards, daring them to come back. Haroun threw his arms around the big man. "I don't believe it," he gasped. "Not again."

Bragi stood there panting, watching the white robes. "I found you, eh? I've been hunting since sundown."

"Just in time. Just in time."

Bragi shuddered. "I didn't think that could happen to me. My father could go crazy when he wanted, but... what's going on? How did they get here? I better get back to camp." He was confused. His voice was plaintive.

Radetic said, "You can't get there from here, lad." There was heavy fighting on the slope below the mercenary encampment. "Stay here. Gamel. Find a Royal standard. Let's give our people a rallying point."

Radetic did his utmost, parlaying the Royal name, but the collapse continued. Al Rhemish was doomed. Even with the mercenaries making vigorous sallies from their encampment, the inertia of the rout could not be turned.

Haroun almost whined as he asked, "Megelin, how could Al Rhemish be overrun so easily? There are too many loyal men here."

"Most of whom ran for it right away," Radetic replied.

A group of youngsters came in led by a wounded officer. "Nobles' sons, sire," he said. "Take care...." And he collapsed.

Haroun stared down, bewildered. "Sire?" he whispered. "He called me sire."

"The word is spreading," Megelin said. "Look. The mercenaries are pulling out. Time we did too. You men. Round up whatever animals and provisions you can."

"Megelin—"

"No room to argue anymore, Haroun." Radetic told Bragi, "Watch him. Don't let him do anything silly." He spoke Trolledyngjan.

"I have to get back to my outfit," Ragnarson protested.

"Too late, son. Way too late." Radetic resumed arguing with Haroun.

Haroun gradually accepted Megelin's truth. Al Rhemish was lost—and with it his entire family. He had no one but Megelin and this strange northern youth. Angry, with hatred knotting his guts, he allowed Radetic to lead him into the night.

Ahmed waited among the dead, holding a limp, frightened Lalla. His personal guards surrounded him, duty-bound despite loathing him for his patricide and treason. A dozen Invincibles watched them, indifferent to the carnage.

Ahmed's heart ripped at him like some cruel monster trying to tear its way out of his chest. "I did it for you, Lalla. I did it for you."

The girl did not respond.

The Invincibles snapped to attention. A darkly clad, hard-eyed man strode in. The hem of his djaballah dragged through a pool of blood. He grunted disgustedly.

There was blood everywhere, on the walls, the floors, the furnishings, the bodies. The bodies were piled deep. More wore white than the bright colors favored by Royalists. Aboud would explode when he saw… Ahmed giggled. For a moment he had forgotten who had died first.

The newcomer asked a question Ahmed didn't catch. He had no attention to spare. Lalla was crying.

A hand closed on his shoulder. Pain lanced through his body. "Stop!" he whined.

"Get up." The newcomer squeezed harder. Ahmed's guards watched, indecisive.

"You can't do this. It's death to lay hands on the King." He reached for Lalla.

"Don't be a damned fool. You aren't King of anything. And you'll never be."

"Who are you?" Though frightened, Ahmed retained the Quesani arrogance.

"The Scourge of God. The man with whom you've been corresponding."

"Then you know I'm King. You agreed to help me take the throne."

Nassef smiled thinly. "So I did. But I didn't say I'd let you keep it." To the Invincibles he said, "Lock this fool up till we can deal with him."

Ahmed was stunned. "You promised…. Lalla…" He had betrayed his family and murdered his father so he could become King and possess Lalla. It had been her idea initially….

"I did promise you the woman, didn't I? Lock her in with him."

"My Lord!" Lalla protested. "No! I did everything you told me."

"Take them," Nassef said. He turned to a man who had followed him inside.

"Get this cleaned up before the Disciple gets here."

"No!" Ahmed shrieked. He stabbed the nearest Invincible, whirled, slashed at another. His bodyguards jumped in enthusiastically.

Ahmed faked a rush at Nassef. The Scourge of God stumbled, avoiding the expected blow. Ahmed swerved toward the exit. His guards followed. "After them!" Nassef bellowed. "Kill them. Kill them all." He faced Lalla. "Get her zils. Can't have her playing tricks on us too." He smiled cruelly. "Save her for me."

Haroun paused halfway up the eastern slope of the bowl, looked back. A third of Al Rhemish was aflame. Fighting persisted, but would not last long. On the far slope the mercenary camp was ablaze. Hawkwind had abandoned it to the Invincibles. "I'm sorry," he told Bragi. "You can catch up with them later, I guess."

"Yeah. I just wish my brother knew I'm all right."

Radetic said, "Let's don't waste time, Haroun. They'll be after us soon."

"Listen!" Bragi said. "Somebody's coming."

Hooves pounded toward them. Swords leapt out of scabbards.

"Hold it!" Haroun ordered. "They're not Invincibles."

Someone snarled, "It's Ahmed." Someone else cried, "Kill him!" Men surrounded the Crown Prince. Curses flew.

"Back off," Radetic snapped. "You don't know anything against him. The rumors could have been planted. Bring him here, Haroun. Let him tell his story." Privately, Radetic believed the worst.

Ahmed scarcely had time to admit his guilt. The party topped the ridge and came face to face with the enemy.

"It's El Murid!" Haroun cried. "Come on!"

The Disciple's bodyguards and household far outnumbered them, but the guards were scattered. The main party was dismounted, either seated or sleeping.

"Maybe there is a God after all," Radetic mused as he spurred his mount. One bloody stroke could turn the war around. Without El Murid there would be no movement.

With Bragi beside him, Haroun slashed through the Invincible pickets. He chopped down at unprotected noncombatant shoulders and heads. Women screamed. People scattered. Royalist war cries filled the night.

The Invincible bodyguards threw themselves at the Royalists with an insane fury. They valued their prophet more than their lives.

"Where are you, Little Devil?" Haroun shouted. "Come out and die, you coward."

Ahmed urged his mount up beside Haroun, opposite Bragi. He fought with an abandon no one would have believed possible an hour earlier.

A boy scampered across the rocks ahead of Haroun. He spurred his mount. Another horse hurtled in from one side, turning his attack. For an instant he looked into the eyes of a girl. He saw fire and iron, caught a glimpse of a soul that could be intimidated by nothing. And something more... then she was gone, dragging the boy toward safety. Haroun shifted his attention to a woman chasing the pair.

He was startled. He knew her. She was the Disciple's wife. Veilless again. He slashed. His blade found flesh. She cried out. Then he was past, wheeling, searching. The Disciple himself had to be somewhere nearby.

Something slammed into him. He felt no pain then, but knew he had been wounded. Bragi hacked at the Invincible responsible while Ahmed engaged another two. A fourth closed in. Haroun forgot the Disciple, fought for his life.

Five minutes passed. They seemed eternal. He heard Megelin shout in a voice filled with pain, rallying the Royalists, ordering a withdrawal. He wanted to overrule Radetic, to stand and fight. This chance dared not be wasted.... But he understood why Megelin wanted to go. Outnumbered, the Royalists were now getting the worst of it. Half were down. Most of the rest were wounded.

"Haroun!" Megelin cried. "Come on! It's over!"

Bragi brushed a sword aside, grabbed Haroun's reins. Haroun wobbled in his saddle. His wound was deeper than he suspected.

Though gravely injured, Radetic directed the withdrawal. "Capture some horses!" he snapped. "Some camels. Anything. We've got wounded with nothing to ride."

The Invincibles might have taken them then had they not been more interested in the welfare of their prophet and his family.

"Let's go. Let's go," Radetic grumbled. "You men. Help those two get onto their animals."

Haroun looked back once. The battleground was littered with dead and dying. The majority were followers of the Disciple. "Did we get him?" he croaked at Bragi. "Do you think we got him?"

"No," the northerner said. "We didn't."

"Damn! Damn damn damn!"

Bragi snorted wearily. "If he doesn't have a god on his side, he has a devil. Ride. They'll be after us as soon as they get themselves sorted out."

FIFTEEN
KING WITHOUT A THRONE

Twenty-one horses, twenty-three men, and eight camels made up the caravan. They straggled across a bleached-bone desert beneath a savage noonday sun. Only the most gravely wounded rode. Those afoot cursed and coerced the faltering beasts along the rocky, dusty, wind-whipped bottom of a dry wadi. Humiliation, despair, and the anticipation of death were their marching companions. Ahmed's treachery was an agony each man bore like a brand, but no man wore it more painfully than did Ahmed himself.

For each man only the will to resist, to survive long enough to avenge, remained. The kingdom had been lost, but its blood, its Crown, lived on and would be preserved against tomorrow.

These things didn't occur as discrete thoughts. The men were too weary. Determination was baked into their bones. Consciously they were preoccupied with the heat, with thirst, with exhaustion. In the short run only one thing mattered: taking another step.

The wadi dissolved into a badland of tent-sized boulders. "This is the place," Ahmed croaked.

"I forbid it," Haroun replied. "I'm King now. You deferred to me. I forbid it."

Ahmed gestured. Men took positions among the rocks. "God go with you, sire."

"Damn it."

"Haroun." Radetic's voice was half whisper, half groan. "Let the man die the death he chooses."

"He's right," Bragi said. He began to collect the remnants of water carried by those who would stay in ambush.

Haroun agonized. These men hardly knew him. It was not meant that he should leave them to die. "Ahmed—"

"Go, sire. Their dust draws close. We die for the Blood. By choice. Just go."

Bragi finished gathering the water. "Haroun, will you come on? Do I have to drag you?"

"All right. All right." He started walking.

There were six of them now, all but Megelin walking. Radetic rode, his guts slowly leaking onto his animal's back. Haroun led his horse. Bragi tried to keep the animals and three youngsters together.

I'm a king, Haroun told himself. A king. How can that be?

Ali was dead. Yousif was dead. Fuad was dead, as were his sons. Ahmed had chosen to die in atonement. Now there was only Haroun bin Yousif. After him, the Scourge of God.

He would not permit Nassef to take the kingdom.

It wasn't much of a kingdom, he reflected. And one he could claim only at the cost of fortunes in blood and tears. If he tried… He glanced back. There was no sign of the ambush. He sent Ahmed a grudging, silent salute.

In the final extremity, in the hour of crisis, Ahmed had shown more character than anyone expected. He had the *mafti al hazid* of old, the high death-pride that had made Ilkazar's legions stand fast even in the face of certain destruction.

The dust raised by the pursuit was close. Nassef himself was on the trail. No one else would press so hard.

Haroun saw Bragi stumble as he forced a recalcitrant camel into line. The youngsters were about done in. There was no hope left. Not if he tried to save the whole party.

"All or none," he told himself. "All or none." He thought he and Bragi could make it if they abandoned the others.

Carrion birds planed the air, patiently awaiting the death their presence guaranteed. Nassef needed but chase them to track his prey. Haroun swung his gaze to the ground ahead. "Step, step," he muttered again and again. Slowly, he coaxed Radetic's mount in the shadows at the bottom of another wadi. How far to the mountains? he wondered. Too far. Already his flesh strove to betray his will, to surrender to the inevitable.

A smile cracked his lips. They had gone after the Disciple like mad dogs, hadn't they? Almost got him, too. Almost got his wife. Almost captured the pearl of his seraglio, the daughter who would finally receive a name this Disharhun.

Her wide-eyed, wild look, struck over awe and determination, all overridden by hard determination to save her brother, haunted him still.

His smile widened. Meryem must have been hurt worse than he had thought. Nassef's pursuit was implacable and tireless, the relentless hunt of a man obsessed with a personal debt. He must be killing his men trying to catch up.

Haroun's wound, on the outside of his left arm, was shallow but painful. He was proud of it, carried it as a badge of courage.

Radetic groaned. Haroun glanced up at the old man. Poor Megelin. So pale, so shaky. He had come so far, in the pursuit of knowledge, and his heart had betrayed him. He should have gone home when his contract expired. But he had lost his affection to a family, and a place, and was about to pay the ultimate price for that indiscretion. Haroun bin Yousif had been forced to become a man and warrior within a matter of hours. Now he faced becoming a leader, a king. While lost in an unfamiliar desert, punished by heat and thirst, aided by one bewildered foreigner, with El Murid's jackals yapping at his heels.

He *would* survive! He *would* avenge his father and brothers, his uncle, and even his mother. And Megelin. Megelin most of all. Beloved Megelin, who had been more father than Yousif…

He paid little attention to his surroundings. He clung to the meandering wadi as long as its tendency was northward, toward the Kapenrung Mountains and the border of Hammad al Nakir. Bragi and the youngsters stumbled along behind, satisfied to follow his lead. Grudgingly, the wadi walls provided protection from the sun and wind.

Haroun's thoughts drifted to El Murid's daughter. What *was* it that he had seen in her face? Someday…

The fall of Al Rhemish would leave one vaguely palatable taste in the Royalist mouth. The Invincibles had been badly mauled. The Disciple would be unable to press his advantage quickly. The scattered loyalists might have time to regroup and counterattack. Ahmed's sacrifice would steel thousands of wavering hearts. It was the sort of gesture Hammad al Nakir loved.

Haroun tried to banish the heat and misery by dwelling on the larger picture. He considered the faithful. Some would scatter according to plans long ago formulated by his father and Radetic. If necessary they could regroup outside

Hammad al Nakir. The gold in the banks at Hellin Daimiel would finance their war of liberation.

If he accepted the challenge of fate, if he became their king, could he gather and wield them? Without Megelin? The old man would not last much longer....

Rationality deserted him when Megelin fell. The old foreigner meant everything to him. Yousif had given him life. Megelin had nurtured and loved him, and had sculpted him into the man he would become.

He tried to lift Megelin and found that the old man's heart had stopped. "Megelin. Not now. Don't give up now. We're almost there. Megelin! Don't die!" But even the command of a king cannot stay the Dark Lady.

Radetic's death was the final straw's weight. He could withhold his grief no longer. "Damn you!" he shouted toward the south. "Nassef! Micah al Rhami! You will die a thousand deaths for this. I will take a vengeance so cruel it will be remembered for a thousand years." He ranted on, madly. One remote, cool part of him told him he was making a fool of himself, but he couldn't stop.

His companions didn't care. They simply sat on rocks and waited for the vitriol to burn away. Bragi did try to comfort him momentarily, ineptly, recalling his own agony at his father's death.

Haroun's recovery began with a fit of self-loathing when he cursed Bragi for showing solicitude. The northerner withdrew, sat on a rock and ignored him. That hurt Haroun, exposing him to yet another level of pain. Was he insane, offending the only friend he had?

In a still moment he heard distant sounds of fighting. Men were selling their lives. He must not belittle their sacrifices. He had to go on and, if it came to that, had to let the desert claim him before he yielded to the Scourge of God.

Eyes still moist, he kissed his teacher's cooling cheeks. "I mourn, Megelin. This wasteland is no resting place for a don of the Rebsamen." Vulture shadows ghosted along the wadi walls. "But I have to leave you. You understand, don't you? You were always a student of necessity." He rose. "Bragi! Let's go. They'll be through the ambush in a few minutes." The sounds of fighting were diminishing already.

He pushed on, into the night, knowing darkness would not stop Nassef. Only the Dark Lady herself would stay the Scourge of God. The three youngsters grew progressively weaker. Horses halted and refused to go on. The camels grew increasingly balky. Bragi became fractious. He did not know how to handle the animals.

Haroun slaughtered the weakest horse, caught its hot blood, passed it around. Their water was gone. He prayed to no certain god for strength, for guidance, for a miracle. His future kingdom became confined to that narrow and perhaps endless passage of the desert.

Deep in the night, under a silver, uncaring moon, the wadi faded. If he paused to listen Haroun could hear men and animals in the distance. Nassef was gaining again.

Moments after he departed the wadi he halted, confused. Before him stood a strange old tower. He recognized the type. Ilkazar's emperors had erected hundreds to house local garrisons. Their ruins could be found wherever the Imperial legions had passed. He was baffled because he hadn't expected to encounter evidence of human habitation in the waste.

Bragi came up beside him. "What's that?"

A sad keening came from the tower.

Haroun shook his head. He glanced back. The boys had collapsed.

The keening came again.

"That's no animal," Bragi said.

"The wind?"

"Maybe it's a ghost."

Haroun reached out with his shaghûn's senses. Incompletely trained, attenuated by hunger and exhaustion, they told him nothing. "I don't get anything."

"Look!" A wan light illuminated a face behind an archer's embrasure.

"That's no ghost."

"Maybe we can get water."

"Could be a bandit hideout. Or a demon's lair. Or a sorcerer hiding from El Murid." But if the magical or supernatural lurked there, his shaghûn's senses should have warned him.

He listened. The sounds of horses and men hung just on the edge of hearing. "I'm going to investigate."

"Nassef is too close."

"I might find something. Water, at least."

"Yeah. Water."

"Let's go." It was hard to get moving again. His joints ached, his muscles begged for respite. His wound sent wires of pain crawling toward his shoulder. He was afraid it would fester. Somehow, he had to elude Nassef long enough to cleanse and cauterize it.

Bragi cuffed horses, camels, and boys and got them moving again. Battered sword in hand, Haroun approached the tower, step by leaden-footed step. Once around the tower he stalked, seeking an entrance.

"Find anything?" Bragi asked.

"No."

"What are you going to do?"

"Look again. You stay here."

"What about Nassef?"

"I won't be long." He went around the tower again. And this time he found a black cavity at its base, facing south. He was perplexed. The opening hadn't been there before, yet he could sense nothing magical. Was he so weak his shaghûn's senses had fled him completely?

The keening resumed. It stirred images of a whole people grieving. It wakened a surge of emotion, of empathy.

Haroun gasped.

In the doorway stood a child, or imp, or cherub, naked, hands on hips, grinning impudently. It demanded, "Candidate, what do you fear?"

Though conventional images formed in immediate response, Haroun suspected the imp meant something deeper, was trying to evoke the nightshapes that lurked in the deeps of souls. Snakes, spiders, El Murid, and the Scourge of God could be handled with boot heels and blades. The devils of the soul were more formidable.

Startled and puzzled, he could think of no appropriate reply.

He glanced at his companions. They had fallen asleep where they had stopped. Even the animals had surrendered to exhaustion. He listened. The pursuit seemed no closer.

The imp grinned again, shrugged, stepped backward, vanished. Haroun was baffled. That was sorcery, yet his shaghûn's senses hadn't detected a thing. He started to follow the imp....

Things exploded from the doorway. The first was a blinking, puzzled lion which, pausing to assess its situation, died under Haroun's blade. Then came vampire bats that ripped and tore and let his blood a dozen times before he finished the last. Then came snakes and scorpions and spiders.

He never considered flight. He defeated each wave by summoning reserves of energy, anger, and courage he didn't know he possessed.

Then came the nebulous thing, the real enemy, the dark shifting form on which he painted his own faces of horror. It flung parts of itself to the sides, to strike from behind. With it came scents and whispers of evil that tore at already tortured nerves.

He stepped back, raised his torn left arm to shield himself. With a cackling, wicked roar the thing doubled in size. Haroun swung wildly. His blade encountered nothing, yet elicited a screech of pain.

Weariness threatened to drag him down. Pain became unbearable. He knew he was doomed. Yet he persisted. The screech convinced him his sole hope was attack. He stumbled forward, sword cleaving Night in wild strokes.

Darkness took him into its gentle arms. For a moment he thought he saw a beautiful, weeping woman approaching, and knew he had glimpsed the face of Death. There was one instant of trepidation and reluctance as he remembered the Scourge of God close behind him, then nothing.

He wakened to warmth and daylight and a sense of well-being. A bent old man stood over him, examining his injuries. Imp-Child watched from a doorway.

He was inside the tower. Its interior was no ruin. He tried to rise.

The old man restrained him. "Let me finish." Haroun found his accent difficult. Sad tones crowded his reassuring smile.

"What time is it? How long have I been here?"

"Three days. You needed the rest."

Haroun surged up. The old man pressed down on his chest with all the weight of the world.

"My people—"

"All safe and well. Resting and healing at the foot of the tower. Your enemies won't find them. Child!"

Imp-Child brought a copper mirror with a surface clouded by age. "Stare into your own eyes," the old man said. He did something strange with his fingers.

At first Haroun was too shaken by changes in his appearance to see anything else. Youth had fled him. The brown of his skin had deepened. His thin, long face had become an emaciated death's head. His hawkish nose had become more shadowed and pronounced. His eyes looked haunted. Anger and pain had etched deep furrows across his forehead.

Then he began to discern the hunters deep in the pools of his eyes. The Scourge of God and two score Invincibles followed a trail implacably.

There was something wrong. Their eyes blazed with madness. They were within a mile of the tower, but never glanced its way.

"They're following their own trail around the stronghold," the old man said. He giggled crazily.

Haroun glanced at him and surprised a malice which instantly transformed into sorrow. "Four hundred winters of despair," his savior said in a voice gone sepulchral. "And finally you've come. I hope it's you. Pray, be the One. This charge has grown tedious. I long for the embrace of the Dark Woman."

Haroun felt he was an audience of one. There was something subtly unconvincing about this old man. "Where am I?" he demanded.

"The place has no name. A watchtower. It had a number once, but I've forgotten it."

"Who are you?" The old man seemed not to hear. "Why are you helping me? *If* you're helping."

"Because you are of the Blood. Because you are the Candidate."

Haroun frowned. "Candidate? For what?"

"For the Invisible Crown."

Each answer left Haroun more baffled. "Why are you hiding out here? This is the least explored part of Hammad al Nakir." The inquisitiveness and skepticism he had acquired from Radetic kept him from accepting the old man's answers. "You'd better tell me a story, old man. A good one. This is all crap and wasted time. I should be heading for the border."

The old man looked surprised and disappointed. "I am the son of Ethrian of Ilkazar, the wise man who predicted the Fall. He was unable to avert that disaster. During the destruction of the Imperial City, hoping to revivify the Empire one day, he smuggled myself and the symbols of Imperial power through the besiegers' lines. He sent me here under a compulsion to await the coming of a suitable Imperial heir. Someone Fate would bring here. Someone of the Blood. I am to test him, and, if he is worthy, to invest him with the Imperial power. My father meant to join me, but he was killed. I've been trapped here for four centuries. Never before has a candidate come."

The story dovetailed with known history and old legend. But when, his head swimming with visions of armies rallying to his Imperial standard, Haroun asked specific questions and received only evasions in reply, his credulity faded. "Get serious, old-timer. You're dodging like a hare chased by a fennec. Give me straight answers or go away."

The old man reddened. He cursed, and stalked out of the room.

Imp-Child giggled, winked at Haroun, followed.

Haroun stared at the bronze mirror, watching Nassef follow an endless trail. He wanted to go down, collect Bragi and move on. Instead, he fell asleep.

The old man returned that night. "Come with me," he said. Puzzled, Haroun followed him to the tower's parapet, which was spectral in the moonlight. He watched distant manshapes doggedly pursue a circular trail.

A milky globe rested atop a tripod standing at the parapet's center. It glowed softly. "Look into this," the old man said.

Haroun looked. And saw the past. He watched his father, brother, uncle, and King Aboud die brave deaths. Aboud fought like the lion he had been as a young man. He watched his mother and sisters die. He watched the confrontation between Ahmed and Nassef. He could not turn away, though each second was an eternity of torture. Something compelled him to study Nassef in action.

The scene changed. He recognized the desert near the ruins of Ilkazar. A horde of horsemen milled nearby.

"Those are Royalists," the old man said. "They began gathering when news spread from Al Rhemish." Flick. A change of time. "Earlier today. These are El Murid's men, commanded by Karim and el-Kader, who on their own initiative followed Nassef and the Disciple."

The enemy spied the Royalist host. They charged. The Royalists scattered like chaff before the wind. In minutes there remained no foundation upon which the Royalist cause could be rebuilt. Haroun sighed. The arrangements his father and Megelin had made, for camps beyond the border, would have to serve to rally the cause.

Haroun divined a bleak future. Exile. Warfare. The constant threat of the Harish kill dagger.

The old man crooned over the globe and showed him what it might be like. Endless flight and fear. Frequent despair. He shuddered at the prospects.

Then the old man said, "But that need not be." Flick, flick, flick. "Here. Here. Here. We can reach back. A moment of blindness. A strayed swordstroke. A captain's horse stumbling at an inopportune moment. Little things can shift the course of history."

"You can do that?"

"If you wish." The battle before the ruins reappeared. "Here. An order mis-interpreted."

"That's too easy," Haroun muttered, though he was not sure why. "But tempting." Was it something Megelin had taught him? "What's the price?" There would be a price. Nothing was free. The more desirable it became, the cruder the cost. It would be more bitter than the price he had paid already.

A childhood memory surfaced. At four he had broken a glass mirror belonging to his mother. His father had had it imported from Hellin Daimiel. He had spent a fortune acquiring it. Haroun's whispered plea to the unseen, then, had been, "Please, make it didn't happen."

In a way, that was what magic was all about. Putting off payments by taking the apparently free route, the characterless route, the easy way. But there were traps and ambushes along that track, cunningly hidden and all unpleasant.

Ahmed had tried the easy way. Ahmed was dead and dishonored. Generations would curse his name.

The old man did not answer his question. Haroun stared him in the eye. "No. The past is done and dead. Let it lie." But it hurt to say that.

The old man smiled. Haroun thought the smile guileful, as though the man had gotten the answer he wanted.

"Nor will I change the present," Haroun said. "I'll make my own future, for good or ill."

"Excellent. Then on to the tests."

"Tests?"

"Of course. I told you the Candidate must be tested. For courage, for wisdom, for… You'll understand in time. My father was determined that there be no more kings like the Golmune Emperors. Come with me."

Haroun wondered what the old man's real stake was. His story became increasingly unconvincing. He seemed, deliberately, to be fostering the fragile, probably futile dream of a Royalist return. And certainly was pushing the fantasy of a resurrected Empire. *That* insanity could be left to El Murid.

Several levels down, Imp-Child lighted candles and stoked up a fire. The old man settled himself on a worn chalcedony throne. Haroun faced him across a dusty table. Atop the table lay three purple pillows. On those rested a bronze sword, a robe of ermine, and, to the eye, nothing. But something heavy had crushed the third pillow deeply. The sword was green with verdigris. The ermine had been the home of generations of moths.

"We begin," the old man said. "Take up the sword."

Puzzled, Haroun grasped the worn hilt.

"This is the sword Ashkerion, forged by Fallentin the Smith, which bought the victory celebrated at Sebil el Selib. The man who bears this blade needs fear no enemy. It defends against all attack. It's always victorious."

Though Haroun had heard of the sword Ashkerion, there was no proof it had existed. He recalled that Fallentin was said to have cast the blade into the sea after securing the throne. He had feared it, for it had developed a will of its own. He thought it might deliver itself into the hands of an enemy.

Haroun let go. "No. Ashkerion had a treacherous reputation. And a man could grow too dependent on a weapon like that. He could grow too arrogant in his power." He envisioned Megelin nodding. Megelin would say something like that.

"Pretty speech," Imp-Child grumbled.

The old man was startled. "You reject the sword? But you have to take it."

"No."

"Take the robe, then. Take up the robe and the authority it represents."

Haroun remained unconvinced that this man had waited four hundred years to crown a new emperor. He suspected motives unrelated to those proclaimed. He could not fathom what they might be, though.

Would it hurt to humor the fellow? That might lead him nearer the truth.

He slung the ratty ermine across his shoulders.

Imp-Child squealed delightedly. "It didn't turn to dust! He *is* the One."

The old man was less exuberant. "The Crown, then," he said. "The Invisible Crown that will fit none but the One. The Crown so heavy only a man determined to fulfill its obligations can lift it. Take it up, Haroun."

Haroun lingered over the third pillow, intimidated by the old man's statement. Finally, he reacted. His fingers touched something his eyes denied. He tried lifting it. It yielded only slightly, slipping sideways. Its weight was astonishing.

"You have reservations," the old man said. "The Crown can tell if you're not wholly committed to people and empire."

"No," Haroun said. "I don't trust you."

Which was true. But the old man was right, too. Haroun faced a tough decision. Was he prepared to pay the dreadful price demanded of a king in exile? He had been too busy staying alive to face that question.

"A king *must* be responsible," the old man said. "He *is* his people and kingdom. Kings are made to put the burden upon."

Not the best argument to sway a wavering youth, surely.

Haroun surrendered. Not to that old man's dream, but to his own. To a dream his father and Megelin Radetic had shaped.

He acknowledged himself King in Hammad al Nakir.

It meant guerrilla camps, grim deeds, and murder done to little apparent purpose, but always with a hope that he would be moving toward peace, unity, and restoration.

The vision both depressed and excited him.

He lifted the crown again. This time it rose as lightly as a wisp of cotton.

"It fits!" Imp-Child squealed, and danced a wild jig.

Haroun snugged the crown upon his head. It bore down so hard he staggered. It suddenly became as light as a silver circlet, then as tenuous as a forgotten obligation.

He had a feeling it would permit no forgetting. He had sold his freedom for a dream.

The old man said, "All men who have an interest in the affairs of Hammad al Nakir, be they friend or foe, now know that a King has been crowned for Ilkazar."

"The King Without a Throne," Imp-Child intoned. "The Lord in Shadow."

Haroun *felt* the knowledge of himself leak into a hundred minds. He felt the rage swell in El Murid and his captains, felt the elation blossom in Royalist commanders riding hard with despair running at their stirrups. Nowhere did he sense a rejection of his right.

The moment faded. The contact died.

"You refused Ashkerion," the old man said. "Beware, then. Turn your back on no man. Choose your successor wisely, and before you yourself depart this pale. Otherwise the Crown will go down with you, and be forgotten again. And I will be recalled from the darkness, to await another Candidate."

Haroun glanced at the old bronze sword. He reached—then drew back. As if sensing final rejection, the blade disappeared. Eyes wide, Haroun turned to the old man.

The alleged son of Ethrian the Wise had vanished too. Only dusty bones sat on the chalcedony throne.

Imp-Child considered him gravely. "Thank you. For the old man's freedom. For mine. Take your people away now. Your pursuers won't see you go."

There was a flash and a pop. When Haroun's senses cleared he found himself alone with bones and dust and three empty pillows.

A hint of dawn rosed the sills of the windows. For a moment he wondered if his visit hadn't been a hallucination.

But no. It had been real. He had healed. He wore a ragged ermine mantle, which he removed. And he felt driven to reclaim the usurped throne he'd never seen.

It was a need he would do anything to fulfill.

He went down dusty stairs and out a doorway which disappeared behind him. Looking north, he saw the dawn-tinted, snow-capped peaks of the Kapenrung Mountains. One day. Maybe two. He surveyed his companions. Bragi, the boys, and all the animals were in a deep sleep beside a pool of water. They all looked healthier than when last he had seen them.

On a distant ridgeline a band of horsemen paused to study the land ahead, then stumbled forward along a trail which had no end.

"Wake up, Bragi. Time to get moving."

The old man stepped from behind the chalcedony throne. He carried a huge cornucopia. He stuffed its bell with pillows, bones, and such. He muttered to himself while he worked.

"The stage is set. The struggle will last a generation."

He whipped around the throne, dragged a squawking Imp-Child from hiding.

"Crafty little wretch. Thought I'd forget you, eh?" He booted the imp into the horn's bell. It tried to scramble out. He grunted as he strained to overcome it. "In, damn it! In!" The cherub squealed piteously and popped out of sight.

The old man leaned against the windowsill and watched the fugitives straggle away. He chuckled malevolently. "Now for Nassef," he said, and crooked a finger at the riders in the hills.

"What happened?" Bragi asked. "It seemed like I dreamed for days."

"I'm not sure," Haroun replied. He told what he could recall. "But I don't know if it was real. I already feel tired again."

They paused atop a ridgeline and looked back. There was no sign of a watchtower.

Haroun shrugged. "Real or not, we have to go on." He seemed to feel a heavy weight atop his head. He glared at the mountains before them, started forward, grimly determined.

With Mercy
Toward None

Contents

ONE
THE DISCIPLE

The moon splashed silver on the waste. The scrubby desert bushes looked like djinn squatting motionless, casting long shadows. There was no breeze. The scents of animals and men long unwashed hung heavy on the air. Though the raiders were still, waiting, their breathing and fidgeting drowned the scattered sounds of the night.

Micah al Rhami, called El Murid, the Disciple, concluded his prayer and dismissed his captains. His brother-in-law, Nassef, whom he had given the title Scourge of God, rode to the ridgeline a quarter-mile away. Beyond lay Al Rhemish, capital of the desert kingdom Hammad al Nakir, site of the Most Holy Mrazkim Shrines, the center of the desert religion.

Micah eased his mount nearer that of his wife Meryem. "The moment is at hand. After so long. I can't believe it."

For twelve years he had battled the minions of the Evil One. For twelve years he had struggled to reshape and rekindle the faith of the people of Hammad al Nakir. Time and again the shadow had forestalled foundation of his Kingdom of Peace. Yet he had persevered in his God-given mission. And here he was, on the brink of triumph.

Meryem squeezed his hand. "Don't be afraid. The Lord is with us."

He lied, "I'm not afraid." In truth, he was terrified. Four years earlier, at Wadi el Kuf, the Royalists had slain two-thirds of his followers. He and Nassef had survived only by cowering in a fox den for days, poisoning themselves with their own urine to stave off thirst, while he battled the agony of a broken arm. The pain and terror and exhaustion had branded themselves on his soul. He still sweated cold when he recalled Wadi el Kuf.

"The Lord is with us," Meryem said again. "I saw his angel."

"You did?" He was startled. No one else ever saw the angel who had chosen him Instrument of the Lord in this struggle for Truth.

"Crossing the moon a few minutes ago, riding a winged horse, just the way you described him."

"The Lord was with us at el Aswad," he said, fighting bitterness. Just months earlier, while besieging the fortress of his most savage enemy, Yousif, the Wahlig of el Aswad, he had fallen victim to a shaghûn's curse. The Wahlig's own son, Haroun, had cast a spell of pain. He could not shake it because a prime tenet of his movement was total abjuration of sorcery.

"The children saw him too, Micah."

The Disciple glanced at his offspring. His son Sidi nodded, as always determinedly unimpressed. But his daughter, who yet bore no name, still had awe sparkling in her eyes. "He's up there, Father. We can't fail."

El Murid's nerves settled some. The angel had promised to help, but he had doubted.... He doubted. The very Champion of the Lord, and he doubted. The shadow kept insinuating itself into his heart. "Just a few days, little one, and you'll have your name."

The Disciple had come to Al Rhemish once before, long ago, when the girl was but an infant. He had meant to proclaim the Lord's Word during the High Holy Days of Disharhun, and to christen his daughter on Mashad, the most important Holy Day. The minions of the Dark One, the Royalists who ruled Hammad al Nakir, had accused him falsely of assaulting Yousif's son, Haroun. He had been condemned to exile. Meryem had sworn that her daughter would bear no name till it could be given on another Mashad, in Most Holy Mrazkim Shrines liberated from the heretic.

Disharhun was but days away.

"Thank you, Papa. I think Uncle Nassef is coming."

"So he is."

Nassef swung in beside El Murid, thigh to thigh. Thus it had been from the beginning. Meryem and Nassef had been his first converts—though Nassef seemed more ambitious than dedicated to a dream.

"Lot of them down there," Nassef said.

"We expected that. Disharhun is close. You heard from your agents?" Nassef deserved his title. His tactics were innovative, his fighting savage, and his espionage activities cunning. He had agents in the Royal Tent itself.

"Uhm." Nassef spread a rolled parchment map. "We're here, on the eastern rim." The capital lay at the center of a large bowl-like valley. "King Aboud's people are camped in no special order. They aren't suspicious. All the nobility have gathered at the King's quarters tonight. Our agents will attack when we do. The serpent should lose its head in the first breath of battle."

The Disciple squinted in the moonlight. "These things you have marked? What are they?"

"That's Hawkwind's camp on the far side." The Disciple shuddered. The mercenary Hawkwind had commanded enemy forces at Wadi el Kuf. His name stirred an almost pathological fear. "This by the Royal Compound is Yousif's camp. I thought both deserved special attention."

"Indeed. Catch me that brat of Yousif's. I want him to take his curse off me."

"Without fail, Lord. I'm assigning an entire company to the Wahlig's camp. None will escape."

"Meryem says she saw my angel. The children did too. He is with us tonight, Nassef."

The Scourge of God eyed him uncertainly. His faith, the Disciple suspected, was entirely of the lip. "Then we can't fail, can we?" Nassef gripped his shoulder momentarily. "Soon, Micah. Soon."

"Go, then. Begin."

"I'll send a messenger when we take the Shrines."

The sounds of battle reflected off the walls of the valley. They could not be heard outside. The voices of nightbirds were louder. One had to go to the rim to hear fighting. El Murid stood there staring at the soft glow of the amulet he wore on his left wrist. His angel had given it to him long ago. With it he could call down lightning from a cloudless sky. He was wondering if he would have to aid Nassef with its power.

Little was visible from his vantage. Only a few fires speckled the soupy darkness below. "How do you think it's going?" he asked Meryem. "I wish Nassef would send a messenger." He was frightened. This was a long chance taken on one pass of the dice. The enemy was vastly more powerful. "Maybe I should go down."

"Nassef is too busy to waste men reassuring us." Meryem watched the sky. War she had seen before, often. Her husband's angel, never. Till tonight she'd never entirely believed.

The Disciple grew increasingly uneasy, becoming convinced the battle was going badly. Each time he rode with his warriors something went wrong.... Well, not every time. Way back, when his daughter was an infant, he and Nassef had overrun Sebil el Selib in a night attack not unlike this. Sebil el Selib boasted the most important religious center outside Al Rhemish. From that victory all else had grown.

"Come relax," Meryem said. "You can't do anything here but upset yourself." She led him back through his white-robed Invincible bodyguards, to a mass of boulders where his household waited. Some were sleeping.

How could they? They might have to run at any moment.... He snorted. They slept now because they knew they would be in flight a long time if the battle went badly.

He, Meryem, and Sidi dismounted. His daughter rode off to inspect the pickets. "She's got the el Habib blood," he told Meryem. "Only twelve and already she's a little Nassef."

Meryem settled on a pallet provided by a servant. "Sit with me. Rest. Sidi, be a dear and see if Althafa made that lemon water." Meryem snuggled against her husband. "Chilly tonight."

His nerves had steadied. He smiled. "What would I do without you? Look. The bowl is starting to glow." He tried to rise. Meryem pulled him down.

"Relax. You hovering won't speed things. How do you feel?"

"Feel?"

"Any pain?"

"Not much. A few aches."

"Good. I don't like Esmat drugging you."

If there was anything he disliked about Meryem, it was her nagging about his physician. This time he ignored her. "Give me a kiss."

"Here? People will see."

"I'm the Disciple. I can do what I want." He snickered.

"Beast." She kissed him, sneezed. "Your beard. I wonder what's keeping Sidi?"

"Probably waiting for the lemon water to be made."

"Althafa is a lazy slut. I'll go see."

El Murid leaned back. "Don't dawdle." He closed his eyes and, to his surprise, felt sleep stealing up.

Screams startled him awake. Where?… How long had he dozed? A strong glow from the valley now…. Shouts. Cries of fear. Charging horsemen limned against the glow, like demons storming from the fires of Hell, swords slashing….

He staggered to his feet, sleep-fuddled, trying to recall where he had left his sword. "Meryem! Sidi! Where are you?"

Must be fifty of the enemy. Coming straight at him. The Invincibles were too scattered to stop them. Already they were slaughtering his household.

The old terror seized him. He could think of nothing but flight. But there was no flying, as there had been none after Wadi el Kuf. He could not outrun a horseman. He had to hide….

A child ran toward him, crying. "Sidi!" he bellowed, fear forgotten.

A horseman swerved toward the boy. Another horse flashed in from the side. "Girl! You fool," El Murid breathed as his daughter blocked the enemy rider. She paused an instant, face to face, while Sidi raced for the rocks.

"Meryem!" His wife was running through the thick of it, chasing Sidi. The rider slid past the girl, slashed. Meryem cried out, stumbled, fell, began dragging herself toward the rocks.

"No!" With no better weapon at hand, El Murid hurled a stone. It missed. But for an instant Meryem's attacker looked his way.

"Haroun bin Yousif!" He swore. Then, "But who else?" His old enemies were always close. Yousif's family were the Evil One's leading champions. This youth had begun doing him evil at age six, when he had caused a horse to throw him. He had broken an ankle in the fall. It pained him still.

His amulet flared, bidding him call down the lightning and end this persistent plague.

The Invincibles beset Haroun and his henchmen. El Murid lost track of the action. It drifted away as the Invincibles regained their composure. They outnumbered the attackers considerably. A half-dozen remained around the Disciple and his wife.

He clutched Meryem to him, ignoring the blood wetting his clothing. He thought her gone till she squeaked, "I did it this time, didn't I?"

Startled, he laughed through his tears. "Yes. You did. Esmat! Where are you, Esmat?" He grabbed an Invincible. "Get the physician. Now!"

They found Esmat cowering in the shadow of an overhang, behind a pile of baggage, and dragged him forth. They were not gentle. They flung him down at the Disciple's feet.

"Esmat, Meryem is hurt. One of those hellspawn…. Fix her up, Esmat."

"Lord, I…."

"Esmat, be still. Do what you're told." El Murid's voice was hard and cold. The physician got hold of himself, turned to Meryem. He was closer to his master than any man but the Scourge of God. Closer, in many ways. His master might collapse if he lost his wife. El Murid's faith, huge as it was, was not sufficient to keep him going.

Nassef rode up to where his brother-in-law paced. "We've won, Lord!" he enthused. "We've taken Al Rhemish. We've occupied the Mrazkim Shrines. They outnumbered us ten to one, but panic hit them like a plague. Even the mercenaries ran." Nassef glanced at the moon as though wondering if some high night rider hadn't stirred the panic on behalf of his chosen instrument. He shivered. He abhorred the supernatural. "Micah, will you stand still?"

"Huh?" The Disciple noticed Nassef for the first time. "What's that?"

The Scourge of God dismounted. He was a lean, hard, darkly handsome man of thirty who bore the scars of many battles. He was a general who rode at the head of a charge. "What's the matter, Micah? Damn it, stand still and talk to me."

"They attacked us."

"Here?"

"The Wahlig's brat. Haroun. And the foreigner, Megelin Radetic. They knew exactly where to come." El Murid gestured, indicating the casualties. "Sixty-two dead, Nassef. Good people. Some were with us from the beginning."

"Fortune is a fickle bitch, Micah. They fled, and by chance stumbled onto you. Unpleasant, but these accidents happen in war."

"There are no accidents, Nassef. The Lord and the shadow contend, and we move at their behest. They tried to kill Sidi. Meryem...." He broke into tears. "What will I do without her, Nassef? She is my strength. My rock. Why does the Lord demand such sacrifices?"

Nassef wasn't listening. He was gone, seeking his sister. His stride was strong and his voice angry. The Disciple stumbled after him.

Meryem was conscious. She smiled weakly, but did not say anything. The physician shook while Nassef questioned him. The Scourge of God had a quick temper and grim reputation. El Murid knelt, took his wife's hand. Tears filled his eyes.

"Not so bad," Nassef said. "I've seen many a man survive worse." He patted his sister's shoulder. She flinched. She had refused Esmat's painkillers. "You'll be up for the girl's naming, little sister." His hand settled on the Disciple's shoulder, gripping so tightly El Murid almost cried out. "They will pay for this, brother. I promise." He beckoned an Invincible. "Find Hadj." Hadj was El Murid's chief bodyguard. "I'll give him a chance to rectify his lapse."

The Invincible gaped.

"Now, man." Nassef's voice was low, but so hard the warrior ran. Nassef said, "We lost a lot of men. Won't be able to follow through. Wish I could go after the mercenaries. Micah, go ahead into the city. The Shrines and Royal

Compound should be cleaned by the time you get there."

"What're you going to do?"

"Go after Haroun and Megelin Radetic. They're all that's left of the Wahlig's family."

"King Aboud and Prince Ahmed?"

"Ahmed killed Aboud." Nassef chuckled. "He was my creature. Was he ever upset when I wouldn't let him become king."

The Disciple smelled the ambition hidden behind Nassef's gloating. Nassef wasn't a true believer. He served Nassef alone. He was dangerous—and indispensable. He had no peer on the battlefield, save perhaps Sir Tury Hawkwind. And that mercenary captain no longer had an employer.

"Must you go?"

"I want to do this myself." Again the wicked chuckle.

El Murid tried to argue. He did not want to be alone. If Meryem died....

His son and daughter arrived during the exchange. Sidi looked bored. The girl was angry and hard. She was so like her uncle, yet had something more, an empathy absent in Nassef. Nassef recognized no limitations or feelings he did not experience himself. She held her father's hand, saying nothing. In moments he felt better, almost as if Esmat had given him a potion.

He realized that he hadn't needed Esmat's painkillers tonight. Stress usually aggravated his old injuries and the curse of that beast Haroun.

The Wahlig wasn't satisfied keeping the movement bottled up in Sebil el Selib for a decade, he had to train his whelps in sorcery as well. The kingdom would be freed of that heresy! Soon, for tonight the Kingdom of Peace had undergone its final birth agonies.

He looked at Meryem, bravely trying to bear up, and wondered if the price of heaven were not too steep. "Nassef?"

But Nassef was gone already, leading most of the bodyguard out after the Wahlig's brat. Tonight the boy had become the last Quesani pretender to Hammad al Nakir's Peacock Throne. Without him the Evil One's Royalist lackeys would be left without a rallying point.

A dark, angry, vengeful sore festered in the Disciple's heart, though love and forgiveness were the soul of his message to the Chosen. The riders clattered and rattled and creaked into the night. "Good luck," El Murid breathed, though he suspected that Nassef was not motivated by revenge alone.

His daughter squeezed his hand, rested her forehead against his chest. "Mother will be all right, won't she?"

"Of course she will. Of course." He sped a silent prayer up into the night.

Two
THE FUGITIVES

The desert smouldered like the forges of Hell, the sun hammering the waste with sledges of heat. The barrens flung the heat back in fiery defiance, shimmered with phantoms of old oceans. Charcoal-indigo islands reared in the north, the Kapenrung Mountains standing tall, forming reality's distant shoreline. Mirages and ifrit wind-devils pranced the intervening miles. There was little breeze, and no sound save that made by the animals and five youths stumbling toward the high country. There were no odors save their own. Heat and the dull ache of exhaustion were the only sensations they knew.

Haroun spotted a pool of shade in the solar lee of a sedimentary upthrust protruding from a slope of bare ochre earth and loose flat stones like the stern of some giant vessel sliding slowly into a devouring wave. A dry watercourse snaked around its foot. In the distance, four spires of orange-red rock stood like the chimneys of a burned and plundered city. Their skirts wore dots of sagey green, suggesting the occasional kiss of rain.

"We'll rest there." Haroun indicated the shadow. His companions did not lift their eyes.

They went on, tiny figures against the immensity of the waste, Haroun leading, three boys straggling in his footsteps, a mercenary named Bragi Ragnarson in the rear, struggling continuously with animals who wanted to lie down and die.

Behind somewhere, stuck to their trail like a beast of nightmare, came the Scourge of God.

They stumbled into the shadow, onto ground as yet unscorched by the wrath of the sun, and collapsed, oblivious of their beds of edged and pointed stones. After half an hour, during which his mind meandered in and out of sleep, flitting through a hundred unrelated images, Haroun levered himself up. "Might be water under that sand down there."

Ragnarson grunted. Their companions—the oldest was twelve—did not bestir themselves.

"How much water left?"

"Maybe two quarts. Not enough."

"We'll get to the mountains tomorrow. Be plenty of water there."

"You said that yesterday. And the day before. Maybe you're going around in circles."

Haroun was desert-born. He could navigate a straight course. Yet he was afraid Bragi was right. The mountains seemed no closer than yesterday. It was a strange land, this northern corner of the desert. It was as barren as teeth in an old skull, and haunted by shadows and memories of darker days. There might be things, dark forces, leading them astray. This strip, under the eyes of the Kapenrungs, was shunned by the most daring northern tribes.

"That tower where we ran into the old wizard...."

"Where you ran into a wizard," Ragnarson corrected. "I never saw anything except maybe a ghost." The young mercenary seemed more vacant, more distant than their straits would command.

"What's the matter?" Haroun asked.

"Worried about my brother."

Haroun chuckled, a pale, tentative, strained excuse for laughter. "He's better off than we are. Hawkwind is on a known road. And nobody will try to stop him."

"Be nice to know if Haaken is all right, though. Be nice if he knew I was all right." The attack on Al Rhemish had caught Bragi away from his camp, forcing him to throw in his lot with Haroun.

"How old are you?" Haroun had known the mercenary several months, but could not recall. A lot of small memories had vanished during their flight. His mind retained only the tools of survival. Maybe details would surface once he reached sanctuary.

"Seventeen. About a month older than Haaken. He's not really my brother. My father found him where somebody left him in the forest." Ragnarson rambled on, trying to articulate his longing for his distant northern homeland. Haroun, who had known nothing but the wastes of Hammad al Nakir, and had not seen vegetation more magnificent than the scrub brush on the western flanks of Jebal al Alf Dhulquarneni, could not picture the Trolledyngjan grandeur Bragi wanted to convey.

"So why did you leave?"

"Same reason as you. My dad wasn't no duke, but he picked the wrong side when the old king croaked and they fought it out for the crown. Everybody died but me and Haaken. We came south and signed on with the Mercenary's Guild. And look what that got us."

Haroun could not help smiling. "Yeah."

"How about you?"

"What?"

"How old?"

"Eighteen."

"The old guy that died. Megelin Radetic. He was special?"

Haroun winced. A week had not deadened the pain. "My teacher. Since I was four. He was more a father to me than my father was."

"Sorry."

"He couldn't have survived this even if he hadn't been hurt."

"What's it like, being a king?"

"Like a sour practical joke. The fates are splitting their sides. King of the biggest country in this end of the world, and I can't even control what I see. All I can do is run."

"Well, your majesty, what say let's see if there's water down there." Bragi levered himself up, collected a short, broad knife from the gear packed on one of the camels. The camels were bearing up still. Haroun drew his belt knife. They went down to the thread of sand. "I hope you know what you're looking for," Bragi said. "All I know is secondhand from your warriors back at el Aswad."

"I'll find water if it's there." While Megelin Radetic had been teaching him geometry, astronomy, botany, and languages, darker pedants out of the Jebal had instructed him in the skills of a shaghûn, a soldier-wizard. "Be quiet."

Haroun covered his eyes to negate the glare off the desert, let the weak form of the trance take him. He sent his shaghûn's senses roving. Down the bed of sand, down, bone-dry. Up, up, ten yards, fifty…. There! Under that pocket of shadow seldom dispersed by the sun, where the watercourse looped under the overhang…. Moisture.

Haroun shuddered, momentarily chilled. "Come on."

Ragnarson looked at him oddly but said nothing. He had seen Haroun do stranger things.

They loosened the sand with their knives, scooped it with their hands, and, lo! two feet down they found moisture. They scooped another foot of wet sand before encountering rock, then sat back, watched a pool form. Haroun dipped a finger, tasted. Bragi followed suit. "Pretty thick."

Haroun nodded. "Don't drink much. Let the horses have it. Bring them down one at a time."

It was slow business. They did not mind. It was an excuse to stay in one place, in shade, instead of enduring the blazing lens of the sun.

Horses watered, Bragi brought the camels. He said, "Those kids aren't bouncing back. They're burned out."

"Yeah. If we can get them to the mountains…."

"Who are they?"

Haroun shrugged. "Their fathers were in Aboud's court."

"Ain't that a bite? Busting our butts to save people we don't even know who they are."

"Part of being human, Megelin would have said."

A cry came from the clustered youngsters. The oldest waved, pointed. Far away, a streamer of dust slithered across a reddish hillside. "The Scourge of God," Haroun said. "Let's get moving."

Ragnarson collected the boys, got the animals organized. Haroun filled the hole he had dug, wishing he could leave it poisoned.

As they set off, Bragi chirruped, "Let's see if we can't pull those old mountains in today."

Haroun scowled. The mercenary was moody, likely to become cheerful at the most unreasonable moments.

The mountains were as bad as the desert. There were no trails except those stamped out by game. One by one, they lost animals. Occasionally, because they were trying to keep the beasts with them, and because they were so exhausted, they made but four miles in a day. Lost, without roadmarks, scavenging to stay alive, their days piled into weeks.

"How much longer?" Bragi asked. It had been a month since Al Rhemish, three weeks since they had seen any sign of pursuit.

Haroun shook his head. "I don't know. Sorry. I just know Tamerice and Kavelin are on the other side." They seldom spoke now. There were moments when Haroun hated his companions. He was responsible for them. He could not give up while they persevered.

Exhaustion. Muscles knotting with cramps. Dysentery from strange water and bad food. Every step a major undertaking. Every mile an odyssey. Constant hunger. Countless bruises and abrasions from stumbling in his weakness. Time had no end and no beginning, no yesterday or tomorrow, just an eternal now in which one more step had to be taken. He was losing track of why he was doing this. The boys had forgotten long since. Their existence consisted of staying with him.

Bragi was taking it best. He had evaded the agony and ignominy of dysentery. He had grown up on the wild edge of the mountains of Trolledyngja. He had developed more stamina, if not more will. As Haroun weakened, leadership gradually shifted. The mercenary assumed ever more of the physical labor.

"Should have stopped to rest," Haroun muttered to himself. "Should have laid up somewhere to get our strength back." But Nassef was back there, coming on like a force of nature, as tortured as his quarry, yet implacable in his hunt. Wasn't he? Why did Nassef hate him so?

A horse whinnied. Bragi shouted. Haroun turned.

The animal had lost its footing. It kicked the oldest boy. Both plunged down a slope only slightly less steep than a cliff. The boy gave only one weak cry, hardly protesting this release from torment.

Haroun could find no grief in his heart. In fact, he suffered a disgusting flutter of satisfaction. One less load to carry.

Bragi said, "The animals will kill us all if we keep dragging them along. One way or another."

Haroun stared down the long slope. Should he see about the boy? What the hell was his name? He couldn't remember. He shrugged. "Leave them." He resumed walking.

Days dragged past. Nights piled upon each other. They pushed ever deeper into the Kapenrungs. Haroun did not know when they crossed the summit, for that land all looked identical. He no longer believed it ended. The maps lied. The mountains went on to the edge of the world.

One morning he wakened in misery and said, "I'm not moving today." His will had cracked.

Bragi raised an eyebrow, jerked a thumb in the direction of the desert.

"They've given up. They must have. They would have caught us by now." He looked around. Strange, strange country. Jebal al Alf Dhulquarneni was nothing like this. Those mountains were dry and almost lifeless, with rounded backs. These were far taller, all jagged, covered with trees bigger than anything he'd ever imagined. The air was chill. Snow, which he had seen only at the most distant remove before, lurked in every shadow. The air stank of conifer. It was alien territory. He was homesick.

Bragi, though, had taken on life. He seemed comfortable for the first time since Haroun had met him. "This something like the country you came from?"

"A little."

"You don't say much about your people. How come?"

"Not much to tell." Bragi scanned their surroundings intently. "If we're not going to travel we ought to get someplace where we can watch without getting caught on the trail."

"Scout around. I'll clean up."

"Right." The northerner was gone fifteen minutes. "Found it. Dead tree down up yonder. Ferns and moss behind it. We can lay in the shade and see anything coming." He pointed. "Go past those rocks, then climb up behind. Try not to leave tracks. I'll come last."

Haroun guided his charges up and settled down. Bragi joined them moments later, picking his resting place with care. "Wish I had a bow. Command the trail from here. Think they gave up, eh? Why, when they were willing to kill themselves in the desert?"

"Maybe they did."

"Think so?"

"No. Not Nassef. Good things don't happen to me. And that would be the best…." Tears sprang into his eyes. He brushed them away. So his family was dead. So Megelin had died. He would not yield to grief. "Tell me about your people."

"I already did."

"Tell me."

Bragi saw his need. "My father ran a stead called Draukenbring. Our family and a few others used to get together to go raiding during the summers." Haroun got little sense from the youth's story, but his talking was enough. "… old king died my father and the Thane ended up on opposite sides… Haaken found what he wanted when we joined the Guild."

"You didn't? You already had your own squad."

"No. I don't know what I want, but it isn't that. Maybe just to go home."

Again moisture collected in the corners of Haroun's eyes. He smote the ferns. He couldn't become homesick! It was too late for unproductive emotion. He turned the conversation to cities Bragi had visited. Megelin Radetic had come from Hellin Daimiel.

Shadows were growing in the canyon bottom when Ragnarson said, "Don't look like we're going to have visitors today. I'm going to set some snares. You can eat squirrel, can't you?"

Haroun managed a feeble smile. Bragi was baffled by the dietary laws. "Yes."

"Hallelujah. Why don't you find a place to camp?"

Unbent by the sarcasm, Haroun levered himself upright, leaned on the fallen tree. Amazing, the changes in life. A king, and he had to do for himself. He'd never had to when he was a Wahlig's fourth son.

"People up ahead," Ragnarson said. Haroun raised a questioning eyebrow. "Can't you smell the smoke?"

"No. But I believe you." Twice Bragi had taken detours around mountain hamlets, not trusting the natives. Inimical or not, their presence was reassuring. Civilization could not be far.

"I'll go scout it out."

"All right." Close now. So close. But to what? Though they had pushed less hard since deciding the Scourge of God had given up, Haroun remained too weary, too depressed, to determine a future course.

Get away from Nassef. Get over the mountains. One down and the other almost accomplished. Vaguely, somewhere in the mists: hammer the Royalist ideal into a weapon that would destroy the Disciple and his bandit captains. But he knew no specifics, had no neat plan ready to unveil. He was tempted to follow Ragnarson when he rejoined his mercenary brethren.

Bragi certainly smelled the end of their flight. He kept talking about getting back to his unit, to his brother, or at least to Guild headquarters at High Crag, where they would know what had become of Hawkwind's companies.

Haroun wanted to be a king less than Bragi wanted to be a soldier. Become a mercenary? Really? It would be a life circumscribed by clearly stated rules. He would know where he stood. "Foolish," he whispered. Destiny had assigned him a role. He couldn't shed it simply because he didn't like it.

Ragnarson returned. "About twenty of your people up there. Almost as ragged as we are. Couldn't tell if they'd be friendly or not. You go take a look."

"Uhm." They should be friendly. El Murid's partisans had no cause to cross the mountains. He crept forward, eavesdropped.

They were Royalists. They had no better idea where they were than did he and Ragnarson. But they did know there were refugee camps somewhere nearby. A chain of camps had been financed by the Wahlig of el Aswad and his friends, at the suggestion of Megelin Radetic, back when it had become apparent that the Disciple was a serious threat.

Haroun stole back and told Bragi, "They're friends. We ought to join forces."

The northerner looked dubious.

"We wouldn't have to worry about natives anymore."

"Maybe. But after what I've been through I don't trust anybody."

"I'll talk to them."

"But…"

"I'm going."

"Hey," Haroun said. "There's one of my father's captains. Beloul! Hey! Over here!" He waved.

They had been in camp half an hour. The two boys had collapsed and been forgotten. Haroun had wandered dazedly, unable to believe he'd made it, looking for someone he knew. Ragnarson had tagged along, eyeing everyone warily.

The man called Beloul set his axe aside, stared. His face blossomed. "My Lord!"

Haroun flung himself at the man. "I thought everybody was dead."

"Almost. I'd feared for you as well. But I had faith in the teacher. And I was right. Here you are."

Haroun's face clouded. "Megelin didn't make it. He died of wounds. Here. You remember Bragi Ragnarson? One of Hawkwind's men? He saved my life at the salt lake, and during the siege of el Aswad? Well, he did it again at Al Rhemish. He got cut off from his outfit." Haroun could not shut up. "Bragi, this is Beloul. He was one of the garrison at Sebil el Selib when El Murid attacked it way back when."

"I remember seeing him around el Aswad."

"He was the only survivor. He joined my father and was one of his best captains."

Bragi asked, "How do I get to High Crag from here? Soon as I rest up a little...." They were not listening.

"Everyone! Everyone!" Beloul shouted. "The King! Hail the King!"

"Oh, don't do that," Haroun pleaded. And, "We got lost in the mountains. I thought we'd never get through."

Beloul kept shouting. People gathered, but with little enthusiasm. Fear and despair stamped every weary face.

"Who else made it, Beloul?"

"Too early to tell. I haven't been here long myself. Where is the teacher?"

Haroun scowled. The man was not listening. "He didn't make it. They all died, except a couple kids. The Scourge of God himself was after us. Took us a month to shake him."

"Sorry to hear it. We could use the old man's counsel."

"I know. It's a weak trade, Megelin for a crown. He saved me for a kingship. So what am I king of? This isn't much. I'm the poorest monarch who ever lived."

"Not so. Tell him," Beloul appealed to the refugees.

Some nodded. Some shook their heads. Which depended on what each thought was expected.

"Your father's party established dozens of camps, Lord. You'll have a people and an army."

"An army? Aren't you tired of fighting, Beloul?"

"El Murid still lives." For Beloul that was answer enough. While El Murid lived Sebil el Selib and his family remained unavenged. He had been at war for twelve years. He would remain so as long as the Disciple survived. "I'll send word to the other camps. We'll see what we have before we start planning."

"Got messengers going west," Bragi said, "let me go along. All right?" No one answered. He spat irritably.

Haroun said, "Right now I'm content just to be here. I'm exhausted, Beloul. Put me to sleep somewhere."

He slept and loafed for three days. Then, so stiff he could barely walk, he left his hut and surveyed his new domain.

The camp surrounded a peak in the northern Kapenrungs. So many trees! He could not get used to the trees. When he stared through gaps created by axes, he saw an endless array of forest. It disturbed him as much as the desert disturbed Ragnarson.

He hadn't seen the mercenary for a while. What had become of him?

Beloul reported, "Forty-three people came in today, Lord. The mountains are crawling with refugees."

"Can we handle them?"

"The teacher's friend knew what he was doing. He put in the right tools and stores."

"Even so, we should move some out. This is a resting place, not the end of the journey." He glanced at the peak. Beloul was erecting blockhouses and a palisade. "Where's my friend?"

"He left with the westbound courier. Very determined lad. Wanted to get back to his own people."

For a moment Haroun felt vacant. The time of flight had created a bond. He would miss the big northerner. "I owe him my life three times, Beloul. And I'm powerless to do anything in return."

"I let him have a horse, Lord."

Haroun scowled. Not much of a reward. Then he indicated the fortifications. "Why all that?"

"We'll need bases when we start striking into Hammad al Nakir. Al Rhemish isn't that far."

"If you know the way through."

Beloul smiled. "True."

Haroun looked at the trees, at the river coursing along the foot of the mountain. It was hard to believe his homeland wasn't far away. "It's so peaceful here, Beloul."

"Only for a while, Lord."

"I know. The world will catch up."

THREE
THE FAT BOY

Sweat rolled off the fat boy. He sat in the dust and mutely cursed the Master. This was the season for the north, not the boiling, rain-plagued delta of the Roë. Necremnos had been bad in springtime, Throyes worse a month ago. Argon, in summer, was Hell. The old man was crazy.

He opened one dark eye, cocked his brown, moon-shaped face, studied the Master.

Was there ever such a wreck? The shadow of the Foreign Quarter Gate helped, but even midnight could no longer conceal his age and debility, nor his weakening mind, nor his blindness.

The old man was napping.

The fat boy's hand darted to a tattered leather bag, whipped back clutching a rocklike bun.

The Master's cane cracked dust. "Little ingrate! Damned thief! Steal from an old man…."

Yes, he was past it. Once getting food had been difficult. Just a year ago the problem had required total concentration.

The old man tried to rise. His legs betrayed him. He tumbled backward, cane flailing.

"I heard that! You snickered. You'll rue the day…."

Passersby ignored them. And that was a dire portent.

Once the Master had drawn them against their wills. With his tricks and banter he had stripped the smartest of their money.

Singsong, the old man called, "Brush aside a veil, see through the eyes of time, penetrate the mists, unlock the doors of fate…." He attempted a sleight-of-hand involving a black cloth and crystal ball, bungled it.

The fat boy shook his head. The fool. He could not admit that he was past it.

The fat boy hated that old man. He had traveled with the itinerant charlatan all his life. Not once had the old man mouthed a kind word. Always he had strained his imagination to torment the child. He had never permitted the boy a name. Yet the fat boy had not run away. Till recently the very idea had been alien.

Sometimes, when he managed the price, the old man would surround prodigious quantities of wine. Then he would mumble of having been court jester to a powerful man. The fat boy, somehow, had been involved in their falling out. Now he paid the price, whether it had been his fault or not.

The old man had instilled a strong guilt in his companion.

He meant it to be his security in his declining years.

The fat boy, brown as the earthen street, sweated, swatted flies, and wrestled temptation. He knew he could survive on his own. He had the skills.

Sometimes, when the Master dozed, he performed himself. He was a superb ventriloquist. He spoke through the old man's props, usually the ape's skull or the stuffed owl. Occasionally he used the mangy, emaciated donkey that carried their gear. When feeling bold he would put words into the Master's mouth.

He had gotten caught once. The old man had beaten him half to death.

That old man wore a list of names, varying according to whom he thought was chasing him. Feager and Sajac were his favorites. The boy was sure both were false.

He chased the secret of a true name doggedly. It might be a clue to his own identity.

Finding out who he was, now, was the main reason he did nothing to improve his condition.

He was unrelated to Sajac, that he knew. The old man was tall, lean, and pale. He had faded grey eyes and blondish hair. He was a westerner.

Yet the boy's earliest memories were of the far east. Of Matayanga. Escalon. The fabled cities of Janin, Nemic, Shoustal-Watka, and Tatarian. They had even penetrated the wild Segasture Range, where the Theon Sing Monasteries, from their high crags, overlooked the shadowed reaches of the Dread Empire.

Even then he had wondered why he and Sajac were together, and what drove the man to keep moving and moving.

Sajac appeared to be sleeping again.

Hunger clawed at the boy's belly. He could not remember not being hungry.

His hands darted.

Nothing. The sack was empty.

The old man did not react. This time he *was* asleep.

Time to do something about their naked larder.

Coming by money honestly was hard enough in the best of times....

He waddled along, looking incomparably clumsy and slow. And, though he was not fast, he was quick. Quick and subtle. And daring.

He took the guard captain's purse with a touch so deft that the man did not cry out till he had entered a sweltering tavern and asked for wine.

By then the fat boy was three blocks away, buying pastries.

His liability was that he was too memorable.

The guard captain, though, committed a tactical error. He shouted his promises of punishment before having his criminal in hand.

The fat boy squealed and took off. He could be enslaved, if not maimed or beheaded.

He made his escape, and returned to Sajac before the old man wakened.

His heart pounded on long after he had regained his breath. This was his third close call this week. The odds were turning long. People would start watching for a fat brown boy with quick hands. It was time to move on.

But the old man would not. He meant to put down roots this time.

Something had to be done.

Sajac wakened suddenly. "What have you been up to now?" he snapped. "Stealing my food again?" He seized his cane, probed the bun sack. "Eh?"

It was full.

The fat boy smiled. He always bought the hard rolls because the old man had bad teeth.

"Thieving, I'll warrant!" Sajac staggered up. "I'll teach you, you little pimple...."

The fat boy hadn't the strength to run. He whimpered. The old man plied his cane.

Something had to be done.

Once his persecutor tired, the fat boy whined, "Master, was man to see you hour passing."

The time had come.

"What man? I didn't see anyone."

"Came while Master meditated. Was great man of city. Offered obols thirty for guaranteed divination of chicken entrail, to choose between suitors of daughter. One poor, one rich. Man prefers rich, girl loves poor. To keep secret from daughter, same said come by midnight. Self, told same Master was in possession of sovereign specific to overcome love, same being available for obols twenty extra."

"Liar!" But the cane fell without force. "Twenty and thirty? At midnight?" That was a lot of wine, a lot of forgetfulness.

"Truth told, Master."

"Where?"

"On High Street. By Front Road, near Fadem. Will leave gate open."

"Fifty obols?" Sajac chuckled evilly. "Get me my potions. I'll mix him something fit to grow hair on a frog."

The fat boy, generally, could sleep under the worst conditions. But he could not doze while awaiting midnight.

The rains came, as always, an hour after nightfall. The old man huddled in his cloak, the fat boy in his rags. The time came to confess his lie or go on.

He went on.

He put the Master astride the mangy donkey, led the animal through silent streets, up hills and down, by back ways, making turns for confusion's sake. Neither robbers nor watchmen bothered them.

Their course took them past the seat of the Fadema's government, the Fadem Still no one challenged them.

Finally they came to the place the fat boy had chosen.

Argon sits on a triangular island, connected to other delta islands by floating causeways. The apex of the triangle points upriver, and it is there that the girdling streams are narrowest. It is there that the ancient engineers built the walls their tallest, with their feet in the river itself.

A hundred feet below, and a quarter-mile south, lay one of the pontoons. It linked Argon with suburbs on a neighboring island. Beyond, in the deeper darkness, lay fertile rice islands, the foundation of Argon's wealth.

The fat boy did not care. Economics meant nothing to him.

"Is necessary to walk from here," he said. "Great Lord say bring no beast to mess garden."

The old man grumbled, but let the boy help him down.

"Is this way." He took Sajac's arm.

"Damn you!" the old man snarled a minute later, rising from a rainwater pool nearly four inches deep. "That's twice." *Whack!* "You did it on purpose."

Whack! "Next time go around."

"Am humblest apologizer, Master. Promise. Will be more careful." A grin tore at the corners of his mouth.

"Woe! Is pool across path again."

"Go around."

"Is impossible of accomplishment. Is flowerbeds on sides. Great Lord would be angered." He paused. "Ah. Is only four feet wide. Self, will jump across. Will catch Master when same jumps after." He positioned the old man carefully, grunted prodigiously.

He cast his voice to say, "Hai! Was easy, Master. But jump hard to make sure."

The old man cursed and thrashed the air with his cane.

"Come, Master. Please? Great Lord will be angry if augurs come late. Jump. Self will catch."

The fat boy's heart hammered. His blood pounded in his ears. Surely the old man would hear their infantry-tramp thundering....

Sajac mouthed a final curse, crouched, hurled himself forward.

He did not begin screaming till he had fallen halfway to the river.

The tension broke. The fat boy flung his arms into the air and danced....

"Here! What's going on up there?"

A police watchman was hurrying up the cline to the ramparts. The fat boy ran to the donkey. But the animal would not move.

He would have to brazen it out.

The watchman walked into a storm of tears. "Woe!" the fat boy cried. "Am foolishest of fools."

"What happened, son?"

The fat boy blubbered. He was very good at that. "Grandfather of self, only relative in whole world, just jumped from wall. Am idiot. Believed same only wanted to look on river by night for last time." He made a show of trying to control himself.

"Only relative left. Was wasting sickness. Much pain. No more money for opium. Self, am stupidest of stupids. Should have known...."

"There, there, son. It'll be all right. Maybe it was for the best, eh? If the pain was that bad?"

That watchman had patrolled the same beat for years. He had seen all kinds go off the wall. Jilted lovers. Dishonored husbands. Guilty consciences. Just plain folks.

Most of them did it by daylight, wanting an audience for their final world-diddling gesture. But a man with cancer would not be mad at the whole world, just its gods. And those little perverts could see just fine at night. His suspicions were not aroused.

"Come on down to the barracks. We can put you up there tonight. Then we'll see what we can do for you in the morning."

The fat boy did not know when to quit. He protested, wailed, made a show of trying to throw himself after his departed relative.

The policeman, deciding he needed detention for his own safety, dragged him to the police barracks.

A less enthusiastic despair would have allowed the boy to have gone his own way. The lawman would not have demurred. His world was filled with parentless, street-running children.

The same watchman woke the boy from his first-ever sleep in a real bed. "Good morning, lad. Time to see the captain."

The fat boy had a premonition. How many guard captains could there be? Not many. He could not risk meeting this one. "Self, am famished. Dying by starvation."

"I think we can arrange something." The policeman gave him an odd, calculating look.

The boy decided he had better show more grief. He turned it on, as if suddenly realizing that he had not just awakened from a bad dream.

The watchman seemed satisfied.

He gorged himself at the mess hall. And filled his pockets while no one was watching. Then, when he could stall no more, he followed the watchman to the captain's quarters.

He got himself out a side door while the patrolman made his report. He had recognized the officer's voice. His premonition had been valid.

They almost caught him in the stables. The donkey did not want to leave such rich fodder. But the fat boy got her moving in time to evade the captain's notice.

He decided to abandon Argon altogether. The captain was bound to do his sums and order a general search. Sajac had taught him long ago that the best way to avoid police was to be out of town when they started looking.

Could he bluff his way past the causeway guards? They might not let a kid leave by himself.

He managed it. He was a crafty and confusing liar.

The child-fugitive from Argon joined the ranks of the visibly unemployed who nevertheless survived. He did so by employing the dubious skills he had learned from Sajac, and others of the old man's ilk whom they had encountered in their journeys.

For several years he wandered the route he had shared with Sajac, from Throyes to Necremnos, to Argon, and round again, with stops in most of the villages between. One summer he traveled to Matayanga and Escalon. Another, he journeyed down the western shore of the Sea of Kotsüm, beneath the brooding scarps of Jebal al Alf Dhulquarneni, but that route showed no promise. The people were too savage and excitable.

They used human skin, back in those dread mountains, to make the parchment on which they scribbled their grimoires.

He picked up several more languages, none of which he learned well. He stayed nowhere long enough to become proficient. Or he simply did not care.

He developed evil habits. Money fled through his fingers like grains of sand. There were girls, and wine....

But gambling was his downfall. He could not resist a game of chance. He left a series of bad debts. The list of places he had to avoid grew too long to remember.

And he persevered in his stealing, thereby committing the double sin, making enemies on both sides of the law.

It caught up with him in Necremnos.

Mornings and evenings he did the usual phony sorcerer spiel.

"Hai! Great Lady! Before eyes of woman renown for beauty and wisdom sits student of famed Grand Master Istwan of Matayanga, self, working way west at Master's command, to seek knowledge of great minds beyond Mountains of M'Hand. Am young, true, but trained in all manner of secrets beauteous. Am also Divinator Primus. Can show how to win love, or tell if man loves already. Have in hand certain rare and secret beauty potions hitherto concocted for wives of Monitor of Escalon only, ladies known across nethermost east for teenlike beauty unto fiftieth year."

The appeal went on and on, tailored to any woman who showed interest. He sold a lot of swamp water and odiferous juices and ichors.

Between his morning and evening shifts he prowled the marketplaces, picking pockets.

And by night he squandered his take.

Then a pickpocket victim recognized him while he was at his more innocent trade.

He tried bluffing it out, packing his gear and loading the donkey while he argued. But when a policeman showed signs of believing his accuser, he fled.

He was no more agile or fleet than he had been in Argon. He relied on cunning. Cunning was his edge on the rest of the world.

Cunning betrayed him.

The place he chose to go to ground was an outpost of a gambler he had bilked the autumn before.

"Seize him!" was his first intimation of disaster.

A pair of hoodlums, one lank and scarred, the other fat and scarred, piled on.

Beyond their flailing limbs the youth spied a man who had promised him a slow flaying at their parting.

He panicked.

From his sleeve he slipped the knife he used to cut pursestrings.

And an instant later his lean attacker wore a second, scarlet-gushing mouth below one opened in a silent scream.

Blood drenched the fat boy. It was hot and salty. He lost his breakfast as he writhed to get away from the other man.

This was nothing like getting an old fool to jump off a wall.

The gambler stared with wide, angry eyes as the fat boy charged him.

The fat hoodlum tripped the boy. The gambler scuttled out the back door. The youth bounced up, discovered that his antagonist had produced a knife of his own.

A crowd had begun gathering. It was time for him to leave.

His opponent would not let him.

He wanted to delay the fat boy till his employer brought reinforcements.

The youth feigned a rush, whipped to one side. He darted out the back door while the fat man was off balance.

It became a hell night. He scrambled across rooftops and crawled through sewers. Half the city was after him. Watchmen were everywhere. Hoodlums turned out by the hundred, lured by a bounty the gambler posted.

It was time to seek greener pastures. But only one direction lay open now. The west to which he had so long claimed to be bound.

He had not yet learned his lessons. He fully intended to pursue his habitual lifestyle once he crossed the mountains.

Even there he would be pursued by a doom of his own devising.

From a safely distant hilltop he laughed at, and hurled mockeries at, Necremnos.

Grinning, he told himself, "Am fine mocker. Finest mocker. Greatest mocker. Is good idea. Henceforth, sir," and he pounded his chest with his fist, "I dub thee Mocker."

It was the nearest thing to a name he would ever have.

He traveled south by remote trails till he reached a staging town on the outskirts of Throyes, where he wrangled a waterboy's job with a caravan bound for Vorgreberg, in Kavelin, in the Lesser Kingdoms, west of the Mountains of M'Hand.

The caravan crossed vast, uninhabited plains, rounded the ruins of Gog-Ahlan, then climbed into mountains more tall and inhospitable than any Mocker had seen in the far east. The trail snaked through the narrow confines of the Savernake Gap, past its grim guardian fortress, Maisak, and descended to a town called Baxendala.

There, after a girl and some wine, Mocker fell to dicing with the locals.

He got caught cheating.

This time he was on the run in a land where he spoke not a word of the language.

In Vorgreberg he lasted long enough to pick up a smattering of several western tongues. He was a fast, if incomplete, study.

FOUR
THE MOST HOLY MRAZKIM SHRINES

Day after day El Murid sat at Meryem's bedside. Sometimes his daughter or Sidi would join him. They would share prayers. His captains sought him there when they needed instructions. It was there that his generals Karim and el-Kader came with the gift-news that they had won an astonishing victory over Royalist forces near the ruins of Ilkazar. That battle's outcome was more significant than his seizure of Al Rhemish. It broke the back of Royalist resistance. Hammad al Nakir was his.

It was at Meryem's side that, in time, an emaciated, desiccated Nassef finally appeared to report, "Yousif's brat eluded me. But Radetic paid the price."

El Murid merely nodded.

"How is she, Micah?"

"No change. Still unconscious. After all this time. The fates are cruel, Nassef. They give with one hand and take away with the other."

"That sounds like something I'd say. You're supposed to put it, 'The Lord giveth, and the Lord taketh away.'"

"Yes. I should, shouldn't I? Again the Evil One insinuates himself into my mind. He leaves no opportunity begging, does he?"

"That's the nature of the Beast."

"It's a hard path the Lord sets me, Nassef. I wish I understood where he's leading me. Meryem never hurt anybody. If she ever did, she paid for it a hundredfold just by being the Disciple's wife. Why should this happen now? With the victory at hand? With the naming of her daughter so near? When we could finally start living the semblance of a normal life?"

"She'll be avenged, Micah."

"Avenged? Who's left to avenge her on?"

"Yousif's son. Haroun. The pretender to the throne."

"He'll die anyway. The Harish have consecrated his name already."

"All right. Someone, then. Micah, we've got work to do. Disharhun starts tomorrow. You can't stay closed up. The faithful are gathering. We've promised them this festival for years. You have to put your personal agony aside."

El Murid sighed. "You're right, of course. I've been feeling sorry for myself. Just a little while longer. You. You look awful. Was it bad?"

"Words can't describe it. They did something sorcerous to us. I'm the only one who survived. And I can't remember what happened. I lost five days of my life out there. There was a tower…." But he wasn't sure.

"The Lord saw you through. He understood my need."

"I have to rest, Micah. I don't have anything left. I won't be much help the next few days."

"Take as long as you need. Heal. I'll need you more than ever if I lose Meryem."

El Murid prayed again after Nassef departed. This time he asked only that his wife be allowed to witness the christening of her daughter.

That had meant so much to her.

It was the wildest, hugest, most joyous Disharhun in living memory. The faithful came from the nethermost marches of Hammad al Nakir to share the victorious holiday with their Disciple. Some came from so far away that they did not arrive till Mashad, the last of the High Holy Days. But that was in time. That was the day when El Murid would accept his victory and proclaim the Kingdom of Peace. And they would have been present on the most important date in the history of the Faith.

The crowds were so huge that a special scaffold had to be erected as a speaking platform. Only a few specially invited guests were allowed into the Shrines themselves. Only the Disciple's oldest followers would witness the christening.

Shortly before noon El Murid strode from the Shrines and mounted the scaffolding. This would be his first annual Declaration to the Kingdom. The mob chanted, "El-Murid-El-Murid." They stamped their feet and clapped rhythmically. The Disciple held up his arms, begging for silence.

The blazing sun flamed off the amulet that had been given him by his angel. The crowd ohed and ahed.

The religion was changing beyond El Murid's vision. He saw himself as just a voice, a teacher chosen to point out a few truths. But in the minds and hearts of his followers he was more. In remote parts of the desert he was worshipped as the Lord in Flesh.

He was unaware of this revisionism.

His first Mashad speech said nothing new. He proclaimed the Kingdom of Peace, reiterated religious law, offered amnesty to former enemies, and ordered every able-bodied man of Hammad al Nakir to appear at the next spring hosting. The Lord willing, the infidel nations would then be chastised and the rights of the Empire restored.

Men who had visited Al Rhemish before, to celebrate other High Holy Days, marveled at the dearth of foreign factors and ambassadors. The infidel were not recognizing El Murid's claim to temporal power.

El Murid was weak when he left the scaffold. Pain ripped at his arm and leg. He summoned his physician. Esmat gave him what he wanted. He no longer argued with his master.

One hundred men had been invited to the christening, along with their favorite wives. El Murid wanted it to be a precedent-setting ceremony. His daughter was to approach the Most Holy Altar attired in bridal white. She would both receive her name and wed herself to the Lord.

He meant it to be an inarguable declaration of his choice of successor.

"She's beautiful, isn't she?" Meryem said huskily as the girl approached the altar.

"Yes." His prayers had been answered. Meryem had come out of her coma. But her limbs were paralyzed. Servants had had to clothe her and carry her here on a litter.

El Murid recalled how proud she had looked on her white camel. How bold, how beautiful, how defiant she had been that first venture into Al Rhemish!

Everything went misty. He took Meryem's hand and held it tightly throughout the ceremony. The girl was nearly an adult. There was little parents could
contribute. She could handle her own responses.

When the newly appointed High Priest of the Shrine asked, "And by what
name shall this child of God be called?" El Murid squeezed Meryem's hand
more tightly. Only she knew the answer. This was the moment for which she
had lived.

"Yasmid," Meryem replied. Her voice was strong. It rang like a carillon. El
Murid felt a surge of hope. He saw another rise in Nassef. "Call her Yasmid,
the Daughter of the Disciple."

She squeezed his hand in return. He felt the joy coursing through her.

Her recovery lasted only minutes more. She lapsed into coma before the
ceremony's conclusion. She passed to Paradise before morning.

The end was so certain that Nassef ordered Al Rhemish dressed for mourning shortly after sundown.

El Murid had been so drained by constant concern that the event itself left
him numb. He could shed no tears. The little energy he had he devoted to
Yasmid, Sidi, and Nassef.

The ever-calm, self-possessed Nassef had gone to pieces.

More than to El Murid himself, Meryem had been all he had had in the
world.

"She is asleep in the arms of the Lord," satisfied no one.

Nassef's response was to plunge into his work with redoubled energy, as if
to take his grief out on the world. Some nights he skipped sleep altogether.

Sidi simply withdrew. And Yasmid became more like her mother at the same
age. She was brash, bold, and fond of embarrassing her father's associates. She
had a low tolerance for pomposity, self-importance, and inflexible conserva-
tism. And she could argue doctrine with a skill that beggared her father's.

For that reason alone the new priesthood gradually accepted the notion of
her succession.

She spent a lot of time dogging her uncle as he pored over his maps and
tactical studies. She knew more about his plans than did anyone else alive. A
half-serious story went the rounds, to the effect that she would succeed her
uncle too.

The wave of the idealist had crested, but had not begun to recede. People
still worried honestly about goals and doctrinal purity. The inevitable, post-
revolutionary wave of the bureaucrat had not begun to gather.

Yasmid would not be challenged till professional administrators supplanted
professional revolutionaries.

Nassef dumped the pacification of Hammad al Nakir onto el-Kader. He made
a crony named el Nadim his satrap on the east coast and Throyen marches. He
and Karim focused their attentions west of the Sahel, on lands El Murid was
determined to restore to Imperial dominion. They spent month after month

in the careful reinterpretation and reiteration of plans Nassef had nurtured for years.

Occasionally accompanied by his son, El Murid sat in on some of their staff meetings. He had his mission and his children, and nothing more. The pain in his limbs was unrelenting. He could no longer pretend, even to himself, that he was not dependent upon Esmat's drugs.

Despite a close watch, he could not resolve his increasingly ambiguous feelings toward Nassef. His brother-in-law was a chimera. Perhaps even he did not know where he stood.

Nassef's headquarters became cluttered with artwork. Years earlier he had employed several skilled artists to travel the west. He had called in their work: detailed maps, drawings and specifications of fortifications, sketches of prominent westerners with outlines of their personal strengths and weaknesses. He adjusted his master plan as information came in.

"The base plan is this," he told El Murid. "An explosion out of the Sahel, apparently without direction. Then one strong force materializing and heading toward Hellin Daimiel. When they think we're committed, we wheel and overrun Simballawein to clear our rear against our push north."

"Ipopotam...."

"Eager to please, my agents say. They'll stay neutral till it's too late. With Simballawein taken, we turn on Hellin Daimiel. But when they withdraw behind their walls we by-pass them again. We push to the Scarlotti. We seize the fords and ferries so help can't get across from the north. All this time raiders will be roaming the Lesser Kingdoms, keeping them too busy to threaten our flank. In fact, after I've got everybody's attention, el Nadim will cross Throyen territory and attack Kavelin through the Savernake Gap. If he breaks through we'll have the Lesser Kingdoms in a vice. They'll collapse. If everything goes right, we'll overrun every kingdom south of the Scarlotti before summer's end."

El Murid examined the maps. "That's a lot of territory, Nassef."

"I know. It's chancy. It depends on the speed of our horses and confusion of our enemies. We can't fight them on their terms. Wadi el Kuf proved that. We have to make them fight our way."

"You're the general, Nassef. You don't have to justify to me."

"As long as I'm winning."

El Murid frowned, unsure what he meant.

Later that day he called for Mowaffak Hali, a senior officer of the Invincibles, who had been conducting an investigation for him. "Well, Mowaffak? It's getting close to the hosting. Am I in the hands of bandits?"

Hali was a fanatic, but he tried to be honest. He did not create answers in hopes they were what his master wanted to hear.

"Nothing damning, Lord. They've given up plundering their own people. I suppose that's a good sign. In private, they're excited about plundering the infidel. I couldn't trace most of the specie that went west. Some apparently went to pay spies. Some apparently bought arms. Some remains in the banks at Hellin Daimiel. And a lot have disappeared. So what can I say?"

"What's your feeling, Mowaffak?"

"I'm baffled, Lord. I lean one way one day, the other the next. I try to leave my personal feelings out."

El Murid smiled. "I've reached this point a dozen times, Mowaffak. And every time I end up doing the same thing. I let it go because Nassef is so useful. I let it go, and hope he'll eventually reveal the real Nassef. I thought an independent viewer might see something I'd missed."

"We don't punish our hands when they fail us by dropping something. I don't like the Scourge of God. I don't trust him, either. Yet he has no equal. Karim is good. El-Kader is good. And yet they are but shadows of the master. I say the Lord wrought well when he brought you two together. Let him undertake to keep you together."

"And yet...."

"The day he becomes a liability will be the last day of his life, Lord. A silver dagger will find him."

"That's a comfort, Mowaffak. I sometimes wonder if I deserve the affection of the Invincibles."

Mowaffak seemed startled. "My Lord, if you didn't you wouldn't have won our love."

"Thank you, Mowaffak. You reassure me, even if you can't ease my confusion."

Disharhun was coming again. Each day made him more nervous. The moment of no return was hurtling toward him like a falling star. It would be too late once the Children of Hammad al Nakir crossed the Sahel. The great war would continue till the Empire was restored or his people had been trampled into the dust.

Warriors were arriving when he asked Nassef, "Should we put it off a year? So we'd have more time to get ready?"

"No. Don't get the jitters. Time is our enemy. The west is weak and confused. Not sure we'll attack. But they're bumbling along, getting ready. In a year they'd know and be organized."

El Murid made his Mashad speech to the assembled host. He was awed by its vastness. Fifty thousand men faced him. They had gathered at *his* command. And as many more were moving toward the Sahel already.

Hardly a grown man would stay home this summer.

He exhorted them to carry the Word, then returned to the Shrines. He was prepared to remain near the Most Holy Altar, praying, till the trend of the campaign became clear.

The first reports seemed too good to be true. Yasmid told him it was going better than Nassef had hoped. Then Mowaffak Hali came to him. "Lord, I need your advice."

"How so?"

"A man named Allaf Shaheed, a captain of the Invincibles, has made a dangerous mistake. The question is how we should react."

"Explain."

"A force of Invincibles encountered Guild General Hawkwind in the domains of Hellin Daimiel. Foolishly, they offered battle. Hawkwind shattered them."

"And that has what to do with this Shaheed?"

"He assumed command of the survivors. While fleeing he chanced on a Guild landhold. He slew everyone there."

"So?"

"We're not at war with the Guild proper, Lord. We're at war with people who employ Guildsmen. That's a critical distinction. They demand that it be observed."

"They demand? Of me, Mowaffak? The Lord makes demands of El Murid. Not men."

"Perhaps, Lord. But should we needlessly incur the hatred of ten thousand men as dedicated as our own Harish? Twice have they invoked what they call the Sanctions of Nonverid and gone to war as an order. Each time they eradicated their enemies root and branch. Were they to muster their full strength and march against Al Rhemish not even the Scourge of God could stop them."

"I think you exaggerate, Mowaffak. And I won't be dictated to by infidels."

"I merely suggest that we not add to our burdens, Lord. That we make a gesture to placate the old men of High Crag. The Guild scattered, taken piecemeal, is far less dangerous than the Guild faced as a body."

El Murid reflected. He saw the sense of Hali's argument. Wadi el Kuf had been impressive. But there was also the fact that petitioning the Guild at any level constituted an admission of weakness.

There was no weakness in the Lord.

"Relieve Shaheed. Return him to Al Rhemish. Otherwise, do nothing but instruct your captains not to let it happen again."

"As you command, Lord." Mowaffak Hali grew pale. He had survived Wadi el Kuf. He hoped never to witness such a slaughter again.

He debated with himself for a day before finding room in his conscience for disobedience.

He sent three messengers by three routes, each bearing letters begging understanding and offering restitution. But the Lord was not with him. Every envoy perished en route.

FIVE

WAR CLOUDS

Bragi reached High Crag after a four-month journey through refugee camps scattered across the Lesser Kingdoms. The castle was an ancient, draughty stone pile perched atop a windy, sea-battered headland jutting from the coast north of Dunno Scuttari. He looked up the long slope to the gates, recalling the misery he had endured during recruit training, and almost turned back. Only his concern for his brother drew him onward.

He explained his circumstances to the gatekeeper. The gatekeeper told him to report to the sergeant of the guard. The sergeant sent him to a lieutenant, who passed him on to a captain, who told him to spend the night in barracks because he could expect to tell his story a dozen more times before anyone decided what to do with him. He was listed missing in action, presumed killed. His death bonus had been paid to his brother. The bonus would have to be repaid.

"I don't care about all that," Bragi said. "I just want to get back to my brother and my company. Where are they?"

"Sanguinet's Company? Down near Hellin Daimiel. Simballawein is negotiating for reinforcements for the Guild garrison there. There's talk that El Murid plans a holy war. Wants to resurrect the Empire."

"Why can't I just catch up?"

"As soon as you've gone the route here."

He remained stuck at High Crag for three months.

Haaken stared. "I don't believe it. Where the hell did you come from?" He was a burly youth even bigger than his foster brother. He approached Bragi warily, circled him. "It's you. It's really you. Damn it. Oh, damn it. After all the heartaches I went through."

Someone hollered back among the tents. "You lying son of a bitch!" A soldier charged onto the drill field. "I'll crap! It *is* him. What the hell are you doing here, Bragi?" He was a tall, lean, tan, ginger-haired youth named Reskird Kildragon, Haaken's friend and the only other Trolledyngjan in the company.

Haaken threw an arm around Bragi. "It's really you. I'll be damned. We were sure you were dead."

"Why the hell didn't you keep riding somewhere?" Kildragon demanded. "Haaken, how are we going to pay back that death bounty?"

Bragi laughed. "Hasn't changed a bit, has he?" he asked Haaken.

"Too damned stupid. Can't *beat* sense into him. Tell the guys, Reskird."

"Yeah." Kildragon winked at Ragnarson.

"So talk," Haaken said. "How did you get out of Al Rhemish? Where have you been? Maybe you *should* have gone somewhere else. We're probably headed down to Simballawein. The Disciple is up to something. We'll probably be in the thick of it. Well? Can't you say anything?"

Grinning, Bragi replied, "Maybe. If you'd shut up long enough. You realize you've said more in the last five minutes than you usually say in a year?"

The rest of Ragnarson's squadmates appeared, ambling out nonchalantly, as if only mildly curious. "Oh-oh," Haaken said. "Here comes Lieutenant Trubacik."

"Lieutenant?"

"Been lots of promotions. Sanguinet is a captain now."

Bragi sucked spittle between his teeth, nervous.

"You're late, Ragnarson," Trubacik snapped. "You were due on guard duty ten months ago." He chuckled at his own wit. "Captain wants to see you."

A messenger came in on a lathered horse. Sanguinet ordered the camp gates closed and the troops into company formation. "Gentlemen, it's begun," he announced. "We're headed for Simballawein. General Hawkwind will join us there."

Five hell-days on the road, marching forty or fifty miles each day. Then a messenger overtook them with word that a regiment of Invincibles had butted heads with Hawkwind and gotten the short end. Only a handful had escaped.

The walls of Simballawein hove into view. "It's as big as Itaskia," Ragnarson muttered to Haaken.

"Bigger, I think." Cheering crowds waited outside the gates. "Think we'd won the war already. Hell, a city ain't nothing but a box trap."

"Gloom, despair, and blessed misery," Kildragon chided. "Come in out of the fog and look around, Haaken. Take a gander at them girls. Check the look in their eyes. I mean, they're ready to attack." He waved at the nearest.

"Sanguinet's going to…."

A girl rushed Reskird. She shoved flowers into his hands, fell into step beside him. She chattered. Kildragon chattered back. Lack of a common tongue didn't hamper communication.

Haaken's jaw dropped. He pasted on a sickly smile and started waving. "Hello, hello," he croaked.

"Smooth," Bragi observed. "You're a real sweet talker, little brother." He straightened his pack and tried to look appealing without showing off. They had given him his squad leader's post back, provisionally, because Haaken would not keep it in his stead. He was supposed to show a certain decorum.

He caught his captain watching him. Sanguinet wore an amused smirk. For reasons Ragnarson could not comprehend he had become a pet project of Sanguinet's soon after he had enlisted. That did not make life easier. Sanguinet rode him harder than he did anyone else.

They had stumbled into soldiers' heaven. The drinking was free, the women were easy, the people were desperate to please, and the duty was light. For the first time Bragi found himself enjoying soldiering.

The idyll lasted two weeks.

The horizons were masked by smoke. Nassef's warriors were not charitable conquerors. Anything they could not drive off or carry away they burned or killed. The Scourge of God appeared to be developing a vicious image deliberately.

"Sure are a lot of them," Bragi observed.

"Too many," Haaken said.

The Scourge of God had been closing in for days. Only a few outlying strongholds remained unsubdued.

"Must be a hundred thousand of them," Reskird guessed.

He was not overestimating much. The excitement of war and easy plunder had penetrated Hammad al Nakir's nethermost reaches. Thousands who cared not a fig for El Murid's revelations had answered his call to arms.

They might doubt his religious pretensions and social tinkering, but they loved his message of Imperial redemption and dominance, of historical rectification. The west had brought Ilkazar low. Now the hammer was in the other hand.

Reskird was having trouble concealing his trepidation.

"Tents like whitecaps on the sea," he murmured.

"Horses can't climb walls," Bragi reminded. And, "We'll make chopped meat out of them if they storm us."

Simballawein's defenders numbered twenty-five hundred Guildsmen and ten thousand experienced native troops. The Grand Council had armed a horde of city folk as well, but their value was doubtful. Even so, General Hawkwind believed he could ensure the city's safety.

"Something will go wrong," Haaken prophesied.

For once his pessimism proved well-founded.

Nassef had laid his groundwork early and well. His agents had performed perfectly. The attack began straightforwardly, concentrating on the south walls, which were held by native troops and city militia. Hordes of desert warriors rushed in to perish beneath the ramparts. As Bragi had observed, it was not their kind of warfare. The few engines they had bothered to build were almost laughably crude and vulnerable.

But Nassef knew his troops. That was why he had begun sugaring the path long before the invasion began.

In Simballawein, as everywhere, there was a breed of man loyal only to gold, and a class interested only in the political main chance. Nassef's agents had structured a pro-El Murid government-in-waiting from the latter. The quislings had used desert gold to hire desperadoes willing to betray their city.

They attacked Simballawein's South Gate from within, while its defenders were preoccupied with the attack from without. They opened the gate.

Scimitars flashed. Horsemen howled through the gateway. Iron-shod hooves sent sparks flying from cobbled streets. Arrows streaked from saddle-bows.

Arrows and javelins answered from windows and rooftops, but the unskilled citizen-soldiers could not stem the flood. They received conflicting orders from conspirators who had infiltrated their organization. Hastily assembled companies raced off to peaceful sectors. Panic spread. And all the while horsemen charged through the lost gate and spread out as swiftly as oil on water.

The panic spread to the rest of the city.

Panic had become Nassef's favorite weapon during his eastern campaigns. He had exploited it in his seizure of Al Rhemish. Now he was intent on teaching the western kingdoms the terror of the horseman who moved like lightning, who appeared and vanished, and struck where least expected.

Simballawein was like a dinosaur. Its immense size kept it from dying immediately.

The youths on the north wall watched the fires bloody the underbellies of the clouds and listened to the moans of a city collapsing.

"I think it's getting closer," Reskird said.

They knew what was happening. This was Simballawein's last independent night. And they were scared.

"How come we're just sitting here?" one of the soldiers asked.

"I don't know," Bragi admitted. "The captain will let us know what to do."

"So damned hot," Haaken muttered. The heat of the fires could be felt this far away.

"I don't want to second-guess Hawkwind...."

"Then don't, Reskird," Haaken grumbled.

"I was just going to say...."

"Ragnarson?" Lieutenant Trubacik carefully stepped over the legs of lounging soldiers. The ramparts were narrow.

"Here, sir."

"Report to the captain."

"Yes sir."

Trubacik moved to the next squad. "Haven?"

Bragi went to Sanguinet's command post. "Gather round," the captain said softly, when everyone had arrived. "And keep your voices down. All right. Here's the word. There's no hope of holding. The situation has deteriorated too much. The general has informed the Grand Council. Come midnight, we're pulling out."

Voices buzzed.

"Keep it down. Somebody out there might speak Itaskian. Gentlemen, I want you to speak to your men. The enemy main force has moved around to the south, but we're still going to have to fight. On the march. Discipline is going to make the difference. And we're going to have to give a little extra. We're green. There's going to be veterans in front of us and behind us, but we've still got to take care of our part of the line."

Bragi did not like it. Hawkwind thought he could fight his way through a larger, more mobile army?

"Maintaining discipline is a must. We're taking civilians with us. The Grand Councilors, their families, and the Tyrant. The Tyrant will bring his own escort, but don't count on them if it gets tight. We're in the narrow passage. We can't count on anybody but our brothers."

Ragnarson began to understand what it meant to be a Guildsman.

He also saw how Hawkwind could justify abandoning a commission. With Simballawein's rulers deserting their people, he would be following his commissioners.

"The march will be short. We'll hit a bay on the coast twelve miles north of here. A fleet is waiting to pick us up."

"Why not sail from here?" somebody asked.

"The waterfront is in enemy hands. That's all, men. There isn't much time. Explain to your people. Discipline and silence. Discipline and silence."

The group dispersed. Similar assemblies broke up elsewhere.

"It's crazy," Reskird protested. "They'll get us all killed."

"How much chance have we got here?" Bragi demanded. "Haaken, find me a dirty sock."

"What?"

"Get me a sock. I'm going to cram it in his mouth and keep it there till we're aboard ship. I don't want him shooting his mouth off out there and getting us wiped out."

"Hey!" Reskird protested.

"That's the last noise I want to hear out of you tonight. Get your stuff. Here comes Trubacik."

"Ready, Ragnarson?"

"Ready, sir."

"Take them down to the street. The captain will form you up."

The wait in the dark street, behind the gate, seemed eternal. Even Sanguinet became impatient. Several Grand Councilors were late.

Native soldiers kept drifting in and joining the Tyrant's bodyguard. The Guildsmen became nervous. News of the proposed breakout was spreading. The enemy would hear before long.

Hawkwind reviewed his troops during the delay. He was a small, slim man in his fifties. He looked like a harmless shopkeeper, not the most devastating captain of the age. Till one looked him in the eye.

Bragi saw raw power in the man. Raw power and pure will. Only death Herself could best a man like General Sir Tury Hawkwind.

Hawkwind completed the review, then informed the Tyrant he would wait no longer. The gates opened. Ragnarson was surprised how quietly they moved.

A moment later he was double-timing into jeopardy. Enemy watchfires formed constellations on the hills and plains. He clutched his weapons and kit to keep them from clattering, and tried not to be afraid.

But he was scared. Badly scared. Again. After all he had survived, he felt his capacity for fear should have been blunted.

They started north on the road that had brought Sanguinet's company south. They would leave it later and follow another to the coast.

First contact came quickly. Nassef's men were alert. But they were not ready for a sally in force. The Guildsmen cut through easily.

Bragi suddenly understood why Hawkwind had chosen to flee at midnight. Darkness negated the enemy's speed and maneuverability. Only suicides galloped around when they couldn't see.

Nevertheless, Nassef's men kept getting in the way. And when they slowed the column, their brethren overtook it from behind.

The fighting seldom reached Bragi's company. He and Haaken occupied themselves carrying a Guildsman who had fallen and nearly been left behind. They did not talk much.

An hour fled. Miles passed. Another hour trudged into the warehouse of time. Hawkwind kept moving. The enemy could not place a preponderance of strength into his path.

Hours and miles. The sky began lightening.

"I hear the breakers," Haaken gasped. Their burden had become agonizingly heavy.

Bragi snorted. "Even if we were close, you couldn't hear the surf over the noise we're making."

But Haaken was right. They tramped through an olive grove and there lay the sea. A galaxy of lanterns sparkled on the water as ships signaled their whereabouts.

"The ships," Haaken muttered to himself. "I see the ships."

The run ended ten minutes later. The secundus and tercio started digging in. Longboats began carrying Councilors to the vessels.

It was a big fleet. Some of the ships had escaped Simballawein. Some, Hellin Daimiel had sent against this contingency. The Daimiellians wanted to salvage Guildsmen who might stiffen their own defenses.

El Murid's men attacked, but without verve or organization. These were not fanatics, they were plunderers. They saw no profit in trying to obliterate a beaten foe. The Guildsmen repulsed them easily.

Bragi's company was one of the last into the boats.

He was digging an arrowhead from Reskird's shoulder when Sanguinet said, "You boys might have the stuff after all."

Bragi was startled. He had not noticed the captain getting aboard.

"Sir?"

"I saw you pick up a man and carry him to the beach."

"He was one of ours."

"You'll make it, Ragnarson. So will your brother. The man was dead the last three miles."

"What? I never noticed."

"What's wrong with your sidekick there? He don't stay this quiet when he's asleep."

"I told him to shut up. He was getting on my nerves."

"Oh? Maybe he'll make a Guildsman too."

"Maybe. You can talk now, Reskird. You made your point."

But Kildragon refused. He was sulking.

The fleet made Hellin Daimiel three days later.

Nassef's horde had raced them northward. The roads out of the city had been cut. A noose was tightening fast. In a few days the sea would be the city's only means of communication.

Hellin Daimiel was not Simballawein. Nassef's confederates were caught and hung before they did any harm.

Bragi's company spent six weeks there, remaining till Hawkwind and the ruling council were sure the city was in no immediate danger.

"Company meeting," Lieutenant Trubacik told Ragnarson one morning. "The rumors were right. We're moving out."

Sanguinet was sour. "The Citadel is sending us to the Lesser Kingdoms. Nassef isn't interested in Hellin Daimiel right now. Meanwhile, Itaskia and the other northern states are raising an army. We're supposed to keep Nassef from clearing his eastern flank, to threaten him into staying south of the Scarlotti till the northern army arrives. It'll be tough, especially if the Kaveliners don't hold in the Savernake Gap.

"We're going to Altea. I guess it's mainly a moral gesture. One company can't do much. My opinion is that we'll be wasting ourselves. The Citadel should assemble the whole brotherhood and take the initiative. But High Crag didn't ask me what I thought.

"We'll board ships in the morning. They'll ferry us to Dunno Scuttari. We'll transfer to river boats there. We'll off-load somewhere in eastern Altea and play hit-and-run.

"Gentlemen, we're the best warriors in the world. But this time I think somebody is a little too sure of us. Break it to your men gently."

Sanguinet entertained only a few questions. He did not have any answers.

Reskird had ended his sulk in the taverns and whorehouses of the city. He was his old self. "You look like death on a stick," he told Bragi. "What's up?"

"They're shipping us to the Lesser Kingdoms."

"Huh?"

"Altea, specifically. On our own. You'd better hope that Sanguinet is as good a captain as he was a sergeant."

Haaken had no comment. He just shook his head gloomily.

SIX

THE WANDERER

The fat youth's arms and legs pistoned wildly. He had done it again. The boys behind him had never heard of the concept mercy.

His donkey, for once, was cooperative. She trotted beside him, eyes rolling forlornly, as if to ask if he would ever learn his lesson. He was headed for an early bout with cut-throat-itis, an often fatal disease.

He was on a downhill slide, this Mocker. The town he was leaving was called Lieneke. It was hardly more than a village. A chance aggregation of bumpkins. And even they had caught on to his cheating.

A fragment of the message had begun to penetrate his brain. He was going to have to do things differently from now on. Assuming he got away this time.

The boys of Lieneke were a determined, persistent lot, but they did not have enough at stake. Fat and lazy though he was, Mocker had stamina. He kept windmilling till they gave up the chase.

He did not go on any farther than it took to get out of sight. Then he collapsed by the roadside and did not move for two days.

He did some hard thinking during that time, and finally convinced himself that he did not have what it took to cheat his way through life.

But what else could he do? His only skills were those he had learned from Sajac and his ilk.

He ought to find a patron, he thought. Somebody stupid but buried in inherited wealth. He smiled wryly, then steeled himself for a serious effort to avoid games of chance and outright thefts.

His visible profession was socially acceptable. Sure, he obtained money under false pretenses, but his customers were fooling themselves. The popular attitude was a tolerant *caveat emptor*. People gullible enough to buy his crazy advice and noxious beauty aids deserved whatever they got.

He finally moved on when a combination of hunger and fear caught up with him. The passage of a party of knights caused the fear.

He had encountered a similar band near Vorgreberg several weeks earlier. The men-at-arms had beaten him simply because he was a foreigner. He had not accepted his beating graciously, and that had not helped. He was a wicked little fighter when cornered. He had hurt several of them badly. They might have killed him had a knight not interceded.

Kavelin was a state typical of the Lesser Kingdoms. Those minor principalities were a crazy hodge-podge where social chaos was the norm. They were lands of weak kings, strong barons, and byzantine politics. National boundaries seldom defined or confined loyalties, alliances, or conspiracies. Wars between nobles were everyday occurrences. Uncontrolled sub-infeudation had reached illogical extremes. The robber baron was an endemic social disease. The blank-shield highwayman-knight was a neighborhood character.

It was the sort of region for which a Mocker was made.

Western Kavelin was in confusion at the moment. The barons there were at one another's throats. Their little armies were plundering the innocent far more often than battling one another. A lot of loot was floating around.

Mocker decided that Damhorst, which appeared to be an islet of peace amidst all the excitement, was the perfect place to launch his abbreviated career.

Damhorst was a town of ten thousand, prosperous, quiet, and pleasant. The grim old castle perched on a crag above the town was intimidating enough to compel good behavior. Baron Breitbarth had a cruel reputation with wrongdoers.

Damhorst's prosperity was in part due to the fact that bands of soldiers from the fighting came there to dispose of their plunder, receiving ridiculously low prices.

A representative cross-section of Mocker's peers had located themselves around the town square. The fat youth moved in and fit in. Even his coloring and accent were unremarkable.

The fates immediately tried his resolve. His traditional pitch was not geared to milking soldiers looking for escape from yesterday and tomorrow. His forte was conning vain women. But the ladies he encountered there were mostly world-wise women of doubtful repute. They did not need his wares to help sell what his usual customers had trouble giving away.

But the fates occasionally relent. And sometimes they try to make amends for dealing out a lifetime of dirty tricks by yielding one golden opportunity.

It was a pleasant day. Mocker had to admit that Kavelin was pleasant most of the time. Politics were the true foul climate plaguing the little kingdom.

The leaves had begun to turn. He found them a great amazement. There were few trees in the lands from which he hailed. The swirls and bursts of color in Kavelin's forests made him wish he were a painter, so that he could capture their fleeting beauty for all time.

It was a warm and listless day. He sat on his mat, amidst his props, and regarded his world with no more than half an eye. Not even the fact that he hadn't a copper daunted him. He was at peace with, and one with, his universe. He was caught in one of those all too rare moments of perfectly harmonious lightness.

Then he saw her.

She was beautiful. Young and pretty and filled with sorrow. And lost. She meandered around the square dazedly, as if she had nowhere to go and had forgotten how to get there. She seemed frail and completely vulnerable.

Mocker felt the touch of a strange emotion. It might have been compassion. He could not have named it himself. The concept was alien.

Nevertheless, the emotion was there and he responded. When her random wandering brought her near he queried softly, "Lady?"

She glanced his way and saw a pair of hand puppets flanking a round brown face. The right hand puppet bowed graciously.

The other whistled.

The first barked, "Manners, Polo, you churl!" and zipped over to wallop the whistler. "Behave before lady of quality."

Mocker winked over his forearm. He wore a thin little smile.

She was younger than he had guessed at first. Not more than eighteen.

The first puppet bowed again and said, "Self, beg thousand pardons, noble lady. Peasant Polo was born in barn and raised by tomcat of more than usual lack of couth or morals." He took a few more whacks at the other puppet. "Barbarian."

When the first puppet returned to Mocker's right, Polo whistled again. The first moaned, "Hai! What can be done with savage like that? Want to slap manners into same?"

She smiled. "I think he's kind of cute."

Polo did a shy routine while the first puppet cried in bewilderment, "Woe! Will never civilize same when beautiful lady rewards crudeness with heart-stopping smile."

"You're new here, aren't you?" The girl directed the question to Mocker.

"Came to town three days passing, lately from east, beyond Mountains of M'Hand."

"So far! I've never even been to Vorgreberg. I thought when I married Wulf.... But it's silly to worry about might-have-beens, isn't it?"

"Assuredly. Tomorrow too full of just-could-be to chase might-have-been lost in yesterday."

First Puppet hid behind his little arms. "You hear that, Polo? Big guy is spouting philosophical nonsense again."

"Will make first class fertilizer when spread on cabbage patch, Tubal," Polo replied. "We ignore him, eh? Hey, lady, you hear joke about priest and magic staff?"

Tubal sputtered. "Polo, peasant like you would disgust devil himself. Behave. Or I ask big guy to feed you to skull."

"Skull ain't biting," said a third voice as Mocker cast his into the prop's mouth. "On diet. Have to lose weight."

Mocker himself said, "Being mere street mummer, have no right to pry. But self sense great despair in lady and am saddened. Day is too fair for grief."

"Oh. My husband.... Sir Wulf Heerboth. He died last night. I didn't sleep at all."

Tubal and Polo exchanged glances. They turned to peer at Mocker. He shrugged. He was at a loss. "Is great pity one so fair should be widowed so young."

"We had such precious little time.... What am I saying? I'm almost glad. He was a beast. My father arranged the marriage. It was two years of torment, that's what it was. Now I'm free of that."

Mocker began to see the parameters. In part she was grieving because she was supposed to, in part feeling guilty for feeling released, and in part feeling insecure in the face of a future without a protector.

"Beautiful lady like you, knight's lady.... Noblemen will come swarming when mourning period elapses. Self, guarantee it. Certain as self is magus primus of Occlidian Circle. Be not afraid, lady. And be not ashamed for glad feelings for freedom from slavery to wicked husband. Never, never make self into what family and friends expect. Is road to misery absolute. Self, speak from certain knowledge."

"Oh-oh," said Polo. "Here we go. Tall tale time."

"That seems like awfully deep thinking for someone your age."

Mocker doubted that she was more than a year older than he, but he did not protest.

Tubal replied, "Big guy was born in hole in ground. Deep hole."

The girl smiled. "Well…."

"Is deep subject, too. Of varying depth. In Shoustal-Watka…."

"What's your name, mummer?"

He could not generate one on the spur of the moment, so confessed, "Self, am ashamed. Don't know. Call self Mocker in own mind."

"What about your parents?"

"Never knew same."

"You were an orphan?"

He shrugged. He did not think so. He liked to believe that Sajac had carried him off out of spite for his parents, that even now they were looking for him. He might be a missing prince, or the lost son of a great mercantile house. "Maybeso."

"That's awful. Don't you have anybody?"

"Old man, once. Traveled with same for while. He died."

A tiny fraction of his mind kept telling him that he was getting himself into trouble. There were two kinds of people in his world: marks, and people he left alone because they could stir more trouble than he could handle. This woman fit neither category neatly. That made her doubly dangerous. He did not know which way to jump.

"That's sad," she said. "My father is still alive, and that's kind of sad too. I just know he's going to try to get his hands on everything Wulf left me."

Ping! went a little something in the back of Mocker's mind. "This father…. Same is superstitious? Self, being most skilled of tricksters…."

"I couldn't do anything to my own father! Even if he did marry me off hoping Wulf would get himself killed. It wouldn't be right…."

Tubal interrupted. "Was remark made, not too long passing, to effect don't allow friends and family to run life. Big guy was close to truth."

"You don't know my father."

"Truth told," Mocker replied. "And same does not know portly purveyor of punditries. So. Things equal to same thing are equal. Something like that. Hai! Lady. Self, being easily embarrassed, cannot forever call conversant 'beautiful lady.' Same must have name."

"Oh. Yes. Kirsten. Kirsten Heerboth."

"Kirsten. Has beautiful ring. Like carillon. Appropriate. Kirsten, we make deal, maybeso? For small emolument, self, being mighty engineer, will undertake to prevent predations of pestilential parent. Also rapacities of others of same ilk. Am easily satisfied, being wanderer mainly interested in visiting foreign lands, needing only bed and board. Would be willing to begin with latter."

"I don't know…. It doesn't seem…. Are you really hungry?"

"Hungry?" Polo said. "Big guy is putting eye on horse across square, same being prizest mount of Chief Justiciar of Damhorst."

"Well, come along then. I don't guess it'll hurt to give you dinner. But you'll have to promise me something."

Mocker sighed. "Same being?"

"Let Polo tell me about the priest and the magic staff."

"Disgusting!" Tubal growled as Mocker stuffed him into his traveling kit. "Absolutely shocking," the puppet muttered from inside.

Mocker grinned.

Kirsten maintained a small townhouse on the edge of Damhorst, in the shadow of Baron Breitbarth's grim old castle. An elderly maid-cook constituted her staff. Sir Wulf had been one of those highwayman-knights, and only marginally successful. He had left Kirsten the house, one gold trade noble, and a small leather bag of jewels she had found inside his shirt after he died in her arms. The gold would carry her a month or two, and the jewels several years more, but she was hardly fixed for life.

Mocker reiterated his remark to the effect that her beauty was her fortune.

The visit for a meal turned into a month-long stay. Daily, Mocker would spread his mat in the square—he insisted that he had his pride—and would pursue his routines. Sometimes he was successful. People enjoyed the entertainment portions of his spiel. More often than not, Kirsten would come and watch. He seemed to have an infinite store of blarney.

Evenings he amused her with tales from the east. She was particularly fond of Tubal and Polo, who were famous puppet-show characters east of the Mountains of M'Hand. The contest of city-slicker with simple farm boy seemed to have a universal appeal. The traditional plays were all adaptable to rural or urban audiences.

Time, proximity, and loneliness worked their devious magicks. Mocker and Kirsten became more than accomplices, then more than friends.

Handling Kirsten's father took little imagination. Mocker used earnings from the square to pay a couple of thugs to escort the man out of town. He had no trouble understanding the message in his lumps and bruises. He kept traveling.

Kirsten never learned about that, of course. She remained *amazed* that the old man had paid but the one friendly visit.

Mocker began to feel vaguely lost. He had had plans. Nebulous things, to be sure, but they had been plans. They were going by the board because of a chance-met woman.

He had become involved with a human being on more than an adversary or use level. He did not know how to handle it. Nothing like it had ever happened before.

The deeper he got, the more uncomfortable he became.

He almost panicked the day Kirsten mentioned that she had been to see a priest, and that the priest wanted to see him too. He barely restrained himself from flight.

A few days afterward Kirsten swore, "Damn! Do you have any money on you? Mine's gone."

He lied, shaking his head. "Has been abominable week. Autumn rains. Getting too cold, too muddy."

"I guess it means selling the jewels. I talked to Tolvar last week. The goldsmith on the High Street. He said he'd make me a good price. Why don't you run them over and see what he'll offer?"

"Self? By night? In town thick with rogues and thieves?" His heart hammered. He could not picture himself lasting five minutes with a fortune like that on him.

His worldview crippled him. He saw in everyone the thief he was himself.

"You can handle yourself, darling. I've seen you. Besides, who would know that you're carrying them?"

"Everybodys. Self, being nervous, would worry too loud…."

"Don't be silly." She shoved the leather bag into his pudgy hands. "Go on. Or we won't have anything to eat tomorrow."

He went. His intentions were honorable. Kirsten was his first love. Temptation did not bite him till he entered the High Street itself.

He froze.

He thought about everything jewels could buy. About Kirsten and an imminent visit to a priest. About opportunities in games of chance opened by unlimited betting funds. About that damned priest….

He panicked. This time he did run.

He did not realize that he had left his donkey and props till he was over the border into the kingdom of Altea.

By then it was too late. He could not go back. He had damned himself with Kirsten forever.

It hurt. A lot. For weeks the pain kept him contained within himself, and out of trouble.

But the ache just would not go away. He began drinking to deaden it. And in Alperin, a small town in southern Altea, while drunk, he wandered into a dice game.

His luck was terrible. His mental state contributed nothing to intelligent betting. Before they let him go he was broke again, having retained just enough common sense to have earlier re-equipped himself with the tools of his dubious trade.

The exigencies of surviving an Altean winter banished Kirsten from his thoughts. He had no time for her. She fled him forever.

With her went his proud resolutions about gambling and thieving.

He ceased giving a damn about tomorrow. His future looked too bleak. He could no longer scrutinize it. And the less he cared, the bleaker it became.

He had fallen into a paradoxical trap. Though filled with a lust for life and learning, he was systematically eradicating tomorrows with wine and stupid crimes.

Tamerice lay south of Altea, a long snake of a kingdom squished between the Kapenrung Mountains and the Altean frontier. Mocker drifted into Tamerice with spring. His successes had been just frequent enough to keep body and soul together. His weight had declined. He had developed a shakiness which occasionally betrayed him when he tried one of his more complicated tricks.

He drew his best response when he stooped to entertaining. Tamericians enjoyed the Tubal and Polo plays. But a false pride or unconscious death wish drove him. He performed only when gnawing hunger compelled it.

He reached the town of Raemdouck the day after a carnival had arrived, and spread his mat beside the road the Raemdouckers followed to the field where the carnival had raised its tents. A preselected traffic helped him marginally.

His third morning there, before traffic picked up, he had a visitor. The man was tall, lean, and had tight, dark eyes in a hard face. Policeman? Bandit? Mocker wondered nervously.

The man sat down facing him, stared for more than a minute.

Mocker wriggled. A demon ground coarse salt into his nerve endings.

"I'm Damo Sparen," his visitor finally announced. His voice was as cold and hard as his appearance. "I own the carnival. I've been watching you."

Mocker shrugged. Was he supposed to beg forgiveness for bleeding off a minuscule portion of the man's revenues?

"You're interesting. One of the nastier cases of self-abuse I've seen. Talent bleeds out of you, and you waste it to the last ounce. Do you *want* to die young?"

Mocker gulped. "Maybeso. In thousand years, or two." He grinned weakly. He was scared. "What is going on here?"

"I wanted to tell you something. I'm no diviner, but this prediction doesn't require the skills of a necromancer. You will die. Soon. Unless you mend your ways."

Mocker's fear tightened its noose.

"You keep cutting purses, somebody's going to cut your throat. Before summer's done. You're too damned clumsy."

Mocker swallowed the lump in that throat. He was bewildered. The man sounded like an evangelist.

"My eastern friend, I'm going to give you a chance to see Old Man Winter again. I'm looking for someone with your talents and not much conscience. I could use you. If we could dry you out and knock a little sense in your head. You've got the skills, but they're in bad shape."

"Self, am unsure hearing is accurate. Explicate, please. Am being offered position?"

"Conditionally. I need a ventriloquist and magician. My performers usually get a share of the net. In your case that won't hold unless you shape up. I'll give you food, found, and lessons in whatever you don't already have. Hypnotism, for instance. Make it a trial period of three months. If you stop the drinking and stealing…. Don't try to bullshit me, my friend. I told you I've been watching you.

"Even without a share it's more than you've got now. Like I said, you won't last the summer this way."

Mocker hemmed and hawed. He could not believe the man was serious. Nevertheless, he decided to take a chance. He could be no worse off.

It was a fateful decision. Damo Sparen would quickly shape the raw Mocker clay into the man he would become.

Sparen was a westerner, and older, but was Mocker's spiritual brother. Their black, lazy souls had been struck on the same dies.

While supervising Mocker's higher education, Sparen became his first real friend.

"One thing you've got to learn," Sparen told him early on. "Discipline. Your troubles all stem from a lack of discipline."

Mocker sputtered.

"I mean self-discipline, not the poundings you got from Sajac. They're part of your problem, too. You don't know how to handle your freedom.

"My friend, you made it this far on sheer talent. But you've got to learn some things that don't come instinctively. You've refused so far. So you've been hungry a lot.

"Sparen's First Law: Always make the mark think he's smarter than you are. Make him think it's him doing the con. Greed will carry it for you then.

"Second Law: Don't work a con where you're boosting. Or vice versa. I warned you before, don't steal around the carnival. Yesterday you cut a purse within a hundred feet of your puppet show. Don't let it happen again. I'm not patient. You could get my whole operation broken up.

"Third Law: Don't aggravate the underworld. You got to stay in good with those guys. They're organized. You leave a bad marker with Three Fingers in Hellin Daimiel and run off to Octylya, when you get there the Dragon's men will be waiting. With knives. They like to do each other little favors.

"Fourth Law: Think big. That crap of sitting in the street selling mud packs made with cat's piss ain't got no future. You'll be doing the same thing fifty years from now. Just like Sajac."

Mocker finally interjected, "Self, am able to do only what is known to self."

"Then suppose you stop scheming and stealing long enough to learn something? You're secure here. You don't have to take risks. Expand your talents instead. Look at me, Mocker. I started out where you are now. Today I've got a villa on the Auszura Littoral. A duke is my next door neighbor. I've got copra plantations in Simballawein. I've got mines in Anstokin."

"Hai! And still…."

"And still I travel with the carnival? Of course. It's in my blood. It's in yours. We can't resist the challenge. Of what the carnival represents. One more sucker taken for everything but his greedy smile. But I don't do that kind of thing as Sparen. Sparen and his carnival are cover. Sparen is an honest and respected businessman. People trust him enough to loan him money."

For once in his life Mocker listened.

"You had what you needed when you got a hold of those jewels. Working capital. More than I started with. How in heaven's name could you have wasted it that way?"

"Self, am mystified. Am bambazoolooed. Am utterly ignorant of course to pursue."

"That's good. That's a beautiful touch. The way you talk. Never change it. If they can't understand you, they can't ever be sure their losses weren't their own fault. At worst, you'll get a little more getaway time. And it'll help convince them they're smarter that you are."

"First Law."

"Exactly."

Mocker's secondary education proceeded apace. He began to learn the self-restraint that had been missing most of his life. Sparen gave a little heavy-handed encouragement, in the form of a gigantic thug named Gouch who was always there, sap in hand, when temptation stalked too close.

"I think we're getting somewhere, my friend," Sparen told him late that summer. And he meant the word friend. They had become as close as two men could. "I think you're ready to be a partner."

"Hai! Good. Self, have several ideas...."

"This war thing has got me scared," Sparen told him, trampling his enthusiasm. "They're bully-ragging Throyes. If those crazies take over and come out of Hammad al Nakir, they'll crawl all over the Lesser Kingdoms. They'll ruin us. I've seen what a war can do to business. Luckily, this carnival business isn't the only one. There're a few better suited to wartime. It's time to start getting ready. Just in case." Sparen downed a long draft of wine. "You know, I never had a son. Not that I could acknowledge. I think I've kind of found one now."

Mocker's eyes narrowed. Was this just talk born of a mating 'twixt wine and melancholy?

"Well, that's neither here nor there. We've got to find you a trade name. Magellin the Magician strikes me. I used to have a partner who went by that. But I caught him shorting the accounts. Had to elevate his spirit to a higher plane and lower his flesh to the fishes. It was a sad occasion. I cried for an hour. I thought he was a good friend. Don't you do that to me, you hear?"

"Is farthest thing from mind, guaranteed. Have developed healthy respect for Gouch and own neck. Have learned to mend ways."

Which was not strictly true. He had learned a lot of wicked and wonderful things from Sparen and Gouch, but mending his ways was not one of them. He never could stifle his urge to cut a purse, or to squander his takings gambling.

What he did learn was how to manage theft with finesse, while Gouch was watching, so that he alone knew what was going on.

SEVEN
THE EXILES

The first assassins reached the mountain camp with the spring thaw. Six good men died stopping them. "Always in threes," Haroun gasped. He was pale and soaked with sweat. "Harish always come in threes. What moves men like that, Beloul? They knew they were going to die."

Beloul shrugged and shook his head. "They believe in their cause, Lord."

A second team materialized almost immediately, and a third followed close behind. Haroun imagined an endless line of smiling, vacant-eyed men coming to die for their prophet, each certain of immediate entry into Paradise.

Distinguishing friend from foe was impossible in the ongoing refugee chaos.

"Beloul, I can't stay here," Haroun declared after the third attack left eight followers dead. "I'm a sitting target. They won't stop as long as they know where to find me."

"Let them come. I'll strip every newcomer and look for the Harish tattoo." The cultists wore a tattoo over the heart. It faded after death, purportedly when the soul ascended to Paradise.

"They'll send men without it. I'm moving out. I'll drift from camp to camp. I have to show the flag anyway, don't I?" Winter boredom moved him as much as did the attacks. He was driven by a youthful eagerness to be moving, to be doing. He selected a half dozen companions and departed.

The camps heightened his appreciation of his mission. He was appalled.

The break with Hammad al Nakir meant a break with a fragile culture and briefly settled past. In some places the ancient desert ways, the nomadic, pre-Royal ways, were reemerging.

"What's wrong with plundering foreigners?" asked a captain in a camp run by an old functionary named Shadek el Senoussi.

"*We* are the foreigners here, you idiot!" Haroun glanced at el Senoussi. The man's face was a mask. "And these people are more understanding than I would be were our roles reversed. I'll tell you a thing, Shadek. If your men bother your neighbors again I'll swing the headsman's blade myself. Quesani law endures, even in exile. Its protection extends to everyone who welcomed us in our extremity."

"I hear, Lord." The old man wore a slight smile now. Haroun had a distinct feeling he approved.

"This is the end of it, then. If it chokes you, tough. Treat your neighbors as equals. We need their help."

Rebellion smouldered in el Senoussi's men. Haroun glared back. The old man needed replacing. He commanded too much personal loyalty.

Few of the camp leaders were enthusiastic about him. Some were spiritual brothers of El Murid's generals: born bandits smelling opportunity in chaos. Others simply did not like being commanded by an untried youth.

He drifted westward, accompanied only by his bodyguards. He met and assessed all his captains. Then he began to seek allies.

He discovered that a claimed kingship opened no doors. "We'll see," he grumbled after yet another rejection. "They'll sing a different song when the Scourge of God begins hammering the Lesser Kingdoms."

"Let them burn," one guard suggested.

"Will he really come?" another asked.

"Someone will. My old teacher called it historical inertia. Nothing can stop it. Not even the deaths of Nassef and El Murid."

"Many men will die, then."

"Too many, and a lot of them ours. The Disciple doesn't know what he's doing."

He tried. He tried bravely and hard, and won no support anywhere. And he went on, his mission driving him mercilessly. His guards began to fear he was obsessed.

Finally, he admitted defeat. There would be no help while the Lesser Kingdoms were not directly threatened. He returned to the camps.

He was in el Senoussi's encampment when Harish assassins found him again. Three teams attacked together. They slew his bodyguards. They slew half a score of Shadek's men. They wounded Haroun twice before el Senoussi rescued him.

"Dismiss me, Lord!" the old man begged. "My failure cannot be excused."

"Stop that. It couldn't be helped. Ouch! Careful, man!" A horse trainer was dressing his wounds. "We have a savage, determined enemy, Shadek. This is going to keep on till we're killed or we destroy him."

"I should have seen through them, Lord."

"May be. May be. But how?" Haroun grew thoughtful. The attack had shaken el Senoussi, yet he seemed more upset because it had happened at his camp than because it had happened to his king.

El Senoussi, Haroun recalled, was an appointee of King Aboud's, a lifelong functionary. He'd spent decades shunning blame and appropriating credit. "Forget the Harish, Shadek. They're like the weather. We have to live with them. Meantime, we have fires to put out." The assassins had started several. Billowing smoke still climbed the sky.

The log blockhouse that was the camp's bailey, and a hutment against the palisade, stubbornly resisted the firemen. The swiftness with which the flames had taken hold bespoke careful preparation.

"Why did they go to the trouble?" Haroun wondered. "They could have killed me if they hadn't wasted the time."

"I don't know, Lord."

The answer came three hours later.

A sentinel called, "Invincibles!"

"Here?" Haroun demanded. "In Tamerice?" He peered over the stockade.

Horsemen were coming out of a nearby wood. They wore Invincible white.

"Must be a hundred of them, Lord," el Senoussi estimated. "The fires must have been a signal."

"So it would seem." Haroun surveyed the encampment. Women and children were moving provisions into the charred blockhouse. They looked scared, but were not panicking. El Senoussi had drilled them well.

"Lord, escape while you can. I only have eighty-three men. Some of them are wounded."

"I'll stay. What good a King who always runs away?"

"He's alive when his moment comes."

"Let them come. I was trained in the Power." He spoke from bravado and frustration. He wanted to hit back.

El Senoussi backed away. "A sorcerer-king?"

Haroun saw the fear-reflections of the kings of Ilkazar gleaming in the man's eyes.

"No. Hardly. But maybe I can blow a little smoke into their eyes."

The Invincibles knew what they were doing. Their intelligence was perfect. Their first attack penetrated the stockade despite Haroun's shaghûnry and a ferocious defense.

"They're getting through where the hutment burned," Haroun shouted. He whirled. El Senoussi was barking orders. Warriors grabbed saddle bows and sped arrows into the throng in the gap, but the Invincibles entered the compound anyway.

"Go to the blockhouse, sire," el Senoussi urged. "You're just one more sword out here. You can bedevil them with your witchery from there."

Haroun allowed himself to be guided through the tumult. He saw the sense of Shadek's argument.

He *was* more effective from the blockhouse. He did little things and quickly betrayed individual enemies. The Invincibles gave up.

"That was close," Haroun told el Senoussi.

"It's not over. They're not going away. They're circling the camp."

Haroun looked over the palisade. "Some are circling. Some look like they're going for help."

"You'd better leave tonight, Lord."

It was the practical, logical, pragmatic course, but Haroun did not like it. "They'll be waiting for me to try. Or for somebody going after help."

"Naturally. But would they expect us to attack? They believe their own reputation. If we sallied without trying to get away...."

"It might confuse them because it doesn't make much sense."

"It does if it gets you away, Lord."

"I don't understand you, Shadek."

"Don't try, Lord. Just go. And send help."

Haroun fled during el Senoussi's third sally. He went afoot, creeping like a thief, grinding his teeth because his wounds ached. He trudged doggedly through the night, ignoring his pain.

Dawn caught him fifteen miles northeast of the encampment. That put him just twenty from Tamerice's capital, Feagenbruch. The nearest refugee camp was more than forty miles away. He decided to try the capital.

It was risky. Tamerice's nobles might be so timorous they would ignore this compromise of the kingdom's sovereignty.

If they did react, though, they would make independent witnesses to an aggression. Tamerice and its neighbors might assume a more bellicose stance toward El Murid.

That chance was worth the risk. El Senoussi's was only an interim encampment. Its loss would not constitute a significant defeat.

The Invincibles wanted to destroy him, not the camp, anyway. The big, important camps they would like to raid were all in the far north.

Haroun was known in Feagenbruch, and not well liked. He had aggravated the lords of that city with his importunities before.

He used his wounds, youth, and title to obtain entrée. He spoke well while explaining to the king's seneschal. He spoke even better once shown into the presence of the king himself.

"It's an outrage, Majesty," the seneschal opined. "We can't let such arrogance go unchallenged."

"Then gather what knights you can muster. Lead them yourself. Cousin," the king told Haroun, "accept my hospitality while this temerity is being rewarded."

"I thank you, Cousin," Haroun replied. He smiled softly. Indirectly, the man had recognized his claim to the Peacock Throne.

At week's end news came that the Invincibles had been defeated and harried back into the Kapenrung Mountains. El Senoussi's people had survived.

The shock waves of the incursion would, in time, course throughout the Lesser Kingdoms, stimulating the growth of animosity toward El Murid.

The Lesser Kingdoms were small and often impotent, but each was jealous of its independence and sovereignty. Nationalism was stronger there than in the larger kingdoms.

Haroun met a man while he was waiting for the news.

It was an inconsequential thing then, but in time would shape the destinies of kingdoms.

Bored with Tamerice's squalid palace, which was a hovel compared even to

Haroun's own boyhood home, he began sampling the excitements of the spring fair set up in the meadow north of town.

One afternoon he was watching the swordswallower when he sensed the approach of a wrongness. He could identify no positive threat. That puzzled him. Usually his intuition was more precise. He looked around.

He had come without guards. If ever there was a time for the Harish to strike, this was it. He damned himself for taking an unnecessary risk.

He reached with his shaghûn's senses.

That godawful palace.... Tamerice's rulers were a barbarous lot. Unlettered thick-wits disguising themselves in the trappings of noblemen. Feh! The only conversationalist there was a treasury clerk hired out of Hellin Daimiel....

Only one individual stood out of the crowd of lean farmers and ginger-haired city folk. Short, fat, brown, apparently of Haroun's own age, he was an obvious alien. There was a hint of the desert about him, yet Haroun could not recall ever having seen a fat poor man there.

He let his senses dwell on the fat youth.

He *was* the source of the wrongness.

He's insane if he thinks he can get away with murder here, Haroun thought. He grabbed that notion, turned it over to look at its belly side.

The fat youth was no Harish crazy. Haroun sensed that quickly. He was up to something else.

Haroun's curiosity rose. He allowed himself to be stalked.

He had seen the fat man earlier. He was one of the carnival performers. He did a good, if sometimes confusing, job of entertaining.

The fat youth was quick and deft. Haroun did not miss his purse for half a minute.

An instant's distraction was all it took, that one brief moment when the swordswallower breathed fire and Haroun was trying to puzzle out the mechanics of the trick.

He whirled when the realization hit him.

The fat youth was gone.

Bin Yousif smiled grimly. This thief was good, but he was a fool.

Haroun loosened his weapons and strolled toward the tent behind the booth where the fat youth had performed earlier.

Coins clinked inside the tent.

Haroun peeped through a tear. The youth was counting and grinning. His back was to the entrance.

Doubly a fool, Haroun thought. He entered the tent with the stealth of a ferret. He waited with his dagger bare.

The youth suddenly sensed his presence. He whirled, trying to rise.

Haroun's dagger pricked his throat. "Down!"

He plopped. Haroun thrust out a palm. His eyes were cold and hard and merciless. The fat youth's were frightened and calculating. "My money." Haroun's voice was soft and dangerous.

The thief started to say something, thought better of it. He handed Haroun his purse.

"The rest." He had seen the gold piece disappear. The youth was good, but he knew the tricks too. "Good. Now tell me why I shouldn't have you hung."

The youth began twitching.

So did Haroun's hand. His dagger pricked a dark throat again. "I was trained in the Power. You can't move fast enough to surprise me."

The youth stared at him.

"Do you know who I am?"

"No."

"Haroun bin Yousif."

The thief frowned, puzzled. Then, "Same being called King Without Throne?"

"Yes."

"So?"

"So you picked the wrong man, Lard Bottom. I could have you dangling from a Royal gallows. But it's just occurred to me that that might be a waste. In my country we learn not to waste anything. I've just gotten the notion that you might be useful. If we could control your thievery."

"Same old song. Am foolishest of fools. Will never learn." The fat youth crossed his legs and folded his arms. "Self, am utterly indifferent to politics."

"The dagger rests in my hand, Tubby. That should make you a little concerned. Your choice is to work or hang. I'll pay you for the work if you do any good." He had been sculpting an odd-shaped little intrigue in the back of his mind for several months. This fat man with the unusual skills might be the character to execute it.

If he failed, so what? The world would be rid of a bandit.

Calculation flickered across the thief's face. He seemed to be thinking of agreeing for the moment so he could run later. Haroun smiled gently.

"Ten seconds. Then I'm leaving. With you, or to call the law."

"Woe!" the fat man cried. "Is infamous riddle of rock and hard place. Am bestruckt by horny dilemma. Am in narrow passage, between devil and deep. Am beset by quandary of epical dimension. Am driven to deepest depths of desperate, despairing desperation...."

"Huh?" Haroun became confused by the verbal pyrotechnics. "Time's running out, Tubby."

"So much for tactic of bogglement and bewilderment. Only one course remaining: last refuge of mentally disadvantaged. Reason. Hai! Lord! Is impossible for self to leave carnival. Am partner in same. Junior partner, very, under closest scrutiny of baleful eye of paranoid senior partner, Damo Sparen, and incorruptible, house-size thug name of Gouch."

"Can't say I blame him. You traveling or hanging?"

"Hai! Lord! Have mercy. Am but humble fool...."

"Pull that knife and you'll be a humble fool with a hole in his windpipe."

"Woe," the youth muttered. "Stars promised evil day. Should have paid attention." He got to his feet slowly. Haroun offered no help. "Will need several minutes to collect accoutrements."

"I'm not buying a baggage train."

"Self, am accustomed to company of certain tools. Am professional, not so? Carpenterses, same need hammers, saws...."

"Hurry it up."

The fat man was gaining confidence. He saw that Haroun was reluctant to strike. "Show some manners, sand rat. Self, am in tight place, maybeso, but can yell and have whole carnival here in minute."

"Including your redoubtable senior partner? How excited would he be about your thieving?"

"Same taught self gentle art." He did not put enough conviction into it to daunt Haroun.

"No doubt. Is that why he watches you?"

The youth shrugged, started packing. "Has strange moments, Damo Sparen. Self, cannot understand same. Is like father sometimes, maybeso, and sometimes like jailor."

"All fathers are that way. What's your name? I can't call you Tubby forever."

"Is all same. Am Magellin the Magician here, sometimes."

Haroun started slightly. "I had a good friend named Megelin. They're too much alike. Try something else."

"Am known to self as Mocker. Same being from inconsequential incident long time passing, in nethermost east, before circumstance brought self on quest to west."

"Quest? And you ended up in a sideshow?"

Mocker chuckled weakly. "Self, must remember conversant is aspirant king. Must select words more precisionly, same being subject to interpretation by noble standard. Not knight's quest. Not holy quest. Simple search for place where enemy blades could not reach."

"Oh?" Haroun thumbed the edge of his knife. "Then you have a habit of making stupid mistakes."

Mocker caught the lilt of danger dancing along the edges of Haroun's words. "Not so! Have turned over new leaf. Have finally learned lesson. Present trap being otherwise impossible to escape, have seen light illuminating great truth heretofore eluding humble, foolish self. Truth is: is nothing free. When same seems in reach, then duck head. Fates are laying trap."

"I hope you learned. But you look too old to teach. How long does it take to stuff that junk in a bag?"

Mocker was stalling while trying to decide if he should yell for help. They both knew it. "Junk?" Mocker wailed. "Lord...."

He looked at Haroun. The thin, leathery-skinned youth did not appear nervous. His self-confidence was too much for Mocker. He jerked his bag shut. "Is enough to get by. Sparen will care for rest. Now, must leave note for same, in explanation, or same will set hound Gouch on trail. Woe be unto man with Gouch for enemy."

"You read and write?"

Mocker held up fingers in a *little bit* sign. "Same skill being courtesy of cruel taskmaster, senior partner. Teaching, teaching. Always is teaching. Everythings."

"Do it quick. Make it good. And honest. You won't be back in a half-hour to tear it up." Haroun could commiserate with the fat youth. How Radetic had driven him in his reading, writing, and language lessons!

Mocker was cunning enough not to assume that his captor was illiterate. He wrote a simple parting note saying that he would return in a few days. He had chanced on an opportunity to profit from the confusion along the border. He wrote in the language of Hellin Daimiel, which was the *lingua franca* of the Lesser Kingdoms, and Haroun's best foreign language.

"Is there anything else?" Haroun demanded.

"Donkey, that is oldest friend of self. Is in corral."

"You lead. I'll be a step behind you." He shook his head, muttering. "Might have known. Best friends with a jackass." He let Mocker leave before sheathing his dagger.

Two men were waiting outside. Mocker stood there with his mouth open, speechless. He seemed caught in the gap between relief and fear.

"What's this?" Haroun demanded.

Mocker found his tongue. "Sparen. Gouch."

Haroun had no trouble guessing which was which. Gouch would be the mountain of beef blocking their way past the performance booth. "Move this creature," he told the smaller man, who was seated on a crate.

"Where're you going, Mocker?" Sparen asked. He ignored Haroun. "Would you be taking anything with you?"

"Donkey...."

Haroun pushed past the fat youth. "Move it," he told Gouch.

Gouch seemed to be deaf. Sparen said, "I wasn't talking to you, boy."

"I have spoken twice. I won't speak again."

Sparen's irritation showed. "You've got a mouth, boy. Gouch, shut him up."

Gouch moved quicker than a snake striking

Haroun moved faster. He cut the big man three times, not too badly.

Mocker tried to run. Haroun tripped him, wheeled on Sparen. "I'd guess Gouch is a valuable property. Move him or lose him."

"You have a point. Gouch, step back. I'll handle this myself."

Haroun took Mocker's elbow, started forward.

"I didn't say you could go, boy," Sparen said. "I just decided to kill you myself."

"Take care, Damo," Mocker said. "Is trained in Power."

"Isn't everybody in this business?"

"Is slight and arrogant, but is one known as King Without Throne."

Sparen spat to one side. "Right. And I'm the Lost Prince of Libiannin."

Haroun took advantage of the diversion of the exchange to palm a blow tube. He raised his hand, coughed.

Sparen saw it coming, but too late. He made one violent thrust, then collapsed. An expression of incredulity contorted his features.

Gouch and Mocker crowded Sparen. "What did you do?" Gouch demanded. He shook Sparen. "Mr. Sparen, wake up." The giant seemed unaware of his own wounds. "Tell me what to do, Mr. Sparen. Should I break them?"

"Come on," Haroun snarled, grabbing Mocker's shoulder. "The big guy's got this figured as your fault." He was thinking he would have to get a lot of use out of this Mocker to repay himself for all this trouble.

A little later, Mocker remarked, "Sparen was friend of self. Not very trusting friend, but best friend even so."

Haroun heard the gentle threat. He saw the promise of murder in his companion's eyes. "I didn't kill him. The dart was coated with a nerve poison that causes temporary paralysis. It comes from the jungles south of Hammad al Nakir. He'll be all right in a couple of hours, except for a headache and a bad temper."

He hoped. The drug was fatal about a quarter of the time.

The more Haroun observed his companion, the more he became sure Mocker would make a dangerous enemy. The fat and incurable optimism hid a lean, conscienceless killer.

They were halfway to el Senoussi's encampment, several days later, when they encountered the refugees. These were not desert-born fugitives from the wrath of the Disciple. They were natives fleeing El Murid's minions.

The El Murid Wars had begun, and troops of desert riders were in Tamerice already.

They gave Haroun a hold on the fat man.

There was no point continuing southward. He turned back, heading for a camp in Altea. Invincible patrols forced them into hiding several times.

North of Feagenbruch they came across the burned wagons of the Sparen carnival. Sparen himself was among the dead, but Gouch had survived. They found him, wounded, lying beneath a mound of desert warriors.

Mocker studied Sparen for a long time. "Was paranoid fool, sometimes, maybeso, this man. But was friend. In some way, even, was like father. There is blood now, Haroun bin Yousif. Same must be cleansed in blood. Self, am now interested in politics." He moved to Gouch. "Gouch. You. Big fellow. Get up. Is work to do."

Incredibly, Gouch rose out of his pile of victims.

"They slew both my fathers," Haroun whispered.

It would be a long time before Mocker understood that remark.

He soothed Gouch's tears and wounds and fears and listened while the King Without a Throne explained the part he could play in bringing about the downfall of the Disciple.

EIGHT

THE LONELY CITY

Al Rhemish was a lonely city that first summer of the wars. All the Disciple's intimates had abandoned him for the excitement and loot of the west.

He often strolled the dusty streets with his children, having trouble accepting his fortune. He ached continuously in the vacuum left by Meryem's passing.

His loneliness grew as the victories mounted and the euphoria of the stay-at-homes transmogrified into a worshipful awe of the man who had dreamed the dream and made the turnaround possible.

"They're trying to make *me* their God," he told his children. "And I can't seem to stop them."

"They already call you The Lord in Flesh some places," Yasmid told him. She not only had the boldness her mother had shown when young, she also possessed that adult self-assurance El Murid had developed after his first encounter with his angel. She seemed an *old* child, an adult looking out of a half-grown body. Even he was disturbed by her excessively grownup perceptions.

Sidi, on the other hand, threatened to remain an infant forever.

"I issue edicts. They ignore them. And the men I set to police heresies become the worst offenders." He was thinking of Mowaffak Hali. Mowaffak was smitten by the man-worshipping disease.

"People want something they can touch, Father. Something they can see. That's human nature."

"What do you think, Sidi?" The Disciple took every opportunity to include his son in everything. One day Yasmid would have to depend on her brother the way he depended on Nassef.

"I don't know." Sidi was surly. He did not give a damn about the Lord's work. The Evil One was in him. He was the antithesis of his sister in everything. He afflicted his father with a desperate pain.

El Murid had trouble handling his feelings toward Sidi. The boy had done nothing blatant. Yet. But the Disciple smelled wickedness in him, the way a camel smelled water. Sidi would be trouble one day, if not for his father, then for Yasmid when she became Disciple.

El Murid felt trapped between jaws of faith and family. Rather than deal with it, he was letting everything slide during the boy's formative years.

He prayed a lot. Each night he begged the Lord to channel Sidi's wickedness in useful directions, as He had done with Nassef. And he begged forgiveness for the continuous quiet anger he bore because of Meryem's untimely passing.

Yasmid had taken Meryem's place, becoming confidant and crying shoulder.

El Murid was strong in his faith, but could never still the lonely, frightened boy within him. That boy had to have someone....

"Papa, you should find another wife."

They were climbing the side of the bowl containing Al Rhemish. Twice weekly he made a hadj to the place where Meryem had fallen. The habit had become part of his legend.

"Your mother was my only love." He had faced this argument before, from Nassef and Mowaffak Hali.

"You don't have to love her like you did Mother. Everyone knows how you felt about her."

"You've been talking to Nassef."

"No. Does he think you should get married too?"

"Then Hali."

"No."

"Somebody. Honey, I know what you're going to say. I've heard it all before. I should wed a woman from the noble class in order to cement relations with the aristocracy. I have to gain their trust so our best people stop deserting to that child-king, Haroun."

"It's true. It would help."

"May be. But I don't compromise with the enemies of the Lord. I don't traffic with the damned, except to punish them for their wickedness."

"Papa, that'll cause trouble someday. You've got to give to get."

"It's caused trouble since the day I met your mother. And today I sit on the Peacock Throne, never having yielded. You sound like your uncle again. You're talking politics. And politics disgust me."

Yasmid was not repeating something she had heard, but she did not tell him so. He had grown argumentative lately. Prolonged disagreement sent him into furies. "Politics is how people work things out," she said.

"It's how they scheme and maneuver to take advantage of each other."

The Lord was the center and source of all power, and El Murid was his spokesman on Earth. He saw no need for any politics but the monolith with himself at its apex, giving commands the Chosen should execute without question.

That vision was his alone. A vicious new politics entered the movement the moment it achieved its initial goal. His captains fought like starving dogs for those crumbs of power which dribbled through his fingers. They savaged one another for the spoils of the new order. Hardly a day passed when he did not have to rule on some dispute over responsibility or precedence.

"They're more interested in themselves than in the movement. Even the old faithful are falling into the trap." He paused to order his thinking. "Maybe we were too successful too suddenly. After twelve years, victory just jumped into our hands. Now things are so good they don't have to stand shoulder to shoulder against the world."

He dreaded the chance that the intrigues and machinations would become habitual. That had happened to the Royalists. During their final years they had done little but accuse one another and indulge their private vices.

He felt impotent. Evil seeds were sprouting, and he could do little to stunt their growth. All the preaching in eternity could not save the man who refused to be saved.

El Murid had grown. He had begun to see the weaknesses in his movement, the potential for evil flanking every inch of the path of righteousness. He had begun to realize that the fall for the true believer could be swift and hard and, worse, unrecognized until too late.

The knowledge did nothing to banish the depression initiated by loneliness.

When he could stand it no more he always called for Esmat.

They reached the site of Meryem's fall.

"Will they ever finish?" Sidi asked, indicating the monument El Murid had ordered raised. A quarter had been completed. Unused stone stood in piles now falling into disordered heaps.

"Even our stonemasons wanted to see the old Imperial provinces. Could I force them to stay when they wanted to carry the Truth to the infidel?"

"They didn't care about the truth, Papa. They just thought stealing from foreigners was easier than working."

El Murid nodded. The Host of Illumination was fat with men whose skills could be better utilized at home. A black, rigid moment of fear enfolded him in cold tentacles. Hammad al Nakir boasted few skilled artisans. A military disaster could destroy the class and shove the nation a long step back toward barbarism. The centuries had not changed his people enough. They still preferred plundering to building.

He altered the course of the conversation. "What I need more than a respite from bickering is water. Millions of gallons of water."

"What?" Yasmid had been about to suggest that he have Nassef send captured artisans to replace native craftsmen gone to war.

"Water. That's the biggest thing we lost when the Empire fell. I don't know how…. Maybe only Varthlokkur himself could bring back the rains."

Sidi showed some interest, so he forged ahead. "The soil is fertile enough some places. But there isn't any water. And because of that there's so little vegetation that what rain does fall just runs away…. You see, in Imperial times they cut most of the wild trees for lumber and firewood. Then the barbarians came. Some places they plowed salt into the earth. Some places their cattle and sheep stripped the land. And then the wizard Varthlokkur stopped the rains…."

Yasmid considered him with a half-amused smile. "What have you been doing, Papa? Going to school on the sly?"

"No, reading some studies done by the foreigner, Radetic. I discovered them after we took Al Rhemish. It's curious. Yousif shared a lot of my goals."

"Haven't you always said that the minions of the Evil One sometimes do the Lord's work unwittingly?"

"And it's true. But don't breathe a word of this. I'm going to adopt the foreigner's ideas. Once the Empire is resurrected and we have the people to do the work. Radetic believed the old lushness could be restored, though it would take three or four generations to get the life-river turned into the new channel. That made him despair. But I like it. I've got to give the Chosen distant goals. Otherwise the Kingdom of Peace will lapse into its old bickering ways."

"You never mentioned this before."

El Murid leaned against the memorial's base and gazed across the valley. He tried to imagine how it had looked in old times. There had been a shallow lake. The Most Holy Mrazkim Shrines had stood on a low, man-made island. The slopes surrounding the lake had boasted rich citrus groves.

Barbarian invaders had cut the trees for firewood.

"It used to be too far away to even dream. Now there's at least a chance. One of these days.... Well, it all depends on your uncle. If he wins the war.... Then we can start."

He looked at the barren valley. For an instant he saw the beauty that had been, and might again be.

"We could bring the water from the Kapenrung Mountains. There're still traces of the old canals.... But enough of that." He turned, knelt, prayed for Meryem's soul. Yasmid and his son joined him, Sidi reluctantly. When he rose, he said, "Let's go jump into the witch's cauldron and see what silliness they're up to today."

Yasmid wore an awed look as she followed her father. She had seen a whole new facet of a man. Her father had depths she had never suspected.

A morning of unpromising beginnings was becoming a cheerful day for the Disciple. He had revealed his most secret dream and no one had laughed. Even unimaginative Sidi had grasped the grandeur of the vision. Maybe, just maybe, he could get through the day without Esmat.

He discovered that Mowaffak Hali had rushed home from the war zone.

"I'm seeing you first because I know your business must be serious, Mowaffak. What is it?"

"Two things, Lord. The least important is that we've lost track of the pretender, Haroun bin Yousif. He's gone underground since the attack in Tamerice. He's contacted only a few rebel leaders, and he no longer haunts the courts of the Lesser Kingdoms. Our agents can't find him."

"Time will deliver him to us. What else?"

"A grave development. I got this from my man in the Scourge of God's staff, who overheard one of your brother-in-law's spies reporting. The Itaskians and their allies have decided not to wait for us to come to them. They're sending an army south. They've chosen the Duke of Greyfells to command it. He's a cousin of the Itaskian king, and reportedly a good soldier."

"That's a pity, Mowaffak. I'd hoped we could finish in the south before we had to deal with Itaskia."

"It's the strongest of our foes, Lord. And the richest. And probably has the best leaders. And they'll have Iwa Skolovda, Dvar, and Prost Kamenets supporting them. The Scourge of God will face tough going north of the Scarlotti."

"Maybe. But I know Nassef. If I were a sinful man and laid wagers, I'd bet that he planned for this before he crossed the Sahel."

"I hope so, Lord. The sheer weight of our enemies intimidates me."

The remark echoed El Murid's fears. He wished he could share them with Hali, but dared not. His absolute assurance made the Invincibles what they were. Doubt would destroy them.

"Let's hope all our friends feel the pressure, Mowaffak. The movement is stumbling over its own success. Spread the news."

"As you command, Lord." Hali's tone betrayed doubts. "Can the Invincibles do something to stem this threat, Lord?"

"Study this Duke, Mowaffak. How competent is he? Would his army survive without him? Who would replace him? How competent is that man? You understand?"

"Completely, Lord. Politics being what they are, his replacement might be a bungler."

"Exactly. Oh. While you're here. I need your advice concerning el Nadim's eastern army."

"Lord?"

"He's gone over the Scourge of God's head. Appealed to me for permission to give up trying to force the Savernake Gap. Yet Nassef told me that maintaining the breakthrough threat is vital."

"What's el Nadim's problem?"

"He claims his enemies are decimating him with sorcery. That his Throyen levies are ready to revolt. They make up most of his army and think we're getting them killed just to be rid of them."

"That's not impossible, Lord. The Scourge of God is using native auxiliaries in the west. I've seen him allow them to take a merciless beating. But I agree when he says we need the eastern threat. It forces the enemy into a static strategy that leaves us the initiative. Once Kavelin and Altea fall, it won't matter. I can muster a few companies of Invincibles and send them east. They'd give el Nadim more backbone."

"And flexibility, I'd think. He hasn't been one of our more imaginative generals."

"Perhaps not. But he's reliable. He'll carry out his orders if they kill him. And he's our only sectarian leader who is a true believer. He came to it late, after he became one of Nassef's henchmen, and I think it's why he drew the remote assignment. The Scourge of God doesn't want him watching over his shoulder anymore."

"You're politicking, Mowaffak."

"Lord!" Hali grinned. "So I am, in my way. I guess it's part of being human."

"Probably. We don't always realize what we're doing. It's the blatant, premeditated backstabbing that aggravates me. Send those companies to el Nadim."

"As you command, Lord."

"Tell Yassir he can start sending in the whiners and complainers."

The following month was a good one. The occupied territories grew more pacified. The conquest of the Lesser Kingdoms proceeded inexorably, though Nassef had given Karim a minimum of warriors with whom to accomplish the task. The Scarlotti fords and ferries, as far east as Altea's western frontier, had been closed. Nassef crossed the river above Dunno Scuttari and completed that city's encirclement. He was achieving objectives ahead of schedule. Even el Nadim's troubles were no cause for despair. His success or failure remained peripheral to Nassef's strategy. Only his presence was essential.

Then El Murid received the letter from his brother-in-law.

"Yasmid. Sidi. Come hear what your uncle has to say." He scanned the letter twice more. "He wants us to come accept the surrender of Dunno Scuttari. He says it won't be long."

"Papa, let's go!" Yasmid enthused. "Please? Say we can! I want to see the west. And think what it would mean to the warriors to see you there with them."

He laughed. "It would be dangerous, Yasmid."

"We could pretend we were somebody else. Somebody who isn't important."

"Salt merchants," Sidi proposed.

"Salt merchants are important," El Murid protested, going along for the fun. His father had been a salt merchant.

"Sure, Papa. Salt merchants," Yasmid said. "You know all about that. We could make your bodyguards dress like merchants and ride camels."

"They'd still look like thugs."

"But...."

"That's enough. Your uncle hasn't taken the city, and I don't think he can. He hasn't been any trouble for Hellin Daimiel, and that should be an easier nut. We'll wait and see."

"Papa, he's just saving Hellin Daimiel for later."

"We'll wait and see. Remember, there's an Itaskian army to worry about now. We don't know what they'll do."

Yasmid smiled. She had the battle halfway won.

El Murid assumed a wry smile. He knew what she was thinking. He decided he was a weak-spined fool. He had so much trouble denying his children anything.

A grave Esmat approached him eleven days later.

"What is it, Esmat? You look grey."

The physician gulped. "Lord, the courier from Ipopotam hasn't arrived. He's four days overdue."

A chill climbed El Murid's spine. "How much of the pain-killer do we have?"

He could not bring himself to call the opiate anything else.

"Perhaps enough for two months, Lord. It depends on the size and frequency of the dosages."

Which depends on how much pressure I have to endure, El Murid thought. "Then the failure of one courier doesn't much matter, does it? If you're afraid your stock will be depleted, send another man. Or double the next regular purchase."

"I intend doing both, Lord. If nothing else, that will answer the critical question."

"Question? What question?"

"Whether or not our enemies have discovered our need and begun intercepting our couriers."

This time the chill grated like the progress of a glacier. "Esmat…. Is that possible?"

"All things are possible, Lord. And this's a fear I've carried for several years. We've reached the point where the drug's withdrawal would leave the movement without a head for some time. It might take months to overcome the withdrawal pains."

"Is it bad, Esmat?" he asked softly.

"Extremely, Lord."

"Esmat, do whatever you have to. Secure the supply. This is a critical hour. I don't dare become ineffective. You should have mentioned our vulnerability before."

"Perhaps. I did not wish to offend…."

"It's too late to take offense. The drug comes from a plant, does it not? A poppy? Can we grow our own?"

"I'm no horticulturist, Lord. And they have a monopoly. They guard seeds and fields…."

"Can they guard themselves against the Host of Illumination?"

"Of course not. But we have treaties of friendship. Our word of honor would be destroyed…. We negotiated them specifically to insure our access to the drug. They might burn the fields if they thought that was why we were invading."

"Nassef negotiated those instruments before we went to war. Does that mean he knows?"

"Many people know, Lord. It's not something that can be kept secret long."

El Murid bowed his head, half in shame, half in fear. "Do what you can. And I'll do what I have to."

"As you command, Lord."

NINE

THE ITASKIANS

Haroun took his leave of Mocker and Gouch in northern Cardine, just east of that kingdom's frontier with the domains of Dunno Scuttari. "The patrols are thick," he warned. "Take care."

Mocker laughed. "Self, will be so circumspect that even eye of lofty eagle will not detect same. Am valiant fighter, true, able to best whole company in combat, but am uncertain of ability against whole army. Even with stalwart Gouch at back."

Bin Yousif had observed the fat man in action the day before, when they had stumbled into one of Nassef's patrols. Sparen had taught him superbly. Mocker's quickness, deftness, and endurance with a blade were preternatural. He was a swordsman born.

"Gouch, keep him out of trouble."

"I will, Mister. He'll be so good you won't even know him."

"Don't let him con you out of the cash." He had given the big man some expense money.

"Don't you worry, Mister. I know him. I watched him when he worked for Mister Sparen. We'll do this job, then come back for the next one."

There was a simple assurance about Gouch that Haroun found both charming and disturbing. Megelin had taught him to see the world as a slippery serpent, changeable, colored in shades of untrustworthiness. Gouch's naive worldview was the antithesis of Radetic's.

"I think you will. Good luck." He turned his back on them and the donkey, strolled to his mount and companions.

"You think they'll do it?" Beloul asked.

Haroun glanced back. The two were waddling south already. The fat man walked that way because of his obesity, Gouch because of his still tender injuries.

"Who knows? If they don't, we're not out anything."

"So. Northward we ride," Beloul mused. "You're sure they'll be waiting across the river?"

He meant the Royalist army, which was supposed to have assembled in Vorhangs, the little kingdom across the Scarlotti. Haroun guessed between one and two thousand men would answer his call to arms.

He hoped, by employing them judiciously in support of the western armies, to make them a bargaining counter in his negotiations for aid in recovering the Peacock Throne.

"We'll find out, Beloul."

A few hours later, as they considered how to cross the Scarlotti, a messenger overtook them. "Lord," he gasped, "the Scourge of God has crossed the river."

"What?" Beloul demanded. "When? Where?"

"Just upriver of Dunno Scuttari. They started sending boats over four days ago. Took the Scuttarians by surprise. He has twenty thousand men on the north bank now."

"He's crazy," Beloul growled. "He's still vulnerable from the Lesser Kingdoms, and the Itaskians will be coming down behind him."

"No, he's not," Haroun countered. "Call El Murid crazy if you want, but not Nassef. He's got a reason if he sneezes."

"The risk is all on the north bank," el Senoussi remarked. "Nobody on this side can challenge him. We'd better find out what he's up to."

"Yes." Haroun told the messenger, "Go back to your company. Tell your captain to find out what Nassef is doing. Tell him to send word to me at the camp in Kendel."

"Kendel?" el Senoussi asked. "We're going that far north?"

"I asked the Itaskian general to meet me. The Kendel camp isn't far out of his way. Somebody trade horses with this man. His won't survive the return trip."

"Thank you, Lord," the messenger said. "Will you take care of her? She's a good animal."

"Of course."

"Isn't that dangerous?" Beloul asked once the messenger departed. "How long before the Harish get wind of your whereabouts now?"

"You think they'd venture that far from home?"

"To the ends of the earth, Lord, if El Murid willed it."

"I guess they would. Guard my back well, then."

They crossed the Scarlotti during the night, the hard way. Still dripping, exhausted, they joined their warriors in the morning.

Haroun was not impressed by his army. It was a ragged mob compared to that his father had commanded. These men had just one outstanding quality: they were survivors.

"Can you do anything with them?" he asked Beloul.

"Of course. Most were soldiers at home. They're still soldiers. They just don't look pretty."

"They look like bandits."

Beloul shrugged. "I'll try to shape them up."

Haroun allowed a day of rest, then led his bedraggled host northward.

The warriors griped. Most had made long journeys south to the meeting place. The biggest refugee camps had attached themselves to the skirts of cities seemingly safe from the Scourge of God.

It took a week of hard riding to reach the Kendel encampment. Twice they were mistaken for Nassef's men and narrowly avoided fighting allies. Nassef had the peoples between the Scarlotti and Porthune spooked.

Haroun reached the camp only to discover that the Itaskian Duke had not responded to his request for a meeting. Yet the combined northern armies were amarch, moving south in small stages, and the main body was just forty miles from the encampment.

"He don't seem eager to make Nassef's acquaintance," Beloul observed. "Even the biggest, heaviest army can move faster than that."

"I smell the corruption of politics on this breeze, Beloul. It stinks like an old, old corpse."

"We'll have to make a showing for the men. It's a pity we came so far for nothing."

"We will. Tomorrow I'll go to him."

"Lord?"

"Let's inspect this camp, Beloul. People ought to know we care."

He had seen more than he wanted already. These people were living in the most primitive conditions imaginable. Their homes consisted of stick piles that did nothing but block the sun's rays.

"This will be a death camp come winter, Beloul. This isn't Hammad al Nakir. The winters get cold. These people will freeze. What happened to that Gamil Meguid who's supposed to be in charge?"

"He disappeared right after we got here."

"Oh?"

"Yes."

"Keep an eye on him."

"I mean to. Wait. I think that's him. With the foreigner."

Meguid was a small, fussy sort from western Hammad al Nakir. He and el Senoussi were old acquaintances. His hands fluttered when he talked, and his left cheek twitched constantly. He was overawed by his King's presence.

"My Lord King," he gurgled. "May I present Count Diekes Ronstadt. Our neighbor and benefactor. Count, His Most Serene Majesty…."

"Enough, Meguid. Ronstadt? I've heard that name before."

The Count was a big man. He had muscles everywhere and an impressive mane of silver hair. Haroun had the feeling that his powerful dark eyes were probing the soft white underbelly of his soul. A quick, warm smile fluttered across the Count's pale lips. It was a smile that proclaimed its bearer an amused observer of the human condition.

"That could be, lad. We had a friend in common. Megelin Radetic."

"Of course! His roommate at the Rebsamen…. You're the one who was always getting him in trouble."

"In and out again. He was the most naive kid…. But brilliant. A genius. He could do anything. I wouldn't have survived without him. We exchanged the occasional letter. I was crushed when I heard what happened."

"The world is poorer for his absence. I'm impoverished. I would have made him my vizier. My marshal."

"A new departure, Megelin as warrior. But there wasn't anything he couldn't do when he put his mind to it. Come with me. Gamil wants to show off our new camp."

"Megelin managed both jobs for my father, in fact if not in name. What new camp?"

"Gamil supposed you'd be put off by this mess. He was scared you'd fire him. So he rushed over and asked me if we couldn't show you what all we've been doing."

"All right. Show me. He's right. This place appalls me."

"Follow me, then. We're building in the valley on the other side of that ridge. The water supply is better, the bottom ground more level, and there's good clay for building."

Haroun went along. Beloul, el Senoussi, and the others crowded around him, their hands near their weapons. "What is your part in this?" Haroun asked Ronstadt.

"This is my county. My fief. It's primitive and sparsely peopled. I'm combining a favor to an old friend with a favor to myself. Megelin wrote a few years back and suggested it. I liked the idea."

Count Ronstadt led them to a man-made clearing in the bottom of a wide, heavily forested valley, on the banks of a small, slow river. The clearing contained dozens of buildings in various stages of construction.

"Getting ready for winter is our main concern this year. Your people are living mostly by hunting. Next spring, though, they should be ready to try farming."

Haroun examined several of the incomplete houses. They were constructed of bricks of sun-baked clay. The refugees were making no use of the plentiful logs. Those they sawed into lengths and rolled into the river.

"I'm pleased, friend of my friend," Haroun said. "I see you have your own people helping. That's really too much."

"They're only teaching. They'll be back to their own work soon."

"How many people can you take here?" The refugees were unpopular everywhere, yet the migration from the desert had not peaked.

"How many here now, Gamil?" Ronstadt asked.

"Nearly five thousand, Count. But the official census lists about eight."

"My arms are open," Ronstadt told Haroun. "My fief is virgin. It could support thousands more. But the King is nervous. He ordered me to make a head count, then freeze it there. He doesn't want me getting too strong. We fudged a little. I want to tame this whole valley. I can't without Gamil's cheap labor."

"That's your deal with Meguid?"

"And a generous one by most standards. Since I'm not bellicose, the feudal burden is light."

"Ah. And their responsibilities to myself as their King?"

Ronstadt became less animated. "They no longer live in Hammad al Nakir. This is Kendel."

Haroun stifled a surge of anger.

Beloul took his elbow gently. "The logic is unassailable, Lord. We can't expect to get something for nothing. And this gentleman seems willing to give more for less."

"I'll let them help you where they can," Ronstadt said. "As long as it's not done at my expense."

Haroun remained angry. This being King Without a Throne was more frustrating than he had anticipated. Too much depended on the good will of people who owed him nothing.

He had to create a political currency before these westerners would take him seriously. He had to have something they wanted to exchange for what they could give.

His absolute imperative would have to be to retain the loyalties of the refugees. He could not permit them to become assimilated, nor to forget their grievances. They had to remain politically viable as contestants for power in Hammad al Nakir.

"Gamil says you want to meet the Duke of Greyfells," Ronstadt said. "Can I give you some advice?"

"What?"

"Don't waste your time."

"What?"

"He's not your man. He's a political animal, a political creation, a political opportunist. He got command only because the Itaskian Crown had to cut a deal with its opposition. You can't help him with his ambitions. He won't give you a place to squat."

"You know him?"

"He's a distant relative. By marriage. So is the man you *should* see. Everybody in the north is related to everybody else."

"Who should we see?" Beloul asked. "If the Duke is no good, who is?"

"Itaskia's Minister of War. He's the Duke's superior, and his enemy. And he has the ear of the Itaskian King. I'll give you a letter of introduction."

Next morning, while riding to meet Greyfells, Haroun asked, "What do you think of our benefactor?"

Beloul shrugged. "Time will tell."

"A not unenlightened man," el Senoussi opined. "Meguid thinks well of him. And trusts him."

The others agreed with Beloul.

"How Greyfells treats us will tell us a lot about him."

The Duke was easy to find. His army had not moved twenty miles in the past three days.

Ronstadt was right. Greyfells would have nothing to do with Haroun. Bin Yousif made it only as far as the entrance to the ducal pavilion, where he waited while an aide tried to get him in.

Radetic had taught him some Itaskian. Enough for him to follow the drift of the abuse Greyfells heaped on the aide for bothering him with the requests of "bandy-legged, camel-thieving rabble."

The aide returned red-faced and apologetic. Haroun said only, "Tell him that he'll regret his arrogance."

"Well?" Beloul asked when he rejoined his captains.

"The Count was right. He wouldn't talk to me."

"Then let's follow up on Ronstadt's suggestion. Itaskia isn't that far."

"I guess a few days more won't matter."

They crossed the Great Bridge three days later, guided by an impatient native sergeant.

"The glory that was," el Senoussi intoned. "Thus it was in Ilkazar in the Empire's prime."

Few of them had seen the like of the waterfront. The river traffic was incredible. Hellin Daimiel and Dunno Scuttari were becoming increasingly dependent on supplies brought in by ship. A river of wealth was flowing from the treasuries of the besieged cities to the coffers of Itaskian merchants.

The sergeant pushed and nagged and finally guided them to a kremlin at city's center. He took them into a building and up several levels to an anteroom where a gimpy old man snatched Haroun's letter of introduction. He disappeared through a fancily carved doorway. He was not gone long. "His Lordship will see you now. You." He indicated Haroun. "The rest stay out here."

"That was fast," Haroun breathed. He started toward the doorway. His followers milled uncertainly, paths blocked by the old man.

A thin, short, middle-aged man came to greet Haroun. He offered his hand. "They told me you were young. I didn't expect you to be this young."

"Count Ronstadt in Kendel suggested I see you."

"And direct. I like that, though you young people overdo it. I presume my cousin disappointed you?"

"The Duke of Greyfells. He was unpleasant."

"He usually is. Somebody forgot to teach him his manners. I never cease being amazed that he's built such a strong following. I was more amazed when he outmaneuvered me on the command appointment."

"I hear he's a good soldier."

"When it serves his purpose. I imagine he'll try to use this as a stepping-stone to the throne. He makes no secret of his long-range goal."

Haroun shook his head slowly. "What's the attraction? It's nothing but headaches and heartaches for me."

The Minister shrugged. "Come. Sit down. I think we've got agreements to agree."

Haroun sat. He studied the Minister. And the thin man considered him from behind steepled fingers.

Haroun saw someone in complete control of his destiny, someone as sure of himself as was El Murid. A hard man. He'd make a bitter enemy.

The Minister saw a boy compelled to become a man. The strain of caring was making him old before his time. Creeping cynicism had begun tightening his brow. It had given his young mouth the lemon-biting look. And he sensed a hardness, an implacability that approached fanaticism.

"What agreements?" Haroun asked.

"First, tell me what you think of El Murid's goals. His war goals. I don't give a damn about the religious issues."

"Restoration of the Empire? It's a fool's dream. This isn't the world of yesterday. There're real countries out here now. And, geopolitically, Hammad al Nakir isn't suited to the role of the great unifier." He recounted some of Megelin's thoughts on the subject, dwelling on his homeland's lack of a centralized administrative tradition and the absence of an educated class capable of administering. Ilkazar had had those, and the peoples the Empire had conquered had, for the most part, been little beyond the tribal stage.

"How old are you?"

"Nineteen."

"You had remarkable teachers, then. I know men with forty years experience in statecraft who couldn't put it that clearly. But you didn't tell me what I want to know. Do you subscribe to the imperial dream?"

"No. The Disciple and I come together only when he says we have to re-establish the dignity and security of the nation."

"Yes. You were well taught." The Minister smiled. "I suppose I can accept that. Let me confess to a small dream of my own. I want to make Itaskia the predominant state in the west. We're already the strongest, but conquest isn't my ideal. More an assumption of moral and mercantile dominion. Today's kingdoms are too diverse for unification."

They were speaking Daimiellian, Haroun's strongest foreign language. The Minister's confession made him determined to improve his Itaskian. "I believe the word you want is hegemony."

The Minister smiled again. "You may be right. Now, to the point. We can help each other."

"I know you can help me. That's why I'm here. But what can I do for you?"

"First, understand that I perceive El Murid as the principal threat to my dream. Yet he's also an asset. If he's defeated before he does much more damage, my hopes might come to life of their own accord. The destruction in the south, and the siege of Hellin Daimiel, have elevated Itaskia to a position of moral as well as military dominance. Economic domination is on its way. Cultural dominance shouldn't be far behind."

"I can help turn him back. But I need money, arms, and places for my people to live. Most especially, I need the arms."

"Even so. Listen. You have enemies who aren't mine. I have foes who aren't yours. And that's where we can help each other. Suppose we trade enemies? If you follow my meaning."

"I'm not sure I do."

"A man is more vulnerable to the dagger of an enemy he doesn't know, wouldn't you say?"

"I see. You want to trade murders."

"Crudely put, but yes. I'll give you arms and money if you'll make three commitments. The first is to go ahead and fight El Murid. The second is to abolish his imperialism if you win. And the third, bluntly, is to provide me with undercover knife work, or whatever, when I need to make a move from which I can dissociate myself."

A classic schemer, Haroun thought. What he wants is his own underground army. "Do you have designs on the Itaskian throne yourself?"

"Me? Good heavens, no! Why on earth would I? I'm safer and happier where I am, pulling the strings. I take it you have reservations."

"It sounds like a sweetheart deal. Too good to be true."

"Maybe from your viewpoint. But you don't know Itaskian politics. Or me. I'm not talking about cutting one throat tomorrow. I'm talking the long run. A lifetime of trade-offs. A perpetual alliance. Our problems aren't going to be resolved in a summer. Nor in ten summers, nor even by our achieving what we think we want. Do you see? Consider, too, the fact that I'm sticking my neck out here. I'm offering you a secret treaty. That could get me thrown out on my ear if certain parties got wind of it."

Haroun knew he might spend his life grasping for something beyond his reach. The old sorcerer in that ruined watchtower had shown him the possibilities.

He turned his inner ear to intuition and the Invisible Crown.

"I'll take the chance. You've got a bargain."

"Forever? It's said your father was a man of his word."

"Yes. And I'm my father's son."

The thin man rose, offered a hand. Haroun took it.

"This is all the contract we'll ever have," the Minister told him. "Nobody but you and me should know about it."

"And I'll never be able to invoke it for immunity, no doubt."

"Unfortunately. That's the nature of the game. But remember, you have me at the same disadvantage."

Haroun did not see it, but refrained from so saying. As the Minister had remarked, he did not know Itaskian politics. And he had searched the west and been offered no other deal at all. Beggars could not choose.

"What do you want right now?" he asked.

"Nothing. Just help stop El Murid. I have to survive that crisis first." The Minister turned, walked to a huge wall map of the west. He examined it briefly, one finger tracing a line from Itaskia toward Dunno Scuttari. "If you'll take some men to Hempstead Heath, about twelve miles south of the South Town Gate on the Octylyan Road, my people will meet you with a shipment of weapons. A gesture of good faith on my part. How does that sound?"

"Again, too good to be true. You don't know the disappointments we've suffered."

"But I do. Why do you think you got in so quickly? I've been studying this thing for eight months. These weapons. They're not the best. They're old, non-standard, captured arms. The kind we use for foreign aid and arming the militia. I can scatter them around without having to account for them."

"Anything is better than bare hands. Not so? I'll be there waiting."

But he was not. He had to deputize el Senoussi for the job.

The messenger had come from Dunno Scuttari. Haroun found Nassef's apparent plans less interesting than the messenger's serendipitous acquisition of facts about Duke Greyfells.

Patiently, probably for the dozenth time, the man told his story. "Lord, as I was passing the camp of the Itaskian host—which I dared because I wanted to see this army that everyone expects to be the salvation of the south—I saw riders come forth. I could not flee without being seen, so I concealed myself in the forest. They passed within ten yards of me, Lord. Their captain was the bandit Karim. He had with him several Itaskians of lofty station. They and Karim's men shared jests as old friends might."

"Karim? You're sure?"

"I have seen Karim several times, Lord. I've heard him speak. This was the same man. There's some treachery afoot."

"Then this Duke.... He wouldn't treat with the legitimate King of Hammad al Nakir. He wouldn't share his thinking with his allies. He practically whipped me from his camp.... No wonder. Karim was there at the time."

Beloul muttered, "A scorpion. Poisonous vermin. He makes common cause with bandits."

"Ah, Beloul. Think. The scorpion dies beneath the boot of the man who knows its ways. Perhaps fate has tossed us a meager gift. Shadek. Meet those men bringing us arms. Beloul. Collect our warriors. Let them know we're on the spoor of the villain Karim. Let them know that it's a hot trail. The rest of us will start after him now. If we catch him before he rejoins his army...." He laughed evilly.

Beloul's grin was as wicked. He had a special hatred for Karim. Karim was one of the butchers of Sebil el Selib.

"As you command, Lord."

The Fates were toying with the young King. Karim led him a merry chase into the south. The old bandit was in enemy territory and knew it. He was wasting no time. Haroun did not overtake him till he was making the river crossing into northwestern Altea. Haroun could do nothing but curse and watch. Six hundred of Karim's warriors lined the south bank.

Haroun had to wait for Beloul before he could force the crossing, hurling all his strength against the handful Karim had left. By then he was a day behind, and Karim was aware of how narrowly he had escaped.

TEN
ALTEAN VENTURES

The arrows made *whisk*ing sounds when they streaked over the riverboat, and *thump*ed when they hit its side. The barrage was desultory. The range was extreme for the short desert bow.

"They're going to follow us to the end of the river," Haaken grumped.

Nassef had tightened his noose round Dunno Scuttari before their departure. They had sailed under fire, and the attack had continued every day since. No damage had been done, but constant pursuit was depressing. Sooner or later the Guildsmen would have to fight, if only to make their landing.

The riverboat was a small galley. Most of its regular crew had been left behind. Guildsmen had to take their turns at the oars. Neither the primus nor even the noncoms were exempt.

The labor left Kildragon surly. "If I'd wanted a career pulling an oar I would've gone home to Trolledyngja," he grumbled every time his turn came up.

"You'll get to put it down quick enough," Bragi promised. "Then you can entertain us with your philosophizing about the life of an infantryman. The captain says we're in for some hard marching."

Haaken and Reskird muttered subversively.

"You had your fun. In Simballawein you chased skirts. In Hellin Daimiel you chased skirts. In Dunno Scuttari you didn't have to do anything but keep the girls happy. Now all of a sudden you start bitching because you have to earn your allowances."

"I think that corporal's belt has gone to his head," Reskird observed.

"I noticed," Haaken said.

"Come on.... Why don't you get your stuff ready? We're going ashore tonight."

They had been delayed five weeks in Dunno Scuttari, first for lack of transport, then to await the proper phase of the moon. The first few hours ashore would be critical. They would need all the light they could get.

Darkness, moonrise, and the hour of peril came all too quickly.

"There it is," Bragi said, indicating the mouth of a tributary of the Scarlotti. "Fifteen minutes."

They landed at a village just above the sidestream, while El Murid's men were scurrying around in search of a ford. Captain Sanguinet hoped his company could vanish into the night before its pursuers got across.

The Altean villagers greeted them as enthusiastically as had the people of Simballawein.

"Keep your hands to yourself, Kildragon," Bragi growled as he formed his squad. "We don't have time for that."

Haaken chuckled softy. In Dunno Scuttari his brother had earned the reputation of being the squad's most devoted pursuer of "split-tail."

"Professional jealousy," Reskird remarked.

"Pot calling the kettle black, for sure," Haaken agreed.

"Come on, guys," Bragi said. "We're in a tight spot." He was edgy, and becoming more so. He had a bad feeling about this Altean campaign. He smelled disaster cooking. And Trolledyngjans were wont to put a lot of stock in omens and forebodings.

"Ready here?" Sanguinet asked.

"Ready, Captain," Bragi replied.

"What's all the hollering over there?" Reskird asked as soon as Sanguinet left. He craned his neck in an effort to see.

Bragi hoisted his pack. "They probably just figured out that we're not going to hang around and protect them." He needed no familiarity with the language to interpret the outrage being vented by the village elders. "Get your packs on."

They moved out to the curses of men and wails of women. Bragi ached inside because the little ones were crying.

They did not even know why.

Sanguinet set a hard pace, heading southeastward. He did not let up often, and then only for a few minutes at a time, to confer with the guides the Altean monarchy had sent to meet them. The march to the Bergwold, the forest they were to use as a base, was almost a hundred miles, and the captain wanted to make it without a major interruption.

Dawn came and the company marched on. Villages, farms, manors, small castles hove up ahead, slipped by, and drifted past like slow, lonely ships. The countryside showed no evidence of the passage of raiders, though the peasants vanished from the fields whenever the weary Guildsmen trudged into view.

Here and there, Sanguinet exchanged news with the masters of the various manors and castles. It was more neighborhood gossip than concrete fact. Karim had not yet turned his attention to Altea. The only real fighting had taken place down along the border with Tamerice. Crown Prince Raithel had beaten back three modest incursions.

Bragi wondered why everything was so quiet. He had expected almost continuous fighting. What Karim was doing to the Lesser Kingdoms had been a constant source of conversation during the trip upriver. Of the little states below the Scarlotti, only Altea, and Kavelin, which Altea geographically screened, remained unsubdued. Bragi had expected to be too late for the whirlwind's passage.

Something strange was going on and the entire Altean nation felt it. Nassef's protégé was not one to lightly abandon the unstoppable inertia his forces had gained.

Twenty-eight hours of grueling marching brought the company to the northern verges of the Bergwold, so-called because of its proximity to Colberg Castle, a ruined fortress which had played a critical role in Altea's early history. The Alteans considered it a national monument. The passing Guildsmen saw nothing but crumbling walls looking spectral in the moonlight.

None of them knew anything about the kingdom they were supposed to help preserve. Of all of them only Lieutenant Trubacik spoke the language.

Those facts had weighed on Bragi throughout the march. As Reskird had observed, his corporal's belt had gone to his head. He had begun to take leadership seriously.

And there was little to do but think while walking.

Even the captain was exhausted. The company broke discipline that first night. Not one spadeful of earth got turned along the camp perimeter.

The lapse lasted only that night. Next day Sanguinet moved deeper into the wood and commenced work on a semipermanent base camp. Scouts made contact with a band of desert Royalists using the Bergwold for the same purpose. Sanguinet concluded a loose alliance.

For weeks they did little but patrol the farmland surrounding the forest. The patrols were halfhearted. The desert horsemen covered more territory faster, and the local nobility went out of their way to keep Sanguinet posted.

Such was the Guild's reputation.

"It feels good," Bragi confided to his brother. "One lousy company and these people figure the kingdom is saved."

"What happens when we don't live up to expectation?" Haaken grumped. Then, "Maybe that's why we're here. Morale. Maybe High Crag knows what it's doing."

"Maybe." Bragi's tone carried the skepticism every line soldier feels for the intellectuals of his trade.

He and his men did a lot of fishing and poking around the Colberg. More interesting diversions were not available.

Word finally came that the enemy was moving. Prince Raithel had met them and been defeated. He was retreating northward and needed reinforcements.

"Here we go again," Haaken grumbled as he shouldered his pack. "Why don't we just wait till they come here?"

"The Master Strategist has spoken," said Reskird. "Bragi, get him an appointment with the captain."

"I got a sock if you want it, Bragi."

Ragnarson ignored them. Haaken's and Reskird's bickering had become ritualized. There was no rancor in it. It had become a time-passing game.

They never saw Raithel's army. The company found its own enemies twelve miles south of the Colberg.

"Oh-oh," Reskird groaned in his soothsayer's voice. "Trouble."

Royalist outriders galloped past the column in a panic, coming from the crossroad the company had passed a half-mile back.

"You the official doom-crier now?" Haaken demanded.

"Company conference!" Sanguinet shouted after stopping one of the horsemen. "Come on! Move it!"

The captain put it bluntly. "We're in for it. There's a mob of El Murid's men coming down that side road back there. We can't outrun them. They've already spotted us." He flung a hand at a brushy sugarloaf hill a mile away. The road snaked around its western base. "We'll go up yon hill and dig in. If you're religious, pray your ass off. There's a thousand of the bastards." He exaggerated.

There were five hundred of the enemy. But that was trouble enough.

Bragi's squad stood to their weapons while their backups dug in. "Some friends," Haaken grumbled, watching the last of the Royalists gallop away. "We might've had a chance with their help."

"We still stand a damned good chance," Bragi said. "We're Guildsmen, remember?"

Reskird glanced over his shoulder. "Look at that dirt fly."

The secundus and tercio flailed at the earth. "Nothing like an unfriendly sword to motivate a man," Bragi observed.

The enemy reached the foot of the hill and halted. His commanders conferred. They seemed reluctant to attack.

"Hey!" Bragi said. "Some of those guys are westerners. Haaken. Can you make out their colors? Aren't they the same as those guys we met in Itaskia wore? Right after we came out of the mountains?"

Haaken peered. "I think you're right. Greyfells. Maybe this is another gang of Royalists."

"How come ours ran off, then?"

Sanguinet came to stand beside Ragnarson. "Itaskians?"

"Yes sir. Those are Greyfells colors."

"Lieutenant Trubacik. Take a white flag down. Find out who they are."

The command argument below continued till Trubacik approached and said something.

It electrified his listeners.

A man with wild grey hair cut Trubacik down.

A deep-throated roar rose from the hillside.

"We did something wrong," Bragi said. "But what?"

"Don't worry about it now," Sanguinet told him. "Worry about staying alive. They've made up their minds. They're coming."

The wild-haired horseman whipped his followers into line for a charge.

"Behind the ditch," Sanguinet ordered. "Primus, stand to your spears and shields. Bowmen, make every arrow count while they're coming through the brush. Men, if we turn their first attack we'll have our bluff in."

The enemy commander sent most of his warriors, holding only about eighty in reserve. Their animals struggled with the brush and the steep slope. The better Guild bowmen began taking them at extreme range. At least fifty did not reach the ditch, which lay just above the worst part of the slope.

The first riders up tried to jump the ditch but their animals had been ridden hard before being compelled to scale the hillside. Only a handful made the leap successfully. The others found their hindquarters dropping into the trench. They floundered around, blocking the progress of those behind them. Guild spearmen filled the trench with dead and dying animals.

The slower attackers walked their mounts into the ditch and up its farther side—into the thrusting spears. More animals went down. Only a handful maintained the momentum to crash the Guild battle line.

Guild arrows kept pounding into those farther down the slope.

Horsemen began leaping from their saddles and throwing themselves at the shield wall.

That was what Sanguinet wanted.

Bragi dropped his bloody spear and started plying his sword. The enemy kept coming. His dead and wounded carpeted the slope and filled the ditch.

Ragnarson pushed an attacker away with his shield. Three more leapt to take the man's place. He took one, but their combined weight forced him back a step. Perforce, Haaken and Reskird adjusted their positions so they could keep their shields locked with his.

A few riders answered the Guild arrows with shafts of their own. They did no damage because the secundus and tercio turtled with their shields.

Though the assault lasted only minutes, Bragi thought it an eternity before El Murid's warriors began to waver. At least a hundred of their number, and as many horses, had fallen.

The man with the wild hair rallied them. They began pressing again.

It was a slaughter without respite. Six, seven, eight of the desert horsemen went down for every Guildsman. But their captain kept driving them forward.

If that fool keeps on, he'll lose his whole command, Bragi thought. *Why's he so desperate to wipe us out?*

Then he heard Sanguinet shouting behind the line.

He dared not turn, but knew what had happened. The warriors who had not joined the initial assault had raced around the hill to attack from the rear. Sanguinet was trying to stop them.

The captain succeeded, but only at the cost of taking his archers away from their bows.

The pressure on the main line redoubled. The shield wall began cracking. Desert warriors pushed into the gaps.

Bragi, Haaken, and Reskird soon found themselves isolated. They backed into a triangle and kept fighting as weary horses pushed past. "Andy! Raul!" Bragi shouted. "Push over here and link back up. Haaken, step backward when I say. Reskird, be ready to fit them in." He kept stabbing and cutting while he shouted.

The cohesiveness of the Guild line continued to dissolve.

A strange, fearless calm came over Ragnarson as death approached. His mind became detached from the body involved in the fighting. He saw what needed doing and tried to get it done.

He managed to reform his squad, having lost only two men.

His calm communicated itself to the others. Their panic declined. They settled down to the grim business of fighting the way they had been taught, maximizing their chances of surviving.

Bragi kept his men in a hard little square, moving when he could to incorporate other members of the company. He kept yelling, "Get their horses! We can murder them on the ground."

The man with the wild hair concurred. Too many of his men were being forced to their feet, where their sabers and small round shields were of little value against heavy infantry. He saw his battalion being destroyed by an inferior force. The gradual regathering of the Guild platoons promised to worsen the casualty ratio.

He was upslope of the company now. He started gathering riders for another charge, one that would shatter the Guild formation more thoroughly and leave the individual infantrymen vulnerable to his horsemen.

Bragi took advantage of the lessening pressure to include more Guildsmen in his little phalanx and move them to a rock outcrop they could use as a core for their formation.

"Get the wounded back in the rocks," he ordered. "Haaken? See those guys over there? Take a couple men and see if you can help them get over here. You. With the bow. Cover them."

He stamped around the rock as if this were his company, gathering more men, recovering weapons and shields, and keeping one eye on the charge the horsemen were about to throw down the hill.

He gathered some forty able men, and a dozen wounded, before the charge. Despite constant harassment, the rest of the company had managed to coalesce into strong knots. Most had moved to the downhill side of the trench.

"Here they come," said Kildragon.

"All right. Reskird, take over on the left side. Haaken, you take care of the right. I'll stay here. You men, don't let them bluff you. They don't have the balls to ride through us into the rocks."

The charge did what the enemy commander wanted, though again he paid a terrible price. It shattered every Guild grouping but Bragi's. The hillside swirled with furious individual combats.

The chances of the company surviving did not look good.

The horsemen sheered round Bragi's group, trying to cut at its flanks. "Get their horses!" he kept shouting. "Somebody with a bow, get that sonofabitch with the grey hair." Nobody did so, so he snatched up a fallen bow and tried himself. He had no luck either.

But a minute later, when the man, cursing, rode closer while trying to force his riders to push straight in, Bragi got his horse by throwing a spear. The animal dropped to its haunches, dumping its rider over its rump.

"Haaken! Grab that bastard!"

Despite furiously raining blows and pounding hooves, Haaken snaked out, grabbed a handful of grey hair, and hurled himself back. He threw the groggy enemy captain at Bragi.

Ragnarson was not gentle with him either. He hoisted the captive overhead so his followers could see that he had been taken.

The Guildsmen cheered.

Bragi did not get the results he wanted. The enemy did not give up. But many of them did back off to talk it over, giving the Guildsmen a chance to reform.

Reskird said, "Those guys aren't going to turn tail just because you got their Number One."

"It was worth a shot. Maybe I shouldn't have. They might take time to think out how to get rid of us easier." Bragi glanced down at the grey-haired man. He had become docile. His lips moved, but no sound came forth. "Hey. He's praying."

"Wouldn't you? Hell, I'd be praying now if I knew a god I could trust."

"Thought you was high on the Grey Walker because he saved your ass when your ship got rammed."

"Yeah? Look what he got me into."

"Bragi," Haaken called. "Come here." Ragnarson pushed to his brother's side. "What?"

"Out there. More of them." Haaken pointed with his chin.

The horsemen were barely discernable. They were not on the road, where dust would have given them away earlier.

There were two columns, splitting from one. They seemed intent on surrounding the hill.

"Damn! And we could've been out of this now if those chicken-shit Royalists had helped. They could've kept that bunch from getting behind us."

"Here they come again!" Kildragon yelled.

Bragi sighed and forced his weary muscles to lift sword and shield once more. This was it. The end. And he didn't even know what he was dying for, unless it were simply brotherhood and the honor of the Guild.

Well, Ragnar had always said you should make your death a moment to remember. And if you couldn't be remembered by your friends, you should leave your enemies with tales they could tell their grandchildren during the long, cold winter nights.

The charge came hard. It should have spelled the end of Sanguinet's Company. But it began weakening almost immediately. Even as he shouted about getting the horses, Bragi sensed the uncertainty of the foe. In minutes their attack became halfhearted. Soon afterward they began showing their backs.

"What the hell?" Bragi asked the air. "Haaken. They're running. Running like hell. What happened?"

Reskird suggested, "Those guys down there must be on our side."

At that most of the Guildsmen surrendered to exhaustion and collapsed on their shields. They did not wait for confirmation. But Bragi dragged himself to the top of the rock outcrop. "Hey, Reskird! For once in your miserable life you guessed right. Whoo-ee! Look at them bastards ride!"

The rumbling of hooves and wailing, hair-raising Royalist war cries swept around both sides of the hill.

"What god did you pick this time, Reskird?" Bragi demanded headily. "We owe him a whole flock of sheep. Wow! I don't think any of them will get away." He eased back down and stretched himself on his shield. "Ah. This sure is nice."

And Haaken, dropping beside him, gripping his upper arm, said, "We made it. I don't believe it. We made it." He was shaking so much he could do nothing but hang on.

"Just lay back and look at that sky," Bragi told him. "Look at those clouds. Aren't they the most beautiful things you ever saw?"

Haaken did as he was told. "Yeah. Yeah."

Bragi let everybody enjoy a few minutes of unexpected life. Then he forced himself to his feet and said, "All right, if you're not wounded, let's start picking up the pieces. We've got a lot of brothers hurt and scattered all over hell. Try to get everybody to gather around here. I'm going to find the captain and see what he wants we should do. Haaken, pick a couple guys with strong stomachs and finish off their wounded."

He found his captain a few minutes later. He was still kneeling over Sanguinet's mutilated body when Reskird shouted, "Hey! Bragi! Come here!"

Ragnarson rose, looked, saw Reskird facing a group of Royalist horsemen. He gathered his sword and shield and trudged back. "Sanguinet is dead," he said in Trolledyngjan. "So are Tomas and Klaus. Who's going to take over?" He surveyed the horsemen. "Well I'll be damned!"

"That's one I paid you back, Bragi." Haroun grinned.

Reskird whispered, "Isn't that that Haroun guy from when we was commissioned at el Aswad?"

"Yeah," Bragi said. "We were handling them, Haroun."

"What are you doing here?"

"High Crag detached us to Altea. To give the locals a little backbone."

An older Royalist asked, "Your men did this?" He indicated the carnage.

"They wouldn't leave us alone," Bragi replied, making a sour joke of it. "We would've cleaned up on them good if your boys hadn't chickened out on us."

Haroun said, "Pardon me?"

Bragi explained that a group of Royalists had left the company to its fate. Haroun's face darkened.

"We met some of them. We thought they were messengers. I'll find their captain. I'll show him this. Then I'll hang him."

Haaken called, "You want I should croak the old guy too, Bragi?"

"No. Give him to these guys. They might get something out of him."

Haaken pulled their captive out of the rocks, where he had concealed himself.

"Wahla!" several horsemen cried.

"Karim!" Haroun shouted. "Ah!" He began laughing. His followers joined in, pummeling one another like joyous children.

"What is it?" Bragi asked.

"You've caught Karim. The great Karim, who is second to the Scourge of God himself. There will be rejoicing when the world hears of this. And many tears will be shed in the councils of the usurper. Oh, how the Scourge of God will rage! My friend, you have given us our first great victory. My spirit soars! I feel the tide turning! The Fates no longer vie against us. But what became of the northern traitors who rode with him?"

"I don't know. I wish I did. I'd like to get my hands on them. They caused this. This Karim didn't want to attack."

"You recognized them?"

"Yes. We thought they were your people at first. Then this Karim killed our lieutenant."

"They wanted no witnesses to their treachery. They were going to meet with Nassef. To betray the northern host. We've been chasing them more than a week."

"You caught Karim. Take him if you want. Will you excuse me? Many of my brothers are injured."

Haroun grinned at Karim. "Beloul. Do you have anything special in mind?"

"Lord, you know I do. All the torments of all the hundreds who died at Sebil el Selib."

Karim sprang at Haaken, seized his sword. He ran himself through before he could be stopped.

"A brave man for a former bandit," Haroun observed.

Because none of the surviving noncoms seemed inclined, Bragi began putting the company together again. One hundred twelve Guildsmen had survived. Fifty-three, miraculously, had come through unscathed.

"We'll shed tears for these for a long time," Bragi told Haaken. He and the young King stood facing the long rank of graves the Royalists had helped dig. "There were some great men among them."

Haroun nodded. He knew what it meant to lose old comrades.

ELEVEN
VICTORY GIFTS

El Murid and his party departed the Sahel at Kasr Helal, traveling as salt-merchants desperately seeking a supplier. The war threatened to destroy the trade. Salt prices were soaring as the flow into the desert dwindled.

It was at Kasr Helal that, unrecognized by the garrison commander, El Murid learned that, to obtain salt, traders had to deal with a Mustaph el-Kader, an uncle of Nassef's General el-Kader. The elder el-Kader was disposing of stockpiles from the captured Daimiellian works.

El Murid had heard of Mustaph el-Kader. He was infamous as a procurer and as a supplier of religiously proscribed wine. What was a man like that doing controlling the salt supply?

"Don't whine at me!" the garrison commander snapped when the Disciple protested.

"But…. To deal with whoremasters and thieves, at usurious prices…."

"You want salt? Good. You buy from who we tell you to. If you don't like it, go home."

El Murid turned to Hali, who was supposed to be his master of accounts. "Mowaffak?"

Hali controlled himself. "We'll do what we have to, and pass the costs along. But nobody's going to love us. I wonder, Captain, what the Disciple would think of your profiteering."

"What he don't know won't hurt him. But complain if you want. He'll tell you to go pound sand. It's his brother-in-law's game. He won't turn on his own kin, will he?"

That was not the desert way. Family was concrete while truth, justice, and sometimes even God's law were subjective.

"Who knows the heart of the Disciple?" Hali asked. "Surely not a bandit disguised as an officer in the Host of Illumination."

"A True Believer, eh? Get out of here. You're wasting my time. You guys are a royal pain in the ass, you know that?"

When they had gotten beyond the captain's hearing, El Murid murmured, "Nassef is doing it again, Mowaffak. If it isn't one thing, it's something else. He's driving me to distraction."

"Something has to be done, Lord."

"Of course. How do these things happen? Why hasn't anyone complained?"

"Maybe they have and the complaint hasn't been passed on. Maybe they never had the chance. Our most reliable people follow the heaviest fighting. Nassef bears your writ of command over the Invincibles. He's been exercising it, possibly to keep them away from evidence of evils such as this."

"Mowaffak, hear me. I speak for the Lord. You will choose one hundred men of irreproachable repute. Men immune to blandishment and extortion. Reclaim their white robes and return them to their original professions. They are to travel throughout the Kingdom of Peace, including both Hammad al Nakir and all the new provinces, unmasking evils such as this. They aren't to distinguish between the grievances of the faithful and the infidel, nor those of the desert-born and foreigner, nor of the mighty and the weak. All men will be equal before their judgment. I will arm them with letters giving them absolute authority in anything they care to judge, and will back them completely, even against my own family. Even if I disagree with their judgments.

This exploitation must stop."

"And who will watch the watchers?" Hali murmured to himself.

"I will, Mowaffak. And I'll be the most terrible judge of all. And Mowaffak. Collect this barbarous captain when we leave. We'll chastise him, and release him to spread the news that El Murid walks among the Chosen, as one of them, hunting their oppressors."

"How much longer will you tolerate the Scourge of God, Lord?" Hali asked, returning to a subject dear to his heart.

"How long will the fighting last? The day we begin beating swords into plowshares, then I'll have no use for captains of war."

It was at Kasr Helal, too, that Esmat told him another Ipopotam courier had failed to return. That made three who had vanished; two regular couriers and the special messenger sent after the disappearance of the first.

"Your worst fears have been realized, Esmat. Three men lost strains a belief in chance. Select six warriors from my bodyguard. Send them. Then another to see what happens to them. Do it right away, and tell them to ride hard. How long can we last?"

"Perhaps forty days, Lord. If luck rides with us."

He wanted to admonish Esmat for the pagan remark, but could not invoke the Lord now. That would be to claim God's countenance of his secret shame.

From Kasr Helal El Murid traveled northwestward, toward Dunno Scuttari and Nassef's promised spectacle. He and his companions often paused to ogle what they thought were great wonders. El Murid lingered over structures bequeathed to the present by the engineers of the Empire. Then the flame of the Empire of tomorrow burned in his eyes, and Hali would remind him that they were traveling incognito. He had had few opportunities to preach since Disharhun. The words piled up within him.

Even the towns and little cities were splendid, despite Nassef's rapine. But never had he imagined such splendor as burst upon him when first he gazed upon Dunno Scuttari.

"Oh, Papa!" Yasmid cried. "It's magnificent! So big and... and magnificent!"

"Your uncle tells me he's going to make it a gift to me. What would I do with a city? You think it's beautiful? I'll give it to you. Assuming Nassef can take it."

"He can, Papa. I know he can."

"What about me?" Sidi demanded surlily.

"There are other cities. Which one do you want? Hellin Daimiel?"

"I don't want another city. I want...."

"Let him have this one, Papa. It's beautiful, but I'd rather have Hellin Daimiel. That's where everything interesting...."

"He said I could have Hellin Daimiel, Yasmid."

"What you're going to get, Sidi, is a taste of the strap. Act your age. You're not four years old anymore."

"How come she always gets her own way? When do we get to see the ocean? I want to see the ocean."

El Murid's hand whipped out. "There are times, Sidi, when you disgust me," he said as the boy rubbed his cheek. El Murid glanced at Mowaffak Hali, who pretended an intense interest in the River Scarlotti. "There are times when I'm tempted to foster you with the poor tribesmen of the Sahel so you'll learn to appreciate what you have and stop whining about what you don't."

El Murid stopped. The boy was not listening.

"Mowaffak, have someone find the Scourge of God and tell him we're here."

Nassef himself came to greet them. He was an adolescent mass of uncontrolled emotion. He had happy smiles and ferocious hugs for everyone.

El Murid easily identified the indelible tracks loneliness had stamped into Nassef's face. He saw them in his own face whenever he glanced into a mirror.

"I'm glad you came," Nassef enthused. "So much work went into this. It would have been a sin if you'd have missed it."

El Murid noted how attentive Nassef was to Yasmid, with his little jokes, his teasing, his mock flirtation. He indulged in an old speculation. Did Nassef have designs on the girl? She was on the brink of marriageability. For Nassef to wed her would be a great coup for the ambitious Nassef who sometimes thrust his head out of the shadows surrounding the several Nassefs the Disciple knew.

There were those who would frown on a man marrying his niece, but it was not without precedent. Many of Ilkazar's emperors had married their own sisters.

A few months earlier Hali had brought El Murid a chart of succession found in the apartment of Megelin Radetic at el Aswad, the fortress the Wahlig of el Aswad had abandoned shortly before the assault on Al Rhemish. What El Murid had seen in that chart had startled him. And had revivified all the specters that had haunted him throughout his association with his brother-in-law.

If Radetic had guessed correctly, Nassef had powerful motives for pursuing Yasmid. Only Haroun bin Yousif stood between Nassef and the throne on that chart. A marriage could lead to Crown and Disciplate conjoined.

El Murid had visited his wife's father on the way west. The old man, who had disinherited his children in the beginning, had been on his deathbed. El Murid had introduced the old chieftain to his grandchildren. They had conquered him immediately. He had recanted. There had been tears of forgiveness and of reconciliation.

"Nassef."

"Lord?"

"I came by way of El Aquila."

A strained longing shone on Nassef's face.

"I saw him, yes. And these two stole his heart. He said they were just like

WITH MERCY TOWARD NONE — 251

you and Meryem at the same ages. He forgave us all. He wanted me to tell you that."

For an instant a tear glinted in Nassef's eye. "Then I can go home? I can see him again?"

"No. You know the Fates were never that kind. He was on his deathbed when we arrived. We stayed till the Dark Lady came for him. He had a gentle, peaceful death."

"And my mother?"

"She abides, but I don't think she'll survive him long."

"I'll visit her as soon as we go into winter quarters. What did he think about me?"

"Pray for him, Nassef. He never accepted the Faith. He died an unbeliever. But he was proud of his son and daughter. He talked incessantly of the things you've accomplished. He said he always knew you'd go far."

Nassef glowed through his sorrow.

Mowaffak Hali watched with the cold eyes of a raptor. For a man who abhors politics, his prophet thought, Mowaffak can play them craftily.

Nassef wasted little time getting on with the event that had drawn the Disciple to Dunno Scuttari. The next day he ferried the family across the river and guided them to a pavilion on a hilltop.

"You won't be able to see much, really," he said. "But what there is you can see best from here. In the morning."

"What is it, Nassef?" Yasmid demanded.

"A surprise, Little Dove. Get up early and you'll see."

"Come on, Nassef," she breathed. Already, unconsciously, she was adopting the little wiles a woman uses to bend a man to her will.

"No, I'm not telling. Not even you. You'll wait like everybody else." He gestured downriver, toward the eastern end of the fortress island. "They'll be the most surprised."

Yasmid's pleading and flirting went for naught. This, Nassef said without verbalizing, would be his greatest triumph. It was his game. It would be played his way, by his rules.

El Murid, uncharacteristically, had an image of an unconfident roué stalking a virgin who had spurned the advances of countless lovers with more to offer. A roué who did not disguise his intent to use her once and pass her on—yet one who had staked his fortunes and ego on the successful outcome of an otherwise inconsequential affair.

And so he gained yet another perspective on this stranger who was his oldest acquaintance. There seemed to be no end to the faces of Nassef.

That night El Murid stood outside his pavilion and marveled at the magnitude of the Host of Illumination. Its campfires covered the countryside on both banks of the river. It seemed that whole shoals of stars had descended to the plains and hills. "So many…." he murmured. "All brought here by *my* dreams."

Nassef had told him that he had recruited almost twenty thousand westerners. The Word, or parts thereof, stirred sympathetic resonances in some western hearts. The New Empire was battling its way from the womb.

Yasmid began tormenting him before sunrise. "Papa. Come on. Come and see what Nassef did. You won't believe it when you see it."

It was hours before his usual rising time. He preferred to work late and sleep late. He fought her till it became obvious that her determination was the greater. Accepting defeat grouchily, he rose. He dressed and followed her to the pavilion's exit.

"All right, brat. Show me this miracle and get it over with. I need my sleep."

"Can't you see, Papa? It's right there. Look at the river, Papa."

He peered down at the Scarlotti.

The river was not there.

The once vast flood had dwindled to a few lakes connected by one murky stream a dozen yards wide. Great expanses of mud lay exposed to the breeze and the rising sun. The breezes shifted while he wrestled with his awe. A foul odor assailed his nostrils.

"How in the world...?"

Nassef came striding toward the pavilion. Weariness seemed to drag him down, yet when he saw them watching, his step took on a boyish bounce. A broad grin captured his face. "What do you think?" he shouted.

The roué has broken his beloved maidenhead, El Murid thought. And now he comes to gloat, to adore himself publicly, to brag....

He snorted softly. "What did you do?" he demanded. "How can you dry up a river overnight?"

"You can't. What you do is impress a couple hundred thousand people and make them dig a new riverbed. I started as soon as we got here. I got the idea from *The Wizards of Ilkazar*. Where the poet tells about Varthlokkur sending the earthquake to demolish the walls and a building collapses into the Aeos and dams it and floods part of the city. I thought, why didn't they dam it upriver? Then they could have gotten in through the water gate. Then I thought, why not reroute the river? It would just spill over a dam."

Nassef babbled on. This ingenious stroke clearly meant more to him than just adding the jewel of another city to his diadem of clever conquests. He had invested of his *self*, like a child undertaking a severely ambitious project in hopes of winning paternal approval.

El Murid remembered Nassef once mentioning his trouble communicating with other children. He realized that in his superbly competent campaigns, and especially in this conquest, his brother-in-law was trying to make a statement to the world.

What was it? A simple, "I exist! Notice me!" Or something more complex? Something more complex, surely. Nothing about Nassef was simple.

"Some of my men are in the city already," Nassef told him. "They went down in boats during the night and waited for the water level to fall below the bottom of the water gate grates. They've occupied the area inside. I had other men laying plank roads across the mud as the river fell. Those should be done by now. The Host should be entering the city. They should surrender before nightfall."

Nassef was overoptimistic. Led, cajoled, and bullied by stubborn Guildsmen, the defenders resisted for nine days, yielding their inner strongholds only when overwhelmed. By the fifth day Nassef was frantic. The stone and earth dam shunting the Scarlotti was weakening. And he had yet to capture one of the fortified causeways connecting the inner and outer islands with the riverbanks.

He drove his forced laborers to prodigies and kept the dam intact. On the seventh day the Invincibles captured a causeway.

That sealed the city's fate. Nassef had acquired indefinite access.

On the eighth day a messenger arrived from the Lesser Kingdoms.

Nassef had no color and was shaking when he approached El Murid afterward. "Micah.... My Lord Disciple. They've slain Karim. Bin Yousif's rabble and some Guildsmen. They got him in Altea. Karim.... He was like a father to me. I'd sent him on a critical secret mission. He was coming back. He may have been successful. If he was, he was bringing us the chance to finish the war before winter."

El Murid frowned as he listened. Nassef seemed lost in the chaos of his thoughts, some of which he was verbalizing. He had never seen his brother-in-law this devastated, this indecisive, this much at a loss for what to do. The possible death of Karim was not something he had calculated into his plans. His habit of anticipating contingencies had failed him. Fate had found his blind spot. He had not taken into account the mortality of himself and his intimates.

"Men die in wartime, Nassef. And they won't all be soldiers we don't know, mourned only in some remote mud hut. Meryem's passing should have taught you that."

"The lesson didn't sink in. One dirty trick.... That whole campaign is going to go to Hell now. Karim was the only one who understood what I wanted. The only one who knew the whole plan. I wonder if they got anything out of him? What kind of an arrangement did he make...? I have to go out there. I'm the only one who can keep it moving. The only one who can get that whoreson bin Yousif. I'll leave el-Kader here. He knows this project. He can finish up."

Before El Murid commented or could ask questions his brother-in-law rushed away. An hour later Mowaffak reported that Nassef had ridden east with a large band of Invincibles.

El-Kader assumed Nassef's role smoothly. He forced Dunno Scuttari's surrender the following day.

Nassef's dam collapsed the day following that. The flood severely damaged the dike facings on the city's outer island. Natives muttered about omens.

We have had too much talk about Fate and omens lately, El Murid thought. And I am as guilty as the worst of them. It's time for a sermon of admonition. We're backsliding.

He was preparing the speech when Esmat relayed the report from the observer they had sent to Ipopotam.

"The lot? All six killed?" El Murid demanded. "That's hard to believe, Esmat. They were the best."

"Nevertheless, Lord. Our man didn't see who or how, unfortunately. He simply found them dead on the road. The natives wouldn't tell him what had happened. He returned before he suffered the same fate."

"All right. It's too late to save the next regular courier. What's our supply look like? We should be in fair shape. Things have been going well. I haven't called you much lately."

"True, Lord. I'd guess sixteen days. Longer if we ration."

"Oh. Not as good as I thought. Too tight, in fact." His nerves began to fray. "Find el-Kader."

The argument with el-Kader became bitter. Stunned by the Disciple's suggestion, the general said, "Just abandon the confrontation line, Lord? With an enemy army on its way? Why? What kind of sense is that?"

El Murid felt foolish as he replied, "The Lord wills it."

"What?" Sarcastically, el-Kader observed, "Then the Lord has become a ninny overnight. And I can't credit that. Lord, we have treaties with Ipopotam. How are we supposed to seduce our enemies if we can't keep faith with our friends?"

"It has to be done," El Murid insisted. But he could muster none of the fiery conviction that usually fueled his statements. El-Kader's resistance stiffened. It was plain that his prophet's demands had nothing to do with the Lord's will. "General, it's necessary that my domains encompass those of Ipopotam."

"Oh?" el-Kader mused. "*Your* domains?" Louder, "I think I understand, Lord. And I suggest you find a diplomatic solution. The Itaskians are moving. Their army is like none we've faced before. I'll need every man to fight them. The future of the Kingdom of Peace will be decided on the Scarlotti, not in Ipopotam."

"There isn't time.... Are you refusing me?"

"I'm sorry, Lord. I am. I must. My conscience won't let me favor one man's vice over the welfare of the Host of Illumination."

El Murid exploded. "How admirable you are, el-Kader. I'd applaud did I not know you a thief and profiteer. I take it that it's within the scope of your conscience to let your relatives plunder their countrymen?"

El-Kader's face became taut. But he ignored the remark. "Lord, if the Itaskians defeat us...."

"I order you to move against Ipopotam!" He was becoming more frightened with every second of delay.

"And I refuse, Lord. With all due respect. However, if you get the Scourge of God to direct me otherwise...."

"There isn't time for that!" El Murid glared at the richly decorated walls of what, till a few days earlier, had been the private audience chamber of the King of Dunno Scuttari. He whirled and stalked to a tall, massive wooden door. He shoved, shouted, "Mowaffak!"

El-Kader stiffened. It was no secret that Hali was El Murid's liaison with the Harish cult.

Hali stepped inside. His eyes were cold. His face was dead.

"Will you reconsider, General?" El Murid demanded.

"I'll give you the western recruits and ten thousand of our own people. Nothing more. I won't go myself. I have to defend the Scarlotti line."

El Murid's jaw tightened. This el-Kader was stubborn. Not even fear of the Harish would compel him to abandon his duty. He would yield nothing more.

He was a valuable man. No need wasting him in anger. "Mowaffak, I appoint you commander of the army just created. We're going to occupy Ipopotam."

Hali's right eyebrow rose almost imperceptibly. "As you command, Lord. When shall we begin?" El Murid glanced away. El-Kader did not. Hali shrugged as if to say, "What can I do?"

"Immediately, Mowaffak. And I'll accompany you." A growing, unreasoning panic taunted him. He felt the walls of the universe closing in. "That's all. Both of you. Get out of here. Give the orders. There isn't much time."

Two days after the Disciple's departure southward, two bedraggled, confused Itaskian survivors of Karim's Altean debacle reached Dunno Scuttari. Their consternation and confusion deepened when they could locate no one who knew anything about the negotiations which had brought them south. El-Kader had them thrown into a dungeon.

The general continued preparing for the advent of the northern army, unaware that its commander and his own were co-conspirators.

Sidi and Yasmid, left behind by their father, drove their Invincible babysitters to distraction with their bickering. They always squabbled when their father was absent.

Sidi was young, but perfectly aware that he was being deprived of his patrimony. He was possessed by a growing, diamond-hard hatred for his sister.

TWELVE
END OF A LEGEND

The death of Karim did not halt the invasion of Altea. The Host of Illumination came on, but its advance became confused, frenetic, without direction. The war bands simply roamed, killed, raped, and destroyed. The warriors did not know what their goals were.

"I'm exhausted, Beloul," Haroun said. "There're just too many of them." He lay back on a grassy hillside, staring at a sky that promised rain. "This charging here to stop this band and there to…."

Beloul settled to the grass beside him, sitting cross-legged. "It's grinding us all down, Lord." He plucked a stem of grass and rolled it between his fingers, squeezing out the juice. "We can't sustain it."

"We have to. If they break through here…. If they finish Altea and Kavelin, and manage their treachery with the Itaskian Duke…. What'll be left? It'll be over."

"I doubt it, Lord. The Guildsmen will continue. We'll fight. And the thieves will fall out soon enough. Can you imagine El Murid being satisfied with half the spoils? When he wants an empire spanning Ilkazar's historical boundaries?"

"Despair stalks me, Beloul. I don't think he can be stopped. He's done the impossible."

"No war is over till the last battle is fought, Lord."

"You begin to sound like Radetic."

Beloul shrugged. "With age comes wisdom, Lord. And Radetic was both old and wise. For a foreigner. Let us recount our victories instead of forecounting our defeats. Karim is gone. The Duke's treachery has been forestalled."

"Who's that there?"

"What?"

"Someone's coming."

"Looks like Shadek."

El Senoussi cantered up. "There's news from Dunno Scuttari, Lord."

"At last. You look grim, Shadek. Is it that bad?"

"It's worse, Lord. A man's face can't express it."

Haroun threw an *I told you* look at Beloul. "Well?"

"The Scourge of God has kept his promise. He took the city."

Haroun surged into a sitting position. "What? Don't joke, Shadek. That's impossible."

"Nevertheless, Lord."

"But how? Where did he get the sailors and boats? How did he scale the inner walls?"

"The Scourge of God sees things hidden from us ordinary mortals, Lord. He does the thing that would occur to no one else. He and the Disciple rode into the city, Lord."

"They surrendered without a fight? You can't make me believe that, Shadek."

"No. They fought. Valiantly. But the Scourge of God changed the course of the river and attacked them through the city's water gate. That huge bridge he was building from the north bank? That engineers said would never work? Just a diversion."

Softly, Haroun asked, "What do you say now, Beloul? You know how that's going to hit them north of the river? They'll give up without a fight. He can't be stopped anymore."

"The final battle isn't lost or won, Lord."

"Yes, yes, I know. Megelin junior. But it's only a matter of time. Shadek.... You have that grey look. I take it there's more."

"Indeed, Lord. There's more. The Scourge of God has decided to replace Karim with himself. He's probably here by now."

"I expected that. He takes defeat personally. What else?"

"El Murid has given his pet Invincible, Mowaffak Hali, his own army. And ordered him to occupy Ipopotam."

Haroun grinned. "Ha! So! You hear that, Beloul? The fat man and his friend did their job. He's desperate. This'll destroy the credibility of his diplomacy. Nobody will believe him anymore. If only the northern army would strike while he's gone and Nassef is out here...."

"I doubt that would help much, Lord," el Senoussi opined. "El-Kader commands the Host. He's no moron. At worst he would persevere till the Scourge of God bailed him out."

Haroun frowned. "You insist on extinguishing every spark of hope, don't you Shadek?"

"I'm sorry, Lord. I but relate the truths I see."

"Yes. I know. So. The Scourge of God has come to our part of the board. How can we make his stay here miserable?"

Sadly, Haroun had to admit that there was little they could do. His army hadn't the strength or the staying power. The predations of the roving war parties were crushing the Altean will to resist. Crown Prince Raithel's army was the sole native force still solid and reliable. The Prince's men, too, were exhausted.

"What about those Guildsmen?" el Senoussi asked.

"Still licking their wounds in the Bergwold," Beloul replied. "I was up there the other day. That boy is trying to rebuild with Altean stragglers. He had a little over two hundred men. Maybe three."

"They won't be much help, then."

"Only as a rallying point. That battle on the hill didn't hurt their reputation."

Haroun observed, "We may all end up hiding in the Bergwold. Shadek, locate the Scourge of God. Keep an eye on him."

Nassef found Prince Raithel first, just fifteen miles west of the Colberg. He shattered the Altean army. The Prince barely escaped with his life. Two-thirds of his soldiers did not.

Nassef then turned to Haroun. He started boxing the Royalists in.

Altea seemed to be taking its last pained gasps of freedom. Only the Bergwold and a handful of fortified towns remained unconquered.

The fat man wakened suddenly, every nerve shrieking that something was wrong. Frozen by fear, he moved nothing but his eyelids.

The campfire had burned low, but still cast a red glow. He probed the shadows. Nothing.

What was it?

There was a frightening stillness to the night. He turned till he could make out the huge, blanket-buried lump of Gouch.

There was a fly walking on the big man's naked eyeball. Its wings caught the glow of the coals, giving the eye an eerie look of motion.

Mocker hurled himself at the big man. "Gouch! You wake up." His hands closed on an arm grown cold. "Hai! Gouch! Come on. Self, am frightened by game."

He knew it was no game. The fly had betrayed the truth.

Gouch had taken terrible wounds in their last fight. They had slain six Invincibles! A half dozen of the most determined fighters in the world. It had been too big a task.

It was a miracle that the big man had lasted this long.

"Woe! Gouch! Please! Do not leave self alone."

They had become close. Mocker, though he had expected the worst, could not accept it.

"Am accursed," he muttered. "Am carrier of death, like bearer of plague. Should be expunged from face of earth."

For a time he just sat beside his friend, damning himself, mourning, and wondering what he would do now. Finally, he rose and began collecting rocks. The cairn he built was not much, but it showed that he cared. He would not have made the effort for anyone else.

He muttered as he worked. "Self, am in no wise able to continue task here. Enemy catching on. Same being intelligent, will send bigger party next time round. Same will be inhamperable. Must assay alternate course, designed to inconvenience religious dolts."

He fluttered round the camp till sunrise. Then he loaded his donkey and headed north, toward lands where he might more effectively prosecute his personal war. He narrowly avoided colliding with El Murid's southbound invasion force.

The Duke of Greyfells, who had moved south slowly while awaiting confirmation of his negotiations with Karim, finally learned of Karim's death. He was furious. Then he learned that Nassef had replaced his subordinate in the Lesser Kingdoms.

Altea was a remote theater. He would not be noticed there.

In disguise, guarded by his most intimate supporters, he rode south to renegotiate treacheries that had promised him the Itaskian Crown and partition of the west.

His second in command, a bitter enemy, allowed him a head start, then rushed the northern army toward Dunno Scuttari.

It met el-Kader and the Host of Illumination on a plain near the town of Pircheaen, twenty-two miles north of the Scarlotti. The armies skirmished throughout a brisk autumn day. Neither commander was prepared to commit himself. The exchanges of the second day were more savage but no more conclusive. Both sides claimed victory.

El-Kader withdrew during the night. But the Itaskians did not follow up with an advance toward Dunno Scuttari. Instead, they turned east, hoping to force a crossing of the River Scarlotti somewhere away from the most heavily defended crossings.

El-Kader recrossed the river, then marched parallel to the Itaskians.

"We're in a bad spot," Beloul told his king. He held a crude map of the area west of the Bergwold. "He's hemmed us in. He has men here, here, here...." One by one, he indicated the locations of eight war bands, each at least the equal of Haroun's own. The Royalists were surrounded on all but the Bergwold side.

"Can we break out?"

"Maybe. But it looks grim."

Haroun sighed, surveyed the countryside. There was not an enemy in sight, yet the cage door had been slammed shut. He glanced down at his hands. They were shaking. He was afraid his nerve was going. He desperately needed a rest. "Which group is he with?"

"Here. South of the Bergwold."

"All right. That's where we'll try to break out."

"Lord? Attack the Scourge of God himself?"

"Yes. We'll just have to fight the harder. And hope. Beloul?"

"Lord?"

"Tell the men our only hope is to slay the Scourge of God. That's going to be the whole point of the attack."

"As you command, Lord."

Sorrowfully, uncertainly, Haroun watched his little army prepare for what might be its last battle. Why did he bother? It seemed every peril he evaded led to a worse. "Let's go!" He swung into his saddle.

"We might do it!" he shrieked an hour later.

The surprised enemy force, backboned by a handful of Invincibles, could not get organized. Haroun flailed about himself, wailing Royalist war cries. His men, smelling success, were hurling themselves on their enemies with more passion than he had anticipated. Some were just yards from the Scourge of God.

Hatred seared the air as he and Nassef glared at one another. The hate drew them like powerful lodestones. But the meeting was not fated. The swirl of battle pushed them ever farther apart.

In time, Haroun moaned to Beloul, "They reacted too damned fast." The tide was turning. And a scout had brought word that another war band was approaching.

"Yet the Scourge of God remains in peril, Lord. Look. The Invincibles keep getting tangled up trying to protect him."

"Don't humor me, Beloul. I have eyes."

The fighting drifted toward the Colberg. All the valor and sacrifice of the Royalist champions was in vain. The Invincibles rallied their less enthusiastic companions and began closing a circle around them. When asked for suggestions, el Senoussi could contribute only, "Maybe we could make a stand in the ruins, Lord."

"Maybe. Where are the damned Guildsmen? Didn't you send a messenger?"

"Beloul did, Lord. I don't know where they are. Maybe they're getting even."

"Not that Ragnarson…. Look. There they are."

An infantry company came double-timing from beyond the Colberg.

"You're right, Lord. And just in time."

"They pay their debts."

Ragnarson opened an escapeway for the Royalists.

"Why didn't you keep after them?" bin Yousif demanded as Ragnarson shepherded him toward the Colberg. "We could have had the Scourge of God."

"Bitch and gripe. How the hell was I supposed to know? Your message said stand by to bail you out if you got in over your head. I barely got here in time to do that. Haaken, get those Altean clowns into close order. Look, your kingship, I just saved your ass. Again. You want me to throw you back? Or to worry about keeping it saved? That isn't the only gang of those guys around. There's one only four miles north of here."

Beloul protested, "Lord, these masterless curs need a lesson in manners."

"Look behind us, Beloul."

He hated looking back himself. That part of his force which remained was no larger than the company led by the young Guildsman. Most of the rest had scattered. It would take days for the survivors to reform.

"Hey, Bragi," a Guildsman shouted. "We'd better get into the woods. They're ready to come after us."

Haroun glanced back. The second war band had arrived. "Your man is right. We'd better run."

They entered the tangle of the Bergwold in time. Nassef's riders showed no inclination to follow them. Ragnarson laughed. "They've tried before. We taught them a lesson. If they're going to come in, they have to get off horses. They don't like that. Move your men ahead. I'll screen you."

"Bragi. They're going to try it after all."

Haroun listened to the courses of men Nassef had ordered into the wood. "You're right. They don't like it."

"They're going to like it a lot less in a little while. Haaken. Reskird. We'll set the ambush at the deep ravine."

The fight was little more than a skirmish. Nassef's men quickly retreated to the forest's edge.

They came again the following morning, this time seriously. The Scourge of God had gathered all his men for the sweep.

"There's way too many of them," Ragnarson told Haroun. "They can cover the whole Bergwold. We can't play hide and seek."

Haroun nodded as he studied the Guildsman's Bergwold maps. "These are good." Megelin would have been pleased with their quality. "You read?" he asked.

"Only enough to follow those. It's part of the training, but the war broke before we got to reading and writing. Captain Sanguinet and Lieutenant Trubacik drew those. They taught all the noncoms how to read them."

"My friend, we've gotten ourselves into a classic situation here. Whatever we do is wrong. We can't run and we don't dare fight."

"Between a rock and a hard place, as we say at home."

"Nassef wants you as bad as he wants me. He was fond of Karim. What do you think we should do?"

Ragnarson shrugged. "You was trained to lead. Now would be a great time to start. I got this job because nobody else would take it. It's all I can do to figure out what to do with the volunteers we've been getting."

"Have you gotten many?"

"A lot. Your friend Nassef has been kicking ass all over the country. Most of them don't seem to know where else to go."

Dawn's light was seeping into the dank, misty forest when Ragnarson's brother appeared. "They're coming, Bragi. Two lines deep. We won't have a chance if they make contact."

"Could we break through?" Haroun asked.

"That's what they want us to try, I think. Then the whole mob could close in."

"And if we run, they'll be waiting on the other side of the forest."

"That's how I'd set it up."

"Let's do it anyway. We'll locate them and I'll attack with my horsemen. You run for Alperin after they start chasing me. It's only twelve miles. Its walls are strong and it has its own garrison. I can circle around and catch up with you there."

"I don't like it," Ragnarson said. "What good will it do? We'll still be surrounded."

"But with a wall to protect us, and people to help."

"The Scourge of God hasn't been intimidated by walls yet." Nevertheless, Ragnarson acquiesced. He could muster no plan of his own. "All right," he grumbled. "I kind of stumbled into this, you know. I kind of hoped I could make some kind of showing before High Crag replaced Sanguinet. I thought this was my big chance."

Haroun smiled thinly. "Look what I'm going to lose. A whole kingdom. It's so huge. It stretches as far as I can throw a rock."

"Yeah. Haaken! Reskird! Let's move out."

Haroun came to respect the Guildsmen even more. The passage through the wood took a day and a night and most of another day. The warrior brothers seldom rested, and frequently spent their own strength to help the weaker of their allies. And many of them were burdened with wounded. He questioned Ragnarson about it, but the youth could not explain. That was the way his brotherhood did things.

Yet the Guildsmen were no less weary than the others, Haroun saw. They just seemed to have more will.

And these, he thought, are the Guild children. No wonder old generals like Hawkwind and Lauder, with their select followers, were so feared.

The sun was well to the west when they reached the nether verge of the Bergwold. Haroun considered the time of day. "We'd have a better chance of pulling it off after dark."

Ragnarson agreed. "We can use the rest. Send some of your people to scout it out. They're better at it than mine. Mine can't see anybody out there, and I think that's too good to be true."

"You're right. Beloul!" Haroun called. "I have a job for you." He explained what he wanted.

The sun had set before Beloul returned to say, "Lord, he's there. The Scourge of God himself, with the Invincibles. They're hiding in a ravine beside the road to Alperin. They don't know that we're here yet. And from what I could overhear, they're exhausted from their ride around the forest."

Haroun translated for Ragnarson. He added, "Let's give it another hour. Then I'll try to draw them off to the south."

"Make it two hours and you'll have the moon."

The time rushed away. The moon seemed to streak into the sky. Suddenly, Haroun was on his mount and Altean countryside was rushing beneath him. He was kicking his mare because she was reluctant to run in the weak light. To his left, one of his followers went down as his mount stumbled.

Nassef was not ready for him. Not for him to come smashing straight in behind a swarm of arrows. The Invincibles remained disorganized for the critical few minutes Haroun needed to lead his band past and take them flying into the night.

Then they came after him.

He could see little, looking back to the northwest, but he could hear the thundering hooves and the exultant war cries.

The Invincibles, like their Guild enemies, were tenacious. Haroun could not shake them. His success consisted of staying ahead. Gradually he swung round northward, circling back toward Alperin.

"Why are we doing this, Lord?" el Senoussi wanted to know. "Why aren't we escaping? Towns are traps."

Haroun did not answer for a while. He did not know how to put it into words. "There's a duty, Shadek. A responsibility. How can I explain? You imply an argument, and the sense of it is incontestable. Radetic would have commended you. Mine is purely emotional. Maybe it's the hand of fate that moves me. But I do have a feeling this Ragnarson might be critical to my future. To all our futures."

"You're the King, Lord."

Haroun laughed. It was a weak, drained gesture. "I love your enthusiasm, Shadek. You're like an oasis after six days of hard desert. You shelter me from the sandstorms of tomorrow."

El Senoussi chuckled. "Thank you, Lord."

Moments later, Beloul said, "Something's wrong, Lord. They're not pushing us as hard as they should be."

"I've noticed. We must be doing what they want."

"I told you, Lord," said el Senoussi.

Daylight arrived. And Haroun learned why the Invincibles had relaxed. He had come back to Alperin.

"Damn! He's outfoxed us again." There was fierce fighting at the town gate. "He let the Guildsmen get there so he could catch them with their gates open."

"Would that we had such a plotter in our ranks, Lord," said el Senoussi.

"Be patient, Shadek. He's teaching me."

"Indeed, Lord. What now?"

"What about our friends back there? In no hurry, eh? Unless we try to break away? Let's see if we can get up on yon hill and watch for a while. Our friends might get so interested they'll give us a chance to get away."

He spoke lightly, as if unconcerned, but he was sure this was the last day of his life.

The Invincibles allowed them the hilltop and did not offer battle immediately. The Scourge of God seemed content to delay his gratification while he dealt with the Guildsmen.

"That's the end of some brave boys," Beloul said gently.

Haroun glanced at the town gate. Fanatics in white were flooding through. "Yes. A pity."

"That Nassef is one crafty bastard," Haaken told Bragi as the Alteans defending the gate collapsed. They had made a valiant stand. Their task had been hopeless, but they had held long enough.

"He thought on his feet," Bragi replied. "He outguessed us. We've got to pay the price. Let's just hope this trick is something he's not expecting. Come on, Reskird!" he shouted. "Quit screwing around over there. They're coming." He could see most of the curved street running from the gate. Horsemen swept toward them like a sudden spring flood, forced on by those behind them.

Alperin was typical of towns that spent centuries constrained within walls. It had had to grow upward and together instead of spreading. Its streets were narrow and twisted. Its buildings stood three, four, and sometimes five stories high, often overhanging the cobbled streets.

It was a bad place for horsemen to engage bowmen who had taken to the rooftops.

Arrows swarmed down onto the Invincibles and their animals. The desert warriors tried fighting back with their saddle bows, but could find few targets. The Guildsmen exposed themselves only long enough to loose their shafts.

The Invincibles still entering the town kept forcing their fellows into the deadly streets.

"Keep it up! Keep it up!" Bragi screamed. He scuttled across a steep slate roof. "We're going to do it, Haaken! We're going to do it! They don't know what's happening."

He was right. The Invincibles, absolutely certain of victory and unable, because of the twisting streets, to see that the slaughter was not localized, kept driving into the killing rain.

"Haaken, I'm going to find that Altean captain. What was his name?"

"Karathel."

"Yeah. Maybe he can rally his men and grab the gates again. We can trap them in here and murder them all."

"Bragi."

"What?"

"Don't push your luck. Things can change. They still outnumber us a skillion to one. We should just worry about getting out alive. Just make them back off."

"Yeah. Okay." But Bragi was not listening. He was too excited to accept the possibility of disaster. He had thought on his feet too. He had turned Nassef's trap into a counter-trap. He was flying high. "Be back in a few minutes."

He scrambled from roof to roof, moving toward the wall, parallel to the street. He paused occasionally to loose an arrow. He had told his men to concentrate on leaders. Confused followers could be dispatched later.

Nowhere did he see anything to warrant Haaken's pessimism. The streets were filled with dead men. It was a target shoot.

His trip proved needless. Karathel's thinking paralleled his own. His was counterattacking when Bragi arrived. The Invincibles at the gate were hard pressed.

Then more Invincibles attacked from outside. They overran the Alteans while Bragi watched, feeling completely helpless.

"Damn!" he snarled. "Damn! Damn! Damn! We had it in the palm of our hand."

Haaken's warning came back. Nassef had thousands of men in Altea. If they kept converging nothing could prevent their victory.

He could see Haroun's men on their hill, watching, unable to help. He sighed. "Just not enough people."

Below, the new wave of Invincibles surged into the deathtrap streets. It was time to rejoin Haaken. If this was the end, they should go down together.

He found his path barred. Some not too bright Invincible had fired a building in hopes of driving the Guildsmen off its roof. He had overlooked the fact that the fire would be as hard on the men in the narrow street. Bragi decided to descend and circle round the burning house.

He dropped into a tight alleyway lying behind a long row of shops and houses. He had taken no more than a dozen steps when horsemen overtook him

He whirled, let an arrow fly. A man groaned. He loosed a second shaft into the flesh under a man's chin as a horse reared over his head. He fumbled for a third arrow, dropped it, clawed at his sword. The certainty of death nearly paralyzed him.

The third rider let out a strangled wail and fled, though he had been in perfect position to split Bragi's head with his saber.

Bragi stood there a moment, stunned. "What the hell?" He glanced at the men he had downed. The Invincible was still alive, groaning. The other was stone dead.

"What the hell?" Bragi said again. Then he shrugged. "Why look the old gift horse in the mouth?" He ran while the running was good.

"Something's happened," Haaken said when Bragi finally found him. "Look how they're howling and carrying on. And hardly fighting back."

Ragnarson looked into the street. He loosed an arrow. "Looks like they've gone crazy. I don't get it. But keep hitting them."

"We won't be able to much longer. We're about out of arrows."

"Use them all. We'll worry about what to do next when we have to."

The arrow shortage never mattered. Within minutes those Invincibles who could were flying out the gate, where Haroun's men took advantage of their confusion and despair to hurt them further.

Haroun rode into the jubilant town an hour later. "Look at his face," Bragi whispered to Kildragon. "He's *glowing*. I never saw anybody look like that."

"I don't know how you did it, my friend," Haroun said softly, awed. "I don't even care. But today will live in memory ever green."

"What? Come on. We didn't…. We survived, that's all."

"No. You did more. Much more. Today El Murid lost his war. The Invincibles have been broken. Now it's only a matter of time till the Disciple has been destroyed."

"What the hell are you raving about? So we finally won one. It didn't amount to that much. And the rest of them will be after us in a day or two."

Bin Yousif considered him momentarily. "You really don't know, do you? I forget, you don't speak my language well. Listen, my friend. Outside. That's a death song the Invincibles are singing. And inside, that's a victory song by my people. They're not singing for today, but for the war. You did two things. You destroyed the biggest band of Invincibles El Murid had left. And you slew the Scourge of God. You. Yourself."

"That man in the alley…?" Bragi muttered to himself. "But…." He sat down on a stone wall surrounding a fountain. "Really?"

"Really. And it'll change the whole shape of the war."

THIRTEEN
THE ENTERTAINER

The fat youth crouched in the scraggly brush and studied the enemy encampment. Fifty Invincibles guarding two children. What made them so important?

He had come close to stumbling into them. He had made cover just in time. His curiosity was aroused. Two children!

He had been headed north, skirting the edge of the Sahel, making for Altea, where he hoped to rejoin bin Yousif. But now the north had fled his mind. This might be a chance to strike a real blow on behalf of Sparen and Gouch.

He shook. "Fat one, O flabby friend, am in no wise able to brave fifty swords of enemies implacable as Lady Death Herself. Only fool would do same.

"Pusillanimous pretender," he answered himself. "Is potential opportunity of unparalleled magnitude. Must at least investigate. Establish identity of protected children. Same might be of tremendous value. Elimination of same might be mighty blow against fell empire of madman El Murid."

Mocker was easily frightened. Sajac had kept him afraid for years. But the constant pressure had schooled him to control his fear.

He was scared silly when he led his donkey into the encampment, pretending less familiarity with the desert tongue than he possessed.

"Go away, vagabond," a sentry told him.

Mocker just looked puzzled and, more brokenly than usual, claimed a right to use the spring. He offered to entertain the band in return for his supper.

He had learned some of the desert tongue during his half-forgotten trek down the coast of the Sea of Kotsüm, and had picked up more while traveling with Haroun. He understood most of what was being said around him.

Thus it was that, shortly after the Invincible commander let him lay out his bedroll, he learned who the children were.

Malicious glee almost overcame him.

They were the spawn of the Disciple himself! Ah, but weren't the Fates playing a curious game? The general at Dunno Scuttari, el-Kader, had ordered them moved to the safety of the Sahel. He was concerned about the approach of the northern army.

What sweet opportunity! The children of El Murid! He nearly forgot his fear.

His devilish mind began darting around like a whole swarm of gnats. How best to exploit this chance encounter?

First he would have to infatuate the children and attach himself to their party.

How? The Invincibles were keeping them carefully segregated.

He opened his packs as evening settled in. He joined some of the younger Invincibles at their campfire. Sealing his eyes, he commenced the dexterity drills he had so often cursed Sparen for forcing upon him. They amounted to little more than making a common object—a copper coin in this case—appear and disappear between his fingers.

"Sorcery!" someone muttered. Mocker heard the fear in the voice.

He opened his eyes, smiled gently. "Oh, no, my friend. No witchcraft. Is simplest trick of prestidigitation. See? Coin is on back of hand. Is finger game. Watch." He pulled a short stick from the fire and made it appear and disappear, slowly and clumsily enough for the warriors to get the drift. "You see?"

Stage magicians were not unknown in the desert, but they had shown no eagerness to perform since El Murid's ascension. The Disciple's followers were too sensitive about sorcery.

"Hey! I think I saw it," said a warrior. "Do it again, would you?" The man squatted in order to see better.

"Self, am humblest of entertainers," Mocker said. "Have been perilously buffeted by winds of war."

"Got you," the warrior said. "That's neat. Could you teach me how to do it? I've got a kid brother who would love something like that."

Mocker shrugged. "Self, can try. But take warning. Is more difficult of achieving than looks betray. Takes much practice. Self, am professional, yet must practice two hours daily."

"That's all right. Just the coin trick. Come on." The warrior, who was hardly older than Mocker, produced a coin of his own. Several others crowded around, equally interested.

Within twenty minutes that fat youth had three students and an audience of a dozen. The watchers taunted the trainees whenever their fingers betrayed them. Mocker provided a natter of invented self-history with his instructions. His biography was an epic of how the war, in the form of marauding Guildsmen, had robbed him of his position as jester to a minor Libianninese nobleman. The Guildsmen, he claimed, had erroneously concluded that the knight was collaborating with the Scourge of God. They had hung the man and burned his manor. Mocker claimed that only a miraculous escape had saved him from the same fate.

"So uncivilized, this west! Understand that war is facet of mankind. Have studied with leading philosophers and know same. But barbarisms practiced by combatants here.... Self, am soured on whole end of earth. Am determined to return to east of childhood, where sanity reigns supreme."

The Invincibles took no offense. He seemed to be condemning their enemies more than themselves.

Their captain heard most of the tale. Mocker kept a close, if surreptitious, eye on the man, but could not detect a reaction. His fireside companions seemed satisfied, but their opinions were not critical. The captain's was.

Then he noticed the face in the shadows. A girl's face. How long had she been watching? And listening?

"Enough of teaching now. Is boring for soldiers out in wilderness, maybeso? Self, will do show. Same being entertaining enough, audience might reward self with copper or two to sustain same during hardship of eastward journey, maybeso." He recovered the rest of his tools and props.

He relied heavily on the stage magic, but after a while broke it up with Tubal and Polo. His audience did not respond. The Children of Hammad al Nakir were not familiar with urban-rural conflicts, and were too conservative to appreciate the ribaldry.

"No fun at all, these people," Mocker muttered to himself. "No imagination. Men of friend Haroun howled at same stories."

Two faces now watched from the shadows. He returned to the stage magic, carefully playing to that select audience.

He studied the children as much as he dared, feeling for something that might reach them. He thought the girl was the one he would win. The boy seemed sour, surly and impossible to impress.

He thought wrong. The boy was the one who defied the captain's glare and came to the fireside. "Can you teach me those tricks?" he demanded.

Mocker scanned the faces of the Invincibles. He found no guideposts. He spread his hands, shrugged. "Maybeso. All things are possible with faith. Show self hands."

"What?"

"Hands. Self, must see hands to say if true skill can be developed."

Sidi offered his hands. Mocker took them, studied their backs, then their palms. "Training is possible," he announced. "Fingers are thin enough. But not very long. Will be problem. Will require much hard practice. Get coin. Will begin...."

"Some other time," the captain said. "He needs his sleep now. We've spent too long on this as it is."

Mocker shrugged. "Am sorry, young sir."

Sidi glared at the captain. Suddenly, he whirled and stamped toward his sister. Mocker thought he heard a muttered, "I never get anything I want."

Mocker turned in with the warriors, but was a long time falling asleep. What had gone wrong? Was it too late to do something more? They would travel on in the morning, leaving him here to watch opportunity vanish into the badlands.... Did he dare try something tonight? No. That would be suicidal. That damned captain would cut him down before he got out of his bedroll.

The captain wakened him next morning. He had been lying there half-awake, trying to ignore the racket made by the rising warriors. "Pack your things, Entertainer," he ordered. "You're coming with us."

"Eh? Hai! Not into desert. Am bound for...."

The captain glared. "So you'll make a detour. The one you were fishing for. That's what last night was all about, wasn't it? So drop the pretense. Pack your things. You've found your new sponsor."

Mocker stared at the ground. He fought fear. This man was dangerously perceptive.

The captain leaned closer. "The Lord Sidi and Lady Yasmid insist on having you. I won't defy them. But I'll be watching, fat man. One misstep and you're dead."

Mocker shook all over. He had had no illusions before, but with the captain having voiced his suspicion he became more terrified than ever. He rushed to his donkey.

He irritated the captain further when the party got under way. He was the only one walking. But Sidi took a proprietary interest in him, shielding him from the Invincible, acting like a child with a new pet.

Mocker faked smiles and mumbled to himself, "Am going to repay this patronization with compound interest, Lord."

The Sahel he liked even less than he did Sidi.

Between Hammad al Nakir proper and the domains of the coastal states lay a strip of land which made the interior desert attractive by comparison. A legacy of the Fall, a natural killing zone, it varied in depth from forty to one hundred miles. Virtually waterless and lifeless, it consisted almost entirely of sharp, low mountains and tortuous, rocky gorges. It was the crudest of lands. The few people who survived there were among the poorest and most primitive alive. They hated outsiders.

And they were El Murid's, heart and soul. Most of the current crop of Invincibles sprang from the Sahel. The sons of the Sahel saw more promise in El Murid's dreams than did the Children of Hammad al Nakir proper.

Mocker walked that barren land and wept for himself. However was he going to win his way back through this maze of dead hills and unseen sentinels? The watchful Sahel tribesmen were everywhere. Lean, ragged savages, they scared hell out of him each time they visited their brethren of the bodyguard.

He tried to keep them out of mind. Sufficient unto the day the evil thereof.

After three thoughtful days he selected the girl as his primary target. El Murid's movement would miss her more than it would Sidi. The heart of the insane beast would not miss a beat if she were to take over when the Disciple's last day came.

The boy was a useless little snot. If he assumed the mantle his father's movement would rush headlong toward the graveyard of history.

The fat man had begun, occasionally, to think politically. Haroun bin Yousif had set his feet upon the path.

He wanted to cause his enemies all the pain he could. Removing their future prophetess seemed the surest way.

He could not get close to the girl. His usual winning techniques seemed wasted on her. Though she often watched his entertainments, and sometimes observed Sidi's private lessons, she never betrayed amusement or delight. The Invincible captain was more responsive.

She had to be an inhuman monster. A child with no child in her at all. That was spooky enough in a grownup. In a kid it was horribly unnatural.

He worked hard with Sidi. The boy had no talent and a lot of impatience. He had to praise him constantly to keep him interested. Sidi was the only channel to Yasmid.

"Self, have decided," he announced one morning, after the Invincibles had set up a semipermanent camp just behind the Sahel. "Will show favorite pupil secret of mesmerism after all." He had decided to go ahead with his final, most desperate, most perilous line of attack.

He had been priming it from the beginning, of course, just in case, mentioning hypnotism, when playing coy. His excuse for dropping the subject was always the best: the Invincibles might accuse him of witchcraft. And there was the problem of finding a reliably close-mouthed subject on whom to practice.

Sidi had been volunteering his sister for almost as long as Mocker had been tempting him.

"Now?" Sidi demanded. He was excited. Mocker watched the green burn in his eyes. Damo Sparen certainly had been a student of the human race, the fat man reflected. He had been guiding the Disciple's son according to the Sparen precepts, letting the boy do all the work. He was ready. A lust for power over people boiled within him.

"Soon, Lord. If same can be managed unbeknownst to white-clad savages. Same being simple skill learnable by anyones, but subject to gross misinterpretation by superstitious, self must protect self...."

"Tonight. Come to my tent tonight. My sister will be there. I promise."

Mocker nodded. He kept his mouth shut, let the boy have his head.

Sidi was the perfect mark, so avaricious and self-centered that he had no time for suspicions. Mocker was ashamed. This was like robbing a blind man.

But the stakes! Oh, the stakes!

He worried about the captain all day. That man was the essence of vigilance. He would have to be the first to die....

He dared leave no one like the captain alive on his backtrail. The captain had that same abiding quality exemplified by Haroun's man Beloul. He would come till he had gotten his revenge.

Not all the Invincibles remained cold and aloof. Several of Mocker's pupils became quite friendly. He swapped jokes and quips with them, and regaled them with endlessly shifting, slippery lies about his misadventures in the east. They answered him with lies of their own.

Darkness finally fell. He let a few hours drag past. Finally, heart hammering, he crept to Sidi's tent. No one challenged him.

It was a night without a moon, but he knew the guard only pretended not to notice him. What if the man suffered a fit of conscience and reported this to his commander?

"Lord?" Mocker whispered, his nerves howling. "Is self. Can same enter?"

"Come on! It's about time. Where have you been?"

Mocker slipped into the tent. "Waiting for camp to fall asleep." He smiled. Yasmid was there.

She had brought one of her handmaidens. That was a complication he had not foreseen.

Could he hypnotize three at one time? He had never tried. And a life or death situation made it a hell of a time to start.

As if to soothe his nerves, he began tumbling a coin amongst his chubby fingers, making it appear and disappear. "All is ready?" he asked. "All are agreed? Lady? Self, will not undertake task if same offends...."

"Get on with it." Yasmid smiled thinly. "Entertainer, I'm here because I'm interested. But we have to finish before the guards change watches."

"Is not so simple like skinning goat, Lady. Stage must be set."

"So set it."

There was no doubt who was in charge here. Not Sidi. Mocker smiled wanly. Had the girl been using her brother all along?

He assumed the lotus position. "If Lady will sit facing self? All right. Lord, will do same here?" He patted the carpeted earth with his left hand. Beckoning the handmaiden, "You, sit here, please." He patted with his right hand. "Lord Sidi, and you, Miss, you must watch self close. See what self does. Is impossible of explaining, but easy to show. Lady Yasmid, you concentrate on coin here. Put all else out of mind. Never let eyes wander from same. See same turn in candlelight? Bright, dark, bright, like day, like night...." His voice became a low monotone. She strained to hear. He stared into her eyes, droning about the coin, and secretly prayed that the other two would be trapped by it as well.

"Now sleep comes. Blessed sleep. Respite from all trials of daytimes. Sleep." He went on far longer than Sparen had deemed necessary. He wanted to be sure. The stakes were high. "Eyelids feel like same are weighted with lead. Unable to open eyes." It began to get to him.

He finally dared glance at Sidi and the maid.

He had them!

His heart hammered. Oh, the wonder of it! He began talking rapidly, first to the maid, then to Sidi, sketching what he wanted remembered should they be interrupted from outside. Yasmid he told not to remember anything. Then, to her, "You will begin to see good side of portly friend of brother Sidi. Will want to ease lot of same…. Wait."

To himself, he muttered, "Is famous case of putting cart before horse. Self, am being too anxious. Must take time, do thing right. First must find true feelings and natural weak points hidden in female mind, same being foundation stones self must assemble into working structure." He began questioning Yasmid about her feelings. About everyone and everything.

"Very interesting," he murmured a half-hour later, having discovered that while she worshipped her father and his notion of a Kingdom of Peace, she secretly loathed her father's war. It had claimed the life of her mother, and that she believed too great a price to pay for a dream.

Her father's warriors, especially Nassef, awed her, but she saw them as instruments of impatience. She was convinced that her father's ideals were invincible in themselves, that they could conquer the world by their own innate superiority. Were westerners not enlisting in the Host of Illumination? Had the Faith not caught on even in Throyes? El Murid needed but give them time.

But she was no pacifist. There was a savage, vengeful strain in her. She wanted the Royalists hunted and slain to the last of their number. They were unrepentant tools of the Evil One, and as such deserved only to be reunited with their dark master.

Mocker strove to reinforce her antiwar feelings. Then he resumed working on her attitudes toward himself.

He wanted her convinced that he was a good and trustworthy friend, that she could confide in him when she dared go to no one else.

Someone stirred outside the tent. "Lord? It's almost time to change the guard."

"Just a minute," Mocker replied, managing a creditable Sidi-like whine. Working hastily, he again told the three what he wanted remembered. Then he wakened Yasmid and her handmaiden with simple fingersnaps.

"What's the matter with Sidi?" Yasmid demanded. The boy was snoring.

"Woe," Mocker said. "Fell asleep short time passing. Self, feared to shake awake lest same be considered crime. In homeland of self touching of royal personage is deemed capital offense. Being cautious by nature, thought leaving same sleep was prudenter course."

"We're not royalty, Entertainer. We've never claimed to be. We're just spokesmen for the Lord. The brat may wish he was a prince…. Nobody would pay attention if he complained."

Mocker watched her carefully. Her reserve seemed to have faded. Maybe he had succeeded. "Maybeso. Still, must ask Lady to do wakening honors. Self would feel more comfortable. Must depart, anyways. Is almost time for watch change. Captain would be irate did same catch nocturnal visitant to beautiful lady in his charge."

He caught her blush as he turned to leave. It climbed her cheeks till it peeped over her veil. He grinned at the darkness as he left the tent.

He had not lost his touch.

In two days he had Yasmid chattering like an old friend. She followed him around the camp, her devotion testing the captain's indulgence. Mocker heard her whole life's tale, and much about her fears and dreams.

As Yasmid drew closer, Sidi withdrew. The boy was selfish and jealous and did not hide it. Mocker was afraid he would backstab him for turning to his sister.

Yasmid came to him the third morning, her face ashen, her mind numb.

"What is problem, Lady?" he asked softly. "Evil tidings? Self, saw messenger arrive hour passing. Am sorry, if so."

"The Scourge of God is dead."

"Eh? Same being famed Nassef, high general to Lady's father?"

"Yes. My uncle Nassef. The man I planned to marry."

"Is sad. Very sad. Self, will do whatever to ease pain of same."

"Thank you. You're a kind man, Entertainer." She seemed compelled to rehearse the details. "It happened at some little town in Altea. The same Guildsmen who killed Karim did it. Only three hundred of them, they say. They slew my uncle and more than a thousand Invincibles, and nobody knows how many regular warriors. The Invincibles haven't been so humiliated since Wadi el Kuf. How can that be, Entertainer?"

He took her pale, cool little hands in his. "Self, am no military genius, admitted. But know strange things happen when men fight. Sometimes...."

She was not listening. She had turned her attention inward. Some of the turmoil there found its way to her lips.

"This is a merciless war, fat man. It claimed my mother last year. It nearly claimed my father at Wadi el Kuf. Now it's taken my uncle. What next? Who? Me? My father again? Sidi? There's got to be a way to stop it. Think for me. Please?"

"Might note, just for purpose of establishing philosophical point, that war is having same effect on many thousands other families. Including family of enemy, Haroun."

"I don't care about...."

"Self, am but humblest wandering mummer, Lady. Simple entertainer. Yet can say this with certitude. Whole war really rests in hands of two men, one being father of yourself, who started same, and archenemy Haroun bin Yousif, who will not let same end." He glanced around to see if anyone were in hearing. In a softer voice, he added, "Make peace between same and peace for rest of world would follow surely as dawn follows night."

She scowled. Then confusion took over. "That's impossible. There's too much blood between them now."

"Not so. Admitted, am not familiar of bin Yousif. But saw same few months passing, at castle of former master of self, where same was seeking aid. Same did not know self was overhearing. Was lamenting war to captain name of Bellous...."

"Beloul?"

"Hai! Just so. Beloul. Old grey-haired guy with nasty temper. Was lamenting to same inability of self to make peace without loss of face to self or El Murid. In meantimes, best young men of desert were dying at hands of one another, and soon none would be left."

"I've heard my father say that. And weep about it. How much more mighty we would be if the Royalists became one with the Kingdom of Peace."

Mocker glanced round again. They were still alone. He whispered, "Sajac the Wise."

Yasmid's eyes went glassy. The fat youth smiled. "Sparen, you were hard master. Am finally appreciating beneficence of same. Lady Yasmid. Hear me. Is good chance of stopping war by meeting with Haroun. Sometime soon, in hour or two, summon self and present idea that self should escort Lady to see same, same probably being in Altea. Sneaky-like, by night, so guards committed to father and war don't prevent." He added a few refining touches, then said, "Will go to sleep now, Lady. Will waken when self asks what is wrong, remembering nothing but agony of uncle's death."

He waited twenty seconds, then plunged forward dramatically. "Lady! Speak! What is wrong?"

Yasmid opened tear-filled eyes. "What?"

"Mercy!" Mocker swore. "Self was frightened…. Seemed Lady was fainting."

"Me?" she asked. Confusedly, "Nassef…. I was thinking about my uncle."

"Is greatest of great shames of great war. Man was genius absolute. Passing of same will be drastic blow to Disciple, maybeso." He settled back onto his boulder seat feeling smug.

Then he noticed the captain eyeing him from the horse picket. The man's expression was inscrutable, but it sent cold-clawed monsters lumbering along his spine. The way the Invincible's eyes drilled into him!

"Is great tragedy Lady has suffered. Self, would suggest time alone, in tent, to deal with grief privately." He moved on to watch several Invincibles practice their swordsmanship. He studied them as if he were unaccustomed to the flash and clash of steel.

The Invincibles practiced daily, both mounted and dismounted, singly and in formation. They were a determined bunch. And Mocker always watched them.

Damo Sparen had been a hard teacher. His lessons had survived his passing well. Among them had been, know your enemy's strengths and weaknesses beforehand.

Mocker knew every man in the encampment now—except that damned captain. He knew he could best any of them except, possibly, the captain. And he had no intention of meeting the man. The captain he intended to share Gouch's fate. Death in the night.

Yasmid summoned him that afternoon. He went reluctantly, no longer certain he wanted to harvest what he had sown.

"Entertainer, are you my friend?" she asked.

"Assuredly, Lady." He tried to appear baffled. Pleasure kept trying to fight its way through. He had not been sure this would work.

"I have a boon to beg, then. A huge one."

"Anything, Lady. Self, exist to serve."

"We were speaking of prospects for peace. You mentioned bin Yousif…. I've had a wild idea. A really insane, improbable idea that just might end this hideous war. But I need your help."

"Aid of self? In ending war? Am entertainer and would-be student philosophic. Lady, not diplomat. Am in no wise able…."

"I just want you to ride with me. To be my protector."

"Protector, Lady? When fifty of bravest men of desert…."

"Those brave men are my father's creatures. They'd never permit what I have in mind."

"Same being?"

"Slipping away from here tonight. Riding hard, northward, through the desert and the Kapenrungs, into Altea, to find the King Without a Throne and make peace."

It was exactly what he wanted to hear. It was hard to pretend shock when he was so elated. "Lady!"

"I know it's crazy. That's why I think it might work. You said yourself that Haroun wants peace as much as I do."

"Truth told. But…."

"Enough. I know the risks, but I'm going to try it. The only question is, will you go with me? Will you help me? Or must I try it alone?"

"Alone, Lady? In this mad world? Would be remiss to permit same, same being suicidal. Am frightened. Am terrified, must admit. Am natural-born coward. But will accompany. For sake of Lady, not of peace." He thought that was a nice touch.

"Then come to my tent after the first watch change. I'll know the guard. He'll do whatever I tell him as long as he doesn't know what's going on. You may have to hit him. Be gentle. He's a good man."

"Self? Attack Invincible? Woe! Lady, am anything but fighter."

"I know. I didn't say you had to fight him. Knock him in the back of the head when he isn't looking."

It was not as simple, of course, as either of them hoped.

Mocker's first move, before approaching Yasmid's tent, was to make an exit without challenge possible. He began with the captain because he wanted no cool head available when it came time to organize a pursuit.

That part was almost too easy. It was anticlimactic. Like plucking a ripe plum. The man was hard asleep. He died without a sound or struggle.

There were six men on perimeter guard duty. Mocker eliminated them next, in the silent way Sparen had taught him. He approached each as a friend, told them he could not sleep, then took them suddenly. That bloody treachery done, he turned to the guards at Sidi's and Yasmid's tents. Finally, he selected two horses from the now restless picket line, readied them, threw what provisions he could behind their saddles, and went to collect his prize.

In his nervousness his donkey and props slipped his mind.

His nerves kept humming like the taut catgut of a carnival fiddle. Every step took time. Each passing minute increased the risk of discovery.

He was almost too scared to think. He proceeded by rote, persevering in an oft-rehearsed scenario.

He scratched on Yasmid's tent. "Lady?"

A head popped out. He squeaked in surprise. "Ready?" she asked.

He nodded. "Have horses set to go. Come. Quietly."

"You're shaking."

"Am terrified, must confess. Come. Before alarm goes up."

"Where's the guard?"

"Bashed same over noggin and dragged behind Sidi's tent. Come. Hurry." He could not give her time to think, to ask questions.

Yasmid came forth. Mocker gawked. She had donned male clothing. She made a passable boy.

A moan came from behind her brother's tent. And a demon with a savage hand seized Mocker's vitals. One of his victims had survived! "Hurry, Lady!" He dragged her toward the horses.

"Captain!" Sidi shrieked, his whining voice tormenting the night. "Captain!"

A sleepy Invincible materialized in Mocker's path. The fat man struck him down, seized his sword, and plunged on. He did not loosen his grip on the girl.

"Why did you do that " Yasmid gasped.

Mocker flung her toward the horses. "Get on!" he snarled. "Talk later." He whirled, crossed blades with the nearest of three pursuers. He dropped the man, and the next, in the wink of an eye. The third backed off, astounded. Mocker scrambled onto a horse. Howling like a damned soul, he tried to scatter the rest. The animals did not go far. They were well trained. He screamed and kicked his mount into motion as a wave of Invincibles appeared. He swatted Yasmid's animal as he passed.

For a long time Yasmid was too busy hanging on and keeping up to ask questions. But she did not forget them. When the pursuit faded and the chance arose, she demanded, "Why did you do that? You weren't supposed to hurt anybody."

He glanced back, expecting the momentary materialization of a horde of vengeful Invincibles. "Self, wonder if bodyguards would play by same rule? Lady, am ashamed. Am coward, admitted. Panicked. Howsomever, retrospectively, must admit same was necessitated. Would not have made escape otherwise. Not so? And Invincibles would have cut self down like cur dog. Not so?"

Yasmid argued, but only halfheartedly. She had to admit that he would have been maltreated had they been caught.

The journey became an epic. The supplies he had secured did not last. Yasmid had brought money, but buying by the wayside was dangerous. It left trailmarkers.

He drove himself and the girl hard. Death was close behind. The Invincibles would neither forgive nor give up.

Weary days came and went. Desert gave way to mountains. The mountains rose, then descended to the farmlands of Tamerice. Exhausted, Yasmid traveled in silence, devoting all her energy to keeping up. Though in friendlier lands, Mocker kept the pace hard, keeping her tired. She was having second thoughts. He did not want her finding the strength and will to slip away.

He stole native garb and made her wear it, that they might become less remarkable. He dressed her as a girl again, hoping fear of being taken for a local maiden would make her avoid her countrymen. Their taste for rape was legend.

He happened to glance back while scaling the first tall ridgeline inside Altea. A heavy dust cloud rose to the south. The riders creating it were too far back to be discerned, but he had no doubt who they were.

He began asking the locals if they knew where bin Yousif was hiding. Most of them refused to talk. He almost panicked.

He had to find Haroun fast. His narrow lead would fade if he spent much time searching.

A garrulous peasant finally told him that bin Yousif was in the Bergwold, trying to rebuild the Royalist force Nassef had scattered before his death.

Neither in Tamerice nor Altea did they encounter an enemy patrol. He could not understand that. Someone should have been there to keep the defeated in line. He had expected to be ducking and dodging all the way.

He added that puzzle to his other worries.

"Almost there, Lady," he announced one morning, pointing. "See hill with ruin on top of same? Is famed Colberg, ancient castle of Altea. Forest called Bergwold lies beside."

"I don't know if I'm glad or not, Entertainer. But one thing is sure. I'm going to be happy to get off this nag."

"Assuredly. Self, am not rider. Am shank's mare man, accustomed to walking. Am going to spend next two weeks lying on ample pillow of stomach." He glanced back. "Hai!"

A low white wave was rolling across the flat green countryside. Their pursuers were just a half-mile behind.

He swatted Yasmid's mount with the flat of his saber, whipped his own, and began the race.

The Invincibles, on fresher animals, closed fast, but the fat man managed to reach the wood several hundred yards ahead. He flung himself off his horse, dragged Yasmid from hers, grabbed her hand and dragged her into the dense underbrush.

FOURTEEN
SUMMER'S END

Mowaffak Hali overcame the army of Ipopotam quite cleverly. He seized the poppy fields before they could be destroyed. But now bands of partisans roamed the countryside.

"They're a stiff-necked people, Lord," he admitted. "They won't accept amnesty."

"I don't want excuses, Mowaffak. I want them brought to heel."

"They're using the tactics we did before coming to power, Lord."

"Not exactly. There's a difference, Mowaffak. Aboud's people didn't know who their friends were. We do. Till they stop resisting slay every man you encounter. Burn their villages. Destroy their fields. Drive them into the forests. Pull down their heathen temples. Eradicate their devil-worshipping priests. And feed and treat kindly those who yield their arms."

"They're not wild dogs, Lord."

"I'm getting old, Mowaffak. There isn't an ounce of mercy in me anymore."

"I have news from the north, Lord. The northern host moved against us there."

A chill crawled over El Murid. His expression betrayed him.

"The news isn't bad, Lord. El-Kader turned them. And the Scourge of God has destroyed the Altean army. It's only a matter of time till he occupies Kavelin and links up with el Nadim."

"El-Kader succeeded without Nassef? This year's campaign is a success?"

"So it would seem. The Scourge of God is preoccupied with bin Yousif and the Guildsmen who slew Karim. He means to have his revenge. And yours, Lord."

El Murid became pensive. Mowaffak was politicking again. "I have my grievances with bin Yousif. But he's only a minor nuisance. Nassef is letting himself be distracted by a side issue. His warriors are needed against the army of the north. This is no time to indulge personal desire."

"My thought exactly, Lord."

Hali's expression betrayed him. Ipopotam was the grossest of side issues, of indulgences. Pacification was tying up thousands of warriors needed elsewhere.

"Go away, Mowaffak. Flog these people. Bring them to heel."

"As you command, Lord."

El Murid glared at Hali's retreating back. Once again Mowaffak had left him to wrestle with his conscience.

Mowaffak was right. But he dared not enter the moral and spiritual lists, to do battle with his addiction, while this war demanded his attention. The war between the soul and the flesh, when it came, would consume him. It would be total and without quarter.

Cued by his thinking, his old wounds began aching.

The Disciple's retinue were worried. Their master seemed to have lost his spirit, his zest, his drive. All too often he retreated into his own inner realms rather than face the crises staring at the Kingdom. Some, like Hali, begged Esmat for help.

What could he do? the physician asked. He simply did not have the personal or moral courage to shed his procurer's role.

And because of that weakness, even Esmat himself held Esmat in contempt.

Altaf el-Kader was not known as an emotional man. His acquaintances knew him as one who let himself be rattled by nothing.

Nevertheless, he blew up when the crows of disaster fluttered in from Altea. Even his boldest subordinates could not approach him. But when the storm blew away, el-Kader was more cool than ever. He had, in a way, been reborn.

He spoke to the assembled captains of the Host of Illumination. "Gentlemen, you've heard the news. The Scourge of God has been sent to his reward by the same Guild scoundrels who robbed us of Karim's songs. The death of this one man, whom we revered and respected...."

An angry mutter began among his listeners.

"Be quiet!" he snapped. "I won't fall into that trap, too. We have people in Altea. Let them deal with the matter. What you and I must do is prove that the Host isn't the Scourge of God. We have to show that we can win without him. Quickly and impressively, for both our friends and enemies. Our foes were wavering. The Disciple's messages have won us converts by the thousand. We can't let the one take heart and the other grow fearful."

He paused to let his words take root. Then, "Prepare to march. We'll make our demonstration by destroying the northern army."

The wings of fear descended, brushing the necks of men who had known no trepidation when Nassef had been in command. El-Kader bore it. He knew the biggest proving would have to be of himself to his captains.

"You have heard me," he said. "Go. Prepare. I'll tell you more as it becomes necessary."

He was adopting Nassef's approach, revealing his thinking to no one. That seemed to reassure them. They were accustomed to operating in the dark.

He had chosen his mission. He attacked it with a flare and determination never before shown. But never before had the final responsibility rested on Altaf el-Kader. Now he had to answer to no one but himself—so he demanded more of el-Kader than ever Nassef had.

Despite his statement concerning Altea, he marched eastward. The immediate assumption was that he meant to punish Nassef's slayers. That had been the style of the Scourge of God, to say one thing and do the opposite. He let his entourage believe that he had had a change of heart. What his followers believed would also be believed by his enemies.

He gathered to the Host all the garrisons along the way, including the men holding the river crossings.

The northern army immediately leapt the river behind him. Its crossing required several days.

El-Kader heard and smiled.

He had planned each move carefully during his day of isolation. He needed only a minimum of luck....

He got more. The Fates, having served the enemy long enough, re-enlisted with the Host of Illumination. The Duke of Greyfells, having learned of Nassef's demise, had abandoned his hunt for the Scourge of God. He rejoined his command during its crossing. The resulting uncertainty at the highest echelon permitted el-Kader to shake the northern scouts.

He immediately turned westward. In hard marches he passed below the northerners and swung back toward the river. He was lying in wait when Greyfells started to march toward Dunno Scuttari.

El-Kader hit him in a land of low hills, attacking from the flanks. He gave his foe no time to organize. The might of the northern knights proved useless. The deadly Itaskian bowmen became scattered before they could bring the punishing power of their weapons to bear. Only the stubborn formations of pikemen from Iwa Skolovda and Dvar withstood the fury of the first charge. They remained brief-lived islands of stability in a maelstrom of death.

The knights of the north, as was the noble wont in defeat, abandoned their footbound followers to el-Kader's untender mercy and flew for the river crossings. But their enemy had anticipated them. His riders were there before them. Not a quarter reached the northern shore.

The men they abandoned fared better.

The infantry fought on, having no choice. Broken into even small units, hunted mercilessly, the soldiers became scattered over a half-dozen Lesser Kingdoms. Their losses, too, were brutal. Only one in three witnessed the coming of winter.

El-Kader called off the hunt ten days later. He wanted to go into winter quarters and to allow some warriors to return to their families.

Then came the news of Yasmid's disappearance.

Hali had debated with himself all morning. How could he tell his prophet? He sometimes let the reports slide, to save El Murid distress, but this time he had no choice. The news was too important. He finally requested an audience.

"Lord." He bowed.

The Disciple knew Mowaffak's bad news now. "What is it?" he snapped.

"An ill wind from the north, Lord."

"I saw that the second you came in. Why don't you just say it?"

"As you command, Lord. There're grim tidings for the Kingdom of Peace, Lord. The worst."

"Out with it, man. Don't play games with me."

Hali, devoted as he was, reached his limit. "Very well, Lord. Two items. The Scourge of God has been slain. And your daughter has been kidnapped."

El Murid did not respond immediately. Nor did he move. His flesh became so pale that for a moment Hali feared he had suffered a stroke. But finally, in a soft, gentle voice, the Disciple said, "I know I've been short-tempered lately, Mowaffak. Sometimes I haven't been fair. But that's no cause to jest so cruelly."

"I wish I were joking, Lord. My pain would be less terrible. But the joke has been played by the Evil One."

"It's true, then?"

"Every word, Lord. And it hurts like my death wound to tell it."

"Nassef. Slain. It doesn't seem possible. And Yasmid carried off. How can that be? It would take an army to reach her, wouldn't it?"

"Guildsmen in the first instance, Lord. The same who slew Karim. They sent more than a thousand Invincibles with him. This has been a hard summer for our brotherhood. There aren't many of us left."

"And Yasmid?"

"The facts aren't clear. A rider brought the news. He was too near death to tell us much. He had ridden too hard with wounds too grave. El-Kader moved your children into Hammad al Nakir lest his confrontation with the north went wrong. Invincibles guarded them. How they failed I don't know. Someone got to your daughter. My brethren who survived the attack are in pursuit."

"That's not very clear, Mowaffak."

"I know, Lord. Yet it's the sum of my knowledge to the moment."

"Are these heathens pacified?"

Hali smiled thinly. "The survivors are behaving themselves, Lord."

"Then I'll get out of your hair. I'm returning north. I leave you and Ipopotam to one another. Decide how many men you need here. Keep as few as you can. El-Kader will need all the help he can get. Mowaffak?"

"Lord?"

"Leave me now. I need to be alone."

"As you command, Lord."

Hali paused at the door, considering the man he loved more than life itself. El Murid sat hunched as if in extreme pain, staring into the gentle glow of the amulet of his wrist. There were tears in his eyes, but his expression remained unreadable. Mowaffak guessed that he was wondering if the game were worth the candle.

He shook his head sadly. His prophet had sacrificed almost everything for the movement. What was left to give? Just himself and that brat, Sidi, who ought to be put out of his misery anyway.

Hali's heart hardened. Heads were going to roll over the Lady Yasmid's disappearance. There was no excuse for so grotesque a lapse of trust.

He ran into Esmat a moment later. "Good morning, Doctor. Give me a boon, will you? Tend our Lord. He's had a terrible shock."

Esmat watched the Invincible depart. He was astonished. Hali never had a kind word…. Something was bad wrong. He rushed to the Disciple's side.

El Murid departed Ipopotam two days later. He rode northward as hard as his old injuries would permit.

Rumor said the Altean Guildsmen carried Nassef's head on a pike, as a battle standard. Elsewhere the Guild seemed to have disappeared, but that band in the outback kept reminding everyone that their brotherhood was fighting its own private war.

What a cruel end for Nassef…. Would his niece join him in the arms of the Dark Lady? Had she done so already?

He would unleash the whole might of Hammad al Nakir if she were still alive.

But the power of the desert might have no meaning now. Its controlling genius was gone. Who could replace the Scourge of God?

El Murid snorted, deriding himself. At least he would not have to worry about treachery, betrayal, or faithlessness anymore. He had no more need to worry about what he would do *with* Nassef, only what he would do without him.

Who would win the impossible victories? Who would give him the Al Rhemishes and Dunno Scuttaris of tomorrow? Who would recover the provinces north of the Scarlotti?

"Lord!" one of his lieutenants shouted. "A rider from the north! My God, Lord, el-Kader's done it! He's destroyed the northern army!"

"Is it true?" El Murid demanded.

"Absolutely, Lord! The message bore the seal of el-Kader himself."

"Find bin Gamel. Tell him to halt the army. We give praise to the Lord of Hosts, from whom all victories flow."

He was astounded. El-Kader? Victorious? The man was but the shadow of Nassef, a crony, a profiteer interested only in making his relatives rich off the chaos of war. The man had no imagination…. But he had won that battle at the ruins of Ilkazar…. Amazing.

Cold autumn winds were blowing when El Murid joined el-Kader. Those who worried about such things predicted an early, bitter winter. The weather had changed rapidly, as if to declare that first savage summer of war over at last.

El-Kader's encampment was nearly naked of warriors. "Where are all our soldiers?" the Disciple demanded. "Was your victory that expensive?"

"Lord? Oh, no. Some are hunting for your daughter. The others went home to their families. The hunters haven't found much, but we're sure she's still alive."

"How so?"

"There's been no news otherwise. And she would be of no value to bin Yousif dead, would she? Our hope is that he'll keep her alive so he can use her against us. If he does, we'll get her back."

"*He* has her?"

"We think so, Lord. We traced the route of her bodyguards, who were pursuing her, into Altea, where they were slaughtered by those Guildsmen he's tied in with."

"Guildsmen? Again? The ones who slew Karim and the Scourge of God?"

"The same, Lord. They're getting to be a damned nuisance."

"I want them a dead nuisance, General. I don't want to hear about them again until you can tell me they're all dead."

"Their chances of survival are poor, Lord. Thousands are looking for them."

"Looking? You don't know where they are?"

"No, Lord. They've vanished. They were operating out of a forest in Altea, but when we went after them there they were gone. So was bin Yousif, who is working with them. They fled about the time your daughter should have reached them."

"You will locate them."

"Of course, Lord."

One of el-Kader's orderlies approached, whispered to his commander. "You're sure?" the general asked.

"Absolutely, sir."

"Interesting." He turned to El Murid. "There's a delegation from the north asking permission to cross the Scarlotti. They want to open peace negotiations."

"Peace negotiations? What have they got to negotiate? They're beaten."

"Perhaps, Lord. But it won't cost to listen."

The thing made more sense when the delegates arrived. El Murid immediately caught the stench of backstabbing politics.

Virtually all the northern states were represented. Only Trolledyngja, the Sharan tribes, and Freyland's kingdom, none of whom had been involved in the fighting, had failed to send someone. And the delegates fell into two obvious parties.

The conciliators represented the small states between the Scarlotti and Porthune rivers, kingdoms which had had a foretaste of Illumination. The belligerents represented Itaskia and her northern allies.

El Murid greeted the ambassadors with benevolent smiles, and western-style handshakes for the conciliators. The Duke of Greyfells seemed puzzled because he drew no special reaction.

El Murid had none of his own people introduced. It was a message to the northerners. He alone spoke for the Kingdom of Peace.

He spoke with el-Kader afterward. "General, is there anything we especially want from those people? Something we can't just take?"

"Not really, Lord. We can keep them divided. Oh. They could give us a little help with a few political problems."

"For instance?"

"The Guild. They could apply pressure to get the Lady Yasmid returned if she's in Guild hands. And you might mention your displeasure about the presence of refugee camps in their domains. While those exist, beyond our reach, they'll remain seedbeds of trouble."

"I see. Wouldn't that give them the impression we don't think we'll be able to break them up ourselves?"

"We will. In time. But what we should be doing here is lulling them. Letting them think they're buying peace. If we make the camps an issue we might get our enemies to pull their teeth for us. You might also insist that they hand over bin Yousif if they get the chance. No harm in getting the Lord's enemies to do the Lord's work, is there?"

"None whatsoever." El Murid rewarded el-Kader with one of his rare smiles. "All right. Let's play their game. And beat them at it."

Next morning El Murid hosted the ambassadors at a lavish breakfast. He had had his people prepare the finest meal possible. Every ingredient came from the recovered provinces. And on the practice fields overlooked by the breakfasters, el-Kader's officers ostentatiously drilled converts from the west.

The Disciple took his meal on a makeshift throne overlooking the assembly. During its course he summoned emissaries individually, and asked each: "Why did you come here?" and "What do you want?" Interpreters translated. Scribes recorded the responses as fast as they could scribble.

Most of the ambassadors admitted that they had come because their lieges had ordered them. In a dozen ways they claimed a desire to end the bloodshed.

"Peace? That has the simplest of solutions. Accept the Truth," the Disciple told each. Then he smiled and offered each emissary a prepared treaty. He had had every learned man in the Host up all night writing. "That, sir," he would say, "is take it or leave it. I am the Hand of the Lord on Earth. I won't dicker like a tradesman. Give me your answer at breakfast tomorrow."

A few, from remote kingdoms, tried to argue. Invincibles intimidated them into silence. Most just returned to their places, surveyed the terms offered, and sometimes seemed surprised.

El Murid was playing a game and enjoying himself immensely. Power could be so diverting…. He frowned, and silently admonished himself. This was no fit behavior for the Hand of the Lord.

In most cases his terms appeared liberal, but he could afford to give away things that he could not possess and to make promises he had no intention of keeping. The Law did not extend its protection to the Unbeliever. The only clause of real weight, with him, was that which permitted missionaries to carry the Truth into the unoccupied territories.

"Did you watch?" he asked el-Kader afterward, almost laughing. "Some of them were ready to kiss my hand."

"Yes, Lord. And they'd bite it if you glanced away. Lord, there was one who approached me privately. He wants to speak with you in his own behalf. I think we might profit."

"Which one?"

"Greyfells. The Itaskian."

"Why?"

"Politics. He claims to have made an arrangement with Karim, at Nassef's request. He says that's why Karim was killed. He could be telling the truth. What we know of Greyfells' movements, and of bin Yousif's and Karim's, would appear to support him."

"Let me see him, then. This might be interesting."

He wished that he had not left Mowaffak in Ipopotam. He could use a trustworthy, discreet sounding board just now.

So. Here was the spoor of another of Nassef's schemes. Greyfells' very involvement suggested its nature. No wonder Nassef had been eager to reach Altea after Karim's death. There had been covering up to do. And bin Yousif, blocking his claim on the Peacock Throne, had been there....

"Nassef, Nassef," he murmured, "you're dead and you're still doing it to me."

Why had el-Kader brought this up? Wasn't he one of Nassef's cronies? Surely he had been tempted to assume the plot for his own.

Greyfells was a spare, hard man with shifty eyes and prematurely grey hair. There was an air of the fox about him. He seemed to be sneaking all the time. "My Lord Disciple," he said, bowing obsequiously.

El Murid told his interpreter, "Tell him to get to the point. I won't play word games. I'll throw him out if he tries that."

Greyfells listened with exaggerated innocence. He minced to the doorway when the interpreter finished, peeped out. "I have to be careful. I have enemies."

"Why shouldn't I let them have you?" El Murid demanded.

Greyfells told him the story that el-Kader had passed along earlier, in more detail. He confessed his determination to usurp the Itaskian crown and carve his own empire.

El Murid was disgusted. If ever mortal woman had borne a child to the Evil One, this man's mother had. "This is all news to me, Duke. Like yourself, my brother-in-law had his own ambitions."

The Duke went pale.

El Murid grinned. Crafty Nassef! He had not been frank with Greyfells.

"I command the allied army, Lord. I decide when and where it fights." Greyfells spoke quickly and nervously, trying to salvage something.

"Then you made a poor decision not long ago." El Murid was on the verge of laughter now.

"That choice wasn't mine. But the political climate compelled me to live with it."

"You no longer have much of an army."

"It can be replaced. A dozen such could be raised. The plans are in the works." A little bluster restored his confidence. "We Itaskians don't make the same mistake twice."

"Perhaps not." El Murid moved the hand that had concealed his amulet. The living stone burned brightly. Its fire reflected off the Duke's eyes. "But others remain to be made. I see no profit in your proposal. If I detect an advantage later, I'll contact you."

"Your profit is the men you won't lose." Greyfells was plainly irked. "You'll have peace while you digest your conquests. Time to clean up loose ends like Altea, Kavelin, and Hellin Daimiel. And you'd have no more worries about those Royalists who've flown into my territories."

The man appalled El Murid. *His* territories! "Produce bin Yousif. Hand him over to me, alive, and I'll give you anything you ask," El Murid lied. He felt no guilt over deceiving a tool of the Great Deceiver. "Deliver me the one thing I most want and I'll talk. Till then you're wasting your time."

Greyfells stared at him, and at the famous amulet. He saw he would never win his point by persuasion. He bowed. "Then I'd better return to my quarters before I'm missed. Good evening."

El Murid allowed a minute to pass. "El-Kader. What do you think?"

The general stepped from behind a concealing tapestry. "He seemed pretty explicit, Lord."

"Will he be of any value?"

"I doubt it. He'd betray us in an instant."

"Have your spies keep an eye on him, but ignore him otherwise. For now."

"As you command, Lord."

During the ensuing week, El Murid concluded treaties which guaranteed peace with all his enemies but Itaskia, Iwa Skolovda, Dvar, and Prost Kamenets. Every treaty contained a provision stating that neither signatory would allow passage to the enemies of the other. The northerners would find it difficult to get at him without attacking former allies.

He was sure that that provision, and the one guaranteeing freedom of movement to his missionaries, would be violated often enough to provide his *casus belli* when he resumed his offensive.

He had no desire for an enduring peace outside the Kingdom's domain. He was negotiating merely to lull tomorrow's conquests.

He did not delude himself. The other signatories just wanted to buy time to strengthen their defenses.

The real puzzle was the wholehearted bellicosity of the Itaskians. Why were they so war-hungry when there was no immediate threat to their territories or people? How were they profiting?

Thus ended the bloody summer known historically as the First El Murid War. Suddenly, the restoration of the Empire looked plausible.

The Disciple returned to Hammad al Nakir, first to Al Rhemish, then to Sebil el Selib, where he shared his griefs with his memories of yesterday. He received weekly updates from el-Kader, who was designing the next offensive according to what he could reconstruct of Nassef's plans.

The general's missives never brought the news El Murid wanted. Never a word about Yasmid.

Even his spies among the Royalists could discover nothing beyond the fact that the girl had, indeed, appeared at the Guild camp in the Bergwold in Altea.

At first the Disciple coped by spending endless hours in prayer. Later, after endowing Esmat with powers rivaling those once given Nassef, he sequestered himself in Al Rhemish's Most Holy Mrazkim Shrines and set about defeating his addiction.

FIFTEEN
CAPTIVES

Four Guildsmen dragged the captives to an outpost. They were none too gentle. The fat man kicked up a fuss, so they bound him, gagged him, and headbashed him several times even though he had been fleeing the Invincibles.

The female remained haughtily silent no matter what language was directed her way.

Kildragon took charge of them, but paid them little heed. He had Invincibles to dispose of. When he finished he detailed two men to escort them to the main encampment. He had listened to the fat man's story, but did not care to sort it out himself.

The fat man started the trip draped across the back of a donkey. His clothing and skin took a beating from the underbrush. He cursed continuously, in a dozen languages.

"Oh, shut up!" Yasmid finally snapped. "You got us into this. Take it like a man."

"Is impossible of doing same thrown across back of animal like sack of corn. Is ignominious fate for…."

"Why don't you knock him in the head again?" Yasmid asked the Guildsmen, using the tongue of Hellin Daimiel.

"She can talk," one muttered in Itaskian.

"I've got a better idea," the other told Yasmid, replying in the language she had chosen. "We'll make him walk. Fat as he is, he'll run out of wind fast."

"You'd be surprised, soldier."

"Better put a choker on him, Karl," the other Guildsman suggested. "So he don't do a fast fade into the woods."

Thus it was that Mocker entered the camp of his ally led like a hound on a leash. The ignominy of it! His captive entered walking tall and proud and free, imperious as a queen, while he entered like a slave.

The Guildsmen took them inside a log stockade and across a compound to where Guildsmen and Royalists were involved in a complicated game of chance.

"Captain, Sergeant Kildragon sent some prisoners."

A big, shaggy youth looked them over. One of the older Royalists said something, then rushed toward one of the shabby barracks. The shaggy youth shrugged. "Hang on to them, Uthe. Beloul wants Haroun to look at them." He returned to his game.

Yasmid flinched, turned pale. She spoke no Itaskian, but had recognized the names. Beloul! The most dangerous of the Royalists. The one most driven by hatred and vengeance. The last vestige of her hope died. Fear replaced it. There would be no peace. Beloul! How could she have been such a fool?

A youth rushed across the compound, dark robes flying. Yasmid remembered his face. That night on the hill overlooking Al Rhemish.... He had aged, matured, hardened....

"Why didn't you cut him loose, Beloul?" Haroun demanded. He applied a knife to the fiber binding the fat man's wrists. Shifting to Itaskian, he told Ragnarson, "The man is an agent of mine. I sent him to the far south. Was there a big man with him?"

"Just the split-tail, sir," one of the escorts replied. "We didn't know who he was. He didn't explain. Not so's anybody could understand, anyway."

"All right. All right. Get that gag off of him."

Mocker could hardly stand. He gripped the expanse of his belly, teetered, and dry-throatedly moaned, "Woe! That self should come to this after fighting way across thousand miles, hazarding life and limb at every step, constantly beset by hordes of desert madmen...."

"You did a good job in Ipopotam," Haroun told him. He used the desert tongue because Mocker had. "Ended up pulling a whole army away from the main action. More than I dreamed. What happened to your man-mountain friend?"

"Do not mention same again. Same met one Invincible too many. Lies buried far from home, not even knowing why. Poor, stupid Gouch. Was good friend. Sparen will rest easy, knowing same has avenged self."

"I'm sorry. He was likeable—in his primitive way."

Yasmid exploded. "Entertainer! You know this.... This....You're working for him?"

Mocker grinned. "Truth told, Lady. Self, am tricksy rogue, more than with fingers. Sometimes do pretty good with girls, too, maybeso."

"What's she talking about?" Haroun asked.

Mocker bowed, still grinning. "Hail, Mighty King. Self, am pleased to present same to genuine princess, same being firstborn daughter of archfoe El Murid, Yasmid, captivated by self, at great peril, and brought forth from very heart of Desert of Death. As small token of appreciation, self would suggestion mighty king bestow upon same huge cash reward. Line up gold pieces, one for every wound, one for every insult suffered...."

Haroun's eyes grew larger and larger. He really looked at Yasmid for the first time. "It's you. You've grown."

Their eyes locked for a long moment, as they had on that faraway night at

Al Rhemish.

Yasmid launched a magnificent, almost artful tantrum. Her shrieks emptied the barracks. In moments she stood at the heart of a circle of two hundred men.

Haroun turned to Ragnarson. "The fat man has brought us the Disciple's daughter. I don't know how.... Can you believe it? It's incredible."

Bragi did not share his awe. But he saw the possibilities. "The Fates have taken a dislike to the man. He was riding high a month ago. Now he's lost most of his family."

Yasmid kept it up. Her anger gave way to hysteria. A sea of evil gloating faces surrounded her. The legions of the Evil One had fallen upon her. What would Haroun do? Throw her to his men?

"Whew!" said Ragnarson. "She does go on, doesn't she?"

"Is in mortal terror," Mocker opined.

"Shut up, girl!" Ragnarson thundered.

She did not. Of course. He had spoken in Itaskian. She would not have had he used a tongue she did comprehend.

The Guildsman was not in the most tolerant of moods. He had been losing badly in the game he had been playing. But it was not anger alone that impelled him to do what he did. Her hysteria had to be cracked.

He grabbed Yasmid, dragged her down, rolled her across his lap, hiked her skirts, and began whacking her bare bottom with his hand. She squirmed and squealed for a moment, then refused to respond.

Ragnarson would never comprehend the indignity he had done her, nor those she had suffered already. In his culture women did not wear veils and girls usually got excited when a guy bared their bottoms.

The fat man had forced her into native dress, and had burned her veils. She had traveled in shame for days. Now another barbarian had exposed her womanhood to the whole camp. His followers laughed and jeered and made crude observations about the hand-shaped birthmark on her behind.

Tears rolled from her eyes, but she refused to pleasure them by begging or crying out.

Haroun was of the desert. He became livid. He slapped Ragnarson's hand aside, yanked the girl to her feet, shoved her behind him. He poised on the balls of his feet, ready for anything. Yasmid crouched behind him, shaking, overcome by shame.

The laughter died. Guild eyes hardened. Ragnarson rose slowly, fists doubling.

"Hai!" Mocker cried. He whirled between the men, his robe flying. As he spun, he yelled, "Self, am wondering when celebration begins. Have made hero of self. Should receive great jubilee in honor, singing, drinking, unfortunately no wenching, but good time for all." He tried to turn a cartwheel, crashed to the dusty earth.

His antics broke the tension.

"Maybe he's right," Ragnarson said, after puzzling out the fat man's fractured Daimiellian.

"Beloul," Haroun said, "take the Lady Yasmid to my quarters."

Beloul's eyebrows rose. But he said only, "As you command, Lord."

Shifting languages, Haroun told Ragnarson, "You should be more careful of the sensibilities of other peoples. You subjected her to unforgivable humiliation. I'll probably have to guard against her taking her own life."

"What?" Bragi asked incredulously.

"That's ridiculous," his brother said.

"Perhaps. To you. You are the children of another land. You do things differently there. My people sometimes find your ways ridiculous."

"You mean she's the real thing?" Bragi asked. "She's not just some tramp your friend picked up on the road?"

"It's her."

"Then we've got some thinking to do. She's trouble."

"Such as?"

"You figure we've had El Murid's men in our hair before? You ain't seen nothing. If we keep her alive—and what good is she dead?—people are going to come looking for her. All of them with hook noses and wearing white. And your friend left a trail good enough for one mob to follow. There'll be more. Which means we've got to disappear. Fast."

"You're probably right. Let me think about it." Haroun strode after Beloul. He met his captain outside his hut. "How is she?"

"Mortified, Lord."

"Uhm. Beloul, find some cloth. Anything, so long as it's something she can use to make a veil and decent clothing."

"Lord?"

"You heard me." Haroun stepped into the shack that served him as home and headquarters.

Yasmid had seated herself on the dirt floor. Her head was down. She was crying silently, her whole body shaking. She did not look up.

"I apologize for my friends. They hail from faraway lands. They have different customs. They weren't trying to humiliate you."

Yasmid did not respond.

"I've told Beloul to find something you can make decent clothing from."

She did not look up, but in a small voice asked, "What are you going to do with me?"

"I? Nothing. Except keep you out of sight. So your father will worry."

"Aren't you going to kill me? Throw me to your men, or those barbarians, then cut my throat?"

"Why would I do that?"

"I'm your enemy. My uncle and my father killed your whole family."

"Your uncle was my enemy. Your father is my enemy. But you're not. I don't make war on women. You didn't...."

"You killed my mother."

Haroun shrugged. "There was a battle on. I wasn't keeping track."

Yasmid pulled her knees up under her chin, hugged them in her arms. "He tricked me, didn't he?"

"Who?"

"The fat man." She knew, of course, but wanted to be told again. That would, somehow, make her feel less like an accomplice in the deceit. "He got me to come.... I thought I could make peace between you and my father."

"That would be difficult. Yes. He tricked you. That's his profession. And he's better than I suspected." Haroun sat on the earth facing her, wondering what made her seem unique.

It was nothing physical. She was an average looking girl, not at all striking. An active, outdoor life had weathered her more than the men of Hammad al Nakir liked. And she was much too assertive.

Yasmid stared into infinity. After a time, she murmured, "It's an interesting dilemma."

"What's that?"

"Whether I should slay myself and thus free the movement of concern and uncertainty, or preserve myself against its need."

The nature of his culture denied Haroun much knowledge of women. He knew them only through tradition and hand-me-down gossip from equally ignorant companions. The last thing he expected of a female was an ability to reason, to sacrifice, to be concerned about tomorrow. He remained silent, awed.

"I guess I should wait for a sign. Suicide is extreme. And if I'm alive there's always a chance of escape or rescue."

"As my fat friend might say, all things are possible." But some are unlikely, he thought. "Ask Beloul for whatever you need for sewing." He left the hut looking for Ragnarson.

"No, no, no," Bragi was telling an Altean who had just sped an arrow into a butt. "You're not remembering what I said about your elbow."

"I hit it, didn't I? Sir."

"Yeah. That time. But you're more likely to hit it every time...."

"Excuse me," Haroun interrupted. "It's occurred to me that our best course might be to move into the Kapenrungs."

"What?"

"We should move to the mountains. They're more suited to the kind of war we'll have to fight now. More room to move around and stay ahead of the hunters. And close enough to Hammad al Nakir to give us the option of striking south. It's only a few days ride from the mountains to Al Rhemish."

"We were assigned to Altea."

"Specifically? Without any flexibility for the commander on the scene?"

"I don't know. They just said we were going to Altea. Maybe they told Sanguinet more. But he's not here to let me know."

"Sent you here and forgot you. Haven't you noticed? They haven't been in any hurry to replace your captain. They haven't even sent any orders. You're on your own."

"How do you figure to get from here to there without getting wiped out? They've got men everywhere."

"Consider our prisoner. They'll know who has her, and where we were last. Anyway, moving was your idea."

"Yeah."

Ragnarson did not debate long. He knew there would be no more miracles like Alperin. The first bands left that evening.

Haroun talked him into sending their men in parties of four, by as many routes as possible, traveling at night, so they would attract minimal attention. Haroun assigned one of his people to each group of Guildsmen, to guide them to Beloul's old refugee camp. Bragi sent his brother with the first night's travelers, and Kildragon with the second's. Bin Yousif, Mocker, and Yasmid vanished sometime during that night. Haroun left no word of his intentions or destination.

Ragnarson left the Bergwold on the last night, riding with Beloul and two young Royalists. None of the three spoke a dialect he understood, and Beloul had wanted to be the last of his.

He looked back once. The Bergwold leaned toward him like a dark tidal wave frozen in mid-rush. He felt a twinge of regret. The forest had become home.

There had been few moments of happiness since fleeing Draukenbring. But he and Haaken were still together, and healthy, and he had never asked the gods for more than that.

Beloul was a crafty traveler. He led them across the nights and miles without once bringing them face to face with another human being. He seemed to sense the approach of other travelers. Always, they were under cover when another night rider passed. Most of those were people of their own persuasion.

It was a skill his own men should learn. How could El Murid find them if even their friends never saw them moving?

These desert men were naturally cunning. Sneakery and deceit were their patrimony.

He wished he could communicate with Beloul better. The captain was one cunning old man.

Bragi had been trying to learn the desert tongue for ages. He had not made much headway. Its rules were different from any he knew, and there were countless dialects.

Thus it was that, when Beloul broke his own rule and stopped a dispatch rider, Ragnarson was bewildered by his companions' behavior. They went into a frenzy of angry excitement. It took half an hour for them to make him understand. El-Kader had destroyed the northern army.

That explained Beloul's sudden haste. This end of the world would fill with warriors hunting the daughter of their prophet. It was time to find a hole and pull it in after. He was glad Haroun had talked him into fleeing the Bergwold.

Four days later he threw his arms around Haaken and said, "Damn, it's good to see you. Good to see anybody who doesn't talk like a coop full of hens clucking."

"You hear? About the battle?"

"Yeah. But you have to fill me in. I missed most of the details."

"El Senoussi and I have been plotting. We figure we ought to recruit survivors. So we can build our own army."

"Tell me in the morning. Right now all I want to do is sleep. Face down. How do you figure to get guys to join when we can't pay? When we can't even guarantee them anything to eat?"

Haaken had no answer for that one.

Eventually, Ragnarson and Beloul did send their boldest followers, in ones and twos, to recruit not only survivors of the battle but anyone who wanted to enlist in the hidden army. That army grew as autumn progressed into winter. The recruits learned Guild ways on the march, while dodging and ambushing el-Kader's hunters.

Those hunters never realized whom they were skirmishing. The search for Yasmid was centered farther north, closer to the Bergwold.

They were turning Altea over.

Mocker turned up after a month, but Haroun remained invisible even to his best friends. He was gone so long that Beloul began worrying about having to find a new king.

It was then that Beloul realized that El Murid's offspring were now closest to the throne, through their mother.

Grinning evilly, he prepared special message packets meant to fall into enemy hands. They contained faked plans for an effort to alleviate Sidi's burden of life lest he be put forward as a Pretender by his father.

Beloul's purpose was to inform Sidi of his standing. The Disciple's son was but a boy, yet from what the fat man said he had qualities that would set sparks flying if he saw a chance for power.

The winter was a cold one and hard on the war-torn lands where marauding troops from both sides stripped the peasantry of its food stores. Anger stalked the snowy land like some hungry, legendary monster.

Everywhere, high and low, men schemed against the coming of spring, when they might seize their own particular breed of fortune and bend it to their will.

SIXTEEN
THE MIDDLE WARS

Assigning blame is not the task of the historian. Neither should he deny guilt where it exists. In later days even the chauvinist historian would admit that the north, personified by Duke Greyfells, provoked the Second El Murid War.

Itaskian apologists pointed at the Guild and Haroun bin Yousif's Royalists and argued that the first summer of fighting did not possess a separate identity because those belligerents never made peace. But the Guild and Royalists were fighting different wars. Theirs merely shared some of the same battlefields as that of the allies. The Kingdom of Peace had established treaties with those enemies who could accept an accommodation short of annihilation. Even Itaskia's highest leadership, despite verbal belligerence, had accepted El Murid's redrawing of the western map. Once winter settled in, the First El Murid War was over.

The real question was when and why the next would begin.

Only the Disciple himself knew his intentions for his second summer of conquest. His warriors came from their homes and tribes, more numerous than ever. Remote, maundering, El Murid blessed them on Mashad, and sent them to join el-Kader in his watch on the Scarlotti. There they were joined by thousands of converts and adventurers from the recovered provinces.

El-Kader waited, daily expecting an attack order from Al Rhemish. The instruction did not come. El Murid had lost interest in the reconquest. His dream of greening the desert and his effort to conquer his addiction had become obsessions.

Among the faithful it was whispered that the Evil One himself had come to Al Rhemish and the Lord in Flesh was wrestling him within the confines of the Most Holy Mrazkim Shrines.

El-Kader distributed the Host along the Scarlotti in accordance with an order of battle mentioned by the Scourge of God months before his death. El-Kader's posture remained strictly defensive.

He sat. He waited.

Lord Greyfells and Itaskia's allies bullied several small states whose lords had concluded treaties with the Disciple. They abrogated treaties at will, at swordpoint crossing kingdoms which had agreed not to permit passage of belligerents. They promoted palace revolutions and imprisoned uncooperative nobles. Greyfells' arrogant treatment alienated the masters of the smaller states.

Emissaries came to el-Kader begging him to withhold his wrath. Some volunteered intelligence in hopes of staying the fury of the Host. A few even petitioned its intercession, begging protection from the arrogance and rapacity of the Duke.

Greyfells did little to conceal his desire to carve out an empire of his own.

El-Kader bided his time, awaiting the will of the Disciple, allowing Greyfells to make himself ever more obnoxious.

His petitions to Al Rhemish went unanswered. El Murid could not stop wrestling the Evil One long enough to concern himself with his opponent's manifestations on the frontier.

El-Kader finally took the initiative. He summoned his captains. He presented them with the order of battle and told them that unless they heard otherwise they were to cross the Scarlotti in fifteen days. They were to speak of the plan to no one till the last minute. Certain kingdoms were to be treated as allies, not foemen.

He waited. He even went so far as to pray for word from Al Rhemish.

Responsibility had changed Altaf el-Kader. His office left him too busy with command to waste time profiteering.

The day came and still there was no command from Al Rhemish. He prayed once more that El Murid would forgive him for taking this on himself. Then he left his tent and crossed the river.

The Host of Illumination rolled north like a great tsunami, unexpected, unstoppable, everywhere swamping its foes. Greyfells, caught unprepared, found his rebuilt army adrift in enemy waters. War bands swarmed around it, nibbling at its extremities. He spent all his energies keeping it intact and avoiding battle with the Host. He showed his positive qualities in retreat.

Suffering inconsequential losses, el-Kader seized all the territories south of the River Porthune. Though the Scourge of God had expected that to take a season, el-Kader finished by Midsummer's Day.

In the absence of contrary instructions, smelling the blood of reeling foes, el-Kader breached that line while momentum and morale remained his allies. Some of his war bands ranged as far as the Silverbind, well within the Itaskian domain. A large force camped within sight of the city walls, and departed only when the whole garrison came out to fight. Panic swept the north. The grand alliance was within a whisper of collapse.

From the south frontier of Ipopotam to the Porthune, the west had been returned to the Empire. Only two small enclaves of resistance remained. Hawkwind's stubborn Guildsmen still directed the defense of Hellin Daimiel. El-Kader ignored the city. It could do nothing to discomfit the Host.

Of High Crag he was not so tolerant. The home and heart of the Guild had to be destroyed. The warrior brotherhood backboned the resistance in the reoccupied provinces.

Ere ever he crossed the Scarlotti, el-Kader summoned Mowaffak Hali from Ipopotam and handed the Invincible the chore of reducing High Crag. Hali accepted the task with reservations. He doubted that it could be accomplished.

Mowaffak Hali was a thorough, methodical leader. He did not hurl the remnants of the Invincibles against High Crag's ancient walls. He gathered information and men of talent, and such additional warriors as he could obtain, for a slow, systematic reduction of the fortress. He built great engines. He employed miners. He did whatever needed doing to neutralize his opponents' advantages.

He might have succeeded had events elsewhere not compelled him to abandon the siege.

Far to the north, el-Kader had the misfortune to, at last, catch the elusive Greyfells.

The nearest town, Liston, gave the battle its name. The engagement was unusual. El-Kader amassed heavy cavalry for the first time in the Host's history. And Greyfells abjured the traditional western use of knights. Once el-Kader closed his trap and battle became unavoidable, the Duke ordered his horsemen to fight afoot.

Greyfells made his stand on the face and top of a rocky hill flanked by woods, with his pikemen and knights massed before his archers. The bowmen of Itaskia were renown, and in this engagement justified their fame. While the pikemen, supported by disgruntled noblemen, valiantly absorbed charge after charge, the archers darkened the sky with arrows.

Had el-Kader not grown overoptimistic, had he not been overconfident, had he listened to his advisers and waited a few days till the whole of the Host had gathered, he would have obliterated the northern might. Liston would have been the battle memorialized as ending the resistance to El Murid's Second Empire.

But he did not wait, and he did not try getting behind his enemies. And still he came within a gnat's eyebrow of success. In the end, he simply ran out of ready bow-fodder before his foes collapsed completely.

Greyfells had the advantage of him in that his troops believed that they had nowhere to run. They believed they had to win or perish. And win they did—in the sense that they compelled el-Kader to withdraw.

The importance of Liston could be weighed only in its effects on the hearts and minds of men. The number of dead on the field was of no consequence. That Greyfells could do nothing but lick his wounds afterward meant little. That el-Kader had not committed his whole strength was overlooked everywhere.

The Host of Illumination had been turned.

Western armies *could* withstand its onslaught. El Murid *could* be stopped.

The effect was magical. Enemies sprang from the earth. Some of el-Kader's allies changed sides again. Resistance stiffened everywhere.

El-Kader coped first by withdrawing across the Porthune, then by summoning every man he could from the south. The siege of High Crag, a project he cherished, he ordered abandoned. He drew strength away from Hellin Daimiel and the captains pursuing the growing guerrilla forces in the southern Lesser Kingdoms.

The summer campaign was in danger of collapse. He had to scatter his strength, flinging lesser armies here and there to stamp out sudden brushfires of resistance. He could not seize the breathing time to rejuvenate the Host and lead it in a grand, finishing surge northward, though he knew the Itaskians could no longer stop such a thrust.

Bin Yousif's Royalists were no help. They had adopted the tactics developed by the Scourge of God in the days when the Kingdom of Peace had been but a dream. There were thousands of Royalists now. They and their Guild allies were keeping the provinces in turmoil. Their raids were becoming ever more widespread, like the growth of a cancer.

There was a bright side to the summer. El Nadim and the armies of the east, receiving no instructions from Al Rhemish either, abandoned their futile siege of the Savernake Gap and turned their attention to the Empire's old provinces behind the Mountains of M'Hand. El Nadim integrated Throyes into the New Empire. He forced pledges of fealty from old eastern tributaries as remote as Argon and Necremnos. His legates collected caravans of tribute and battalions of mercenaries. His missionaries carried the Truth to the masses, and were well received.

El Nadim's successes amazed the Faithful. He was the least regarded of the generals Nassef had created. Now, suddenly, with only a few thousand men actually of Hammad al Nakir, with almost no fighting, he had recovered territories more vast than the whole west.

Some whispered that el Nadim had been successful because he was a true believer, because he followed El Murid's teachings in handling his foes. There were those who said that el-Kader's troubles were the Lord's punishment for associating with profiteers.

El-Kader ignored the whispers. El Nadim's successes pleased him. The tribute of the east could be used in the west. Two summers of fighting had left a lot of desolation.

He, too, was applying El Murid's precepts—to the extent that they won favor amongst the populations of the recovered provinces.

He drove his warriors and allies hard, extinguishing any resistance he could identify. He recovered several bridgeheads across the Porthune, but the enemy regained a couple below the river. Both sides retained isolated pockets within the other's territory. Their smaller allies remained evanescent in their loyalties, shifting allegiances with each breath of fortune.

Winter, the season of peace, set in. It became the season of negotiation, the time of secret treaties and not so secret betrayals. Always there was an agent of the Itaskian Duke around, ever with an offer of double-edged treason.

And still el-Kader had received no orders from Al Rhemish.

None that he considered genuine, anyway. None signed in the Disciple's own hand.

Orders did come. From someone. He ignored them. They were not from his prophet.

Nassef's death had been the signal for the formation of new cabals, for the beginning of the institutionalization of the movement. The greatest, the most praised and heroic of the revolutionaries was gone. The sedentary administrators-potential perceived a vacuum and were trying to fill it.

It was a foreshadowing of the social inevitability of all revolutions, though Altaf el-Kader could not understand.

He saw a gang of stay-at-homes isolating the Disciple and presuming to speak in his name, perverting his pure vision.

He knew a cure.

He had a few words with Mowaffak Hali, a man he did not like but who possessed the specific for this disease. Hali agreed. Something had to be done.

Hali bore el-Kader no love either, but in this they had to be allies. He gathered a few tattooed white robes and rode for the capital.

He was shocked by what he found. The Disciple was a ghost of a man, drained, without spirit. His struggle with the evil within him was consuming him.

Mowaffak spent one afternoon with the master he loved, then went into the desert and wept. Then he instructed the Harish and returned to the west. He redoubled his prayers on behalf of the man who had been, in hopes he would be again.

The third summer of fighting began like the second, with el-Kader trying to avoid his old mistakes. He began by making big gains, but bogged down just thirty miles from the Silverbind and Itaskia the City. For four grim months he maneuvered, met the enemy, maneuvered, and skirmished in an area of barely a hundred square miles. Greyfells had spent the winter preparing, screening the approaches to Itaskia and the Great Bridge with countless obstacles and redoubts. El-Kader could not break through.

It was some of the bitterest, most sustained, deadly, and unimaginative fighting ever. The Duke pursued no higher purpose than stalling el-Kader. Defeating him would have obliterated any chance of profiting from the threat to Itaskia.

El-Kader strove to bleed the north till it could no longer withstand him.

Both generals spent lives profligately, though the Duke was the worst. A worried king resided less than a dozen leagues away, and willingly raised fresh levies.

El-Kader's failing was an inability to adjust to the changed nature of his army. He was a desert captain, born to the warfare of the wastelands. But the Host was no longer a horde of nomadic horsemen, riding like the wind, striking where it would, then melting away. That element remained, but in this third summer more than half the troops were westerners whose lack of mobility el-Kader abhorred and whose tactics he could not entirely encompass.

He considered throwing the known quantity of his countrymen like chaff into the wind, to let the breezes carry them where they would, behind Greyfells and along the banks of the Silverbind. But he did not. He did not trust his allies, and the defeat at Liston still haunted him.

So he endured four months of attrition, and, if grave-markers were the totalizers of success, he was winning. But the Great Bridge seemed to arch into a bottomless pool of replacement battalions.

It was a pity that he had lost touch with Nassef's spy networks. The news of political conditions north of the Silverbind would have heartened him. Itaskia's peasantry were on the verge of revolt. The nobility were demanding Greyfells' recall. Bankers were threatening to call in their loans to the Crown. Merchants were howling about the interruption of overland trade. City dwellers were angry about rising food costs caused by exports to Hellin Daimiel and reduced production due to conscription of peasants into the replacement levies. Fathers and mothers were bitter about the losses of their sons.

Itaskia was as taut as a bowstring stretched till it was about to snap. El-Kader needed to give just the right nudge.

His choice of campaign style was an error. By letting the Duke set the standard of battle he had permitted himself to be diverted from his strength to a form of warfare he did not understand.

Then, as autumn approached, he made every soldier's most dreaded mistake. He stepped into the shadow of the outstretched left hand of Fate.

He was doing what needed doing, directing an attack against a stubborn earth and log redoubt, when a random arrow struck his mount in the eye. The animal threw him, trampled him, and dragged him. Altaf el-Kader was a stubborn man. He held on for four days before finally yielding to the Dark Lady's charms.

His passing broke the will of an already dispirited army. Bits and pieces broke away. The most fanatic Faithful were dismayed.

The wrath of the Lord was upon them, and their hearts were filled with despair.

The Host was an eager, conquering horde no more. It had become a huge mob of war-weary men.

Mowaffak Hali assumed command, after riding all the way from Al Rhemish. He bore the mandate of the Disciple himself. But he arrived only after a chaotic, month-long interregnum.

He found the Host in disarray, dissolving, retreating, its captains squabbling amongst themselves instead of fighting the enemy.

He summoned a council. A Harish kill-dagger thrust into a balk of oak formed an intimidating centerpiece for the meeting. Hali spoke. He brooked no questions.

He told them he would be a hard taskmaster. He told them they were going to turn the campaign around. He told them he would have no patience with defeatism or failure. He told them that the Lord was with them even in their hour of despair, for he had descended upon the Most Holy Mrazkim Shrines and the Disciple and had renewed his pledge to the Faithful. He told them to keep their mouths shut, to listen, and to do what they were told when they were told. He caressed the kill-dagger with each of his directives, and each time that silver blade glowed a gentle blue.

He got his message across.

Methodically, Hali studied the situation and took hold of its problems. Systematically, he carved off chunks of northern strength and obliterated them. He was not a man of inspiration like Altaf el-Kader. He was no genius like Nassef el Habib. He was, simply, a determined workman. He knew his tools. He knew their limits and his own. He strained both. Animated by his will, the Host stopped, ceased falling apart, and brought the enemy to a halt on the Porthune.

Winter came once more.

El Murid attained his victory over the demon within him. It was a long, grueling battle. Esmat served as his eyes and ears in the world. The physician screened his master from anything even mildly disturbing.

Even after El Murid recovered, Esmat confined outside news to the huge irrigation project El Murid had ordered begun before going into seclusion.

The drive had gone out of the Hand of the Lord on Earth. He knew the physician was intriguing, but did not protest. He *wanted* to escape his role as Disciple, and Esmat had deprived him of his chemical escape....

He told himself he could quash Esmat's ambitions whenever he wanted.

He knew the movement would suffer during his absence. The Al Rhemish factions would play at a hundred intrigues, trying to push into the power vacuum, perhaps even attempting to suborn the generals in the field....

He could not bring himself to care. With Yasmid gone, and no news of her fate.... He did not have much to live for anymore.

One man kept the Faith. One man kept the schemes and intrigues from becoming a gangrenous wound in the movement's corpus. One man battled and controlled the forces of devolution. Mowaffak Hali, Master of Assassins.

Hali did not like Esmat, but he did trust the physician. More than he should have. When Esmat said the Disciple was still fighting his addiction, Hali took his word. He would preserve the movement while it awaited the return of its prophet.

He did much of his waiting in Al Rhemish, in a big white tent from which grim-faced, fiery-eyed men ventured with silver daggers next to their hearts. The daggers had a habit of finding the hearts of the more dangerous conspirators.

Even the least of men shrank from the Invincible when they encountered him in the street. Esmat was terrified of him.

El Murid spent all his time sequestered in a vast suite hidden deep in the Shrines. He had had Esmat assemble a dozen tables in what once had been the priests' dining hall. He had shoved them together and covered them with maps and crude models reflecting northern Hammad al Nakir. Upon that vast board he planned his dream reconstruction.

He could wander round for hours, making marks, shuffling models, building his vision of the desert's tomorrow. Citrus groves. Lakes. Renewed forests. All to be created with the water that western prisoners were canaling down from the Kapenrung snows.

It was the day that el-Kader fell. His amulet began vibrating. It became hot. He cried out in surprise and pain. The jewel's glow intensified. Then it flashed so brightly that for a time he was blind.

A voice thundered through the Shrines: "Micah al Rhami, son of Sidi, that was named El Murid by mine angel, where art thou?"

The Disciple collapsed, burying his face in his arms. For a moment he could do nothing but shake in fear. Then, "Here, O Lord of Hosts." His voice was a tiny mouse-squeak.

"Why hast thou forsaken me, Chosen of the Lord? Why hast thou abandoned me in the forenoon of mine triumph? Why dost thou lie in indolence, surrounding thyself with the wealth of nations?"

The fear ground him down. He groveled and whimpered like a puppy at the feet of a cruel master. The voice boomed on, chastising him for his sloth, self-pity, and self-indulgence. He could not force a word of rebuttal past the whiteness of his lips.

"Rise up, Micah al Rhami. Rise up and become El Murid once more. Shed thy robe of ungodliness and minister to the Chosen once more. The Kingdom of Peace doth lie in great peril. Thy servant el-Kader hath been slain."

Five minutes passed before El Murid dared peep out of the shelter of his arms.

The light was gone. The voice had departed. His amulet had returned to normal. His wrist was an angry red.

He rose, looked around. He was badly shaken. The first time he called out his voice cracked. It was the mouse voice again.

Then the mouse roared. "Esmat!"

A terrified Esmat appeared instantly. His furtive gaze darted from shadow to shadow.

"Esmat, tell me the situation in the provinces."

"Lord..."

"Did you see a light, Esmat? Did you hear a voice?"

"I heard a thundering, Lord. I saw lightning."

"You heard the voice of the Lord of Thunders telling me I was failing Him. You heard Him setting my feet on the Path once more. Tell me what I need to know, Esmat."

The physician started talking.

"Thank you," El Murid said when he finished. "It's worse than I thought. No wonder the Lord is vexed. Where is Mowaffak Hali these days?"

"He's in the city at the moment, Lord."

"Bring him. I need him to take command of the Host."

Esmat was puzzled, but asked no questions. He went for Hali, and as he walked told his friends what had happened in the Shrines. Few were pleased.

The news of el-Kader's passing reached Al Rhemish eleven days after Hali's departure. The Disciple's foreknowledge further dismayed those who had been profiting from his seclusion.

Three weeks later El Murid changed his mind. "Esmat, find me a messenger. I want to move el Nadim west. He's finished in the east, and I need Hali here."

302 — Glen Cook

"As you command, Lord." Esmat left looking pale. It looked like the profitable days were done.

El Murid did not rush Hali's recall. The threat of the man's return was enough to purge Al Rhemish of parasites. Nor did he hasten el Nadim's transfer. El Nadim and his strength would not be needed till spring.

The Disciple was, simply, proclaiming his return. He wanted the world to know that he was in command again, that he was El Murid once more, that the hiatus of will had ended.

The word spread across the Second Empire like ripples across a pond. An upswing of morale accompanied it. Countless believers reaffirmed their faith.

The era of stagnation ended. The movement took on new life. The gloom of the future vanished like a fog burned off by a hot, young sun.

Nevertheless, the Disciple could not expunge the gloom of the past from his own heart. His losses were a soul-burden he could not shed.

SEVENTEEN
THE GUERRILLAS

Between them, Ragnarson and bin Yousif recruited seven thousand men in three years. The enemy no longer came to the Kapenrungs hunting them. They were all hardened veterans with nothing to lose.

Haroun directed field operations throughout the Lesser Kingdoms, through a score of sub-commanders. Many were men he had never met, men who had allied themselves with him because of his guerrilla successes.

He had learned the lessons of Nassef's campaign in Hammad al Nakir. Now, in the Lesser Kingdoms, the nights were his. He had begun to believe that he was at least the ghost of a king.

He selected the targets and chose the men who would attack them. He ran the spies and assassins who were making the enemy miserable. When a big operation came up he took the field himself.

His partner, Ragnarson, trained recruits.

Ragnarson was not happy. He had seen no real action in two years. The world had forgotten that he and his Guildsmen existed. He worked his tail off to make stubborn fighters of the hungry, ragged, dispirited leavings of lost battles, then Haroun sent them off to skulk in the woods like bandits.

"I just don't feel useful anymore," he complained. "My men don't feel useful. None of us have wielded a sharpened sword in so long that we've forgotten how."

"Uhm," his brother grunted. "Nor sheathed a sword of flesh in its proper place." Women were scarcer than gold in the mountains. The occasional wild hill woman stopped by and made sure gold and silver did not accumulate.

"We're not ready for heads-up fighting," Haroun insisted, as he had been doing since they had come to the mountains. "You keep looking at it like we should fight in one big mass. We may someday. If the war goes on long enough.

But not yet, damn it! It'd be our last battle if we did."

"This hiding in the bushes and stabbing guys in the back is getting to me, especially since I don't get to do even that. It's not getting us anywhere. Ten years from now we're still going to be hiding in the same bushes."

"It worked for Nassef and it'll work for us. You just have to be patient."

"Bragi was born impatient," Haaken said. "Mother told me he was a month premature."

"I can see that. Well, I've been thinking about the problem. You may see action sooner than you want, my friend."

Ragnarson perked up. "How so?" His brother and Kildragon looked interested too. Beloul and el Senoussi continued to look bored.

"I got us together because I've had some news from Al Rhemish. Seems El Murid had a visit from his angel."

Ragnarson shuddered. He became uneasy whenever facing the notion that there might be something to El Murid's religious claptrap. "How does that do us any good?"

"It doesn't. My spy says that the Disciple came out of seclusion spitting fire. He's ready to go again. He's going to recall Hali and replace him with el Nadim—and the eastern army."

"Sounds grim."

"Worse than grim. It'll mean the whole war. Some of us like to think the tide's turned. But we're deluding ourselves. My friend the Itaskian Minister is scared silly. Greyfells hasn't broken the Host. He's just squandered lives and wealth. Itaskia's allies are muttering about a separate peace. Any big setback will knock everything apart. And Itaskia can't go it alone."

Ragnarson frowned and shook his head. "We supposedly had them when we finished Nassef and Karim. It was a sure thing after el-Kader fell." He looked at Haroun sourly. "Now we have friends Mowaffak Hali and el Nadim and...."

"I'll eliminate them."

"Exactly what I thought you'd say. And then what?"

"What do you mean?"

"I mean that this's one of those dragons that grows heads as fast as you chop them off. You're going to tell me that we'll have them by the shorthairs if we get rid of Hali and el Nadim. And I'm telling you that's a load of horse manure. There'll be another one step in just like el-Kader and Hali and el Nadim."

"You overestimate them. They weren't that good. They were lucky, and their opponents were that bad."

"And Nassef picked them all. Except Hali. Who are you kidding, Haroun? You know your own people and you know the west. The Host has always been outclassed in weapons and training, and a lot of times outnumbered. They've had more than luck going for them. The only guy who can handle them is Hawkwind, and nobody'll give him enough men to do any good."

Haroun shrugged. "Maybe you're right. Still.... Here's why I want to talk to you. I'm leaving you in charge here. I'm sending Mocker after el Nadim. Shadek, Beloul, and I are going to be away on personal business."

"Eh?"

"Beloul and Shadek have been nurturing a scheme. I can't tell you more right now. Except not to believe everything you hear the next couple of months."

"What am I supposed to do here? Sit and twiddle my thumbs all winter?"

"My spy system needs running. The raids have to be directed. Somebody has to take charge. Don't worry about it. I have faith in you. You'll manage."

Haroun looked around to make sure no one was eavesdropping. "Just ignore any strange stories you hear about me, Beloul, and Shadek."

The would-be king drifted away in his mind to happier times to come. He had to sometimes. He had to remind himself that these grim todays would be worth the pain and deprivation. He had found little happiness in this struggle.

He vanished one winter night, taking with him Beloul, el Senoussi, and a dozen of his toughest supporters. He left behind less than a ghost of an idea of his plans.

That was his way. Like his onetime archfoe Nassef, he could not share his thoughts. Ragnarson said he would have fought his war alone had it been possible.

Mocker departed later that same week, leading a mangy-looking donkey loaded with ridiculous impedimenta. For six months, through the length and breadth of the Lesser Kingdoms, Haroun's men had been risking their lives to accumulate that collection of junk.

"That's one guy I'm not sorry to see go," Kildragon observed. "I'd have killed him myself if it wasn't for Haroun protecting him. He can't do anything without cheating or stealing."

"He has his uses." Ragnarson rather liked the fat man, who could be entertaining. A man just had to have sense enough not to trust him.

"What're we going to do?" Kildragon asked. "I mean, we've got the whole thing to ourselves. We can try it our way now."

"Sit tight. Wait."

"You mean keep doing it his way?"

"For now. Because he's right. We'll just get ourselves killed doing it any other way."

"Well damn! Are we Guildsmen or are we bandits?"

"A little of both. I don't recall any Guild rule that says we have to do things thus and so, Reskird. Remember your first mission?"

"Stay alive. All right."

For two months Ragnarson let Haroun's organization, of which his Guild-oriented infantry made up a lesser part, roll along on its own impetus. Various war bands made desultory raids on remote outposts and terrorized natives who favored El Murid. Taking Haroun at his word, Bragi tried to ignore rumors that bin Yousif and Beloul had been slain.

The stories were dreadful. Some said el Senoussi had turned on his king, that he had made a deal with El Murid's son, Sidi.

"It's getting hard to keep those guys interested," Kildragon said of the Royalists. "They're ready to fall apart. You think el Senoussi really was playing a double game?"

"Nothing political surprises me anymore. But I never figured Shadek for smarts enough to work something that complicated."

"How do we make the troops believe?"

"We don't try. El Murid and Sidi have spies too. We want them to believe they're dead."

Haaken ducked into his brother's headquarters. "Hali's on the move, Bragi. Messenger says he got wind of the rumors about Haroun and decided to head home early. He figures it's some kind of trick."

"Damn! But he is the Disciple's moral and political enforcer, isn't he? Got anything more? Like what route he's taking?"

"No. You're not thinking of trying to stop him?"

"Damned right I am. It's just what we need. Get our old bones loosened up."

"But...."

"This is what we've been waiting for. Don't you see? It's a chance to do something."

"If you're going to do anything you'd better move fast. This messenger only had a couple of days head start. Hali doesn't piddle around when he decides to go somewhere."

"Get the maps. Let's find the fastest roads to Hammad al Nakir. Reskird, go tell our people to get ready. Rations for two weeks, but otherwise we're traveling light."

Haaken spread the maps. Bragi considered them. "I only see three roads that look worth worrying about. We can get to these two ahead of him, but it'll be a footrace."

"Send Haroun's boys to that farthest one. They're used to long, hard rides."

"They might refuse."

"Take a chance. You're supposed to be in charge."

"Who should lead them? Who do you trust?"

"I'd say Metillah Amin."

"All right. Tell him to move out today. We'll start tomorrow."

"It's going to snow tonight."

"Can't help that. I'm going to have Reskird take care of this eastern road. You and me will take the middle one."

"That's a lot of walking. Let me have the east road."

"Nope." Bragi grinned.

All day, along the way, the locals came out to watch. The Guildsmen bowed their heads and slogged on. None of the watchers spoke. Very few smiled. The occasional snowball flew from a youthful hand.

"Haaken, Reskird, we'd better be nice to these folks."

"Aren't exactly friendly, are they?" Kildragon asked. "Guess you could say they're not on our side."

"Guess you could say."

A light snow began falling as they parted with Kildragon and his three hundred men. By noon next day Bragi and his three hundred were fighting a blizzard.

"Just like home," Haaken growled.

"It's a part of home I don't miss," Bragi replied. "I've never seen it this heavy in these parts."

"Nobody else has either. So naturally we've got to be out in the middle of it. We're crazy. You know that?"

"We should be there pretty soon."

"And then what? Sit and freeze our butts off till we find out that this Hali had an attack of smarts and holed up by a fire somewhere?"

"Nice to see you in a good mood, Haaken."

"Good mood?"

"I can always tell. You talk more. And it's all bitch-craft."

They would have missed their road had it not been for the town and a soldier who knew it. "That's Arno yonder, Captain," he said. "Right where we want to be."

"Here's where we make ourselves unpopular," Bragi said. And they did, by forcing the townspeople to quarter them while they waited. Nearly a thousand people lived in Arno, and none of them welcomed the Guildsmen. It was not a good feeling.

Bragi paid what he could, and made his men meet Guild behavior standards. It did little good.

Four days passed. The townspeople grew increasingly resentful. Like common folk everywhere, they just wanted to be left alone.

"Riders coming," a chilled and winded scout reported the fifth afternoon. "Four or five hundred. Look like Invincibles."

Haaken glared at his brother.

"Another fine mess I've gotten us into, eh?" Bragi asked. "Pass the word. And tell the civilians to get into their cellars."

Arno had no walls. What a place to die, Bragi thought as he hurried toward the church. Its belfry commanded a good view of the countryside.

The afternoon sun blazed off fields of snow. He squinted. The Invincibles were hard to see. They blended with the background. They were walking, leading their animals.

He spied one man clad all in black. Curious. Black was not popular with El Murid's followers.

"How am I going to work this?" he wondered aloud. "They're not going to let us pull another Alperin."

A horseman forged ahead. Bragi galloped downstairs. "Haaken! They're sending a guy to scout. Have a couple men make like townspeople. Tell him everything's wonderful."

Haaken waved acknowledgement from the loft of the town inn. A few minutes later two men stepped into the road.

By then Ragnarson was back in the belfry and wondering if he should avoid a fight. He had a hollow sensation. Something was wrong. This one did not feel like a winner.

The north wind picked up. He shivered. This winter was getting bad. People in these parts did not know how to handle the cold and deep snow. Most of his men did not.

He could not picture them surviving a long retreat. Not harried by an enemy and burdened by wounded. "But Hali won't be used to it either," he reminded himself. "It'll be harder on his men."

The fighting would be savage. Refuge from the weather would be the prize. The loser would be out in the cold literally.

He watched as several Invincibles gathered around the returned scout. The man in black joined them, gesturing emphatically.

The meeting broke up. Invincibles readied weapons and spread out for an advance upon the town.

"So much for that idea," Bragi growled. He plunged back downstairs. "They're coming in ready, Haaken," he shouted. He glanced up and down the road, at windows where his men waited with ready bows. "Damned weather. Maybe he'd have gone around."

Back up the tower he went, puffing and snorting. "This has got to stop," he gasped.

The Invincibles reached the first houses. They were careful. Each carried a bow or crossbow. "Maybe I should get out after dark," Bragi muttered.

It began. And it looked bad from the beginning. The Invincibles were cautious, determined and as systematic as their commander. They cleared the buildings one by one.

Hali did not try to obliterate anyone, just to get hold of warm quarters. He did not surround the town. His men did not prevent Bragi's from fleeing a building they could not hold.

A third of Arno belonged to Hali when Haaken clumped into the belfry. "Looks like we lose this one."

"Don't it?"

"We've got a problem."

"Besides looking at a cold night, what?"

"They're using sorcery."

"I haven't seen any.... They wouldn't. They're El Murid's men."

"Yeah? Go remind them. The one in black turns up anywhere we're doing okay."

"Hmm. Well. Get the wounded ready. We'll get out after dark."

Haaken thudded back downstairs. Bragi looked into the road. Several Invincibles were in easy range. He let fly. His arrows stalled their advance.

The man in black appeared. Bragi sped a shaft that missed.

The man turned slowly. His gaze climbed the church tower. His left hand rose, one finger pointing. A bluish nimbus surrounded him.

A monster voice bellowed in the belfry. Flat on the floor, Bragi clapped his hands to his ears. It did no good.

The sound went away.

A quarter-inch layer of blue haze masked everything in line of sight of the man in black. Sorcery! Bragi thought, *Haaken, I'm convinced!*

The haze faded. He examined the wood underneath. It had turned an odd grey color. It flaked when he touched it.

He examined his bow. It looked sound. He peeped outside. The wizard faced the inn, his arm extended again.

"You sonofabitch, you asked for it."

His bow creaked at its moment of greatest tension. His arrow did not fly true. It smashed through the man's elbow.

"Well, damn my eyes! I never seen such whining and carrying on."

Several Invincibles hustled the wizard into a captured house. His departure did not alter the outcome. The expulsion of Guildsmen continued.

Bragi nearly waited too long. He had to fight his way out of the church. Haaken's only comment was, "We've got to quit fooling around here, Bragi. We're going to have too many people hurt to get them all back to camp."

"Scavenge all the warm clothes and blankets you can. And tools so we can build shelters. Find some harness animals and carts…."

"I took care of it already."

"You're not supposed to plunder…."

Haaken shrugged. "I'll worry about it when they court-martial me. What's the difference? These people will hate us no matter what. Which you already thought about or you wouldn't have told me to clean them out."

"I got that wizard."

"Shaghûn."

"What?"

"Shaghûn. That's what they call a soldier-wizard."

"Like Haroun is supposed to be? What's he doing here? With Hali, of all people?"

Haaken shrugged.

"He's going to be damned mad. Who's in good shape? We've got to let Reskird and Amin know what's going on."

"I sent Chotty and Uthe Haas right after Hali showed."

"You're getting too damned efficient."

A soldier approached them. "Captain, they're moving into this block."

Ragnarson withdrew as the sun set. The Guildsmen marched dispiritedly, sullenly, weakly. The cold was gnawing their wills. Bragi had to remind them that they *were* Guildsmen.

Several of the wounded died during the night. The company paused to bury them next morning. A messenger from Metillah Amin overtook them while they were chopping graves in the icy earth.

Amin had heard that Hali was on the middle road. The messenger bore a belated warning and the news that Amin was on his way to help.

"We're back in business," Bragi announced. "Haaken, take some men to those woods over there and start building shelters."

"You're not serious." Haaken wore a look of disbelief. "You are serious."

"Damned right I am. And get some fires going first thing."

Haaken grumbled away with the men. Their disenchantment was unanimous. For a moment Bragi feared he faced a mutiny.

Guild discipline held. He concluded his conversation with the messenger.

He joined his men at their hastily built fires. They huddled near the flames, taking turns rushing into the cold to assemble shelters of boughs and packed snow. When he felt half-toasted on each side he rose and trudged toward Arno, to see for himself what Hali was doing.

Twice he had to hide from Invincible patrols. They were not strong and not enthusiastic about their job. They were not ranging far from town.

Hali was doing nothing but keeping warm. He seemed content to wait till the cold spell passed. Neither his men nor his animals were fit to face prolonged exposure.

Bragi crawled into a haystack to sleep that night. When he finally returned to camp he found Amin and his men crowding the fires and looking forlorn. He decided to give them a day of rest.

The temperature did not drop that night, and it rose next day. It kept rising and the snow began a fast melt. The ground was soggy during the march on Arno.

"Looks like the cold is over," Bragi observed.

"Yeah," Haaken replied. "Our buddy, Hali, will be getting ready to move."

Hali was getting ready, but not to move. He had his shaghûn, and the shaghûn could see beyond the range of mortal eyes. The Invincibles were cooking up a little surprise.

Bragi walked into it. The fighting became savage. Amin's men were in a bloody mood. Hali's people, backboned by the shaghûn, stomped the eagerness out of them. Come nightfall, with only a few houses retaken, Ragnarson sent a whole train of casualties back to his camp in the woods.

"This is stupid, Bragi," Haaken declared. "It's like the time Father got into it with Oleg Sorenson."

"What?" Amin asked.

"My father and another man got into a fight one time," Bragi explained. "They were both too proud to give up and neither one was strong enough to drop the other. So they beat each other half to death. They couldn't get out of bed for a week. And nothing had changed when they did. They went right at it again."

"That shaghûn has to go," Amin said. "They'll eat us alive if he doesn't. We can eat them if he does. It's that simple."

"So go do something about him."

Amin smiled. "You mock me. All right. Loan me three of your best bowmen."

Bragi peered at the man. "Do it, Haaken."

"You sure?"

"He is. Give him his shot."

"Whatever you say." Haaken went looking for men.

"Still testing?" Amin asked.

"Always. You know it."

Amin was one of those curiosities which turn up in every war, the soldier of schizophrenic loyalties and ideals. He was twenty-seven years old. He had been fighting for ten years. For the first seven he had served El Murid. He had been one of the Scourge of God's Commanders of a Thousand.

He had become disenchanted with his fellow officers during the invasion of the west. They were making a mockery of the Disciple's law, and he saw little evidence that El Murid himself cared. When Nassef perished and el-Kader assumed command, Amin expected wholesale looting in the recovered provinces. He deserted.

Time had proven him wrong, but by then it was too late for Metillah Amin. He went to the mountains and swore allegiance to the King Without a Throne. His name was entered on the Harish lists.

Metillah Amin was an unfortunate man, and the more so because he knew no life but that of the warrior. In the tale of the El Murid Wars he was to have little significance save that he symbolized all the thousands of young men who found the conflict a slayer, not a mother, of dreams.

Bragi and his brother watched Amin's team vanish into the darkness. "That's a man looking for death," Haaken observed.

"It's his only way out," Bragi replied. "But he's got that fighter's determination, too. He can't just let it happen. He's got to earn it. Keep an eye on him. We'll hit them with everything if he gets lucky."

Haaken returned an hour later. He hunkered down and held his hands out to the fireplace. Bragi heard a rising clamor. "Well?"

"He earned it. But he got the job done. The shaghûn is gone."

"Dead?"

"As a wedge. For whatever good it'll do."

It did little immediate good. Hali's men were stubborn and desperate.

Uthe Haas, Haaken's messenger to Kildragon, returned next morning. He reported that Reskird was on his way.

"Ha!" said Bragi. "We've got them now." He sent another messenger to tell Kildragon to dig in across the road near the encampment in the woods. Then he gradually surrounded Arno, sneaking his strength to the north clumsily enough to be sure he would be detected. When he launched his "surprise" attack next morning Hali broke out to the south, driving down the road toward Hammad al Nakir and imagined safety.

The weather remained warm. The snow was almost gone. The earth was mush. The race was a slow one. Ragnarson and his infantrymen shambled along, pausing each few paces to knock the mud off their legs. Each time a man lifted a foot there was a *schlock!* as the mud surrendered its grip.

The Royalists and their foes exchanged the occasional arrow, but there was little fighting. From above, the road would have looked like a disorganized ant trail. The columns became ever more extended.

Bragi discovered some stony ground to his right. He guided his men into it and began gaining on Hali. Then his path suddenly dipped to a narrow, icy creek. By the time he crossed, Hali was in a brisk fight with Reskird and the Royalists. His men charged through the mud and closed the circle around the enemy.

Here Hali's men were at a disadvantage against Guild bows. The encounter was bloody and did not last long. Only a few dozen Invincibles escaped.

Ragnarson prowled the field with the Royalists, trying to find Hali's body. Night fell without his being able to determine if the game had been worth the candle. Investigations next morning proved nothing either.

"Ah, damn, Haaken. All this for nothing."

"Maybe. And maybe he died in the town."

Bragi would know nothing for sure for months. By then he would be back in the Kapenrungs, engrossed in another matter and indifferent to Hali's fate.

EIGHTEEN
THE ASSASSINS

Haroun knelt beside the brook, drinking from cupped hands. He shivered in the chill mountain breeze. Beloul said, "Lord, I'm not comfortable with this."

"It is risky," Haroun admitted. "Beloul?"

"Lord?"

"Guard my back well."

"You think Shadek would...?

"I don't know."

"But...."

"In politics you never know. He kept me informed all the way, but I'm still not sure. The question is, did he do the same with Sidi?"

Beloul smiled thinly. "Shadek is my friend, Lord. But even I couldn't say. Who knows a man's secret ambition?"

"Exactly. And in this case that's what's going to count. He's set it up so he can jump any way he wants. Just the way I would have done. I admire him for that. I didn't think he had the imagination."

Beloul smiled again.

"Now I'm wondering if I'll ever trust him, assuming he does jump my way."

"We shouldn't waste time worrying, Lord. Just be alert. We'll all know when his moment of no return comes."

"Maybe. Do you think he'd be fool enough to trust Sidi's gratitude?"

"He would arrange some sort of self-protection, Lord."

"Uhm. I thought so."

Next day, even deeper into the mountains, Haroun told his companions, "I have to leave for a few days. Make camp here. Wait for me." His tone brooked no questions. Aside, to Beloul, he said, "Take care, my friend. Most of these men were chosen by Shadek."

"I know, Lord. I know."

The snows in the Kapenrungs were deep. Haroun found the going heavy. Most of it was uphill, which did not help.

He located the cabin more by the smell of smoke than by memory or sight. It was as white as the rest of the landscape and virtually invisible. A dog howled, protesting his presence. He approached cautiously.

It had been months since he had come here. Anything might have happened. He reached with his shaghûn-trained senses, feeling for a wrongness. There could be no better place for the Harish to lie in wait.

The door creaked inward. He stared at the rectangle of shadow, probing for a trap.

"Come in, damn it! You're letting all the warm air out." The unveiled face of an old, old woman drifted across the doorway. He pushed inside, slammed the door. One hand rested on his sword hilt.

Nothing. No danger.

He stamped the snow off his feet. A thin layer of white remained. It faded in the heat.

After the bitter cold the cabin was overpoweringly warm. He shed clothing fast, feeling slightly faint.

"How is she?" he asked.

"Well enough, considering she's trapped here a hundred miles from the Lord alone knows where." There was no deference in the woman's harsh old voice. "She's sleeping now."

Haroun glared at her.

She was his uncle Fuad's first wife's mother, the nearest living relative he could claim. She looked like a pessimistic artist's conception of Death. Wrinkled, bony, toothless, all clad in black. And mean as a snake. She resembled the harridans guarding the gates of Bragi's version of Hell, he reflected. He laughed softly. "You're a sweetheart, Fatim."

A ghost of a smile crossed her colorless lips. "You're here now, make yourself useful. Throw some wood on the fire. I'll have to cook extra tonight."

"That any way to talk to your king?"

"King? Of what?" She snorted derisively.

A voice squeaked in the loft.

"Nobody. Just your uncle, Haroun," the old woman replied.

A thin, dark, strange face peered down from the gloom. The firelight made it appear diabolic. "Hello, Seif," Haroun said. Seif was the son of Fatim's brother's son, and all she had left of her blood. He helped around the cabin.

A slow smile fought the half-dead muscles of Seif's face. In a moment he began working his way down the ladder. Haroun did not help. Seif insisted on doing for himself.

Reaching the floor, Seif turned, started toward Haroun. He dragged one leg. He held one clawed hand across his chest. It shuddered with effort. His head lolled to one side. A tail of spittle fell from the corner of his mouth.

Haroun concealed his aversion and threw his arms around the youth. "How have you been, Seif?"

"Well?" the old woman snarled. "Are you going to see her or not? Your timing is good, anyway."

Haroun released Seif. "I suppose I should. That's why I came."

"And about time, I'd say. What kind of man are you? It's been almost a year."

"I have my problems. Where is she? Hiding?"

"Asleep, I told you. Go see her, you fool."

The youth said something. Haroun could not make it out.

"And you keep your mouth shut, Seif. Let him find out for himself. It's his fault."

"Find out what?"

"She's not going to come to you. So go."

Haroun bowed to her superior wisdom and pushed through the hangings that divided the cabin.

She was lying on her back in the crude bed he and Seif had worked so hard to build. She was sleeping, smiling, her left arm flung above her head. She looked sweet and vulnerable. A month-old child lay cradled in the crook of her right arm, head near her breast. She seemed content.

"Well, I'll be damned," he whispered. He knelt and stared at the infant's face. "I'll be damned. Girl or boy, Fatim?"

"A son, Lord. An heir. She named him Megelin Micah."

"How beautiful. How thoughtful. How absolutely perfect." He reached out, touched the girl's cheek. "Darling?"

Her eyes opened. She smiled.

They were on the downside now, getting near the desert. There was just the occasional patch of snow, in the shadows of the trees. "Lord?" Beloul queried softly.

"Yes?"

"What's happened?"

"What? I don't follow you."

"You've changed. Somehow, while you were away, you became a different man. More whole, I think you'd say. Perhaps matured."

"I see."

Beloul awaited something more. Haroun said nothing, so he asked, "Might I know?"

"No. I'm sorry, old friend. Maybe someday."

"As you will, Lord."

He *had* changed, Haroun reflected. The birth of a son gave the world a different look. It made a man a bit more inclined toward caution. For three days he had been considering canceling the expedition

"Lord," el Senoussi called from up the column. "We're here."

Haroun scanned the mountainsides and canyon. He saw nothing unusual. "Now's the time, Beloul. He's got to jump one way or the other. Be ready."

Beloul pointed. "Down there, Lord. Smoke."

"I see it."

Shadek led the way down the steep trail. Haroun eyed his back, trying to postulate his thoughts from his posture.

No matter his intent, Shadek knew the significance of the moment. It would be too late to change his mind once he brought his king and Beloul into Sidi's camp as simple bladesmen.

Unless he were making a delivery.

Haroun grew more tense. That possibility had not occurred to him earlier.

El Senoussi's hand snapped up, signaling a halt. Haroun dropped his fingers to his sword. Shadek made his way up the file. "Lord, this is going to be tricky. I don't know what they plan. It could be a trap."

"It could be. Take a couple men down and find out. I'll wait here."

"As you command, Lord." El Senoussi picked two men and departed. They disappeared among the trees whence the smoke rose.

Haroun and Beloul waited with their swords lying across their laps. The rest of the men dismounted.

El Senoussi returned two hours later. He came all the way up instead of signaling from below. Beloul whispered, "I'm inclined to think he's sticking, Lord."

"We'll see."

El Senoussi arrived. "It looks like they'll play it straight, Lord. There's only ten of them, and Sidi himself."

"Let's go, then. Make sure he dies first if they try anything."

"That goes without saying, Lord. Listen up, men! We're going down. And I'll cut the heart out of the man who forgets and gives our Lord away. This is just a warrior named Abu bin Kahed." He started down the trail again.

They clattered into Sidi's camp, suspiciously eyeing Sidi's men, who watched them suspiciously. This would be an uneasy alliance, Haroun reflected.

El Murid's son awaited them, his face a stony mask. He made no move to greet them. The war truly claimed the young, Haroun reflected. The boy had the look of a cruel, miserly old man.

They set out for Al Rhemish next morning, riding fast. El Murid had ended his seclusion. He was watching everyone. The night-stalking Harish were busier than ever before. Sidi did not want to be away long enough to invite unwelcome questions.

The parties traveled without mixing. There was little intercourse between them, and less trust.

Haroun and Beloul performed the chores of ordinary warriors. They did their turns cooking, currying animals, standing sentry duty. Sidi's people paid them no heed. Shadek's men showed them no special respect. He had selected smart, vigilant, veteran guerrillas.

It was noon of a warm winter's day when Haroun once again saw the Holy City, the city of his dreams, the city of the kings of Hammad al Nakir. He had to struggle to keep his feelings hidden.

The great bowl had changed. There was a broad, shallow lake where once pilgrims had camped during Disharhun. The Shrines and city now stood on an island reached by a rickety wooden causeway. The old ruins had been cleared. New structures had been raised. More were under construction, including giants that looked worthy of the capital of a new Empire. The stone piers of a permanent bridge were in place beside the wooden causeway.

The inner slopes of the bowl were covered with green grass. Camels and goats, horses and cattle grazed them. At the points of the compass four small sections had been enclosed with fences built from the rubble of the leveled ruins. Each enclosure contained arrow-straight rows of seedling trees. The all important moisture descended the slopes from a ringing irrigation canal. Haroun could only guess whence the water had come.

He exchanged glances with Beloul.

"It's changed remarkably," Shadek told Sidi.

"The old fool's hobby," the boy said. "Greening the desert. A damned waste of money and manpower."

"It would seem a worthy goal, Lord."

Sidi gave Shadek a cruel look. "Perhaps. But it would consume the labor and wealth of a dozen generations, General."

Haroun knew the numbers. Megelin had shared them with him back when, while preparing suggestions for his father.

He sensed that Sidi was parroting something he had been told. There was a strong flavor of rote recital in his phrasing.

What fell puppet-masters were filling him with contempt for his father's dreams? And with insidious schemes for murder?

No doubt Sidi believed he was his own creature, was making his own decisions and pursuing his own ambitions. The poor naive child.

Sidi was a dead puppet and did not know it. How long would he last once his manipulators eliminated El Murid? Till the first time his will crossed theirs.

While he wallowed in the privileges of power, they would sink their claws into its instruments. If Sidi asserted himself he would find himself standing alone.

Would the Invincibles support the slayer of their prophet? A parricide? Never.

There was no one on whom Haroun would rather see the jaws of fate close. Sidi impressed him that negatively.

He looked down as they crossed the rickety bridge. The water made a nice moat. There were fish in it. Big ones. It was a shame El Murid could not have remained a loyal subject.

They wound through Al Rhemish past sites hard to recognize but difficult to forget. There…. That was where he had unhorsed the Disciple when he was six. His uncle Fuad had died yonder. And his father and brother Ali and King Aboud had made their stand against this wall….

"Lord!" Beloul cautioned softly. "Take care. Your memories are showing."

Haroun stifled the emotion, became as much a gawker as his companions.

He did not like all he saw. There were too many white robes. Getting out would be difficult.

Sidi led them to a stable belonging to one of his backers. He told el Senoussi to sit tight till he was needed, and to keep his men off the streets.

They moved into the loft over the stable. "Not exactly where you'd look for a nest of assassins, is it?" Haroun murmured.

El Senoussi held a finger to his lips. "The walls have ears in this town. There were too many intrigues during the Disciple's seclusion."

"When do we act?" Beloul asked.

Shadek shrugged. "He needs time to arrange it. He'll want it to happen when he has an ironclad alibi. And he'll probably try to arrange it so something happens to us, whatever the outcome. We'd make dangerous witnesses. It might take him a month."

"One thing, Shadek," Haroun said. "Be obsequious. Fawn on him. Be the desert's number one lickspittle if you have to. But make believe he's taken us in, that he needn't fear us."

"That is my plan, Lord." El Senoussi looked like an artist watching a very personal piece of work, wrought with loving care, being reshaped by another artist. "I'm going to make him so sure of me that when the day comes he'll come tell me himself. We'll slay the pup then leap at the throat of the sire. I trust that meets with your approval, Lord?"

"Pardon me, Shadek. I worry. About everything. What about escape? That bridge will be trouble if they're chasing us."

"That was an unforeseen complication, Lord."

Haroun gave him a name and address and had him bring the man to the loft.

Nine weeks ground away. Haroun and Beloul spent every minute of every one inside that stable. "I'm going out of my mind," Haroun moaned. "The Disciple is going to die of old age before we move."

Beloul started to say something. A stir below interrupted. Shadek growled something. Men scrambled into hiding. "Sidi's coming," Beloul whispered.

"Another false alarm," Haroun predicted. "Just checking up on us."

The boy visited once a week, growing bolder each time. Only two bodyguards accompanied him now. Shadek met him on the ground level.

Men watched from every shadow. Sidi and el Senoussi spoke in low tones, Shadek apparently growing excited, Sidi baffled.

Thus it had gone every time, with Shadek throwing his arms around as he spoke.

In the middle of a sentence he grunted and began to dig at his ear with the nail of his little finger. Then he dropped like a stone.

Arrows flew. Sidi and his bodyguards flung about in a grim, drunken *danse macabre* under the impact of the shafts. Shadek snaked away. His men leapt from the shadows, made sure of their victims.

"Quick, quiet, and easy," Haroun told Beloul. "We couldn't ask for anything more." He scrambled down and joined el Senoussi, who was slapping off dirt and straw.

"Shove them under that pile of hay," Shadek ordered "You, you, get the horses saddled." He turned to Haroun. "Lord, we're expected at the Shrines in an hour."

"Who are we supposed to be?"

"A delegation of salt merchants presenting a petition for redress. The Disciple has a soft spot for the trade. We're supposed to raise hell about the officers managing the Daimiellian salt works. Sidi said it was a pet peeve."

"Good enough. Anything to get past the Invincibles." Haroun thumbed his dagger.

They all made sure their hidden blades were accessible. Their more obvious weapons they would surrender before being permitted to approach the Disciple.

"Let me do the talking," Shadek said. "I know a little about the salt trade. I'll scratch my ear again."

Every man appeared pale and nervous. The one Shadek assigned to manage the horses was visibly relieved.

Haroun surveyed the others. They looked too hardened to be simple caravaners. Nobody would believe their story.

Throats tightened and stomachs churned as they passed through the series of guardians shielding the Disciple. Haroun was baffled. The white robes seemed unsuspicious. Hidden weapons got by them, apparently because they surrendered blades almost as well concealed and, perhaps, because no one had ever dared stalk the Disciple in the sanctity of the Shrine.

Haroun hoped his own bodyguards never became as complacent. The Harish had struck too close too often already.

He hung back a little when they entered El Murid's throne room, keeping his head down. Beloul lagged with him. The others masked them with their bodies. El Murid knew Haroun and might recognize Beloul.

Haroun could not avoid a hungry glance at the Peacock Throne. *That* was his self-proclaimed destiny....

It was called the Peacock Throne because its tall back resembled the fan of a peacock displayed. The twelve-foot plumes had been fashioned of planks of rare woods. Over the centuries they had been set with gold, silver, gems, ivory, jet, pearls, turquoise, and semiprecious stones in contrived, garish patterns. Dynasties of Ilkazar's emperors and generations of Quesani kings had contributed to the gaudy mosaic. The Throne was the heart and symbol of power in Hammad al Nakir, as it had been for the Empire before.

And now this usurper, this jackal without a drop of royal blood, defiled the seat of kings. Haroun stifled his anger.

Another rose to replace it. This beast had slain his family. This monster had destroyed everything worthy and dear and had unleashed the hounds that dogged him even now.

He counted bodyguards cautiously.

Shadek halted a dozen paces from the Peacock Throne. After the courtly courtesies, he advanced a few steps. He began talking in a low, persuasive voice. El Murid leaned forward to listen. He nodded occasionally.

What was Shadek waiting for? Let's do it! Haroun screamed inside.

Shadek's hands flew as if in emphatic support of his argument, as they had with Sidi. Haroun tried to relax, to still his fears. He dared not let tension betray him.

A door burst inward. A man in tatters staggered through. A pair of ranking Invincibles supported him. Rag-man croaked, "No, Lord! Beware!"

Not a soul moved for a bewildered moment. Then El Murid yelped, "Mowaffak! What are you doing here? What's happened to you?"

"Assassins, Lord," Hali croaked, extending a shaky arm to point. "They're assassins."

Haroun dove for his dagger.

"Hali!" Beloul squealed. And charged.

Men flew this way and that. El Senoussi rushed the Disciple, got sidetracked. Haroun flung himself after Shadek, only to have his path blocked by Invincibles. The white robes had been taken off guard. They began going down. Soon they were outnumbered.

Haroun dispatched the man blocking his path. He skipped the body and started toward his old enemy. He met El Murid's gaze. There was no fear there.

"You're a bold one," the Disciple said. "I never expected you here."

Haroun smiled. It was a thin, cruel, wicked little smile. "It saddens me that you'll never see me on the Peacock Throne, usurper. Unless you manage from the Other Side."

"Your father and uncle were wont to speak in that vein. Who is watching whom from where?"

Haroun sprang.

El Murid raised his left hand. The glow of his amulet shown into Haroun's eyes. He spoke one word.

Thunder rolled. A brilliant flash filled the room. The Shrines quivered on their foundations.

Haroun's knees gave way. A darkness stole his vision. He tried to shout but his mouth was numb.

El Murid did not laugh, and that infuriated Haroun. The Disciple was the villain of the piece. Villains were supposed to crow in triumph when they won.

Hands seized his arms, lifted him. A remote voice said, "Get him out of here." Haroun tried to help. His feet would not untangle. His supporters slung him around helter-skelter as they fled along a stormy shore. Every breaker smashed in with a metallic roar and muted shouting. Twice they dumped him while they hurled back the waves.

His vision began to clear. His legs worked a little. His mind regained its ability to grasp sequential events.

Shadek's men were fighting their way out. They were good, hard men but they had failed in their mission. They were leaving no one behind to be captured and tortured into betraying those who did escape. They might have to slay a few of their own to manage but that had been understood beforehand.

The city seemed unnaturally calm after the chaos of the Shrines. "Let's don't anybody get in a hurry," el Senoussi cautioned as he helped Beloul hoist Haroun aboard a horse. "We don't want to attract attention."

Beloul laughed. "Somebody's bound to figure there's something wrong." He indicated a pair of Invincibles howling at the entrance to the Shrines.

Haroun tried to tell Shadek to get a move on. His tongue was not yet fit for duty.

Shadek led them toward the bridge spanning El Murid's lake, saying, "They didn't have any horses around. It'll take them a while to get the word out. We'll be long gone before they do."

He was wrong.

There was a new order in the Kingdom of Peace. Secretly, El Murid had withdrawn his ban on the practice of the dark arts. A few former shaghûns had rallied to his standard. Most were in the capital city with the Invincibles. They were not the shaghûns of old but they had their uses.

Like getting swift orders to the bridge defenders.

The assassins reached the city's edge and found the causeway held by two score alert and angry white robes. "So we turn back to Bassam's," Haroun told el Senoussi.

Excitement was afoot in the city now. Those first wild rumors which come before slower-footed truth leapt from house to house like flames through a dry, brushy canyon. People moved with more speed and less purpose, certain something was wrong but unsure what it was. The Invincibles were more in evidence, though not yet asking questions. "Shadek, we'd better ditch the animals. We're too memorable this way."

"Aye, Lord." El Senoussi returned to the stable. What better place to abandon horses?

Now to move to the place his agent Bassam had prepared…. The wounded were a problem. They would be more memorable than any number of horses.

The pragmatic course was obvious. Dispatch the badly injured. Hide them with Sidi and his bodyguards.

There were only two men to consider, men whose lives Haroun did not want to squander. Too many had been wasted in this cruel war. "Shadek, we just became lepers. We'll bind ourselves in rags and go by twos and threes. People will be too busy getting out of our way to look us over."

"Excellent idea, Lord."

Haroun walked with a man named Hassan who had taken a saber's bite in his thigh. "Unclean!" he moaned. "Lepers!" In a softer voice, he told his companion, "I'm starting to enjoy this."

The nervous mobs scattered ahead of them, reformed behind. People cursed them. Some muttered that the Disciple had extended his protection too far, that lepers should not be allowed to befoul the City of God. One overly bold child chucked a clod. Haroun shook a gnarly stick and howled incoherently. The child scampered away. Haroun laughed. "This is fun."

"Have you ever known a leper, Lord?"

"No. Why?"

"It's no fun for them. They rot. They stink. Their flesh falls away. They don't feel anything. If they're not careful they can injure themselves fatally. That happened to my sister."

"Oh. I'm sorry, Hassan." What else could he say?

Bassam, a long-time Royalist agent, had prepared them a place in the cellar beneath his house. Something of an innovation for a poor shopkeeper, he had begun digging it the day of their arrival. He had made no effort to conceal the work, going so far as to brag that it would be the finest cellar in the city.

He had lined its walls with sun-baked brick, then had erected a cross wall that concealed a narrow portion.

The surviving assassins moved in. Haroun's agent started bricking up the hole through which they had entered. "I stocked food and water for a month, Lord. Nothing tasty, but it'll keep you. I expect the stench will bother you most. People would wonder if I dumped too many chamberpots. Your fresh air will come through that wooden grate. You can see the street through it. Try not to get caught peeking."

Bassam left one loose block that could be removed for communication purposes. He did not take it out again for four days. "They've searched the house," he announced. "They're searching them all. El Murid has decreed that no one will enter or leave Al Rhemish till you're caught. Mowaffak Hali died yesterday, but you can't claim him. It was gangrene. He was attacked by Guildsmen coming home. The same band that accounted for Karim and the Scourge of God a few years ago."

"That damned Bragi," Haroun muttered. "Who told him he could leave camp?"

"Begging your pardon, Lord," Beloul said. "Did you think you could tell Guildsmen what to do? Consider their viewpoint."

"I can see it, Beloul. I don't have to like it."

"There's more, Lord," Bassam said. "El Murid rescinded the ban against shaghûnry. He admitted he's been trying to recruit them since his God visited the Shrines. The first division of el Nadim's army passed Al Rhemish today. He sent all he had with it. Lucky for us."

"Send down some wine," el Senoussi muttered. "We'll celebrate Hali's passing and mourn everything else."

"Wine is proscribed," Bassam retorted. "I follow the Disciple's law to the letter."

"No sense of humor, eh?"

Bassam ignored Shadek. "You may be here a while, Lord. He's damned angry. The Invincibles prowl day and night. You can't travel a hundred feet without being questioned."

Bassam paid his second visit three days later. The Invincibles had discovered Sidi's body. "He's more excited than ever, Lord. Crazy with grief and rage. Someone whispered in the right ears. News of the boy's plot reached him the same afternoon they found the corpses. He's tearing the city apart looking for the conspirators. They've caught a bunch trying to get out. The Invincibles are making them sing. The Disciple thinks they're hiding you."

"I wish him luck. I hope he hangs them all." Haroun laughed wickedly.

"I won't be down for a while, unless there's crucial news. I have to mind the shop every second. Half of our good citizens have turned thief."

Nine days passed. The cellar began to wear. Nerves frayed. Tempers flared. It promised to get worse. Haroun collected the weapons and piled them in a corner. He and Beloul took turns guarding them.

Bassam came in the middle of the night. "It's gotten no safer, Lord. If anything, it's worse. They're calling it the Reign of Terror. The Invincibles have become a pack of mad dogs. Their killings make less sense every day. I don't know how long it'll last. People are getting hungry. There'll be riots. And my own days may be numbered. If they take one of my men and he talks…."

"Then we'd better get out now."

"You wouldn't have a prayer. They'd cut you down before you got out of sight of the shop. It's worth a man's life to walk the streets in broad daylight, Lord. Sit tight and hope it runs its course. Or that the riots start before they get on to us. They might even get sick of it themselves."

"And if they do take you?"

"I'll hold out as long as I can."

"And we'll be buried down here without knowing anything is wrong," el Senoussi growled. "Like sleepy birds caught in their nests."

"We'll fix that. Right now." In less than an hour Bassam rigged a bell that would ring at a tug on any of several cords concealed around the shop. Its installation required making a small hole through his expensive new wooden floor. He bemoaned the vandalism the whole time he was drilling.

"I won't ring unless I'm sure I'm caught," he said. "Can't guarantee I'll be able to then. I'll only do it if it won't give you away. If I do ring, you're on your own. I don't know how long I can hold out. I've never faced any real test of courage."

"Of course you have, Bassam. No coward would have hidden himself in the Disciple's shadow all this time."

"One last thing, Lord. El Nadim is camped outside town. His is the last division of the eastern army. It'll be a tough spring for the Disciple's enemies out west."

"That's the way it looks."

"That's a good man," Shadek said a moment after Bassam departed. "And a scared one. He's sure he won't last much longer."

"He's the best," Haroun agreed. "Beloul? You think our fat friend failed?"

"It does look like his luck ran out."

That cellar became worse than any prison. A prisoner had no hope, no essential belief in his existence as a free man, no knowledge that he could break out at will. The days were interminable. The nights were longer. The stench was as bad as promised. Haroun began worrying about disease. He made everybody take turns exercising.

Bassam seemed to have forgotten they existed.

Twice they heard the mutter of searchers beyond the false foundation wall. They held their breaths and weapons and waited for the worst.

The bell tinkled gently eight days after its installation. Its voice was so soft Haroun was not immediately sure it was not just his nerves.

"They've taken him!" Shadek snarled. "Damn!"

"How long will he last?" Beloul asked.

"I don't know," Haroun replied. "He was right, in a way. Good intentions don't count for much if there's a hot iron gnawing on you. Hoist me up to the grate."

He peered into the dusty street. He watched the white robes take Bassam away. They had bound him so he could not fight and force them to kill him.

"They did get him. Damn! Brave in the shop and brave in the Shrines, when they're breaking your fingers and toes, are two different things."

"We'd better move out."

"Not before dark. We wouldn't have a prayer before then. Get with the exercises. We'll need to be loose."

"At least let's get out where we can give them a fight if they come back," Shadek suggested.

"All right. Knock the wall apart. Carefully! Keep the noise down. We'll put it back together. Make them break it down to find out if we're gone or not."

The foul tempers and abysmal morale evaporated, to be replaced by anxiety.

They spent a tense afternoon waiting for Invincibles to appear. None came. Beloul and Shadek took turns studying the movements of the patrols in the streets. Haroun and the others continued their exercises.

There was no moon that evening. The winter moon would not rise till early morning.

They moved out right after sentry change. Shadek and Beloul said the watch officers would not check back for at least an hour. They had determined that there were both posted sentries and walking patrols. The latter were the greater danger. They roamed at random, in twos and threes.

Shadek said, "Let's hope they've gotten a little lax. They've had their own way for a long time. They can't keep on edge forever, can they? When every civilian practically kisses their toes?"

"Uhm," Haroun grunted. "Beloul, go get your man."

Beloul would slay the nearest fixed guard and don his robe. Haroun would steal up on the next and do the same. The two were the party's masters of the deadly sneak.

Together they would approach additional guards acting as a random patrol. They would clear the way and provide disguises for their henchmen.

Had there been an early moon they could not have done it. The sentries were posted within sight of one another.

Beloul was as slow, patient, and deadly as a serpent. He performed his task to perfection. Haroun had more trouble but managed without alerting the enemy.

Fourteen Invincibles perished. The band reached the new circumferential street El Murid was paving around his island. A garden strip twenty to fifty feet wide would lie between it and the water's edge. No alarm had risen.

They were discussing how best to get the non-swimmers across. A pair of Invincibles materialized. "What's up?" one asked.

Haroun started a casual reply. One of Shadek's men panicked, threw a swordstroke that missed.

The group exploded.

Too late. One of the white robes got his whistle to his lips before he went down.

"Into the water," Haroun snarled. "Help each other the best you can." Softly, to Beloul, "I knew it was going too well. Damn! I thought we might have time to steal horses."

The water was cold. Haroun cursed as he towed one of the non-swimmers across those places where the man could not touch bottom.

He forgot the chill once he heard the clamor of pursuit, once the torches began appearing on the island shore.

NINETEEN
THE SORCERER

The miles grew longer every day. The hills grew steeper. Mocker worried about getting through Kavelin without being remembered, but Fate overlooked him.

The weather caused him misery enough.

He was in no real hurry. He spent the worst days holed up at wayside inns. Haroun had given him money, but where he could he paid his way by entertaining. He wanted to get his touch back. It had been years since he had played to strangers.

Not once did he allow himself to be drawn into a game of chance.

Three years in the witches' cauldron of war had matured him more than had three with the dubious Damo Sparen.

Slow as he traveled, winter was slower. He climbed into Kavelin's eastern mountains and the Savernake Gap during the worst time of year. At the last town, Baxendala, they warned him not to go on. They told him the pass would be snowed in, and the gods themselves only knew what awaited him beyond the King's last outpost, the fortress Maisak.

But Mocker recalled Baxendala, and was afraid Baxendala might remember him.

When he reached Maisak he was cursing himself for not staying. Winter in the Gap made winter in the Kapenrungs seem mild.

The Maisak garrison would not let him inside. El Nadim had assailed them with a hundred wiles. They were not willing to take a chance on so much as one little fat man.

He hunched his shoulders and trudged eastward, his donkey following faithfully.

Winter was not so harsh east of the mountains. He left the snow behind before he reached the ruins of Gog-Ahlan.

The nearby traders' town had become a ghost village haunted by a few optimistic souls trying to hold on till war's end. The fat man got good and drunk and warm there.

El Nadim, the townspeople assured him, had established his headquarters in Throyes. "Curious," Mocker mused, tramping down the road leading to that city. "Time and greed make friends of old enemies."

El Murid's faith had swept Throyes like the plague. The resulting changed political climate baffled the fat man. He did not understand religion at all. For him gods were, at best, excuses for failure.

He found Throyes in a state of high excitement, eager, already spending the riches el Nadim's troops would bring home. He was amazed. This was the Host of Illumination, in its halcyon days, all over again.

And he was supposed to stop it? Alone?

It looked like trying to stop an earthquake with his bare hands.

Nevertheless, he went to work.

He had been to Throyes before. Memories of him might not have faded. He changed careers, becoming, instead of a con artist, thief, and street mummer, a faith healer.

The eastern part of El Murid's empire was more tolerant than the rest. El Nadim had made no effort to exterminate its wizards and occultists. In fact, he maintained a personal astrological adviser.

The fat man's little devil eyes glowed when he heard that. A chink! An avenue of approach. If he could eliminate that astrologer and appear at the right moment....

He was out of practice. And the eastern astrology differed from the western.

He located an old woman willing to tutor him in exchange for his faith-healing tricks.

Getting the patter down and becoming deft took three weeks. He was beginning to fear he would not get near el Nadim in time. Elements of the eastern army were drifting west already, into Hammad al Nakir.

There remained the problem of approach. No street corner stargazer was going to get past el Nadim's guards.

Eliminating the general's starry-eyed adviser beforehand was out. He was a mystery man. Nobody knew who he was or what he looked like. His very existence was little more than a rumor. Some people thought he was an invention of el Nadim's enemies, meant to discredit him with El Murid.

Whatever, getting close quickly had become the priority.

The parting was almost painful, but Mocker finally turned loose some of Haroun's money. A tailor outfitted him in superb imitation of a sorcerer's apprentice. Another gentleman, of less savory profession, forged him letters of introduction, in Necremnen, over the dread signature Aristithorn.

Aristithorn was a Necremnen wizard. His reputation was not a pleasant one. El Nadim would have to become very suspicious before bothering him with authentication requests.

Everything was ready. His excuses for vacillating had been exhausted. He had to move or confess himself a coward. He had to march up to the sentries outside el Nadim's headquarters and start lying, or to forget Damo, Gouch, and his promises to Haroun.

He did not tuck his tail and steal away. He marched.

His costume made an impressive rotundity of him. Walking tall and arrogant, he seemed to rise above taller men. Curious eyes followed him, wondering, *Who is that important young man?*

He hoped.

He presented himself and his letters. He told the sentries, "Self, am called Nebud, apprentice primus to Lord Aristithorn, Mage of Prime Circle, Prince of Darkling Line, Lord of Foul Hills and Master of Nine Diabolisms. Am sent to Lord el Nadim by same, to assist in great work."

He spoke with all the hauteur he could muster, fearing the soldiers would laugh. Even his toes were shaking.

They did not laugh. Aristithorn was no joke. But neither did they seem impressed. Their senior disappeared briefly. He returned with an officer who asked a lot of questions. Mocker responded with odds and ends from his carefully rehearsed store of answers. The officer passed him on to a superior, who also asked questions.

And so on, and so on, till the fat man forgot his fear in his preoccupation with keeping his lies straight.

He thought himself free of preconceptions about el Nadim, but was not prepared for the creature who received him. The man was almost a dwarf. He was not old, but so hunched away from the world that oldness seemed to envelope him. He shook almost constantly. He looked no one in the eye. He stammered when he spoke.

This was a mighty general? This was the genius who had conquered the east? This little guy was scared of his own shadow.

This little guy had a mind. The Scourge of God had had faith in that. And from beyond timidity a man's brain had brought forth the miracle, uniting the middle east virtually without bloodshed.

El Nadim had to be taken seriously, no matter his appearance. He had done what he had done.

"I understand you were sent by the infamous Necremnen, Aristithorn."

Not sure if he were being interrogated, Mocker did not speak.

"I received no prior warning of your arrival. I did not request your presence. The wizard isn't one of my allies. So why are you here?" El Nadim seemed almost apologetic.

"Self, have asked self same question since moment Lord Aristithorn informed self that self would be coming to Throyes. Wizard is master of closed mouth. But was very explicit in orders. Aid el Nadim in all ways possible, as if same were true master of self, for period of one year, then return to Necremnos. Opinion of self: Master is well-known for interest in international affairs. Also for despite of problems born of needless conflict. Is aficionado of Old Empire. Would suspect Lord will ask self questions to decide if El Murid and movement of same are worthy heirs to mantle of Ilkazar."

"I see. Some of my brethren in the Faith would consider that an insult to our Lord. A Necremnen wizard judging his fitness to found the New Empire. Moreover, the Disciple has banned all traffic with their ilk."

"Self, would think that time has come for same to recognize reality. Will need help of thaumaturgic nature, absolute, to achieve temporal goals. Is fact. Western kings and captains have been petitioning western wizards for years. Now same are beginning to see El Murid as genuine threat, same being inflexible in hatred for Wise. Same have voted to ally with enemies of Disciple come summer should Host of Illumination manage big success early."

El Nadim smiled a secretive smile, then frowned, looking over Mocker's shoulder. He seemed both amused and slightly puzzled. And Mocker was slightly amazed when the man said, "We've heard something of the sort ourselves. Frankly, I'm worried. But the Disciple isn't. Yet your sources among the Wise would be better than ours."

Mocker gulped. Had he made up a truth out of whole cloth?

"But what could you do for me?" el Nadim asked. "That my captains and astrological adviser cannot?"

"Am only apprentice, admitted. Still, am skilled in numerous minor wizardries and expert at various divinations. Could assist adviser."

El Nadim's eyes narrowed.

"Liar!" someone squealed behind Mocker.

He began turning. Too late. The blow smashed his rising hand back against the side of his skull. Head spinning, he dropped to his knees, then pitched forward at el Nadim's feet.

He could not see. He could not move. He could scarcely hear. He could not curse the malicious fate that had brought him to this improbable pass.

"That's enough, Feager!" el Nadim shouted. "Explain yourself."

"He's a fraud," said Mocker's one-time companion Sajac, the general's half-blind astrologer. "A complete fraud."

This can't be happening, Mocker thought. The old man could not have survived that fall. Yet he had. So why hadn't time finished him by now?

Mocker should have understood necessity. He was its child himself. Crawling from the Roë, battered and no longer able to compel someone to care for him, Sajac had had to adjust to survive. The need had had a remarkably rejuvenating and regenerating effect.

"Explain," el Nadim insisted.

Mocker could neither move nor speak, but his debility and pain did not prevent him from being amused. Sajac would not expose him. By doing so he would betray himself.

"Uh...." Sajac said. "He was my assistant once. He tried to murder me."

Mocker was coming back. He croaked, "Is partial truth, Lord. Was traveling companion of same long ago. More like slave, in truth."

His remark initiated a battle of wits and half-truths. Student and teacher ingeniously skirted betraying themselves. And Mocker gradually got the better of it.

He knew El Murid's law. It shielded children well. He kept describing the maltreatment he had suffered at Sajac's hands. The old man could but answer his charges with lies. El Nadim sensed them.

"Enough!" the general snapped, for the first time sounding like a commander. "You each hold some of the right. And neither of you is telling the whole truth. Feager, I won't anger Aristithorn needlessly."

Mocker sighed, smiling. He had won a round. "Self, am grateful for confidence, Lord. Shall endeavor to requite same with quality of service."

El Nadim summoned a lackey. The man led Mocker to the finest room he had ever seen. Sequestered there, he went around and around and around in his mind, trying to figure out how Sajac could have survived. And how he could finish what he had started without getting himself shoved six feet under.

He would have to stay a quick step ahead of the old man.

He ought to say the hell with it. He had done his share in Ipopotam and with Yasmid. Yasmid. What the devil had become of the girl? Haroun had made her disappear…. He imagined human bones scattered among the trees somewhere in the high Kapenrungs.

He received a summons from el Nadim next morning. "I want a divination," the general told him.

Mocker was puzzled. "Divination, Lord? What sort? Self, am poorly skilled as necromancer, entrail-reader, suchlike. Am best with stars, tarot, ching sticks."

"Feager gave me a reading earlier. Concerning my enterprise in the west. I want a second opinion. Even a third and fourth if you're willing to pursue more than one method."

"Will need to spend much time obtaining particulars to properly consult stars," Mocker said. "Preferring not to take word of colleague for same. Understand? So, for moment, we try cards, maybeso, same being quickest and easiest under circumstances."

He drew the book of plaques from within his robes, offered them to el Nadim. "Touch, Lord. Take. Mix up good, thinking questions while doing same."

El Nadim glanced at the expressionless guards spaced around the chamber walls. The Hand of the Law should not be seen flouting it.

The guards stared into nothing, as they always did.

El Nadim took the deck. He touched. He mixed. He returned the cards. Mocker hunkered down and began laying them out at the general's feet.

He had five cards down. His heart hammered. The sixth was a long time coming.

It was another bad one. He glanced up. Did he dare start over?

Subsequent cards made a worse picture still.

He could not lie outright. El Nadim might know something about reading the tarot.

"Bad, eh?"

"Not good, Lord. Great perils lie ahead. Self, would guess same not to be insuperable, but very unpredictable. Would like to do astrologic chart now, stars being more exact."

"That bad? All right. Ask your questions."

El Nadim's stars were no better than his cards. Mocker was sure Sajac had derived similarly bleak forecasts; el Nadim had sensed it and had hoped that an alternate divination would prove more hopeful.

"Nevertheless," el Nadim mused after the fat man had reported his findings. "Nevertheless, we're going. Tomorrow. El Murid himself has commanded it."

He seemed so sad and resigned that Mocker momentarily regretted having to make his prophecies become fact.

There were always good men among the enemy, and el Nadim was one of the best among today's foe. He was a genuinely warm, caring, and just man. It was his humanity, not his battlefield genius, that had melded the middle east into a semblance of the Old Empire. He truly believed, in his gentle way, in El Murid's Law—and he possessed the will and might to enforce it.

The disease of nationalism had not yet infected the east. El Nadim's vision of Empire met needs there that had died long since in the fractious west.

Mocker could see that. Perhaps el Nadim saw it. But Al Rhemish did not. El Murid expected his general to plunge into an alien civilization, comprised of scores of divers cultures and kingdoms, and repeat a success he had wrought in an area where only three significant cultures existed.

"Foredoomed," Mocker muttered as he dogged el Nadim through Throyes' western gate. El Nadim would find suasion and right dealing of little value beyond the Kapenrungs. The lords of the west spoke and understood only one language, shared only one reality, one right, and the sword was its symbol.

Each day the fat man grew more nervous. Sajac lurked like death in the shadows, a constant reminder that the past has a way of coming back. To the west there were Invincibles who might remember him, who had less to lose than did the old man.

Sajac made his move after a lulling week.

Mocker guided his mount off the trail, swung down, hiked his robe, and squatted. And it was while he was in that inelegant pose that the Dark Lady reached out and tried to tap his shoulder.

A foot crunched gravel. A shadow moved swiftly, like nothing of the desert.

The fat man moved faster, diving, rolling, and springing to his feet with blade in hand.

The assassin, a young Throyen soldier, gaped. No human being ought to move that fast, let alone a fat man.

Mocker moved in. His blade danced in the sunshine flinging sprays of reflected light. Steel sang its song meeting steel. Then the soldier was staring forlornly at an empty hand.

"Self, am perplexed," Mocker said, forcing the man to sit on a rock. "Am beset by epical quandary. By all rights, should slay attacker as example to vituperative old man who sent same. Not so? Terrify greedy instantly? But am afflicted by disease called mercy. Will even withhold curse of revenge…." A wicked smile danced across his round face. "No! Will not withhold same."

He began to whoop and holler and dance, though his sword's point remained unerringly centered on the soldier's Adam's apple. He howled out a few spirited, obscene tavern songs in guttural, fractured Altean while gesturing as if summoning up the Lords of Darkness.

"There. Should do job. Have set curse of leprosy, my friend, same being very specific."

The soldier flushed. He could imagine no worse fate.

"Very specific," Mocker reiterated. "Same becomes incumbent only when recipient tells lie." He laughed. "Understand? One lie and curse begins to take effect. Within a few hours skin yellows. Within a few days flesh starts to fall away. Smell grows like stench of old corpse. Listen! Should lord general summon erstwhile assassin as witness, report whole truth of situation, exact. Otherwise…."

The fat man whirled, sheathed his blade, caught his mount, finished his wayside business, then returned to his place in the column. He kept bursting into giggles. That fool soldier had fallen for it.

The fat man muttered and cursed as the column approached Al Rhemish. His companions fussed and bothered. They were eager to visit the Holy City and Shrines. Mocker sweated constantly. This was the critical period. It was here that he was most likely to encounter a familiar face. It was here that Sidi now resided. It was here that Sajac would find his best opportunities.

El Nadim's army assembled on the lip of the bowl, looking down on Al Rhemish.

"Where are the divisions I sent ahead?" el Nadim asked no one in particular. They were nowhere to be seen. They were supposed to have awaited him here.

A lone Invincible came galloping across the bridge and upslope. "You're not to enter Al Rhemish," he shouted "Our Lord bid me tell you to go on westward."

"But…."

"That is the command of the Disciple." The messenger seemed uncomfortable. He was relaying orders he did not himself approve.

"We've come a long way. We want to pay homage at the Shrines."

"Perhaps when you're returning."

"What's going on? What's happened?" el Nadim demanded. "Something has, hasn't it?"

The messenger inclined his head slightly, but said only, "The Disciple has barred outsiders from the city." He indicated the bowl's south rim. "Even the pilgrims, who are old folks, women, and children."

"Even his generals? Will he see me?"

"No. I'm to offer his apologies and tell you that you'll understand in time.

He said to remain steadfast in the Faith. He said his prayers will go with you."
The messenger then wheeled and descended into the valley.

El Nadim waited a long time before saying, "We'll camp here tonight. He may change his mind."

There was no change of heart. Al Rhemish ignored the army's existence.

Mocker sighed after the column began wending through the desert once more. He was safe. He could concentrate on Sajac.

The crazy old man was careful. He had received a convincing lesson in Argon.

Mocker found scorpions in his boots. He found a poisonous snake in his bedroll. A flung stone narrowly missed his mount while he was negotiating a particularly nasty piece of mountainside trail. He found doctored water in his canteen, and feared his food would be poisoned if he stopped eating from the soldiers' common mess.

Sajac had his bullies. They made sure Mocker got nowhere near him.

The problem became a challenge. Poison would have suited Mocker's sense of propriety perfectly. An agent that would cause heart failure....

Heart failure. Sajac was old. His heart might be weak. Scare him to death? Using sympathetic voodoo magic like he and Gouch had seen in Ipopotam?

Notions and schemes fluttered through his head like drunken butterflies. He was supposed to be a sorcerer, wasn't he? Why didn't he get with the hoodoo and the mojo and make the old bastard think he was on his way out? Sajac could never be sure he *wasn't* Aristithorn's apprentice.

In minutes Mocker was telling a soldier, "Self, am tired of constant sniping." Sajac's attempts had become common knowledge. "Look!" He held up a hideous, venomous little lizard that looked more like an example of primitive beaded artwork than it did an animal. "Found same snoozing in donkey pack. Patience is at end. Am casting curse taught by master Aristithorn. Will gnaw heart of squamous old buzzard. Is slow curse. Sometimes takes months to kill victim. Beauty is in torture of waiting. Will end come immediately? Tomorrow? Will hurry to settle affairs maybe hasten same? Hee-hee. Was exceedingly difficult of learning said curse, but am glad today. Is even more beautiful because same curse can be hastened any time with proper cabalistic processes. Friend, self is not cruel. Do not like harming even monsters like bilious little villain of lizard. But, and am ashamed to admit same, am going to enjoy watching agonized waiting of nasty old backstabber."

He careened around the force making similar declamations. He let his imagination run with the nastiness of the curse, till he was sure Sajac would hear of it from a dozen sources and be scared out of his pantaloons.

Still.... The news might have no impact. The old man was as cynical a nonbeliever as he.

Once his excitement waned he became certain that he had chosen the silliest possible means of striking back.

Yet Sajac began watching his every move, squinting his myopic little eyes. Mocker grinned a lot, wondered aloud when the end would come, organized a betting pool that would pay the man guessing the correct moment, and occasionally pretended to be aggravated enough to consider hurrying matters. Sajac began to cringe, to become defensive and irritable. His forecasts for el Nadim degenerated.

"See?" Mocker crowed all over camp. "Curse is devouring wicked old man."

El Nadim became critical of Sajac's work. He had Mocker second-guess every reading. Which only made the old man more nervous.

There were no more attempts on Mocker's life. Sajac shifted to attempts at negotiation and bribery. The fat man dismissed these with derisive laughter.

Sajac lost his eyesight suddenly, completely. Mocker moved closer, began tormenting him verbally. The old man's protectors faded away, sensing the shift of power.

The Kapenrungs were in sight. When el Nadim summoned him, Mocker fought down his evil glee and began marshaling the courage needed to lead the general astray. Blind, Sajac could no longer dispute his readings.

The general did not want a divination. He said, "I want you to stop persecuting the old man. He's tormented enough, don't you think? El Murid teaches us not to answer cruelty with cruelty, nor to prey upon the old simply because they're weak. You may have been justified in what you did in Argon. You saw yourself trapped. But that excuse no longer obtains."

Mocker sputtered in protest.

"Go. And cease tormenting that pathetic old man."

Mocker went. And, in spite of his hatred, he thought about what el Nadim had said. He took a look at himself. And he was not pleased.

He saw a cruel thing no better than the Sajac he had known back when, feeding its insecure ego on its ability to injure someone weaker.

The fat man was not given to extended introspection. He did not examine himself for long. He simply decided to pretend that Sajac had perished in his leap from Argon's wall.

He caught a taste of the cool breeze off the mountains, grinned, went off to badger one of el Nadim's captains.

When next he presented himself for a reading, he went armed with a crude map. "Lord," he said, "have been on job, guaranteed. Have come up with plan for circumventing dread forecasts of past. Relies on very positive attributes of Hammad al Nakir, for outflanking Fates. Can move too fast for same to keep track. Before same catch on, voila! Here is new general in back pastures of enemies." He waved his map wildly. "Hai! New Empire is victorious! Tiresome war is finished. Self, being genius to suggest plan, receive great reward, am finally able to leave employ of penurious wizard and go into business for self."

"Let's see the map. And let's hear your suggestion. Not about it."

Mocker surrendered the map. "See how Kapenrungs cut across to west, forming barrier? Suppose way could be found through same? Exiting in Tamerice, crossing Altea, Host could be over Scarlotti and far north before enemy spies realize same is coming. Same spies will be far to west watching traditional routes from Sahel. Not so? So...."

"There are no passes through the Kapenrungs. And I don't have the whole army here even if there were." El Nadim's force, a quarter of his army, numbered twenty thousand.

"Latter is immaterial," Mocker said. "Spies can dog forerunner forces, thinking same are whole army, thinking new general is there. As to pass, self did not come unprepared to reveal same." He sketched a jagged line with a pudgy finger. "So." The route was identical to that he and Yasmid had followed earlier. And it passed within fifteen miles of Haroun's present main camp.

"Last night, while army slept, notion came upon self. Ran round it like silly dog on leash, getting tangled and snarled. Then decided to take first-hand look. Hai! Leaving body was difficult of accomplishment. So much body to leave. But managed same, and flew to inspect mountains, discovering route just outlined. Will be difficult of crossing, assuredly, but not impossible of achievement."

He had concluded that he'd never manage to eliminate el Nadim himself. Not with any hope of getting out alive. So he had decided to lead the man into a position where Haroun could do his own killing. The presence of the army would be noted quickly if it entered the mountains.

"I like the basic notion. As to its practicality.... Let me think it over."

Did the general know these were Haroun's mountains? Mocker hoped not. But el Nadim never said anything about bin Yousif. It was almost as if he were pretending Haroun did not exist.

And what of these wild rumors they had been hearing, about Haroun and Beloul being dead, having been betrayed by Shadek el Senoussi? If they were true he might be guiding el Nadim to a toothless tiger, truly giving him the surprise maneuver he was promising.

"Must waste no time, Lord. Point of entry to mountains is near."

"I can read a map. Go away and let me think."

Next day the van turned northward. And Mocker found himself riding point, charged with showing the way and using his alleged thaumaturgic powers to anticipate danger.

Days crawled by. The mountains rose ever higher. The air grew colder as the wintry north wind leaked between the peaks. They began to encounter snow. The fat man's nerves grew ever more frazzled.

They were out there watching. He could feel the touch of their eyes. He had seen signs no one else had recognized.

What would he do when the hammer fell? One side or the other, or both, would label him traitor.

Even he was surprised when the boulders began thundering down the canyon walls.

Men shouted. Horses reared and bolted. Boulders started knocking people around. Arrows zipped out of the sky. Mocker flung himself off his mount and scurried to the shelter of an overhang. He crouched there momentarily, getting the lay of his surroundings. Then he started creeping up the canyon. He wanted to disappear before anyone noticed.

He glanced back after he had crawled three hundred yards.

The canyon floor was a mess, and the mess was getting worse. Yet el Nadim's soldiers were counterattacking. They were headed upslope, darting from the protection of one tree to the next. El Nadim himself had arrived and, oblivious to stones and arrows, was whipping them on.

He spied Mocker among the rocks ahead. He intuited what had happened.

His arm snapped up. A finger pointed. His mouth worked. A dozen soldiers started toward the fat man.

The fat man hiked the skirts of his robe and ran.

TWENTY
END OF A LEGEND

"Suppose they get past Reskird?" Haaken asked.

"Suppose. Suppose. All the time with the supposes," Ragnarson growled. "If they do, then we've wasted our time."

He was shaky and irritable. He had looked el Nadim over and now doubted his trap would work.

Kildragon, commanding a force of Royalists, was to attack el Nadim's van in a narrow place ten miles to the north. He was to use boulders and arrows till el Nadim decided he could not break through. When the general turned back he was to find escape to Hammad al Nakir cut off here. Ragnarson had assembled six thousand men, rushed them through the mountains, and gotten them into hiding barely in time to let el Nadim pass. Now he was digging in.

"Let's check the works," he said. He could not stand still. He was too worried about Kildragon.

"They should've reached Reskird yesterday," Haaken said, following his brother. "We should've heard something by now."

"I know." Ragnarson slouched, stared into a narrow trench.

At that point the canyon was two hundred yards wide and had a relatively level floor. Its walls were sheer, towering bluffs of granite. There was a small, cold stream and dense stands of pine. Ragnarson's line lay across a meadow before one such stand.

He had assembled his infantry there and backed them with a few hundred Royalist horsemen. The remaining Royalists were either with Kildragon or hidden in a side canyon slightly to the north.

"The golden bridge," Haaken muttered. "Not to mention that we're outnumbered."

"I know." Ragnarson went on worrying. The golden bridge was a Hawkwind concept. It meant always showing the enemy an apparent route of flight. Men who saw no escape from a poor battle situation fought more stubbornly.

Ragnarson's dispositions left el Nadim with no easy avenue of flight. And the general had the numbers.

"Here comes Reskird's messenger."

The courier reported that Kildragon was holding. But, he announced, el Nadim had smelled the trap. A quarter of his force was headed south to make sure of his line of withdrawal.

"Maybe that's a break," Bragi mused. "If we can finish part of them before the main mob shows...."

"We'll just tip our hand," Haaken replied.

"No. Send somebody over to tell those Royalists to stay out of sight unless this first bunch starts to whip us."

Haaken's courier vanished into the side canyon just in time. El Nadim's horsemen appeared only minutes later.

Bragi's men scurried around, getting to their places. El Nadim's men halted. They sent skirmishers forward. Nothing happened after the probe had been repulsed.

"Sent for instructions," Ragnarson guessed. "Should we stir them up?"

"Let's don't ask for trouble," Haaken replied. "They look too professional."

The casterners pitched camp in the Imperial fashion, surrounding themselves with a trench and palisade. They were equally professional in mounting their morning attack.

The westerners repelled them easily. The easterners retired to their encampment and stayed put till the balance of el Nadim's force joined them.

"Guess they found out what they wanted to know," Bragi said when it became clear that no new attack would develop.

The damned easterners bounced from rock to rock like knobbly old mountain goats. The rate they were gaining, Mocker thought, he might as well sit down, save his breath, and be fresh when they arrived.

He scooted between two jagged hunks of granite and headed for the nearest tangle of brush. He would ambush them. He squirmed in with the grace of a panicky bear cub.... And found himself face to face with a Royalist warrior.

The man knocked his sword away. Glee animated his leathery face. "You!" He grabbed Mocker's clothing and yanked him forward onto his belly. He jumped astride. The fat man protested, but without much volume.

"You cheated me one time too many, tubbo."

El Nadim's harriers charged into view. Not seeing their quarry, they paused to talk.

A blade caressed Mocker's throat. "One peep, fat boy, and it's all over."

Mocker lay very still. The soldiers began probing hiding places.

An arrow streaked off the mountainside. Then another and another. The soldiers fled whence they had come.

"Bring them out of there," someone ordered. He had an abominable accent.

Mocker felt his captor tense, torn between obedience and a lust to use his knife. Mocker's life hung in the balance. The balance needed tilting. "Hai!" he moaned. "Self, thought same was goner. Thought knives of pestilent foemen would drink blood sure. Months of labor to bring same into trap wasted in blood. Would have been sad end for one of great heroes of war against madman of desert."

The someone who had spoken waded into the brush. Mocker's setting hen rose from his plump nest. A boot pushed against the fat man's side, rolled him over. He stared up into the unfriendly face of Reskird Kildragon.

"Hai! Arrived in nick, old friend. Not so happy about self anymore, men of el Nadim. For some strange reason have decided former master magician betrayed same into trap." He forced a laugh.

"I'm no friend of yours, fat man. Get up."

Mocker rose. Kildragon bent and recovered his sword. Mocker reached for it. The Trolledyngjan refused to yield it. "Sorry. Thank your heaven that I'm going to go against my better judgment and let you live. Come on. Before your playmates come back with help."

"Is wise decision," Mocker averred. "Self being intimate friend of Royalist chieftain Haroun. Like so." He held up a pair of chubby fingers pressed tightly together. "Same would be displeased to learn that old friend and chiefest agent met misfortune at hand of professed ally."

"I wouldn't lean on his protection too much, was I you," Kildragon told him, urging him up the mountainside with an ungentle shove. "The last word we had was that he's dead. That's been months, and nobody has said different since."

The fat man shivered despite the warmth generated by his exertion. He was going to have to get himself onto his best behavior. A lot of these people would be hunting excuses to pound him.

It just was not fair. Everywhere he went somebody was out to get him. The whole damned universe had it in for him.

Kildragon herded him up and across the mountainside and before long he was half-convinced the man was trying to work him to death. "Sit down," the Guildsman told him suddenly, planting him on a boulder. "And stay put."

He stayed put, more or less, for the next four days.

That mountainside provided a fair view of the canyon floor He watched el Nadim make repeated, valiant, futile efforts to break through. The general finally reached the not unreasonable conclusion that doing so would not profit him anyway. It was well known that there were no decent passes through the Kapenrungs. Why believe one assertion of a man proven faithless in other ways?

Mocker tried to determine the fate of Sajac by examining the dead after el Nadim departed. He found no sign of the old man. Prisoners could not tell him anything. His Royalist companions would not deign to answer his questions.

He needed to know. Despite el Nadim's admonitions, blind or not, he did not want that nasty creature skulking around his backtrail.

"Woe!" he muttered after el Nadim cleared out. "Back along same old route. Is becoming boring routine, back and forth through mountains. Self, am more profound, being of broader adventurousness, wishing to see new lands. Same motivation brought self to west in first place."

He had lost his audience before he began. What was the point of a declamation when nobody was going to listen?

Kildragon's force followed el Nadim's rearguard without any great enthusiasm or alacrity. Four days of heavy fighting seemed an adequate contribution to the cause.

Four of them rode stumbling horses. Haroun and Beloul walked. They took turns falling and helping one another up.

They were the survivors, and not a one was not wounded and perilously exhausted. The Invincibles had hunted hard and well, and hunted still, but they had shaken the white robes for a while. The Invincibles needed a day or two to work themselves up for a charge into the enemy mountains.

"I heard a trumpet," el Senoussi muttered from his animal's back. "A long way off."

"The bugle of the angels, maybe," Beloul replied. "We're halfway between back there and nowhere. They never even heard of bugles out here."

El Senoussi was right. An hour later everyone could hear the occasional braying of trumpets and what sounded like a distant crash of battle. Sound carried well through the cold, still canyons.

"It's a big one," Haroun guessed. "Up here? How can that be?"

"Been seeing a lot of horse droppings since we got into this canyon," Beloul said. "Too many for our side."

The others had noticed too. No one had wanted to be first to mention a bad sign.

"We're getting close," el Senoussi observed a little later. "Someone ought to go take a look before we walk into it."

"He's right. Beloul, take Hassan's horse."

Beloul groaned but did as he was told. He returned soon. "The Guildsmen and our warriors have part of el Nadim's army trapped," he reported. "It looks nasty."

"Who's winning?"

"I didn't ask."

Haroun groaned as he climbed to his feet. He ached everywhere. "What I need is a week to do nothing but sleep, but I guess I'd better show my face. Heaven knows what they've been thinking since we disappeared."

His companions sighed and slowly clambered into their saddles.

It took but a moment to discern what Ragnarson had done. He had drawn a kill line across the easterners' path and was trying to wipe them out.

"It didn't work like I figured," Ragnarson admitted once nightfall provided a moment to visit.

"How so?" Haroun's followers were ecstatic about his return. He was using the meeting as an excuse to escape their attentions.

"That charge from the rear. I don t know if it was ill-conceived or just came too soon. It looked like it was going to work, then el Nadim made a comeback. He's got your men trapped in that side canyon now. And there isn't a damned thing I can do."

Haroun replied, "They can abandon their animals and climb out. If they don't, they're so stupid they deserve whatever happens. I'll go over myself come morning."

"Don't know if we can hold *here*."

"Think positive. You've gained us another victory. Maybe our most important since Alperin. El Nadim himself is trapped here. Imagine the impact. He's El Murid's last great general. The hero of the east. The end of the legacy of the Scourge of God. Mowaffak Hali, too, is a tale that's reached its end. He made it to Al Rhemish, then the gangrene took him. The Disciple was furious."

Ragnarson grinned. "We wondered what happened to the sonofabitch. We ragged his gang pretty good, but couldn't find him afterwards. So tell us about your pilgrimage to the Holy City. I take it your scheme didn't work."

"We came this close." Haroun held up a thumb and forefinger spaced an inch. "Then the Disciple used his amulet. Damned near wiped us out." He told the story to a quiet, sometimes incredulous audience.

"Get some sleep," Ragnarson advised when he finished. "I'll get you up if we have to run for it."

"Thoughtful of you."

Haroun and his traveling companions slept through most of the next day's fighting.

The Royalists fought like a new army. Their King had returned. Fate was on their side.

El Nadim's men fought well. It did them no good. They could not break out. Ragnarson began talking about asking el Nadim to surrender.

A refreshed Haroun disabused him of that daydream. "Some of his least enthusiastic soldiers might sneak over and give up. Don't look for him to. He's a true believer. He'll fight till we kill him. Or till he wins."

"I don't know if we can whip them," Bragi said. "We might end up getting hurt worse than they do if we try."

Haroun shrugged. "You're the one put his back to the desert."

El Nadim mounted his most ferocious attack yet. The Guild lines bowed and buckled and would have broken but for a timely rear attack by Kildragon.

Spent, the easterners· withdrew into their encampment. Not a man was seen for days. "Looks like we play see who gets hungry first," Ragnarson said.

"I damned sure ain't going after them. My momma's stupid babies all died young."

A Throyen officer came out under a white flag five days later. He asked for bin Yousif.

"News gets around, doesn't it?" Haaken muttered.

"Seems to," Bragi replied. He and his brother watched over bin Yousif's shoulder.

"We're ready to talk terms," the Throyen told Haroun.

"Why? You came out here looking for a fight. You get one and right away you want to call it off."

"There's no point fighting when there's nothing to gain. Were we to win, you'd just fade into the mountains. Were you to win, you'd have spent most of your men. It would be best for everyone if we disengaged."

Haroun translated for Bragi, who could not follow the Throyen dialect. Ragnarson said, "This guy is dangerous. He's got an off-center way of looking at things. Keep him talking."

Haroun asked questions. He translated the answers. "He's pretty much said it, Bragi. We quit fighting and go our separate ways."

"Where's the profit? He must have a good reason for this. Like maybe el Nadim is dead or hurt. Push him."

"Don't be too eager. They've still got the numbers." Nevertheless, Haroun pressed.

The Throyen responded, "I'll come see how you feel in a week."

Haroun translated. "I pushed too hard. I think they'd give up their weapons if we let them go."

"What's to keep them from hiking around the Kapenrungs and joining up with the rest of their mob?"

"What's to keep you from wiping them out once they give up their weapons?"

"We're Guildsmen. We don't operate that way."

"Maybe they have a sense of honor too. Look, all they're going to do is sit and wait us out. Right?"

"Looks like. And yes, we'd be better employed somewhere else."

"Ask for their parole. Weapons and parole. That's good enough for me." Haroun planned an active summer campaign. Having seen the chaos in Al Rhemish, he believed the tide of war had turned. He wanted to get into the thick and make so much noise his claims would catch the ears of all his allies.

"All right," Bragi said.

Haroun resumed dickering with the easterner.

El Nadim's force filed out of the trap next morning, leaving their arms in their encampment. Ragnarson and bin Yousif watched closely, ready for any treachery.

Ragnarson was depressed. "Another inconclusive contest, my friend. When are we going to make some real progress?"

Haroun insisted, "We've set another stone in El Murid's cairn. Be patient. This summer, or next summer at the latest, his house of sticks will fall. There's nothing to hold it together." He was bubbling. Could the Second Empire long endure now that its last hero had fallen?

Ragnarson believed it could. "It's not as easy as you pretend, Haroun. I keep telling you, it's not just a few men. But my big problem is I don't like what trying to stop them has done to us."

"Done to us? It hasn't done anything."

"If you believe that, you're blinder than I thought."

"What?"

"I don't know you well enough to tell about you. You're a closed person, and you've lived this all your life. But I can see what it's done to my brother. Haaken is a good mirror that shows me what it's done to me. I'm twenty, and I'm an old man. Anymore, my only concern is the next battle, and I don't much care about that. I'm just staying alive. There's more to this world. I can remember a time when I was supposed to get married next summer. I can't remember the girl's face, though. I've forgotten the dreams that went with her. I live from day to day. I can't see the end. I can't see it getting any better. You know, I really don't give a damn who sits on the Peacock Throne, or which god gets declared head honcho deity."

Haroun considered Ragnarson thoughtfully. He was afraid Bragi might be right. Megelin would have agreed. His father would not have. It was to their often antagonistic memories and shades that he answered.

They'd certainly lost their illusions, he thought. And maybe more, that they hadn't known they had. Bragi was right about one thing. They were just surviving, trying to get through a winnowing of survivors.

What Bragi didn't see was that it couldn't end till El Murid was overthrown. That beast would never stop fighting. He would do anything to make his mission bear fruit. Anything.

Ragnarson marched toward Hellin Daimiel. The lands through which he passed were preoccupied with spring planting. War was a terror of long ago or far away. There was little evidence of El Murid's occupation.

Each town had its missionary, and each county its imam, trying to convert the unbeliever. They had had their share of luck. Bragi saw scores of new places of worship built in the desert style.

The occupation had had its greatest impact on civil administration. The Disciple's followers had started from scratch in the desert and had brought new concepts with them, bypassing traditional forms. Though the feudal structures persisted, the old nobility was in decline.

Ragnarson found scant welcome along the way. The Disciple's propaganda effort had been successful. People were content with El Murid's Kingdom of

Peace, or at least indifferent to it.

Ragnarson was near the bounds of the former domains of Hellin Daimiel when the rider he had sent ahead returned. The man had gotten through. Sir Tury Hawkwind agreed with Haroun's strategy.

Haroun and his Royalists were somewhere to the south, moving faster. They would deliver the first blow against Hellin Daimiel's besiegers. Curving in from the north, Ragnarson would deliver the follow-up. While the besiegers reeled, Hawkwind would sally with the city garrison.

El Murid's force at Hellin Daimiel was not big, nor was it comprised of the desert's best. Native auxiliaries, old men, warriors injured elsewhere…. Its value was psychological. Haroun figured its defeat would have repercussions far beyond the numbers involved.

Ragnarson encountered fugitive desert warriors while still a day away from the city. Haroun's punch had been sufficient. He and Hawkwind had broken the siege.

"I'll be damned!" Ragnarson swore. "We run our butts off and we're still too damned late. What the hell kind of justice is that?"

Haaken peered at him. He wore what looked like a sneer. "Be grateful for a little good luck, nitwit."

"That any way to talk to your captain, boy?"

Haaken grinned. "Captain for how much longer? We get to the city, you're going to come down a peg or nine. We'll be back with the real Guild. And real Guild officers. No more of this Colonel Ragnarson stuff."

Ragnarson stopped walking. His troops trudged past. He had not thought of that. He was not sure he could handle falling back to corporal. He had been on the loose too long, running things his own way. He watched his men march by. They were not real Guildsmen, despite the standard heading the column. Not one in fifty had ever seen High Crag. Only sixty-seven of his original company survived. They were the officers and sergeants, the skeleton but not the flesh of his little army.

"You planning to make a career of blocking the road?" Haaken asked.

"It just hit me how much has happened since we left High Crag."

"A ton," Haaken agreed. Something struck him. "We haven't been given our allowances for three years. Man, can we ever have a time."

"If they pay us." Suddenly, Bragi's world was all gloom.

He did not find himself deprived of his makeshift army. When he reached Hellin Daimiel, Hawkwind and bin Yousif were already headed south, intent on liberating Libiannin, Simballawein, and Ipopotam. "Guess they're trying to draw strength away from the fighting in the north," he hazarded.

Haaken did not care about the big picture. His attention was taken with the city.

The siege had been long and bitter. Some all-powerful monster of a god had uprooted all the happy, orderly, well-fed citizens of yore and had replaced them with a horde of lean, hard-eyed beggars. The rich merchants, the proud scholars, the bankers and artisans of olden Hellin Daimiel had come into a ghastly promised land. It flowed not with milk and honey but with poverty, malnutrition, and despair.

"What happened?" Ragnarson inquired of a girl not yet too frightened to talk to strangers. He had to explain several times to make her understand that he wanted to know why the city was in desperate shape when the Itaskian naval and mercantile fleets had been supporting the city all along.

"Our money ran out," the girl explained. "They wanted our museum treasures too. They forgot who we are," she declared haughtily. The Daimiellians long had arrogated to themselves the roles of conservators and moderators of western art and culture. "So they send just enough to keep us barely alive."

"Thank you. I taste politics, Haaken."

"Uhm?"

"The Itaskians have destroyed Hellin Daimiel more surely than the Host could have by sacking it. Wearing a mask of charity. That's bloody cruel and cunning."

"What do you mean?"

"Remember Haroun telling about that Itaskian War Minister? He got what he wanted. He's let the siege ruin Hellin Daimiel. And all the time he was probably reminding their ambassadors of the great things Itaskia was doing for them. Maybe that's why Greyfells piddled around."

"Politicians," Haaken said. He expressed an extreme disgust with that word.

"Exactly." Bragi was just as indignant. "Let's see if we can't find someplace to get crazy. I've got three years in the woods to get out of my system."

The vacation lasted only two days. One of Ragnarson's men brought the bad news. "El Murid has left the desert, Colonel. They don't know where he's headed. The Daimiellians are in an uproar. They figure he'll come straight here."

"Damn! Well, let's see if we can't give him a warm welcome."

TWENTY-ONE
HIGHWATER

Hard-eyed, El Murid glared at the pylons bearing the names of those who had died for the Faith. There were too many. Far too many. The obelisks formed a stone forest atop the south lip of the bowl containing Al Rhemish. The presence of his family stelae only worsened his mood.

It had taken a great act of will to lay Sidi beside his mother. He had been tempted to throw his traitorous get to the jackals.

"Esmat."

"Lord?" The physician was not pleased that his master had resumed his pilgrimages to his family's graves.

"The Lord charged me with bringing the Truth to the nations. I've been delegating that task. That is why so many have died. The Lord is reminding me of my vocation."

"I don't follow you, Lord."

"I began alone, Esmat. I was a child dying in the wastes when I was called. I brought the Truth out of the badlands. Hearts opened to it. I used them. I wasted them. I'm alone again. Alone and lost in the Great Erg of the soul. If I remain here again this summer, the entire Host of Illumination will be taken from me. More and bolder bands of assassins will remind me that the time allotted for my work is both borrowed and limited. This summer, Esmat, the Disciple becomes a warrior for the Lord, riding with the Host."

"Lord, you swore never to go to war again."

"Not so, Esmat. I vowed not to determine strategy for the Host. I swore I would leave the management of war to my generals. Assemble us an escort when we go back down."

"As you command, Lord."

"If the Lord calls me before thee, Esmat, lay me down beside Meryem. And if ever Yasmid should be found, let her lie at my other hand."

"So it shall be, Lord. Was there ever any doubt?"

"Thank you, Esmat. Come. Let us gird ourselves, for we face the hour of our trial."

"And the Lord our God, Who is the Lord of Hosts, shall trample thine enemies, O Chosen, and they shall drink the sour wine of their unbelief, and they shall be vanquished."

"Esmat! You amaze me. I thought you indifferent to the Teachings. I didn't know you could see beyond your own small ambitions."

The physician shook. How subtle the Disciple was, chiding him in this gentle way! His transgressions were known! They had been forgiven, but not forgotten. "I'm not well enough known, Lord, and by myself least of all. I'm so foolish I try to be something I'm not."

"That's the curse of humanity, Esmat. The wise man leashes it before it leads him into the shadow where pretensions are of no avail."

"I am a child in the light of thy wisdom, Lord."

El Murid gave him a hard look. Was that quote a gentle mockery?

His venture west did not begin immediately. News of el Nadim's demise delayed it. "The Lord has written the final paragraph of his message, Esmat," he said. "I stand alone on the battlefield, naked to the Evil One. I must wrestle his minions now, as I wrestled the Dark One himself in the Shrines."

"Hardly alone, Lord. The Host of Illumination is more vast than ever before."

"Who will wield it, Esmat?"

"Convene a council of leading men, Lord. Let them name candidates."

"Yes. Good. Gather the right people, Esmat."

He selected Syed Abd-er-Rahman, the man least popular with functionaries who obviously wanted a general they could manipulate. El Murid could not recall ever having met the man or even having heard of him. But he was popular with the military.

El Murid started west two days after he granted the appointment.

The news of his coming swept ahead like a scorching wind. It blew his enemies into shadowed corners. It brought his friends forth. Crowds cheered his passing. In town after town he slowed his progress so he could touch the reaching hands of the Faithful, and bless them and their offspring, and sanctify their new places of worship.

"We'll ignore it," he decided when Esmat brought news of the collapse of the siege of Hellin Daimiel. "Let bin Yousif run himself ragged trying to distract me. His conquests mean nothing. He'll win no new followers. We'll eradicate his bandits after we've dealt with the Evil One's northern minions."

Syed Abd-er-Rahman was energetic. He wasted no time putting his own strategy into effect. He kept el Nadim's eastern army separate from the western, ordering it to advance up the coastline from Dunno Scuttari. The other army he sent directly toward Itaskia, after assembling it in the Lesser Kingdoms. He scattered a dozen smaller divisions between the armies, their mission to drift north unnoted. He fought his first battle before El Murid joined him.

Like so many before, it was inconclusive. Greyfells stalled the western Host without shattering it. The Duke had not yet abandoned hope of a successful treachery.

Abd-er-Rahman had predicated his strategy on the Duke's political tunnel vision.

Hardly had Greyfells blunted the interior thrust than he had to rush west to forestall the coastal. In his absence Rahman rallied the western Host for another thrust.

El Murid joined him at that time.

He attended all the conferences. He listened to all the discussions and studied all the maps. He kept his opinions to himself. Wadi el Kuf still haunted him.

News came that Libiannin had fallen to Hawkwind and bin Yousif. The fighting had been bitter. El Murid shrugged the loss off. "They suffered heavy casualties. Let them spend their strength. If we send more men they'll just flee into the mountains. Let's worry about finishing Itaskia."

Greyfells halted the army on the coast. He had to extend himself to do so. The eastern troops were outnumbered but not war-weary. Their officers were eager to win themselves names.

Abd-er-Rahman started north again.

Greyfells finally recognized the trap. The two armies were going to slap him back and forth like a shuttlecock while Rahman's smaller divisions slipped past and created havoc behind him. If he withdrew and took up a defensive position along the approaches to Itaskia, one or the other army would bypass and cross the Silverbind. If the city itself were threatened he would lose his command and all hope of profiting from it.

He was in a corner, on thin ice, already. He no longer dared visit the city. The mob jeered and threw brickbats. The news from the south, about guerrillas and Guildsmen liberating coastal cities, worsened his position. People wanted to know why bin Yousif and Hawkwind could capture great cities while he could do nothing. Itaskia's allies were near the limit of their patience.

He had to win a big one.

Esmat stole glances hither and thither as he approached his master. There were no witnesses he could detect. "Lord," he whispered, "There's an enemy delegation to see you."

El Murid was startled. "Me?"

"Yes, Lord. The ones who contacted you several years ago."

"That Duke?"

"His people."

"Show them in." This might lead somewhere. If Itaskia's stubbornness could be neutralized.... Endless warfare did no one any good. His dream of greening the desert would never bear fruit if all the empire's energies had to be devoted to reducing intransigent enemies.

The Greyfells proposal remained unchanged. El Murid did not. His readmittance of the shaghûn to the army was but one sign.

"What I'll do," he told the emissaries, "is nominate the Duke viceroy over all the northern territories. Not just Itaskia, but Dvar, Iwa Skolovda, Prost Kamenets, and Shara. He'll have plenipotentiary powers within the scope of the Empire and Faith. In return he must acknowledge the Empire's suzerainty, allow free movement of missionaries, and produce a modest annual subscription for the restoration of the great works of Ilkazar. In time of war or unrest he'll have to produce levies for the defense of the Imperium."

The emissaries looked dubious, though El Murid was practically offering Greyfells an empire within his Empire. They said they would relay the proposal.

The Duke found it better than he had hoped. He was composing his acceptance when events intervened.

Abd-er-Rahman overtook the Itaskians at the Five Circles.

The Five Circles were the remains of a vast prehistoric monument. They formed a cross in the center of a grassy plain astride the main road from Itaskia to the Lesser Kingdoms. The plain was surrounded by hardwood forests. The natives avoided the megaliths. The Power was strong there. Witch covens gathered among them for their bizarre midnight rituals.

Neither Greyfells nor El Murid could halt events once the armies sighted one another. Abd-er-Rahman was anxious to bring the battered Itaskians to battle. He knew one sharp defeat would strip them of their allies. He accepted the plain as a site of battle, though the circles would serve the enemy as strongholds if their formations broke.

He hit fast and hard, sending the whirlwind of his light cavalry first, following with his heavy horse. The northern knights scattered. Rahman's horsemen plowed into the Itaskian infantry. But for the circles, they would have been slaughtered.

The fighting continued till dusk. The Itaskians could not escape. Rahman's men could not overrun the outer circles. Wherever they threatened to do so, troops from the larger central circle sallied in support of their comrades.

El Murid abandoned all thought of negotiation. At the evening council he announced, "Tomorrow we eschew the mundane. Tomorrow I call down the might of the Lord of Hosts and seal the northern doom."

A hundred eyes stared curiously.

El Murid stared back. These men were warriors before they were disciples. Their faith was incidental to their profession. The spirit of the Lord no longer impelled them.

He would refresh their ardor.

"Tomorrow I shall challenge the heathen. I shall show them the wrath of the Lord. I shall smite them with the fire of retribution and leave them weeping for their dark master's protection. I shall set them running like whipped dogs. Shaghûns, attend me."

There were but a handful of the witch-brethren with Abd-er-Rahman's force. They were so few and their wizardry so pitiful, Rahman seldom bothered using them. El Murid spent an hour closeted with them.

Morning came. The Host arrayed itself. The Disciple strode forth clad in purest white. Two Invincibles accompanied him, bearing the standards of the Lord and of the Second Empire. The black-clad shaghûns followed. El Murid halted on a mound a long bowshot from the southernmost circle. The shaghûns formed a shallow crescent cupping him and his standard-bearers.

Enemy faces lined the top of the tumbled rock barrier. The Itaskians had felled the megaliths during the night. The Disciple felt the full weight of their nervousness and fear.

He dropped to one knee, bowed his head, offered up a prayer. Then he rose, surveyed his enemies, flung arms and face toward the sky.

"Hear me, O Lord of Hosts! Thy servant beseechest thee: Empty the cup of thine wrath upon these who cast dung upon thy Truth. Lend thy servant thine immeasurable power that he might requite them for their iniquity. Hear me, O Lord of Hosts!"

Few of his enemies understood who he was or comprehended what he screamed. But they did not need that knowledge to realize that a mighty doom was upon them.

El Murid's amulet blazed, cloaking him in blinding light. Cries of despair rose within the circle. Panic-driven arrows darted toward the man of fire. The Disciple's shaghûns turned the shafts.

El Murid flung his hands downward. Thunder groaned across the sky. The earth trembled. Stones cracked, broke, tumbled, crumbled, flew into the air and plunged down again. Lightning stalked the plain. Men shrieked.

El Murid lifted his arms and flung them down again. Again the sky spoke and hurled down its spears. Again mighty rocks cracked, broke, flew about, collapsed into mounds of gravel. The surviving Itaskians shrieked and wailed and looked for places to run.

El Murid signaled Abd-er-Rahman.

A light horse regiment swept forward. It scoured that circle clean. The men cowering in the other circles were too stunned to support their fellows.

El Murid and his escort stalked to a hummock facing the westernmost circle.

Arrows darkened the sky before the Disciple commenced his prayer. The shaghûns were hard-pressed to turn them. One did crease a standard-bearer as El Murid flung his fiery hands at the world's blue ceiling.

The Host scoured that circle. And the eastern one too. And cheered their Lord almost continuously. At long last this stubborn foe was to be put away.

Some of the men in the northern circle tried to flee. Rahman flung his cavalry after them. They died before they reached the woods, before comrades who could do nothing to save them.

The plain stunk of fear. The Host was showing no mercy at all, even refusing to take knights and lords for ransom.

The Host grew quiet. The Disciple had turned his eye to the central circle, where half the northern army awaited its doom. He took his station atop rubble left from the scouring of the southern circle. The Host crowded up behind him, eager for blood and plunder.

The Duke and his captains were waiting. As the arrows began to fly and the light to surround the Disciple, a dozen bold knights charged.

Rahman sent men to meet them. But not in time. El Murid's shaghûns were compelled to shift their attention to stopping them. The last fell twenty feet from El Murid.

The arrows fell like heavy winter snow while the witch-men were distracted.

The standards went down. Two shaghûns fell. The arrowstorm thickened. The remaining shaghûns could not turn it all.

El Murid's blazing power did not shield him.

His concentration was such that the first shaft bothered him less than a bee's sting. He brought the lightning down. Inside the circle a hundred men died.

A second arrow passed through the Disciple's upraised right hand. Again he brought the fire down. Boulders hurtled about. Men and animals screamed. Rahman's riders moved up close enough to use their short saddle bows.

The third arrow buried itself in El Murid's left breast. Though it missed heart and lung, its momentum spun him around and flung him to the earth just as the lightning came down again and shattered the last of the megaliths protecting Greyfells' army.

Abd-er-Rahman attacked immediately, hoping to finish the enemy before his own men realized what had happened to their prophet. The Host swarmed into the central circle.

Esmat reached his master before the glory of the amulet faded. He shielded his eyes with his hands. "Lord?"

El Murid groaned. He should have been dead. The terrible vitality that had seen him through the desert in his youth and through the hellish aftermath of the defeat of Wadi el Kuf remained with him. Perhaps his amulet assisted. Esmat grabbed the fallen standards. He snarled at the shaghûns, "Help me make a stretcher." The witch-men stared dumbly. "Strip one of the bodies, you nitwits!" He glared toward the central circle.

The melee was wild and bloody. The warriors of the Host continued pouring in. Some quick-witted foeman was howling, "The Disciple is slain!"

Too many warriors saw Esmat and the shaghûns flee with the stretcher. They believed the cries.

Shouting, the physician tried to assemble El Murid's bodyguard. A handful of Invincibles remembered their honor.

Fickle, insane panic filled the Host as it teetered on the brink of final victory. Victory slipped away.

Esmat concealed himself and his master in a woodcutter's cottage ten miles south of the Five Circles. A dozen Invincibles accompanied him. Most remained in the woods watching for enemy patrols. Two he retained for their muscles.

Out in the dusk the Host was in dismayed flight, small bands of warriors flying hither and yon to escape the Itaskians, who were so bewildered by their good fortune they were doing nothing to follow up.

"Hold him!" Esmat snapped. "Forget who he is. We're trying to save a man, not a myth." The white robes remained unconvinced. Esmat argued, "If we don't save him, who will speak for the Lord?"

The Invincibles leaned into it. Esmat began with the simplest arrowhead.

El Murid groaned and screamed.

A sentry burst in. "Can't you keep him quiet?"

Esmat sighed. "The will of the Lord be done." He took drugs from his kit. He had wanted to avoid them. The Disciple had had so much difficulty whipping his addiction.

El Murid bled a lot, but remained too stubborn to die. Esmat removed four steel barbs.

"How soon will we be able to move?" the leader of the bodyguard asked.

"Not soon. He's hard to kill but slow to mend. We might have to stay here for weeks."

The white robe grimaced. "The will of God be done," he whispered.

They stayed put a month. Twice the Invincibles exterminated small Itaskian patrols. They endured. The Disciple banished his despair with repeated pretenses of agony. Esmat gave him drugs out of fear of the Invincibles. His master became an addict once more.

The Host had collapsed. The survivors had fled so swiftly their enemies hadn't been able to overtake them. Abd-er-Rahman had been unable to rally them. But the collapse affected only the one force.

Where there were commanders of will and energy the Faithful hung together. Two of the small divisions penetrated the domains of Prost Kamenets. Another crossed the Silverbind and brought fire and sword to the unguarded Itaskian midlands. The army on the coast, after one savage encounter with the remnants of Greyfells' force, stunned the Itaskians by driving north and occupying their great harbor city of Portsmouth, where they settled in for a siege. Other divisions lurked near Greyfells, harassing his foragers.

A stalemate, of sorts, had been achieved.

Greyfells could not move south while strong formations threatened his homeland. The Faithful hadn't the will to resume the offensive.

In the south, Haroun and Hawkwind continued to whoop from town to castle, cutting a broad swath, rooting out supporters of the Disciple. They captured Simballawein and roared on into Ipopotam.

The military governor of the occupied provinces let them spend their vigor and spirit. Once they were far away, he collected scattered formations and reoccupied Libiannin, putting all unbelievers to the sword.

An overconfident Haroun badgered Hawkwind into racing north to recapture the city.

The trap snapped shut in a narrow valley a day's march from Libiannin. Hawkwind and bin Yousif left eight thousand dead upon the field. They had had only twelve thousand men going in. The survivors managed to get inside the unguarded walls of Libiannin. They were not welcomed as liberators. The enemies leagued them up.

"News of a great victory, Lord," Esmat said, having heard of southern events in the village he had just visited. They were moving south in small stages. "The Royalist and Guild forces were all but destroyed in a battle near Libiannin. The survivors are trapped in the city."

The Disciple was alert and lucid. He saw the ramifications. And yet he could not rejoice.

He had done the Lord's work and the Lord's will and the Lord had betrayed him. The Lord had allowed him to be struck down an instant before the moment of victory. He had endured every possible humiliation, had suffered every possible loss for the Faith.... He had left the corpse of his belief sprawled between the bodies of his standard-bearers.

"Where are we now, Esmat?"

"In Vorhangs, Lord. Just a few days from Dunno Scuttari. We can convalesce there."

"Send a message to the garrison commander. Tell him I'm alive. Tell him to send couriers to all our captains apprising them of that fact. Tell him I want a general armistice declared. Tell him to announce my offer to hold a general peace conference in Dunno Scuttari next month."

"Lord? Peace? What about the new Empire?"

"We'll settle for what we get out of the negotiations."

"We have enemies who won't make peace, Lord."

"The Guild? Bin Yousif's bandits? You said they're all but destroyed. We will invite High Crag, by all means. They must be war-weary enough to give up the sanctions they declared when the Invincibles massacred those old men. But there will be no peace with Royalists. Ever. Not while bin Yousif and I both live.

"Esmat, that battle is all I have left. They've killed everything else. My wife. My babies. Nassef. Even my faith in God and my Calling."

Esmat responded with quotations from his Teachings.

"I was naive then, Esmat. Sometimes hate is all a man has." And maybe it was that way for everyone he had labeled a minion of the Evil One. The drunk, the gambler, the whoremaster: maybe each gravitated to his niche not because of a devotion to evil—but because of some need only an odious life could fulfill. Maybe some men needed a diet rich in self-loathing.

His entrance into Dunno Scuttari made a grand excuse for a holiday. The Faithful turned out in their thousands to weep and cheer as if he had brought them a triumph for the Chosen. There was a threat of carnival in the river-tainted air. The happy-storm was not long delayed. The costumes and masks came out. The bulls were run in the streets. Believer consorted with infidel and shared tears of happiness.

El Murid blessed the revelers from a high balcony. He wore a thin smile.

Esmat wondered aloud at their joy.

"They rejoice not for me but for themselves, Esmat."

"Lord?"

"They rejoice not for any accomplishment, nor for my return. They rejoice because by surviving I've put the mask back over the secret face of tomorrow. I've relieved them of uncertainty."

"Then they'll be disappointed when they find out how much you'll yield to make peace."

The Disciple had decided to defy his God. His mission, he told himself, was to establish the Kingdom of Peace. He had been unable to do that sending men to war....

"What of the painkiller?" he asked as an aside. "Is there a supply?"

"You once called me a confounded squirrel, Lord. We held Ipopotam for years. I acquired enough to last several lifetimes."

El Murid nodded absently. So long as there was enough to divert him from thoughts of his true motive for defying the Lord: pure childish spite for the arrows of betrayal that had fallen upon him at the Five Circles.

He returned to Esmat's earlier question. "They don't care which mask the unknowable wears. They just want it to wear one."

Allied emissaries began arriving two weeks later. "They seem serious this time," the Disciple observed. "Especially Greyfells."

"Perhaps they sense your own determination, Lord," Esmat replied.

"I doubt it." Already they were hard at their backstabbing and undercutting. Yet he was impressed. He would be dealing with men honestly able to make commitments and undertake obligations, all in an air of great publicity. Even the Guild had entered its delegation, captained by the formidable General Lauder. The Itaskians had sent their redoubtable War Minister as well as the slippery Greyfells. Something solid would come out of the sessions.

Within the formal process there was little dissent or maneuver. No one held a position of strength. After a week, El Murid told Esmat, "We're going to get there. We can wrap it in a month. We'll be in Al Rhemish before your old cohorts can put back everything they stole when they heard I was dead." He chuckled.

He had become an easier El Murid, taking a juvenile pleasure in disconcerting everyone with his frankness and new cynicism. People recalled that he was a salt merchant's son and muttered that blood would tell.

"Not long at all, Esmat. The only real thieves are the Itaskians, and they defeat themselves by working at cross-purposes. We'll come out better than I anticipated."

He had concluded a covert, long-term understanding with Duke Greyfells almost immediately. In private, the Duke showed a pragmatic honesty El Murid appreciated.

"And what of the Second Empire, Lord? Do we abandon the dream?"

"Not to worry, Esmat. Not to worry. We but buy a breathing space in which the dream may build new strength. The Faithful carried the Word to the shores of the Silverbind. They have sown the thunder. Those fields will yield up a rich bounty when next the Chosen come harvesting."

Esmat stared at his master and thought, Yes, but.... Who would provide the magnetism and drive? Who would deliver the spark of divine insanity that made masses of men rush to their deaths for something they could not comprehend?

Not you, Lord, Esmat thought. Not you. You can't even sell yourself anymore.

He looked at his master and felt a great sorrow, felt as though something precious had been taken away while he was distracted. He did not know what it was. He did not understand the feeling. He thought himself a practical man.

TWENTY-TWO
LAST BATTLE

Haroun and Beloul stared down at their enemies. The encircling camp grew larger every day.

"This could get damned nasty, Lord," Beloul observed.

"You'd make a great prophet, Beloul." Haroun glanced along Libiannin's crumbling wall. Heavy engines would have no trouble breaching it.

The enemy really needn't waste time on engines. A concerted rush would carry the wall. He and Hawkwind hadn't the men to defend it, and the natives refused to help.

"What's happening, Beloul? Why haven't they attacked? Why hasn't the Itaskian fleet shown? They must know what's going on. They'd want to take us out, wouldn't they?"

He had had no contact with the world for weeks. The last he had heard, El Murid was reported slain in a huge battle with the Itaskians. His hopes had soared like exultant eagles. He had sent out messenger after messenger, till it seemed an endless parade of fishing smacks were leaving harbor, never to be seen again.

"We're marooned, Lord," Beloul said. "The world is getting on with business and has forgotten us. Maybe on purpose."

"But with the Disciple dead…."

"Lord, nobody but us Royalists gives a damn if you ever sit the Peacock Throne. The Itaskians? They're glad to have us howling around down here keeping the Disciple's men busy. But are they going to spend lives for us? It wouldn't profit them."

Haroun grinned weakly. "Have mercy, O Slayer of Illusions."

"Here comes Shadek. He looks like a man about to slay a few dreams."

El Senoussi's face did have a grim cast. Haroun trembled. He smelled bad news.

"A boat came in, Lord," Shadek puffed.

"Well?"

"It brought a Guildsman, not one of our men. He's with Hawkwind now. He had a funny expression when he looked at me. Kind of a sad, aching look. Made me think of a headsman about to swing his sword on his brother."

Haroun's back suddenly felt cold. "What do you think, Beloul?"

"I think we better take care to watch our backs, Lord. I think we're going to find out why our messengers never came back."

"I was afraid you'd say that. I wish I'd pursued my shaghûn studies to the point where I could perform a divination…. Would they really turn on us?"

"Their interests aren't ours, Lord."

"I was afraid you'd say that, too."

Haaken and Reskird looked like men standing at the graveside of a friend suddenly struck down. Ragnarson was so angry he could not speak.

Orders had come. After all these years.

Bragi compelled himself to calm down. "How many people know about this?"

"Just us. And the courier." Kildragon indicated the man who had brought the message from General Lauder.

"Reskird, take that sonofabitch somewhere and keep him busy. Haaken, hustle down to the barracks and sort out everybody who was in our company when we left High Crag. Get them out of the way, then tell the others we've got a full kit formation in two hours. Ready to march."

Haaken eyed him suspiciously. "What are you up to?"

"Let's just say a permanent commission as captain isn't a big enough payoff for selling out a friend. Do what I told you."

"Bragi, you can't...."

"Like hell I can't. I resigned from the Guild five minutes before that guy got here. You and Reskird both heard me."

"Bragi...."

"I don't want to hear about it. You gather up your Guildsmen and hike them up to High Crag. Us non-Guildsmen are going to take a hike of our own."

"I just wanted to say I'm going with you."

Bragi studied him a moment. "Not this time, Haaken. You belong in the Guild. I don't. I've been thinking about this a long time. I don't fit. Not in what it would be in peacetime. I want to do too much that the Guild wouldn't allow. Like lay hands on lots of money. You can't be rich and be a Guildsman. You've got to give it all to the brotherhood. You, you don't need the things I do. You belong. So you just stay. In a couple years you'll have your own company. Someday...."

Ragnarson's voice grew weaker as he spoke. Haaken was looking hurt. Bad hurt. He was trying to hold back tears.

They were brothers. Never had they been separated long. He was telling Haaken it was time they went their own ways. Haaken was hearing that he was not needed anymore, that he was not wanted, that he had been outgrown.

Bragi felt the pain too.

"I have to do this, Haaken. It's going to ruin me with the Guild, but I have to. I don't want to drag you down too. I'll be back after it's over."

"Stop. No more explaining. We're grown men. You do what you have to do. Just go.... Get away...."

Bragi peered at his brother intently. He had injured Haaken's pride. The man behind that taciturn exterior never forgot that he was adopted, never let himself think he was as good as other men. The little rejections became big in his mind.... Best to just end it now, before they said something that would cause real pain. "Gather your men, Haaken. You have your orders." Bragi walked away. There were tears in his eyes too.

He managed to round up enough mounts for his men, more by theft than legitimate means. He hustled his baffled troops out of town before news of the treacherous peace could reach their ears.

His outriders captured an enemy courier almost immediately. "Read this," he ordered his interpreter, handing him a captured dispatch.

"Let's see. All the usual greetings and salutations. To the Captain of the Host at Libiannin…. It's from El Murid himself. Here's the gist. The Disciple is heading south to participate in the final solution to the Royalist problem. His own words. That's it. He probably sent several couriers, just in case."

"Uhm? He would be ahead of his messenger, would he? Boys, we're going to double-hustle now. Let's see if we can't have a little surprise waiting for the sonofabitch."

Haroun placed a gentle, restraining hand on Shadek's elbow. El Senoussi was ready to launch a one-man crusade against Hawkwind's Guildsmen. "It wouldn't do any good, Shadek. They have their orders, like them or not."

The Guildsmen were trooping aboard ships that had come to take them out of the city. An embarrassed and displeased Sir Tury had posted guards to make sure no Royalists joined the evacuation. The guards would not look their former comrades in the eye.

"So it goes, Shadek," Beloul observed. "The waters of politics run deep and dark. Occasionally there has to be a sacrificial lamb."

"Now's a damned poor time for you to go philosophical on us, Beloul," el Senoussi snapped. "Stop jacking your jaw and start finding a way out of this."

"I wonder what El Murid gave up to get us?" Haroun mused.

"I'm sure he gave the Guild and Itaskians their money's worth, Lord."

"I didn't think he cared anymore. He's ignored us lately."

"Maybe getting three-quarters killed gave him a more intimate perspective," Beloul suggested.

"Don't be facetious."

Hawkwind had stretched the letter of his orders and filled them in on current events. His news hadn't been good for the Royalist cause.

Haroun glanced across the far curve of the harbor. A pair of heavily fortified hills stood there. They were connected with the city by a long wall guarding a strip of coast only fifty yards wide. Many smaller ships were beached there. Quietly, Haroun's men were seizing those in hopes some Royalists could follow the Guildsmen to sea.

"How many can we get out?" Shadek asked.

"Maybe a thousand," Beloul replied. "If the Guildsmen's brave rescuers don't stand off the roads and keep us bottled."

Haroun glared at the troopships. "Think the treachery runs that deep?"

Beloul shrugged. "Time will tell, Lord."

One by one, the transports stood out to sea. Haroun, Beloul, and el Senoussi watched in silence. Shortly after the last warped away from the quay a runner arrived. He gasped, "Lord, there're warships ready to come into the channel."

"Uh-huh," Shadek said, congratulating himself.

Haroun felt the color leave his face. "What flag?"

"Scuttarian, Lord."

"And Dunno Scuttari is in the Disciple's bag. Beloul, forget your little navy. Looks like our only choice is to take as many with us as we can. Shadek, round the men up and send them to the wall. It won't be long."

"Maybe we can negotiate something," Beloul suggested.

"Would you bargain with them if the roles were reversed?"

Beloul laughed sourly. "I see what you mean, Lord."

Push as he might, Ragnarson could not match El Murid's pace. The Disciple reached Libiannin fifteen hours ahead but too late in the day to launch the attack he had come to enjoy.

Ragnarson's outriders captured a courier who apprised them of the true state of affairs.

"We keep going tonight," Bragi announced. "Maybe we can get there in time to do some good. I'm going to ride ahead."

He gathered a small band and surged ahead, outdistancing his main force. He scouted Libiannin's environs, found what he wanted and rejoined his command as the sky began to lighten.

The hill he had selected overlooked the enemy main camp. Its base was just a mile from Libiannin's wall. The remains of an Imperial fortification crowned it. A small party of desert scouts occupied the ruins.

Ragnarson sent his sneakiest people forward. His main force reached the peak of the hill fifteen minutes later. The enemy there were all dead. "Perfect." He assembled his captains. "What I want is...."

El Murid and his people had their attention fixed on Libiannin. Ragnarson's men dug in for an hour before they were noticed. By then the Host had arrayed itself for the assault on the city.

Bragi went downhill, well below his foremost trench. He stood with hands on hips and said, "You folks go right ahead. Don't mind us." No one could hear, of course, but that was unnecessary. His stance conveyed his message. "But be careful about turning your backs on me."

He walked back uphill, listened to his men cuss and grumble as they deepened their trenches. They were not pleased by what they saw below. They were badly outnumbered.

One of Ragnarson's officers who was in the know asked, "What kind of standard should we show? We need something new if we just represent ourselves."

Despite his weariness and concern, Ragnarson was in a good mood. "Should be something unique, right? Something that will puzzle hell out of them. Tell you what. See if you can't find some red cloth. And some black. We'll make a flag like my father's sail. It'll drive them goofy."

Several officers got into the act, creating bizarre standards of their own.

The Host vacillated, racked by indecision. Bragi raised his standard, a black wolf's head on red. Baffled, the Disciple sent a deputation to investigate.

Bragi laughed at their questions while carefully concealing his true strength. He said, "The way I see it, you men have three choices. Attack Libiannin and have us jump on your backs. Attack us and have Haroun do the same. Or you can get smart and go the hell home."

One envoy glanced at the banner and for at least the fifth time asked, "Who are you?"

"I should let you find out the hard way." He could no longer resist a brag. "Ragnarson. Bragi Ragnarson. The Ragnarson that got rid of the Scourge of God, Mowaffak Hali, and el-Nadim. Not to mention Karim. There's one name left on my list. Tell your nitwit boss I'll scratch his off too if he doesn't get out of here."

"That Guildsman from Altea? The Guild has made peace. You're out of line. This is between our Lord and bin Yousif."

"And me, Wormface. And me. I'm no Guildsman now."

One of Ragnarson's officers whispered, "Don't push them, sir. They may go."

"I'll carry this news to my Lord," an Invincible said. "It will help him reach his decision." He spun and raced down the hill.

"I don't like the way he said that," someone muttered.

"I think I goofed," Bragi admitted. "My name is right up by Haroun's on the Disciple's list. Stand to arms. Double-check the arrows."

"Can you tell what's happening, Lord?" Shadek asked. "My eyes aren't what they were."

"Mine aren't that good. Looks like somebody's dug in on that hill out there."

"Must be on our side," Beloul guessed. "Else they'd be all over us by now."

"But who? We have no friends anymore."

They waited and watched. The Host waited and baked in the increasingly uncomfortable sun.

"Couldn't you reach out with your shaghûn sensing, Lord?" Shadek asked.

"I don't know. I haven't used it for so long…. I'll give it a go."

Beloul and Shadek shooed the nearer warriors. Haroun seated himself, bent forward, sealed his eyes against the sun. He murmured poorly remembered exercises taught him long ago. A fleeting memory of el Aswad fluttered across his mind. Had that been him? That innocent child? It seemed like another boy in another century, roaming those desert hills with Megelin Radetic, spending those miserable hours with the lore-masters from the shadowed valleys of Jebal al Alf Dhulquarneni.

Slowly, slowly, the chant took shape. He took hold and repeated it till his mind had shed all distractions, then he reached out, reached out….

A sound like a mouse's squeak crossed his motionless lips.

"All right." He lifted a hand. El Senoussi helped him rise. "I'll be damned," he muttered. "I'll be damned."

"Not a doubt of it, Lord," Beloul chided. "But did you learn anything?"

"I did indeed, Beloul. I did indeed. That's our fool friend Ragnarson out there. He's come to save us from the fury of the madman of the wastes."

Shadek and Beloul looked at him oddly. Beloul said, "Ragnarson? But he's Guild."

"You think we should tell him to go away?"

"Not just yet, Lord. Him decorating that hill improves the view marvelously."

And Shadek, "It gives a man a good feeling here inside, knowing there are people who will stick."

"Don't forget it if we get out alive, Shadek. We'll owe him bigger than ever. Let us, too, be men who can be counted upon by our friends."

"Not only our friends but our enemies, Lord."

"The Disciple must be in a dither," Beloul observed. "Like a starving dog stationed between two hunks of meat. Which should he jump first?"

"Except these two hunks will bite his behind if he turns his back."

"Take not too much heart, Lord," Shadek cautioned. "Ragnarson would have far fewer men than the Disciple. And El Murid has his amulet."

The Host went into motion. It split like some weird organism giving birth to another of its kind. Half came toward the city. The remainder faced about and advanced on Ragnarson's hill.

"And there's the answer," Beloul quipped. "The dog turns into two dogs."

"Tell the men they have to hang on till our allies finish their share of the Host," Haroun said.

"Let me be the first to congratulate you on your newfound optimism, Lord," Shadek said.

"No need to be sarcastic, Shadek."

"There's good and good, Lord, and some things could be better than they are. I'll speak to the men."

Haroun nodded. He returned to his semi-trance, supposing that, in this extremity, his small talent as a sorcerer would be more valuable than his talent as a swordsman. He tried to lay a slight, small cloud upon the minds of the men about to attack Libiannin.

At least six thousand horsemen swarmed up Ragnarson's hill. "Oh, damn!" he swore. "I didn't count on them splitting." He shouted and waved, letting his people know they could loose their shafts at will. Clouds of arrows arced toward the riders.

Few of these horsemen had faced the arrowstorms so often seen in the north. They received a rude shock.

Every man of Ragnarson's carried a bow. The pikemen and swordsmen of his front ranks loosed several shafts apiece before hefting their weapons and bracing to receive the charge. The regular archers never slackened fire. These infantrymen had borne the charge of el Nadim's cavalry and had survived. They had confidence in themselves and their officers. They faced the human tidal wave without losing their courage.

The Host left thousands dead on that hillside and countless more heaped before the trenches. The pikemen fended them off while the archers plinked. Yet the impetus of the attack was so massive, Ragnarson's front began to sag. It seemed the surviving horsemen might yet carry the day.

He committed his small reserve, ran back and forth behind the line cursing his bowmen for not shattering the attack.

For half an hour it hung in the balance. Then, here, there, a few of the enemy began to slip away. The larger mass, almost entirely unhorsed after Ragnarson had ordered his bowmen to redirect their fire against the animals, began to give ground. Ragnarson ordered his wings forward to give the impression he meant to encircle.

Panic hit the enemy. They blew away like smoke on the wind.

"That was close," Bragi muttered. His men were exhausted but he had no mercy. "Sort out the wounded and get them up to the ruins," he ordered. "Archers, get down the hill and recover arrows. Move it! Come on, move it! Officers, I want to form for the advance. We've got to challenge them before they get their balance."

He had drums pound out the message of his coming. He had his men beat their shields with their swords. He hoped nerves in the Host would be so frayed his enemies would scatter.

El Murid had other ideas. He detached men from the assault on Libiannin and sent them to reorganize the survivors of the first wave for a second attack.

Ragnarson did to that second wave what he had done to the first, more thoroughly. The horsemen were less enthusiastic about facing the arrowstorm. They took longer reaching his pikemen and as a consequence suffered more from the blizzard of shafts. The enemy coming up afoot never closed with Ragnarson's line.

More drums. More shield banging. And again El Murid did not bluff. He pulled all his men away from the city.

This time he spearheaded the attack himself, pounding the hill with bolts of lightning called from the cloudless sky.

Ragnarson was proud of his soldiers. They did not let the sorcery panic them. They took cover and tried to hold their ground. When compelled to fall back they did so with discipline, fading toward the ruin.

They wrought incredible carnage while their arrows lasted. But this time the supply ran dry.

Bragi heard a distant whinny and sudden pounding of hooves. The Disciple's men had captured his mounts. "Looks like I miscalculated this time, don't it?" he told one of his officers.

"You're damned calm about it, Colonel."

Surprised, he realized he was calm. Even with the lightning stalking about. "Get back into the ruins. They'll have to come after us on foot. They're no good on the ground."

He ran hither and thither, establishing his companies amidst the tumbled stone. The majority of the foe were hanging back letting their prophet hammer the hill. El Murid was not much of a sharpshooter. Satisfied with his new dispositions, Bragi climbed to the ruin's highest point and stared toward the city. "All right, Haroun. This is your big chance."

Haroun surveyed his men. Their mounts pranced as if eager to be off to the fray. The warriors wore grins. They could not believe their good fortune. An absolute certainty of destruction had turned into a chance for escape.

"How soon, Lord?" Shadek asked.

Haroun peered at the hill. Ragnarson was in bad trouble. "A few minutes yet. Let a few hundred more dismount." He considered the street below. Beloul had finished passing along the line, vigorously pointing out that there was to be no run for freedom while El Murid's back was turned. They were to jump the Disciple from behind.

The more Beloul talked the fewer were the grins.

"Now, Shadek. Take the left wing. Beloul will go to the right."

"I'm thinking we ought to head east, then north, as hard as we can ride."

"What about our friends?"

El Senoussi shrugged.

"Who was it said something about people sticking? Sometimes I wonder how much I dare lean on you myself, Shadek."

"Lord!"

"The left wing, Shadek. Go after them as hard as you can, as long as you can. Let's not let El Murid duck the Dark Lady again."

"Suppose he won't let *you* duck?"

"Shadek."

"As you command, Lord."

Haroun led them out, spread them out and trotted them toward Ragnarson's hill. His coming was not wholly unanticipated. Many of the Disciple's horsemen came to meet him.

The lines crashed. Horses reared and screamed. Men shouted war- and death-cries. Lances cracked, swords clanged, shields whumped to the impact of savage blows. Dust rose till it choked the combatants, coating their colorful clothing a uniform ochre. And the Disciple's horsemen gave way.

Haroun howled and wailed, urging his men to finish it for once and all. His blood was up. He never thought to appeal to his people with arguments more convincing than love for their King. What matter to him that one man's death would mean they could return to loved ones unseen for years? *He* had no loved ones waiting in Hammad al Nakir. What matter that the passing of El Murid would permit their escape from sad roles as unwanted strangers in lands with grotesque customs? *He* was a stranger everywhere.

For Haroun—and Beloul—home was the hunt for the hated foe. Family were the men who shared the stalk.

A hand of fear passed over the battlefield. Its shadow fell heaviest upon the Chosen.

Haroun crowed and whipped his men forward.

The enemy broke and flew away like autumn leaves scattering in a sudden cold wind.

Beloul and Shadek drove their wings forward. Haroun, wounded, kept pointing with his blade and cursing his men because they would not hurry.

Spears of lightning fell upon the battleground, failing to discriminate among targets. Horsemen pelted away from every point of impact.

Haroun tried to locate the Disciple. He descried a large band of Invincibles, but could not determine if El Murid was amongst them. He tried to force his way closer.

More and more of the Disciple's horsemen fled. Some flew eastward, toward Hammad al Nakir. Some galloped across the narrow plain and got inside Libiannin's undefended wall.

The fighting rolled this way and that, up and down Ragnarson's hill. All order vanished. Immense confusion set in. The dust made it difficult to distinguish friend from foe. Neither side could guess who might be winning. But the longer it went on, the more the once stout members of the Host chose the better part of valor.

Late in the afternoon the big band of Invincibles lost their nerve. They scattered. The morale of the Host collapsed. It dissolved in minutes.

"Enough," Haroun told Beloul, who wanted to give chase. "We got out alive. That's enough." He dismounted with exaggerated care. His legs quaked with weariness and reaction. He lowered himself to the earth and began cataloging his injuries.

Twenty minutes later Ragnarson limped down the hill. He was covered with gore. Some was his own. He rolled a corpse aside, seated himself on the trampled earth, loosed a weary sigh. "I'm going to be too stiff to move for a week. If they come back…."

"They won't," Haroun promised. "They're going home. They've had enough. This was the last battle." Despair shadowed the corners of his soul. "The last battle. And the desert is still theirs." The groans and cries of wounded men nearly drowned his soft, sad voice. "I should have seen it before."

"What?"

"It will take more than killing El Murid to recover Hammad al Nakir."

He stared down the hill. The fallen lay in mounds and windrows, as though a big, wild tornado had slapped down in the midst of a parade. People from Libiannin were hurrying toward the field to join the looting. "Beloul, run those people off. You needn't be polite about it." A handful of Royalists, apparently with energy to spare, were working the dead already.

Haroun turned to Ragnarson. "My friend.... My friend. What are you doing here? Sir Tury had more room to refuse than you did."

Ragnarson wrapped his arms around his knees, rested his right cheek atop them. "What orders? This is *my* army." He tried to smile. It was too much work. "I'm my own man now."

The setting sun painted the seaward sky a fitting shade of blood. A cool breeze came off the water. Bold gulls drifted inland, curiosities aroused by the gathering ravens.

"They wouldn't be too harsh with you," Haroun guessed. "You won. Winners are easily forgiven."

"I don't want to go back. I wasn't born to be a soldier. Not the Guild type, anyway."

"What, then, my friend?"

"I don't know. Not right now. There'll be something. What about you?"

Haroun glanced at Shadek, at Beloul returning across the field of death. "There's a usurper on the Peacock Throne." A vast weariness entered his voice. He was tired unto death, and still the ghosts whispered in his ears. His father, Yousif, to his right, his uncle, Fuad, to his left. Contested by Megelin Radetic. "Still a usurper."

"There's one in my homeland too. The way I figure it, time and his own stupidity will take care of him."

"I'm not made for waiting."

Ragnarson shrugged. "It's your life. What ever happened to the fat guy? He was weird, but I liked him."

"Mocker? I thought he was with you."

"I haven't seen him since we split up. I figured he went with you."

"Curious."

"Maybe he headed east. He talked about it enough."

"He talked about everything. Probably somebody finally stuck a knife in him." Ragnarson shrugged again.

Below, the groans and cries continued. More of their men were finding the ambition to search the dead.

TWENTY-THREE
GOING HOME

El Murid flung both hands skyward, beseeching another bolt from the firmament. He was half-mad with frustration. The bandit Royalists were not overawed by his power.

The blow felt like a hammer stroke against his ribs. He felt bone crack. A whine ripped through his lips. The earth hurtled up. He tried to reach, to soften his fall. One arm would not respond. He hit the ground hard. His bodyguards wailed in dismay.

As consciousness faded he heard hooves racing away. He cracked one eyelid and watched his Invincibles flee.

The darkness came.

And the darkness went away.

A foot pushed against his ribs, rolled him over. A scream boiled in his throat. He swallowed it, did not breathe while the warrior went through his clothing. The man cursed him. He carried no wealth upon his person.

The warrior's eyes brightened when he discovered the amulet. He removed it quickly and furtively, instantly concealing it within his clothing.

The jewel had ebbed low. The looter never noted its weak gleam.

El Murid confined his curses to his heart. The choice was the amulet or life. That was no choice.

A second warrior called, "You find anything?"

"Two lousy pieces of silver and a handful of copper. These guys are poorer than we are. This one's got decent boots, though. Look like they might fit."

The Disciple ground his teeth while the man yanked his boots from his feet.

The second warrior joined the first. "I found one of those silver kill-daggers. That ought to be worth something."

"Yeah? Let me see."

"Like hell."

"All right. All right. Hey, this one has a pretty fine sword here."

"Better than that nicked up hunk of Itaskian tin you're carrying."

El Murid wanted to laugh. The weapon had been given him in Dunno Scuttari only days ago. He'd never had it out of its scabbard. There was something ironic in that.

Even more ironic, he concluded after the warriors moved on, was the fact that his enemies were making no effort to learn if he were among the fallen. He did not understand their political apathy. They had him at their mercy.

How ironic it would be, too, if he were slain simply because he was found alive, with his killer never realizing the importance of the deathblow he dealt.

Darkness took the field into its arms. For a time, the more ambitious Royalists plundered by torchlight but eventually even the greediest opted for sleep.

The battlefield grew still and silent. El Murid waited. The pain kept him awake. When he was certain he would not give himself away, he began dragging himself from the field.

He had gone no more than a dozen yards when he came upon his physician. "Oh, Esmat. What have you done? I thought you were one of the immortals and here you've abandoned me. My old friend. My last friend. Lying here for the ravens. It's cruel. All I can do is raise a stele for you."

Someone or something stirred a short way down the slope. El Murid froze. He did not move for a long time.

Somehow, the plunderers had overlooked Esmat's bag. He took it with him when he resumed dragging himself from the field. When he felt safer he crawled to a tree and used it to pull himself to his feet. He began stumbling eastward by the light of a crescent moon, his feet bleeding. Twice he paused to draw strength from the medicines in Esmat's bag.

Near dawn he encountered a riderless horse. He caught and calmed the beast and dragged himself into the saddle. He walked his new mount eastward.

Two weeks of agony brought him to the Sahel, where he fell into the arms of devoted followers. They nursed him and eventually carried him back to Al Rhemish where he secluded himself in the Most Holy Mrazkim Shrines.

His high ambitions had died their final death.

The Royalist warrior who plundered the Disciple's amulet sold it to a goldsmith in Libiannin after the Chosen there withdrew. The goldsmith in turn sold it to a woman of quality returning south to reclaim family estates near Simballawein. She had had the amulet for two months when it came to sudden life, cursing in a foreign tongue. Terrified, certain the thing was some dread sorcerer's toy that had been fobbed off on her by a dishonest artisan, she had her servants hurl it into a deep well. The well she ordered filled with earth and planted over.

So El Murid's amulet vanished from the earth, to the bafflement of historians, the Faithful and, most of all, of him who had presented it to the Disciple.

The magic had gone out of El Murid's movement. Literally.

TWENTY-FOUR
REVELATION

The fat man was never more circumspect. He traversed an inhospitable land infested by piratical deserters from both the Itaskian army and Host of Illumination. These renegades preyed on everyone. The locals therefore greeted any stranger with violence, fearing he might be scouting for one of the bands.

Disorder held sway from the Scarlotti north to the Silverbind. He had survived that chaos. He had evaded misfortune week after week, making his way toward Portsmouth where the remnants of el Nadim's army yet awaited the Disciple's command.

"Self, am cast-iron fool," he berated himself at one juncture, forty miles from his destination. "Should be bound for easternmost east. Should be headed for lands where good sense is rule rather than exception, where man of skill and genius would have half chance to prosper."

His talents were wasted on this mad country. Its people were too damned suspicious and too impoverished. The to and fro of armies had destroyed tens of thousands of farms. Plunderers had carried off any wealth that had existed there. The natives had to scratch and fight to survive.

He was losing weight. Hunger was a monster trying to gnaw its way out of his guts. And he had no props with which to ply his trade even had he been able to gather the marks. He had had no time, and no money, to assemble a new inventory.

He never stopped asking himself what he was doing in this mad country, and still he went on. He had to get close to the eastern army. He had to *know*. He could not go on wondering if Sajac were out there somewhere, stumbling along on his backtrail, closing in for the kill.

That need to know had become an obsession. It drove him more mercilessly than any slavemaster's whip.

For the first time in his life he fell into the habit of introspection, trying to discover *why* this was so important to him. He encountered the shadowed reaches of his soul and recoiled. He dared not believe that such darknesses existed within him. He found his love-hatred for the old man the most repulsive monster hidden there. He wanted to be possessed of no feelings for Sajac at all. He wanted to be able to exterminate the old man like the louse he was—if he still existed.

He did not want to care about anybody but Mocker.

Yet he did care, not only about Sajac but about the friends he had made during his wartime adventures. He had grown fond of Haroun and Bragi, both of whom had treated him well and who had been understanding about his constant making an ass of himself.

Often, late in the night, he would waken and find himself afraid. It was not a mortal fear, a fear of this enemy land, nor was it a dread of specific enemies. It was a fear of having no more cause and no more friends and being totally alone.

He did not like that fear. It did not fit his image of himself as a man at war with the universe, beating it again and again by acuteness of wit. He did not want to be dependent on anyone, especially not emotionally.

He began to hear news of the eastern army as he neared Portsmouth. That last remnant of El Murid's might was preparing for a homeward march. An Itaskian force was camped outside the city ready to assume control when the easterners departed.

News was always a few days old. He lengthened his stride. He did not want to arrive only to discover that his quarry had departed by another route.

His always inimical fate must have dozed off. He ran head on into one of his rare strokes of fortune. He reached the city the morning the easterners departed. He ensconced himself on a rooftop for four long hours, reviewing the Host.

Nowhere did he see a blind old man.

The thing that drove him was not satisfied. It wanted the where, the why, and the how of the old man's separation from the Host. Cursing himself for a fool, he stalked the easterners down their road toward home.

On three different occasions he isolated a soldier and put him to the question. Two had not known Sajac. The third remembered the astrologer but had no idea what had become of him.

Mocker squealed in exasperation. He cursed the gods, one and all, with a fine impartiality. They were toying with him. They were playing a cruel game. He demanded that they cease their torment, and that they let him *know*.

He became so frustrated that, in one of the Lesser Kingdoms, after failing in a fourth attempt to isolate a soldier, he went to a priest for advice.

The priest was no help. Mocker refused to reveal enough of the story for the man to hazard offering advice. He simply told the fat man, "Nothing is certain in this life, my son. We live with mystery. We share a world shrouded in uncertainty. For those without faith, life becomes an interminable journey fraught with the perils of being unsure. Come. Let us pray together. Put your trust in the Lord."

Salvation was not what Mocker had in mind. He stamped out of the rectory snarling about not getting caught in the world's oldest scam, about the effrontery of a priest who tried to con a master con artist.

He trailed the eastern army all the way to the Sahel.

He stood on a low swale staring at the barren hills, recalling what it had been like passing through them, going into the desert with Yasmid and the Invincibles. He could not penetrate those badlands without attracting the attention of the savage Sahel tribesmen.

"Woe!" he cried, after debating with himself for half a day. "Self, am accursed. Am doomed to remain wanderer in fear, ever watching backtrail lest doom steal upon self unnoticed." He again cursed all the gods and devils he knew, then turned westward, shambling shoulders slumped. Bragi and Haroun would be somewhere along the coast, he supposed.

Two days later he entered a village unscathed by war. The dogs did not growl and attack. They just barked out his arrival. The villagers did not rush out with hammers and knives and threaten to make pet food of him if he did not make himself scarce.

The townspeople were adherents of El Murid's Faith. He arrived during an hour of worship, while the muzzain was singing a prayer from the steeple of a church that once served another god. When prayers were over the villagers received Mocker with charity, offering him food and drink and asking only that he repay their kindness with a few hours of labor.

Work? Mocker? That was as implausible as asking the sun to stand still. Yet work he did, and marveled at himself as he helped clean a stable. He tried entertaining with a few tricks but was admonished because they smacked of sorcery. The townsfolk were conservatives who hadn't warmed to the Disciple's shift in attitude toward the dark arts. In any case, the old man who lived in the temple had shown them all those tricks already.

Mocker's eyes grew huge. Old man? Tricks? Temple? But.... Could it be ... ? No. Impossible. Not a chance. Things did not happen that way. The gods did not torment you mercilessly, dangling your heart's desire just out of reach only to throw it into the dust at your feet, contemptuously, when you abandoned all hope. Did they?

He was so nervous and eager that he went to the extreme of taking a bath before attending the next service. He had learned that the old man in question was blind and on his last legs. The temple had taken him in out of charity. He had helped the priest where he could, which was very little, and in return received a place to lay his head, two meals a day, and someone to bury him when he died.

A strong emotion hit Mocker when he heard this. He could not identify it immediately. Then he realized he was sad for this unknown old man, crippled and dying alone and unloved, nurtured only by the charity of strangers.

That feeling grew stronger as the hour of worship approached. It baffled him when he tried to probe it in an attempt to unearth its genesis and meaning. He became confused and, in an odd way, frightened. And he wondered constantly if this really could be Sajac.

He joined the worshippers as they drifted toward the temple. Several remarked on how clean and shiny he looked. He grinned idiotically and responded to a few feeble jests.

The nearer he approached the temple the more difficult it became to keep going. More and more of the villagers passed him. In the end, he stood a pace outside the temple door, alone, motionless, wondering what he would see when he stepped through. A feeble Sajac helping the priest? Or some complete stranger?

Three times he tried to take that last step. Three times something held him back. Then he turned and walked away.

In the final summation, he did not need to know. He could walk away and let the pathetic creature in the temple be whomever he wanted.

The need had left him. Empathy had banished hatred.

He resumed his westward journey.

TWENTY-FIVE
FINALE, WITH KING

"There's an Itaskian wants to see you, Lord," Shadek announced from the entrance to Haroun's tent.

"Itaskian?" Haroun exchanged glances with Ragnarson. "What's he want?"

"An audience, Lord. He didn't say why."

"Who is he?"

Shadek shrugged. "A gentleman of quality. An older man."

"Uh-huh. Bring him here, then." Haroun's voice betrayed a great weariness.

"Now what?" Ragnarson wondered aloud.

"Who knows."

Their encampment was a hundred miles northeast of Libiannin. It lay a far ride from anywhere for anyone. The nearest known Itaskians were at Dunno Scuttari, not yet having returned north after their negotiations with the Disciple. The reports suggested that, despite the terms of the peace, they were trying to shake the hold the Faithful had on the kingdoms south of the Scarlotti.

Haroun was drifting toward the Kapenrungs, having nowhere to go but the old camps. Ragnarson had joined him because he, too, had nowhere to go. He had disbanded his little army. His men had been anxious to return home, to resume interrupted lives. Fewer than twenty-five had remained with him. None knew what they would do with their tomorrows.

Shadek returned. "The Itaskian, Lord." He held the flap for a thin old man.

Haroun rose, face reddening. "My Lord Minister," he growled, restraining himself with difficulty. "I am… shall we say I'm boggled by your audacity. Or stupidity. Only a bold rogue or an idiot would come here after what you did to us." Shifting to his own tongue, he identified the man for Ragnarson.

"I?" the Minister asked. "Bold? Hardly. I'm in the grip of an immense trepidation. My advisers are astonished that we lived long enough to reach you. They don't believe you're sophisticated enough to distinguish between this Itaskian and that."

"Why make distinctions?" Ragnarson growled. "One father of lies is like another. The gods have blessed you, Haroun. They've given you a peace offering. I know the perfect way to dispose of this worm."

Haroun eyed the Minister. "I'm open to suggestions."

"In Trolledyngja we carry traitors from town to town in a cart, hanging them gently. Just enough to make them dance a little. When the traitor reaches Tonderhofn, we draw and quarter him and send the quarters out to the four winds as a warning."

"An interesting custom. I'd be tempted had I villages through which to parade and a capital to call my own. Had a snippet of treachery not arisen, I'd have the villages and capital. But nobody to slay. It's a problem. I fear we'll have to settle for something less flashy."

The Minister refused to be intimidated. His stance and gaze were those of a brave man who had undertaken a hazardous mission willingly.

"I'm not pleased with you," Haroun told him. "But you helped once. I'll let you say your piece."

"These are the facts, then. Whether you believe them or not. During the negotiations in Dunno Scuttari my cousin managed a secret understanding with El Murid. His agents then isolated my party for several days. During that time the articles of peace were implemented. The Guild came to shameful terms in return for a guarantee of their properties and livings south of the Scarlotti. My cousin then issued the orders that resulted in you becoming entrapped in Libiannin. I confess shame, sir, but I deny responsibility."

Haroun glared. The man did not respond.

Ragnarson said, "It *is* your fault. It's been clear since the wars started that Greyfells was dealing with El Murid. You didn't stop him."

"Who is this?" the Minister asked.

"My partner," Haroun replied. "Bragi Ragnarson. I want you to answer him."

"Ragnarson? Good. I've wanted to meet him. I'll answer him thus: He doesn't know Itaskian politics. It's impossible to control Greyfells without civil war."

Ragnarson snorted. "A dollop of poison."

"We'll let the question slide," Haroun said. "Get to the point. You want something."

"To reaffirm our private treaty."

"What treaty?"

"The one we made four years ago. I don't want it to fade away because the fighting has ended."

"Your war has ended. Not mine. Go on."

"El Murid is still El Murid. He hasn't given up. He's just backed off for a breather. He controls most everything south of the Scarlotti and has planted his ideals in fertile soil north of the river. If he tries again he may conquer us."

"So?"

"You said your war hasn't ended. I'm offering continued support. A strong Royalist movement will hamper El Murid. It might nibble away at his bastions outside the Sahel. And I still have those hidden ally needs I spoke about before. My cousin will change his strategy now. The occasional knife in the dark would be an invaluable tool."

"And, I guess, this aid wouldn't be sufficient to put me on the Peacock Throne. It'd be just enough to keep me going, to keep me a useful tool."

"We're getting bitter and cynical, aren't we?"

"You don't deny it."

"I have an operation in mind. It could net you the wealth to make you a power with which to be reckoned."

"Talk. I haven't yet decided to cut your throat."

"This is down the road a way, of course. Because the war has tied up the fleet, pirates have established themselves in the Red Isles. Their leader is a renegade wizard. We need somebody to go in and kill him. If that someone were nimble enough, he could escape with the pirate treasure before the fleet arrived to mop up."

Haroun glanced at Bragi. Ragnarson shrugged.

"You'd let this treasure get away?"

"It belonged to Hellin Daimiel."

"I see. Shadek, take the gentleman somewhere and make him comfortable."

El Senoussi took the Itaskian away.

"The man is cunning," Ragnarson observed.

"Oh?"

"He shined a pot of gold in your eyes and you forgot about Libiannin."

"Think he was telling the truth?"

"Anything is possible. Even that."

"You've got connections in Hellin Daimiel. Find out if they lost any treasure ships."

"Now?"

"You had something else to do?"

"I guess not." Creaking, Bragi rose. "Watch out for him, Haroun."

"I'm done with him. He won't see me again. I'm leaving too. Beloul! Sentry, find Beloul."

"Where you heading?"

"Nowhere important. Personal business. Take care."

Beloul pushed into the tent.

"I'm going away for a while, Beloul. You and Shadek take over. Move back to the camps. Do whatever seems appropriate. Try not to attract too much attention. The next few years will be hard. It'll be a struggle to keep the movement from falling apart."

"Where will you be, Lord?"

"Out of touch, Beloul. Use your own judgment."

"How long, Lord?"

"I don't know. It all depends."

"I see." Beloul's tone made it clear he did nothing of the sort.

"Have a horse readied. And send someone to help with my things."

Haroun climbed the mountain gingerly, feeling both anticipation and guilty reluctance. He made a poor father and husband.

The old woman and her nephew were out gathering firewood. They fled to the cabin when they spied him. He made his approach openly and slowly, not wanting to be taken for one of the Harish. He reached the cabin. Its door stood open, presenting a dark and uncertain rectangle.

"Yasmid?" he called. "Are you here?"

Minutes later he was seated with his woman beside him and his son in his lap. He was free for a few hours, days, or weeks. For the moment he was a husband, not a king without a throne.

He would be happy here in his sanctuary. For a while. Till his thoughts turned to the outer world once more. He would try to stay, to be a simple husband, but the Peacock Throne never ceased its night-whispered calling. One day he would sally forth to battle again.

They knew, did Yasmid and little Megelin, but they pretended his stay would last. They always pretended. They always would, and would live each minute as if it might be their last.

"He's a sturdy little rascal, isn't he?" Haroun asked. Little Megelin gripped his forefingers and stared up with wise infant's eyes. A smile teased the child's soft, moist little lips.

Haroun wept. For all the children, he wept.

Night Shade Books Is an Independent Publisher of Quality SF, Fantasy and Horror

ISBN 978-1-59780-104-1
Trade Paperback; $16.95

Before there was Black Company, there was the Dread Empire. *A Cruel Wind* is an omnibus collection the first three Dread Empire novels: *A Shadow of All Night's Falling*, *October's Baby* and *All Darkness Met*.

> "The thing about Glen Cook is that... he single-handedly changed the field of fantasy something a lot of people didn't notice, and maybe still don't. He brought the story down to a human level... Reading his stuff was like reading Vietnam War fiction on Peyote."
> — Steven Erikson, author of *Gardens of the Moon*

An Empire Unacquainted with Defeat collects all of Glen Cook's short fiction set in the vast world of the Dread Empire, from "The Nights of Dreadful Silence", featuring the first appearance of Bragi Ragnarson, Mocker, and Haroun bin Yousif, to the culture-clashing novella "Soldier of an Empire Unacquainted with Defeat"; from "Silverheels", Cook's first published work of fiction, to "Hell's Forge", a haunting tale of cursed pirates and strange lands, appearing here for the first time.

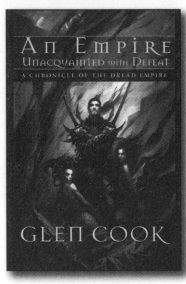

ISBN 978-1-59780-140-9
Hardcover; $24.95

Also including a detailed introduction and extensive story notes by Glen Cook, *An Empire Unacquainted with Defeat* charts the development of this influential American author and the massive, multifaceted world that he created.

Find these Night Shade titles and many others online at http://www.nightshadebooks.com or wherever books are sold.

Night Shade Books Is an Independent Publisher of Quality SF, Fantasy and Horror

"A master realist of the Imagination" — *LOCUS*

GLEN COOK

THE DRAGON
NEVER SLEEPS

ISBN 978-1-59780-148-5
Mass Market; $7.99

Glen Cook delivers a masterpiece of galaxy spanning space opera. For four thousand years, the Guardships ruled Canon Space with an iron fist. Immortal ships with an immortal crew roamed the galaxy, dealing swiftly and harshly with any mercantile houses or alien races that threatened the status quo. Now the House Tregesser believes they have an edge; a force from outside Canon Space offers them the resources to throw off Guardship rule. Kez Maefele must chose which side he will support; the Guardships, who defeated and destroyed his race, or the unknown forces from outside Canon Space that promise more death and destruction.

"One of the best evocations of life in close quarters onboard a spaceship... the *Das Boot* of SF." — JEFF VANDERMEER, SF SITE

GLEN COOK

PASSAGE
AT ARMS

ISBN 978-1-59780-119-5
Mass Market; $7.99

The ongoing war between Humanity and the Ulat is a battle of attrition that Humanity is losing. Humans do, however, have one technological advantage — trans-hyperdrive technology. Using this technology, specially designed and outfitted spaceships — humanity's climber fleet — can, under very narrow and strenuous conditions, pass through space undetected.

Passage at Arms tells the intimate, detailed and harrowing story of a climber crew and its captain during a critical juncture of the war. Cook combines speculative technology with a canny and realistic portrait of men at war and the stresses they face in combat. Passage at Arms is one of the classic novels of military science fiction.

Find these Night Shade titles and many others online at http://www.nightshadebooks.com or wherever books are sold.

Night Shade Books Is an Independent Publisher of Quality SF, Fantasy and Horror

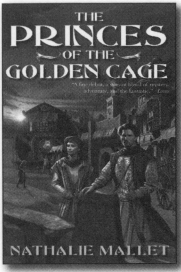
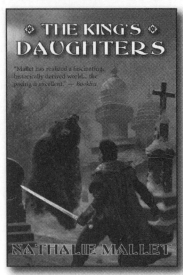